RED ZONE

A Calvin Watters
& Charlene Taylor Mystery

Luke Murphy

RED ZONE
A Calvin Watters & Charlene Taylor Mystery #1

www.authorlukemurphy.com

FIRST EDITION
July 2020

Published by ANM Books

ISBN: 978-1-7753759-9-9

Cover designed by Casey Snyder Design
info@caseysnyderdesign.com

Praise for *Red Zone*

"Luke Murphy ramps up the thrill factor with RED ZONE—an awesome, gotta-know-what-happens-next novel. Murphy knows how to entertain. I tore through RED ZONE in a single sitting, and didn't want the book to end. This should be on your Do-Not-Miss list to read this fall."

—Linda Castillo, NYT bestselling author of the Kate Burkholder series

"Well-drawn characters and an interesting premise—Luke Murphy is a mystery writer to watch."

—DV Berkom, USA Today bestselling author of the Leine Basso series

"Red Zone is another winner for Murphy! Thrilling...riveting...a stay-up-all-night-read."

—Kim Cresswell, bestselling author of Deadly Shadow

"Luke Murphy creates a gritty and compelling murder mystery with 'Red Zone'. Calvin Watters and Charlene Taylor are the complex and real characters we search for in our stories, and their lives add the perfect amount of seasoning to the soup. Watching them move through the mystery is just as entertaining as trying to figure out who did the heinous deed...which you won't, but it's fun to try. Great story and I hope to see more from this talented author."

—S.L. Shelton, bestselling author of the Scott Wolfe series

"In Red Zone, Luke Murphy gives us a thoroughly enjoyable read. As authoritative about forensics, college football, cheerleaders and murder in LA as he is in creating richly developed characters, snappy dialogue, and a plot to keep the reader guessing, he takes this story into the end zone for a touchdown."

—Peter Clement, bestselling author of the Earl Garnet series

For my readers:
You helped bring Calvin and Charlene together.

Acknowledgements

Bringing a book together takes many hands, and I'm indebted to many people. If I miss someone along the way, then I apologize.

The most important people in my life: my family—Mélanie, Addison, Nève and Molly.

I'm the first to admit that this novel was not a solo effort. I've relied on many generous and intelligent people to turn this book into a reality. I'd like to thank the following people who had a hand in making this novel what it is today.

Always a big thank you to my editing team: Mrs. Joan Conrod, Ms. Lisa Murphy and Mrs. Tracy Davis.

Special thanks to my beta readers: Mrs. Amy Patton and Ms. Vikki Faircloth.

These individuals were an integral part of my research: Ms. Joanna Pozzulo, Dr. Keith MacLellan, Officer Laura Meltzer (Retired), Mr. Darron Barr, USCTrojans.com, LAMC Customer Service and Mr. Kevin Daly.

Another amazing book cover designed by Ms. Casey Snyder.

Any procedural, geographical, or other errors pertaining to this story are of no fault to the names mentioned above, but entirely my own, as at times I took many creative liberties.

And last but not least, I'd like to thank you, the reader. You make it all worthwhile.

Book I

The Prodigal Son

Chapter 1

"What do you think? Nineteen? Twenty?"

Detective Charlene Taylor turned around and shaded her eyes with one hand, noticing her partner for the first time at the crime scene. She hadn't seen him when she'd first arrived, but his large frame was hard to miss amongst the number of law enforcement who graced the freshly laid turf of the Los Angeles Memorial Coliseum.

It was still too early in the morning for Larry's hair to be combed, and the messy gray mop was too thick around his ears.

"Eighteen maybe," Charlene whispered.

She looked back at the body, on its back, eyes locked open in a death-stare. The LAPD Medical Examiner, who had been called in to determine a preliminary cause of death, hovered over the body. The detective knew that at any crime scene, the ME took precedence, and Charlene would have to wait her turn, but she scanned the girl over the examiner's shoulder.

The African-American female had a pretty face, long curly black hair, almost crimped. No makeup, her complexion and clear skin showed off her natural beauty.

"Got a name?" Charlene asked.

The medical examiner, a personal friend of Charlene's, turned around and gave the detective a 'what do you think' look.

"No ID on her. No pockets. Soft kill, no gun or knife used."

"You found nothing on her?"

"Nothing."

"No phone?"

"That's the definition of nothing."

Kids went nowhere these days without their phones.

The victim wore a cheerleader uniform. The white shell had the USC letters displayed across the chest. Underneath the sleeveless top the young woman wore an athletic tank top, showing a section of midriff. The thirteen inch white skirt had a cardinal and gold trim, and covered white spandex briefs, known as spankies in the cheerleading world.

"Those uniforms don't leave much to the imagination," Larry said. "Not much money spent on material."

"They wear short skirts like that for a couple of reasons."

Larry raised his thick eyebrows. "I can think of one."

Charlene squeezed her lips together. "Yes, for horny old bastards like yourself. But some coaches and team sponsors encourage wearing shorter skirts due to safety reasons. Too much fabric can be dangerous while tumbling."

"You seem to know a lot, Taylor. Former cheerleader?"

Charlene rolled her eyes. "Hardly."

"Oh, that's right, I forgot. Daddy's little tomboy."

She grinned. "And don't you forget it, Larry."

The medical examiner stood up and snapped off his rubber gloves. He had a thin, sharp face, strawberry blond hair parted to the left, and extremely small hands.

"From my preliminary assessment, she's been dead about ten hours. Once I get her back to the lab, I'll be able to tell you more."

"Cause?"

The ME pursed his lips. "I'd say asphyxiation. But there is also evidence of blunt force trauma to the left side of the frontal bone."

"Could that have killed her?"

"Maybe."

"Object?"

"No idea. Like I said, I'll know more once I get her back and wash her up. You can have your photographer snap some shots now before we move her."

"Thanks, Doc." Charlene looked around the football field, where hordes of officials walked the grounds. She turned back to Larry. "Let's get to work."

Calvin Watters laid his smoothly-shaved scalp back on the airplane seat headrest, closed his eyes and gripped the armrests until his knuckles turned white, as the plane's wheels lifted off the ground.

The seat rattled slightly when the immense metal object suddenly left the ground, and rose on its own. Calvin's two-hundred and twenty pound frame flexed tensely to fight off the nausea that developed. He ground his teeth.

"Isn't this exciting?" The enthusiasm in Rachel's voice was obvious, as she sat beside Calvin, her arm snaked inside and around his bulging biceps.

Calvin didn't share her enjoyment. In fact, he had never gotten used to flying.

The large black PI held his breath and didn't exhale until the plane leveled off, gained speed, and the vibration stopped completely.

He let out his breath, his shirt damp with sweat. "We're good now," he said, more to himself, for comfort.

Rachel smiled. "You need to get over this fear of flying. I thought that your trip to South America would have cured that."

"I don't have a fear of flying. I have a fear of crashing."

"But what happens when I want to travel?"

"We have everything we need in Vegas."

Rachel pouted her lips. She lifted her legs onto the seat and crossed them Indian-style. At five foot four, she could afford such luxury. For Calvin, at six-five, he didn't have that option, as he had his bulk already uncomfortably squeezed into an economy seat.

"I can't wait to see your old school."

Calvin turned to look at his girlfriend. He had been with Rachel for a while now, and it still made him feel good to see her smiling. With everything she had been through in her life, from an abusive stepfather, to working the Vegas streets as a prostitute, to now being not only Calvin's steady girl, but also his secretary, she deserved some happiness in her life for once. They'd already been through so much together.

But no matter what life threw their way, Rachel always seemed to maintain that optimism. At times it even wore off on Calvin, who had a tendency to worry about even the smallest of things, a trait he'd inherited from his single-parent mother.

Calvin didn't tell Rachel, but he wasn't looking forward to his return to USC. He hadn't exactly left the school on the best of terms. Even though he still had many friends there, he had burned some bridges and, for the former USC running back, those eyes would be hard to look into.

Sure, there were some good memories, but as well there were many lasting ones that had been a chapter in his life he had hoped to leave behind, forget about, and move on. But he had to admit to himself, you couldn't run away from your past, and eventually, all things caught up with you.

"You know that I'm going there to work, right?"

Rachel shrugged her slender shoulders nonchalantly, as if lost in her own little world, practically vibrating on the seat beside Calvin.

Once the electronics light came on, Calvin removed the cellphone from his belt. He plugged in his ear buds and placed them in his ear, then listened again to the message that had been left on his phone earlier this morning, only a few hours before Calvin had booked this flight.

"Cal, it's Nick." The voice sounded scared. *"The team needs your help. They found a body this morning. A girl, killed, right here at the stadium. I know I haven't been good to stay in touch, but we could really use your help right now. You know what the cops will do to this program. We need you. Call me."*

Charlene stood back and watched as two uniformed men transferred the body into a black bag and zipped it up. Then they placed the bag on a gurney and transported the victim from the premises.

Her gaze wandered around the Coliseum field, where only twelve hours ago the USC Trojans had played, and won, an NCAA collegiate football game. It still amazed the detective that things could actually get accomplished in the chaos of a crime scene, but she knew that everyone present had his or her job to attend to, and they were some of the very best at what they did.

The usual suspects were present:

Uniformed police officers, the first to arrive at the crime, secured the area so no evidence was destroyed.

The CSI unit, including her good friend Dana Davis, documented the crime scene in detail and collected any physical evidence.

Since this happened at USC, which meant big news for the city of Los Angeles, the district attorney, Jeffrey Clark, a well-known bachelor throughout the city, was present to help determine if the investigators required any search warrants to proceed, and obtain those warrants from a judge.

Forensic specialists had been called just in case the evidence required expert analysis.

And along with Charlene and Larry, there were three other detectives on hand to interview witnesses and consult with the CSI unit. It was her job to follow leads provided by witnesses and physical evidence.

The detectives approached the spot where the body had been located.

"Twenty yard line," Larry said. "Any significance?"

In gridiron football, the area of the field between the 20-yard line and the goal line was known as the red zone.

Charlene shook her head. "No idea. Who found her?"

He checked his notepad. "Groundskeeper. Francisco Sierra."

Charlene eyed Larry. "He legal?"

"Good question."

"Where is Sierra now?"

"He's waiting for us."

"Let him wait. How many people approached the body this morning?" Charlene asked.

"More than a few."

"Let's get some molds of the prints done."

"There are a lot."

"That's what I'm afraid of. We'll get a list of everyone who came near the victim. When was she found?"

"First thing this morning. Grounds crew came in to work on the field, guess Sierra was the first one out here and saw her from where they enter. He came over, and then called it in."

Sunday morning, early, a day after a Trojan home game—even worse, a Trojan win. The bleachers and field were still littered with garbage—crumpled up game programs, discarded drink cups and food wrappers, and anything else college kids would leave behind.

USC was one of seventeen out of thirty-four schools that didn't sell beer at their football games. Many schools refused to sell alcohol at games and on university premises because so many college students were under the age of twenty-one, and schools must adhere to standard laws regarding alcohol sales. That helped reduce the amount of trash in the stadium, which made the detectives job a little easier.

But the fact that the Trojans had won their home opener last night, meant that many fans rushed the field to celebrate after the game. That led to many sets of footprints going in multiple directions, including football cleats ripping up sod, so the detectives had to distinguish between those made late last night at the time of the murder, and others from earlier on in the day.

"Ever been to a game before?" Larry asked.

Charlene nodded. "A few."

Actually, when Charlene had first moved back to LA she had been a big Trojan football fan and follower. She had attended a few games and had followed their team through those so called glory years—individual record breakers, Heisman trophy winners and championship teams. But she hadn't been interested in the team over the last few years, as her life as a cop got in the way.

"Over ninety-thousand screaming fans. Must be crazy."

"You've never been to a game?" This surprised Charlene, since Larry was a football fanatic.

"Never."

"You're missing out. All those college girls in skimpy clothing and bare flesh. You'd be in heaven."

"Up yours, Taylor."

"Did you see last night's game?"

Larry grunted acknowledgement. "Pathetic."

"They won."

"Yeah, last second field goal. They were favored by eighteen points. Turner flopped last night, he threw four picks."

"He's a Heisman candidate."

"True. Last night he was just off his game. He'll turn it around, it's still early."

"Let's get to it."

Most of what people learned about police work came from watching movies and TV, a thin line between police fact and police fiction. In reality, police investigations were nothing like on TV or in movies. Police didn't mark murder sites with chalk outlines. The tape or chalk silhouette is a nice visual crutch for a cop movie or TV show, but the police didn't outline murder victims because it contaminated crime scenes.

Instead, photographs were taken of the body and its surroundings, along with a series of measurements to fixed reference points. Occasionally dots, lines, or boxes of fluorescent paint might be used to make photos clearer, especially when the victim was a traffic fatality, on dark pavement, at night. But those weren't really outlines, and crime lab employees got very annoyed if any of the paint touched any actual evidence and interfered with their work.

Because of that, Charlene programmed herself to work-mode. She had a routine when investigating a murder at the scene. She closed her eyes, picturing the exact location and positioning of the body. When she opened her eyes, it was as if the victim's body remained.

She walked around the invisible body, circling it in a five-foot radius. Numerous footprints went in every direction, both away from and towards the victim. Different shoes sizes, brands, stride-lengths, and gaits were arranged in no particular order.

Charlene got down on one knee, bending her head as low to the ground as possible, trying to reach eye level with the grass.

"These prints look significantly deeper than the others."

"Bigger guy? Some of these football players are massive."

"Not cleat marks. He could have been carrying something, extra weight on his shoulders."

"You think this is a drop site? You think she was killed somewhere else?"

Charlene shrugged her shoulders. "I'm just thinking out loud here."

Even though they'd only been partnered a short time, Charlene and Larry worked out a system where Charlene spitballed ideas and Larry contributed his thoughts in some back and forth banter.

"What else is on your mind?" Larry asked, apparently detecting something in Charlene's posture.

"Hey, you," she yelled across the field to a CSI member.

He jogged over. "What's up?" The man had gelled-back hair and a pointy nose.

"You got a measuring tape or ruler?"

The tech pulled a metal ruler from his belt and handed it to her.

The detective got down on her knees and measured the depth of the shoeprint.

From the ground she said, "I know it's a stretch, but I first thought what looked to be the same shoe print and size, going in the other direction, isn't as deeply indented into the group." She got to her feet. "I was right."

She gave the ruler back to the CSI tech and walked with Larry. From the corner of her eye, she noticed the techie get down and start measuring the same prints.

"He carried something out here, but empty-handed on his way back?" Larry asked.

"Maybe."

The shoe imprints that Charlene had recognized as being deeper into the ground approached the body from the dressing room exit, where the players entered the playing field from the locker room.

"If the killer carried the victim and dumped her here, that would rule out a woman," Larry said.

"Not necessarily. There are some strong women in the world. I'm sure many of the female athletes even at this school might be strong enough. Our vic is petite, I'm sure not even a hundred pounds."

They were quiet for minutes, thoughts circling the detective's mind.

"You have your lip lodged between your teeth," Larry said. "What are you thinking?"

Charlene was no longer embarrassed when it was brought to her attention. When in the zone, she didn't realize she bit down on it.

"I'm thinking we need to find out who our victim is and inform her next of kin. Was she really a cheerleader or just wearing a costume?"

"You mean like some kind of role-playing game?"

Charlene let out a breath. "Oh, my God, that's all you think about."

"I'm a man, of course, it is."

She shook her head. "We'll come back when CSI and everyone else have completed their tasks so we can be alone, and work in a quiet space."

"What about Sierra?"

"We know where to find him. It's not like he saw the murder happen, did he?"

"I don't think so."

"Let's go."

The Los Angeles International Airport buzzed, per usual.

"Is that him?" Rachel strained her neck, eyeing the crowd that had gathered at the baggage terminal retrieving their luggage.

Calvin grinned. "Still no, Rach."

She asked at every black man who passed. Calvin didn't realize he had never shown Rachel a picture of Joshua.

He hadn't seen his brother in years. They'd talked on the phone frequently, but neither of them had reached out to make the trip to see each other.

The fallout had started with Calvin's spiral from USC, after a freak, on-field knee injury. Calvin's knee had been scoped twice, and doctors said he'd never play football again. The USC running back had lost the scholarship he'd worked so hard for, and that had angered him even further.

Calvin lost all touch with reality after that, wound up on the Vegas streets and in a bad place. He seethed about losing his scholarship, but it was more self-denial than anything. One selfish act, putting himself ahead of the team, so maybe he had gotten what he deserved. The only person to blame for his predicament was himself, and it had taken Calvin a long time to realize that.

While at USC, Josh had been Calvin's biggest fan. The football star had left tickets for Josh at every home game, and his brother had attended most of them. But when Calvin took a job with a Vegas bookie, after losing his scholarship, hired as the man's muscle, breaking legs and dishing out punishment to collect payments, Josh had lost all respect for Calvin, and the two had drifted apart, not just geographically.

Rachel had never met Josh, Calvin's brother who was an LAPD detective. Calvin knew he hadn't put his brother in the best position, a detective with a brother as a bill collector. His brother had probably gone to bat for Calvin more times than not, just to keep the large leg-breaker out of jail. Looking back now, Calvin didn't blame Joshua for cutting all ties.

The PI didn't like his life back then, wasn't proud of the things he had done. It was a job, a source of income and a means to an end. That's all. But he had turned the page. He and Rachel had moved on.

"You want this?"

Calvin looked at the cane in Rachel's hand, his 'walking stick'. "No."

"The doctors said you should use it, just in case."

His last case, a trek to South America, hadn't been gentle on his knee. "I'm fine, Rachel. I don't need it."

"Okay, but—"

"I'd recognize that bald head anywhere."

Calvin and Rachel spun around. Calvin came eye to eye with his brother, and they shared a smile.

"Hey, Cal."

"Hey, Josh."

They slapped hands together, and then pulled each other in for a hug, holding it for a few seconds, then pulled apart.

"You look good," Josh said.

"Thanks." Calvin poked his brother's soft gut with his finger. "What's this?"

Josh swiped Calvin's hand away, grinning. "That's called old age, having a wife, kids and a sixty hour a week job. You'll get there someday."

Calvin snorted. "Sounds pretty lame." He took a step back and turned to his side, to allow Rachel to step in, which she did. "This is Rachel."

Josh stuck out his meaty palm and Rachel shook it, her fine-boned fingers disappearing inside his large black mitt.

"Nice to finally meet you. Calvin has told me a lot about you."

Josh looked at Calvin. "Has he? Don't believe a word of it." He smiled.

"How are Alexis, Caleb and Kayla?" Calvin asked.

"Alexis is fantastic, and the kids drive me nuts."

"Good to hear." Calvin grabbed his bags from the baggage claim and heaved them over his shoulders.

"Let me take that for you." Joshua took Rachel's carry-on bag from her.

"Thanks." She looked at Calvin. "Such a gentleman."

"See," Josh said. "I told you not to believe what he told you."

They started walking. Rachel lagged behind, wheeling a rolling suitcase, seeming to appreciate the beauty of the LAX airport that Calvin had grown accustomed to during his college days.

The marble floor under their feet gleamed as herds of people rushed by them on either side. They gazed up at the blue Californian sky, out through the full ceiling skylight, the clouds floating lazily.

"Did you get the case?" Calvin asked.

The first thing the PI had done after receiving the phone call from his former equipment manager, right after booking their flights, was to call Josh and let him know. As a private investigator, having a brother inside the LAPD was very beneficial, and Calvin planned to take advantage of that. Plus, a common professional courtesy to let a police department know.

"No. USC is designated to West LA."

His brother worked at the Central Bureau. "Do you know who is working it?"

They exited the airport terminal and headed for the parking lots, which were four levels high. Rachel exhaled loudly to show her satisfaction, taking in the warm sun and admiring the well-built structures and oversized LAX letters.

"Detective Baker and Taylor."

"What are they like?"

"Baker's a veteran. He's a lifer, been on the job a long time, and has a successful track record. High clearance rate."

"What about Taylor?"

"She's a rookie. Started out as a Blue Flamer."

Because Calvin had worked so much with the LVMPD, he knew that Blue Flamer meant a rookie officer who felt like he or she had a mandate to save the world and bring all evildoers to justice.

"She?" Calvin had nothing against women, but Taylor's gender had thrown him for a loop. He was aware that very few female detectives existed, and he knew the kind of person it took to work the streets, especially the LA streets.

"Don't let her gender fool you. She's as tough as nails, and has a bit of a chip on her shoulder. She definitely doesn't shy away from the shit, and has already solved a couple of high profile cases. If she's anything like her father, she'll be one hell of a detective."

Josh pulled a set of keys from his pocket and unlocked the car, using the remote.

"I'd like to go to the crime scene, if that's okay?"

Josh smiled. "I think I can pull a few strings and get you in."

They got in the car.

"What about me?" Rachel asked from the backseat.

Calvin looked at his brother. "Do you think Alexis wants some company?"

"Absolutely."

"You're pawning me off?" Rachel seemed upset.

Calvin turned in his seat and looked back at her. "Just for the afternoon. Then I'll pick you up and we'll go somewhere nice to eat. How about—"

"No way," Josh cut in. "First night in LA, we're having you guys over for supper. Plus, you have a lot of catching up to do with your niece and nephew."

Calvin grinned. "Deal."

Chapter 2

It only took a quick phone call.

The victim, Samantha Baylor, was indeed a USC Song Girl, a term they used to refer to cheerleaders—an eighteen year old freshman, majoring in Economics.

Baylor was born and raised in San Francisco, where her parents still resided. Her mother worked as a law clerk and her father a computer software engineer. The Baylors were currently in the air, on the earliest flight towards LA.

Samantha was an only child.

Charlene snapped off her phone. "Motive might not be an easy one here."

"There's always a motive," Larry answered.

"Let's talk to the groundskeeper."

Francisco Sierra stood a head shorter than Charlene. He had weather-beaten skin, slicked-back shoulder length hair, callused palms and lines at the corners of his mouth. The Mexican sat in a first row seat, behind the Trojans bench, waiting for the detectives.

The man fidgeted nervously in his seat, and it could have been for a number of reasons—finding a dead body, the sight of a detective badge, possibly an illegal immigrant fearing deportation, or maybe he did know something about the murder. Charlene doubted it was the latter.

Larry stooped down beside the groundskeeper and Charlene remained standing, leaning back against the guard rail that separated the bleachers from the field.

"Mr. Sierra," Larry started. "Are you a legal citizen of the United—"

"Mr. Sierra," Charlene cut off Larry. "I'm Detective Taylor, this is my partner, Detective Baker. We'd like to ask you a few questions about this morning."

The groundskeeper nodded.

"Anything unusual happen this morning, before finding the body?"

"No. We come in like always, change clothes in back and come out on field." A heavily accented voice.

"Were you the first one out here?"

"Si."

"Are you always the first one out here?"

"Not always, but sometime."

"When did you first notice the girl?"

"As I come through entrance, I see something on field. I get close and see girl."

"Did you touch the body?"

"No."

"Did any of your colleagues touch the body?" Larry asked.

"No."

"What did you do?"

"I ran tell boss. He call cops."

Charlene tucked her hair behind her ears. "Did you notice anything else unusual when you first got to work? Any of your workers acting strange? Maybe something on the field that normally isn't there?"

The man shook his head. "No. Lots of grass trampled down around body, but day after win, field always messed up."

"How long have you been working here?" Charlene asked.

"Two year."

"You like it?"

"Si."

"Do you recognize the girl?"

"Si. She cheerleader."

"Do you know her name?"

"No."

"Were any of the locks broken? Did you notice the entrances tampered with, damaged in any way, as if someone had broken in here last night?"

"Didn't notice nothing."

Charlene looked at Larry. "Anything else?"

"Nah."

"Thank you, Mr. Sierra. If you think of anything that might help, please let us know."

The Mexican stood from his seat and walked away, a slight limp in his gait.

Charlene sat down beside her partner. "What do you think?"

"He doesn't know anything. That murder happened long before Sierra even woke up and thought about work."

"We didn't find any evidence of tampering with locks or breaking in. Does that mean the killer had access to the field? Could be a worker."

Larry nodded. "Could be. We'll have the whole staff backgrounded and checked. But what kind of motive would a groundskeeper have to kill a cheerleader?"

"What kind of motive would anybody have to kill a cheerleader?"

"Lust? Money? Greed? Revenge? Hate? Sex? Jealousy? Personal Vendetta? Who knows? Murder is murder; there's always a reason behind it."

"Do you think her race is significant?"

"Oh no, Taylor, don't start that. Let's not jump to conclusions that this is a race issue."

Now it was time to start spit-balling ideas, as Charlene and Larry liked to do when they got into work-mode.

"So the Trojans have a game last night. They win. People storm the field. I assume they all go to a party afterwards, at least that's how it used to be. After the crowd files out and the Coliseum is shut down, someone, or a group of people, come back here, or are still here, and kill the cheerleader."

Larry scratched his thick sideburns. "But why here? Was she still here after the game?"

"We have a few hours before the Baylors arrive in town, so let's go back to the precinct and see what we can dig up on the family," Charlene suggested.

"You think this is some sort of revenge killing for something they've done or gotten into?"

She folded her arms over her chest. "I have no idea."

"I don't think an eighteen year-old cheerleader has too many enemies, yet."

"Don't underestimate the college social scene, Larry. Women can be overprotective with boyfriends, jealousy can be a motivating factor. And cheerleading can be just as intense, competitive and cut-throat as any college athletic team."

After dropping Rachel off at his brother's house, and making the introductions to the rest of his family, Calvin left his girlfriend, and he and his brother hit interstate 110 heading towards the LA Memorial Coliseum.

Calvin vibrated slightly in the passenger's seat, in anticipation of visiting the cathedral, the place that had created a mix of emotions for the large black former running back. On that very field, he had broken records, won championships, and went to war with his football brothers. But it had also been the location of the biggest setback of his life, a play that had turned his whole world upside down, and had caused so many sleepless, nightmare-filled nights.

How would it feel to once again step onto the green grass of the football field? To walk the sidelines, make that memorable trek from hash mark to hash mark, as he travelled the gridiron that had made him famous, and then took him down.

Mixed emotions for sure.

"Thanks, buddy, I owe ya one." Josh clicked off his cellphone and set it in the coffee holder between the seats. He turned to Calvin. "The victim is a USC Song Girl."

"Really? That's why Nick was so adamant about my joining the investigation."

"Freshman, African-American."

He scratched his cleanly-shaven head. "Is Makayla still the team advisor?"

Josh smiled sneakily. "I believe so. Why?"

"Does she still live in the same house?"

"Will only take one call to find out."

Makayla Thomas had been a first year cheerleading team advisor, normally held by a USC cheer alumni, when Calvin first met her. He was in his junior year at USC, a star running back and worshipped by thousands of USC fans and students. Even though a few years older, Makayla had caught the running back's eye one day at practice, and a fling ensued.

Both were young, lustful, and without expectations.

He allowed himself a small grin, thinking about his time with Makayla.

"I see you smiling over there."

His brother's voice shook Calvin out of his time-travelling journey. "What do you mean?"

"You're thinking about Makayla."

"So?"

"So? You told me she had one of the healthiest sex drives you had ever seen in a woman. It was all she thought about. You told me that *you* even had a hard time keeping up. Flexible, eager, intense, erotic. You said—"

"Ya, ya, ya, I get it."

"Hey, I'm just repeating your words, brother."

"If you didn't notice that blond bombshell I had with me earlier, that is called a girlfriend."

Josh grunted. "So that's who that was."

"Anyway, last time I heard, Makayla got engaged. She's probably happily married now."

"Divorced."

Calvin looked at his brother, who still wore a large smile on his face, "Really?"

"Yep, and just recently."

"You're enjoying this, aren't you?"

"I think it will be entertaining."

"Just drive."

Makayla Thomas *did* live in the same townhouse on West Forty-First Street, a few blocks from the Coliseum, as she had when she and Calvin had hit it off all those years ago. Joshua had called ahead to let the cheerleading advisor know they were coming, so she waited outside when they pulled the car into the driveway.

Physically, the cheer advisor had changed slightly. She'd put on about twenty pounds, now a shapely size twelve, but still had curves in all the right places. She sauntered down the concrete drive towards them, her hips swaying, a full-bosomed woman flaunting what God had given her.

Her hazel eyes still danced. She had small frown lines around her mouth, and her nails looked manicured and buffed.

They got out of the car.

"Calvin Watters, as I live and breathe. I heard you were dead."

"You heard right."

"Come here." She summoned with those long, perfect red fingernails and wrapped him in an embrace.

Calvin pulled away. "You remember my brother, Josh."

Josh nodded.

"Of course I do. The detective. Come on inside."

"Actually I have to go," Josh said, looking towards Calvin, an obvious smirk hidden behind his big brown eyes.

Calvin squinted a glare towards his only brother. "What do you mean?"

"I gotta get back to the precinct. My partner is gonna come with me to get you a car, and then I'll bring it back here and leave it for you."

"We can do that later. I can come with you."

This time Josh smiled wide. "No need, I have it all worked out."

Calvin knew his brother, knew the warped sense of humor. This was a preplanned sabotage to get Calvin alone with Makayla. Calvin looked at Makayla who stood with her legs crossed, hands perched on wide hips, and smooshing her lips together, a knowing look in her eyes.

A set up?

"You're not afraid to be alone with me, are you, Calvin Watters? I guess times have changed." A wink teased at the corner of her eye.

Calvin stood speechless, indeed afraid to be alone with his ex, but it had nothing to do with not trusting himself. He had self-control, tons of it. He remembered Makayla's aggressive nature, and Calvin worried that she'd flat out pounce once his brother vanished.

Calvin licked his dry lips. "Of course not."

She stood with one leg bent, and a hand lodged on the curve of her hip. "Good."

Makayla moved quickly, three strides to get to Calvin's side. She bent her arm at the elbow, as if summoning for Calvin to snake his arm inside hers and follow obediently.

"You two have fun," Josh said, lobbing a slight smile Calvin's way.

"Oh, we will," Makayla replied, seduction oozing in her voice.

As they walked towards the house, Calvin wrapped his free arm behind his back and flipped the middle finger to his brother, who responded with a honk of the car horn, before backing out.

She led him inside, through the front door, ushering him in and insisting Calvin leave his shoes on. They sat in a large, open-plan living room with little wall space. The back wall had a run of doors, and the varying floor height created a natural, cozy home for seating. The living room was a carbon copy of the 1970's era, when the notion of the sunken living space was in style. It no longer was. A dark colored armoire leaned against a wall looking completely out of place.

"Drink?"

"No, thank you."

"Don't tell me Calvin Watters has gone boring on me?"

Calvin flushed.

"Mind if I have one?"

Calvin shrugged his broad shoulders. "Help yourself."

She left the room. Calvin wiped his sweaty palms on the leg of his pants. He looked around the room from his place on the sofa, shaking his head at what few changes Makayla had made to the place over the years. Almost as if she was still reliving her college days. Calvin knew a lot about how that felt.

"How long have you been back here?" Calvin called out.

Makayla re-entered the room holding a tall glass with light brown liquid swirling around ice cubes.

"Moved back in after my divorce. My former roommates had never moved out, so it worked."

"Still drinking the Long Island Ice Teas?"

Makayla nodded. "You remember."

He remembered what booze did to her. It could go two ways: it might loosen her tongue so she would share more pertinent inside information on the cheerleading squad, or it would loosen her clothes, which Calvin was in no position nor did he want that.

She slinked down next to him, close, and seductively tucked her legs under her, sitting on her knees. She took a sip of her drink, sucking on an ice cube and then dropping it back into the glass.

Calvin tried not to stare as Makayla openly flirted with the man with whom she had shared some epic memories, in this very area of the house. He shook his head to snap himself back to the present.

"I guess you've heard about Samantha Baylor?"

She swallowed, and set her glass gingerly on the table at the end of the couch. "I did." There was a slight quiver in her voice.

He waited, but she didn't say more.

"Can you tell me a bit about her?"

Makayla stared at her drink on the table, the sweat streaking down the side of the glass. She rubbed it away with a swipe of her thumb. When she finally turned her head and looked in Calvin's direction, her eyes had moistened.

"Sam was a sweet kid."

Calvin reached for a tissue box and tugged one free, handing it to her. She took it without saying anything, or even looking at Calvin, and dabbed her eyes softly.

"Just a freshman, new to cheering. She said she didn't cheer in high school, but she definitely had a talent for it and was enthusiastic to learn and improve. Flexible, and her athletic ability and coordination were second to none. Her coach-ability, and competence to learn on the fly were exceptional. She owned a genuine smile, and perfect muscle tone."

Even though Makayla wasn't the head coach of the cheering squad, she had been in the game long enough, as a cheerleader and an assistant coach, so when she spoke with the tone of a proud coach her years of experience made her an expert.

The information Makayla gave Calvin wasn't exactly what he hoped for, but he let her go on about cheering. It was her passion, and he knew that if he waited her out, eventually she would open up and he could find out more about Samantha Baylor the person.

"Samantha wasn't even supposed to be on the team."

"What do you mean?" Calvin asked.

"She didn't try out." She hesitated, bringing the tissue to her face. "Oh my God, do you think if she wasn't on the team she'd still be alive?"

She sniffed, a slight snort, and wiped the tears rolling down her cheeks.

"I'm sure that has nothing to do with it, Makayla." Although Calvin wasn't convinced, yet. In fact, he had nothing yet on the murder to lead him in any direction. He had to get her back on track. "How was she on the team? I thought tryouts were mandatory?"

Makayla nodded. "They are. But like I said, she hadn't cheered in high school, so why would she attempt to cheer at the college level?"

"So what happened?"

"Sam came to our first practice with her roommate, Rory Cummings. Rory is a sophomore, came to us on an academic scholarship, had a great freshman year, and Sam decided to tag along to watch Rory practice. I remember noticing her in the stands. She was so into our practice, studying the moves, imitating the actions. She didn't think anyone was watching, but she had the rhythm, even just sitting in the stands and mimicking the moves."

Calvin leaned back and listened. Makayla was on a roll, so he wasn't going to slow her down.

"Halfway through practice one of our girls went down, twisted an ankle as we were attempting one of our more challenging stunts. We only had one alternate at the time and she wasn't at practice because her GPA had dropped under 3.0 so she was on a leave from us."

Calvin knew, as a former player, all athletes had to maintain a 3.0 grade point average to remain eligible to be a part of a college athletics team—one of the reasons why he had lost his scholarship his senior year. When he had been injured, he sank down into the swirling vortex of his funk, he ignored his studies—something he'd always regret. That had given *them* more fire power against him.

Makayla continued. "Rory suggested Samantha step in, just to fill in for practice. Rudy, as head coach, hesitated, but he really wanted to continue practice so agreed to work on the smaller points of our routine. When Makayla stepped onto that floor, it was as if she belonged. She fit right in from the get-go."

"What was her relationship with the rest of the team like?"

"Everyone loved her. How could they not? She was so easy to love. Sweet, genuine, easy to get along with. Once we checked her out—GPA and everything, we offered her the second alternate position. Of course she knew that the only way she'd ever get to cheer was if someone got hurt, but she seemed okay with that. She actually seemed quite pleased and excited to be a part of our team."

Calvin had a hard time believing that with all of those cheerleaders, men and women who had worked their whole life at cheerleading, those who had been scouted, recruited by scholarship, either athletic or academic, or walk-ons, would be okay with someone just stepping in with no experience. Cheerleaders could be just as vicious, if not more, than any other college athlete.

"What about off the field. What about Sam's social life?"

She shook her head. "I don't get involved in that."

"Come on, Makayla, you're in the change room. Girls talk, especially college girls. You must have heard things. Did she have many friends? A boyfriend? What was she into?

"I know she dated a football player."

Calvin had his notebook out. "Which one?"

"I'm not sure about that. But I overheard Sam and Rory talking one day."

"When was the last time you saw Samantha?"

"Friday's practice."

"Did you notice anything different about her? Maybe a change in her attitude? Like maybe something bothered her?"

Makayla leaned back into the sofa, sinking into the soft cushioned-back. She paused, quiet, as if thinking back to that scene.

"Now that you mention it, I remember Rudy stopping one of our stunts because Sam missed her cue."

"Is that unusual?"

"Very. Sam was usually spot on, flawless technique and her timing like clockwork. But I don't know, she just seemed off, as if unfocused, her concentration elsewhere."

Calvin noted this. "Why full-practice mode? Do alternates practice like the regulars?"

"Everyone has to be prepared, but Sam was a regular."

"Really? How's that?"

"An injury to a regular girl."

"What about alternate number one?"

"Still hadn't passed our GPA requisite."

"So Sam just stepped in and took the place, passing two cheerleaders in the process?"

"Pretty much."

"How did they feel about that?"

Makayla shrugged. "It wasn't up to them."

"What are their names?"

Calvin wrote down the cheerleaders' names and closed his book. He checked the time on his phone, wondering about his brother.

"Any more questions?"

"You know," Calvin said. "You haven't really given me anything to work with. This wasn't really worth my while."

"That can be changed."

She slid closer to Calvin on the couch, a twinkle in her eye, and rested her hand upon his shoulder.

Calvin shrugged her hand away gently, not wanting to offend Makayla and lose any kind of cooperation she could offer. He knew that he would need her. A cheerleader was dead, and Makayla spent more time with those girls than anyone else.

"I mean, do you have any gossip, pertinent information about either Samantha Baylor or any of the other cheerleaders on the squad. Come on, Makayla, I know things happen and words are exchanged behind locker room doors."

Makayla eyed Calvin, as if sizing him up. "What's it worth to you?"

"Depends what you have."

She grinned slyly, a half-smirk, one side of her lips curling up playfully. "Could be something, but could be nothing."

"What do ya got?"

"A couple of weeks ago I walked in on what looked like an argument. Samantha and her roommate were in the hallway heading out, and they were talking to two other girls from the team. They were heading out the back way from the change rooms, and the only way I saw them was because I left Dan's office."

"What day?"

"I can't remember the exact date, but it was either a Sunday or Wednesday, because it was late, and our practices end at eleven and ten on those days."

Calvin scribbled notes. "What exactly did you see?"

She shook her head. "Not much, because when one of the girls spotted me making my way down the hallway towards them, they all hushed up and looked towards the floor. I asked if everything was okay and they said they were fine. But if you ask me, it looked like a confrontation."

"So you didn't hear anything?"

"Nope, as soon as they saw me everyone stopped talking. Kind of suspicious, but some girls prefer their privacy and don't like their dirty laundry aired."

"Damn. Write down the names of those cheerleaders."

He handed her the notebook and pen and she scribbled the names quickly. She handed the book back, but not the pen right away. She raised it to her mouth and seductively ran it over her lips, tugging her bottom lip down and stroking the pen slowly.

"So, was that worth anything?" she asked.

Calvin didn't reply, too busy thinking. He didn't have any more questions for Makayla, but a lot were running through his mind, a lot of processing to do. The PI was sure cheerleaders didn't like their toes stepped on, or rookies moving in and being handed their jobs. But how far would a cheerleader go to keep or regain her status on one of the top cheerleading teams in the nation, a team which competed across the country, with a shot at competing in Nationals?

"Any other questions?"

"I don't think so," he told Makayla.

"Well then," she said, sliding closer to Calvin. He could smell the light floral fragrance of her perfume. "What should we do now?"

Calvin stood up. "I think I'll wait outside for Josh."

Makayla stretched out on the couch, slinking to the sofa arm and propping herself up, her hips raised in the air. She pouted her lips. "Are you sure?"

"Thanks for your help, Makayla." Calvin turned and walked away.

As he let himself out, he heard Makayla's voice.

"You owe me one, Calvin."

Calvin opened the door and stepped out into the sunlight, raising his notepad above his eyes to shield them from the brightness. A silver Hyundai Elantra was parked in the drive-way behind Makayla's red Jeep Cherokee. Calvin's brother stayed in the patrol car, with his partner in the passenger's seat.

Calvin walked towards the cop car, shaking his head as he moved. He couldn't see Josh's face, as the sun's glare caught on the windshield on the driver's side. But when he reached the driver's door and looked through the open window, Josh still had that same smile fixed on his black face.

"How'd that go?"

"How long have you been out here?" Calvin asked.

"We just got here," Josh replied. His partner snorted a laugh.

"Liar." Calvin gritted his teeth and squeezed his fists playfully.

"Here." Josh tossed a key with an electronic car lock out the window.

Calvin snatched it athletically. "Thanks."

"See you at home."

Calvin again gave him the one finger salute.

Chapter 3

"Mr. and Mrs. Baylor, thanks for coming. I'm sorry it's under these circumstances."

A solemn-faced, African American man and Caucasian woman sat at a table. The couple was middle-aged, probably early to mid-forties, and still had much of their youth in their eyes and skin. But Charlene knew, as a cop, that this incident, losing their only child, would age them.

Samantha Baylor's mother had smooth, makeup-less skin and sharp cheekbones. Her eyes were red-rimmed, and she held a tissue to her face. The man of the Baylor family had a full head of black hair, dark framed glasses and a square jaw. He looked to be in shock.

Their plane had landed less than an hour ago and the LAPD had had a car meet them at the airport to offer the now childless parents a ride to the headquarters. Charlene met them downstairs in the parking lot and escorted them upstairs, where they had secured a tiny room to be alone. The detective wanted the parents to feel welcomed and wanted, and for them to understand that their daughter's murder was a priority and being given everything they had.

"You're never prepared for a phone call like that," said the shaky-voiced, fragile woman who looked on the verge of cracking. "When the police calls and says your only daughter was murdered."

Michael Baylor wrapped an arm around his wife's shoulders and pulled her close. Mrs. Baylor let herself semi-collapse into her husband's embrace.

"You're not supposed to outlive your children. It's not right for a parent to put their child into the ground." His voice trembled, and his upper lip quivered.

Larry joined them and set two steaming Styrofoam cups down on the desk in front of the Baylor parents. Kimberly Baylor picked up the coffee and cupped her hands around the warm Styrofoam, as if hoping the heat could scorch through her body that had been chilled by the news.

Larry had advanced to a D-3, and Charlene a D-1, but since accepting her promotion to detective not long ago, replacing her father who had been murdered, Larry had treated Charlene as an equal, and sometimes even let her take the lead.

She'd been concerned about being partnered with Larry Baker, an old-school cop who hadn't changed his approach with the times, but Larry hadn't been thrown off by his first female partner. After a rocky start, Charlene and Larry now had a great working relationship.

"Can you tell us about your daughter?" Charlene asked.

"Are there any leads?"

Charlene shook her head. "We're working on it. It's still very early in the investigation."

A moment of silence ensued, and Charlene wondered if the Baylors remembered the detective's original question. But she didn't need to re-ask, because Kimberley Baylor spoke.

"She was always hard-headed." She forced a smile. "We had wanted her to stay around San Fran, wanted her to attend a college close to home. She insisted on coming to LA, always dreamed of attending USC."

"We knew she needed this," Michael cut in. "As they say, she needed to spread her wings, get away and see the world through her own eyes, away from the careful watch of mom and dad."

His face twisted, as if battling with the thought that perhaps if he had been more persistent, his daughter would have gone to a local college and still been alive today.

Kim blinked her wet eyes. "She was a beautiful person, inside and out." She hesitated. "Not to boast, but my daughter had it all in high school. She was top of her class in academics, popular in her circle of friends, boys calling all the time, athletic, just someone easy to get along with who people gravitated towards."

Charlene remembered Samantha Baylor's body on the twenty yard line. She had indeed been a beautiful girl—flawless skin, a round, young face, a kid yet to become a woman.

A glint in her eye and the pride in her face and voice, told Charlene that Samantha Baylor meant everything to her parents—an only child who had probably been spoiled.

"What about college?" Larry asked.

"What do you mean?"

"Transitioning smoothly?" Charlene added.

"Do you mind?" Kim motioned to a box of tissues on the table.

"Please." Charlene handed the box to Mrs. Baylor, and the woman pulled one out softly, and dabbed her eyes.

"We gave Sam a few weeks to adjust. I know Sam, she was independent, wanted to prove to us she could make it on her own. For her first time away from us, I knew she wanted us to see we didn't have to worry about her." He stopped, shook his head and closed his eyes.

His wife placed a hand in his lap and spoke. "We visited for the first time a few weeks after Sam moved in and got settled. I'd never seen my daughter happier. When she spoke, she glowed. According to her, everything was perfect: the campus, classes, friends. She didn't have one negative comment on anything related to USC."

"Did she mention any friends she was particularly close with?"

Michael shook his head. "No names. She seemed really close with her roommate, Rory Cummings. She went on and on about how great Rory was."

"What do you know about Rory?"

He shrugged his shoulders. "We met her when we dropped Sam off and helped her move in. Seemed like a really nice girl, quiet, down to earth. Didn't have much time to spend with her."

Charlene knew, from experience, that college kids, especially girls, acted totally different around adults than they did in their social circles and full party mode. The detective doubted the Baylors would have seen any side to Rory to cause them concern.

"Our second weekend visit gave us the opportunity to learn more about Rory, plus, Sam spoke about her all the time during our phone calls."

"Sam made an instant connection with her," Kimberly said. "She was a sophomore, had a lot of friends who she'd introduced to Sam, and she even had a hand in getting Samantha on the USC cheerleading team. I believe she's from the Los Angeles area?" She looked at her husband.

He nodded. "I believe so."

This wasn't anything that Charlene and Larry couldn't have found out by looking up Cummings themselves, but it at least gave them a sense of her interactions with adults and her roommate, and a bit of a 'where to start'.

Kimberly choked on a sob. "Sam was so proud to be a part of the cheerleading team. She talked about it constantly; it consumed her. When our daughter got something in her head, she stopped at nothing to achieve it. And I could tell that the cheer team had a hold on her and she had a determination to be the best at it, as she did with everything in her life. And she usually succeeded, too."

"What about other friends? Did you get a chance to meet anyone else?" Larry asked.

"No. We had only visited twice since she'd moved in. We were planning another trip next month."

"Was Sam seeing anyone romantically?" Charlene inquired.

"She never had any boyfriends in high school, nobody she left behind." She smiled. This time it wasn't as forced, as if recalling a fond memory. "I always questioned her about it. Urged her to go out and meet some boys. But that never seemed to interest her. She was never into boys."

"Nobody at USC caught her eye?"

"Not that we knew of."

"Is that something Samantha would share with you?"

"I would hope so. We always encouraged her to tell us everything, and to keep no secrets from us. We are a religious family, detective, and we are an open family."

Charlene remembered her own life in college. She told her parents absolutely nothing. What they didn't know couldn't hurt them, or her. Even now, although she had gotten better, sharing feelings and secrets with family wasn't something she was totally comfortable with.

The detective knew she wasn't the typical daughter, but she also recognized that many college students didn't exactly share everything about their college life with their parents. Some things would need to come from Samantha Baylor's close friends, and Charlene had a name to start with.

"Can we get the name of Samantha's cheerleading coach?"

"Sure." Mrs. Baylor pulled out her phone and tapped in a passcode. She scrolled down with her thumb, navigating through the pages, her lips moving as she read in her head.

She handed Charlene the phone. The detective jotted down the name and handed back the phone.

Charlene wanted to ask more, but turned towards Larry. "Anything else?"

"Nothing right now."

She looked back at the parents, who were still huddled closely. To Charlene, they seemed like a close couple, and they would hopefully use each other for support and stability to get through this devastating time. This would be unlike anything they had ever endured in their lives.

Charlene looked back at the parents. "I think that's all for now. I know it was a long flight and you must be tired. You probably have a lot to take care of. I'll take those contact numbers, and make sure you leave us with where you'll be staying here in LA. Thank you for your time."

Charlene stared blankly at her computer screen, biting her lip.

"That wasn't the time to ask them about potential enemies," Larry said. "We can do some digging into their lives if it comes to that. What are you thinking?"

"They don't know their daughter as well as they think they do." Charlene looked at Larry, who had just turned on the computer on his desk.

Larry had his usual grey hair messed and the front cowlick everpresent, his gut nestled comfortably on the keyboard to his computer.

The detectives had exchanged contact information with the Baylors. The couple were staying at the Radisson Hotel Los Angeles Midtown at USC.

"You think she's more than they say?"

"Maybe not. But according to her parents, Samantha Baylor was a straight "A", Bible thumping, do-gooder who had no enemies and no interest in boys."

"Well, she pissed off someone." Larry pursed his lips.

"And what was she doing on the football field that late at night?"

"What are the facts we know about Samantha Baylor?"

"She was an eighteen year-old freshman."

"Cheerleader."

"Only child from a good family."

"According to her parents, she had no boyfriend."

"That's not a fact; that's from her parents. Very few college kids reveal such information to their parents, until it's something serious."

Larry grinned. "You sound like you're speaking from experience."

"If I had told my parents everything I'd done at college, my dad's heart would have stopped. I am still very cautious about what I tell my mom."

"I agree."

It was true, Charlene hadn't been the easiest daughter. She had lived the "college life" long after graduating, with very few worries or cares about who she hurt with her reckless actions. The drinking, the sex, the carefree lifestyle had been dangerous for Charlene and anyone close to her. She tried hard to be a better person, but it was an everyday struggle to hold it all together.

"You know, Brady still wants to see you."

She knew. She didn't need to be told again. Just the mention of his name dredged up heated memories.

Darren Brady, AKA the Celebrity Slayer, one of her first 'unofficial' homicide cases, never strayed far from Charlene's thoughts. It was one crazy case full of double-crosses and near-death experiences.

The man, a former LAPD officer, a bent cop, who had worked directly with Charlene on the detective's first homicide case, had been secretly killing 'B' list celebrities throughout LA. He had been one of the biggest and most gruesome serial killers the city had ever seen.

Charlene tried desperately to put the whole ordeal behind her. Frequent trips to a psychiatrist, heavy doses of medication, sleepless/ dream-filled nights, booze, anything she could do to help herself move on. Nothing worked, but at least knowing that Darren Brady was dead and gone had somewhat lightened the burden.

Then, weeks ago, Larry revealed to her that Brady was in fact not dead, but alive, living on life support in a coma at the Cedars-Sinai Medical Center. Brady had woken up a couple of weeks ago, and he requested to see Charlene.

She wasn't sure how to react, what to say. Charlene had been putting it off, and she had no idea if she could ever stir up the nerve to see him face to face again. So many memories, so many thoughts, so many questions. She had thought she'd gotten past it, but Dr. Gardner said that her scars had only healed superficially, and there was still a lot to confront.

Charlene drew a calming breath. "I know, Larry."

She didn't know what else to say to the man who had stepped in to be not only her partner, but also a father-figure and mentor to her. How could she tell Larry that she was scared, and for the first time, unsure as a cop.

Her partner laid a concerned hand on Charlene's wrist. "You know I can go with you if you want, right?"

"I know."

"I can just tell him flat out 'no' if you want me to."

"I know, Larry. I just need time to think."

"It's been a couple of weeks."

"I realize that."

"He'll be moved soon."

Since the cases were local, and the arresting/involving officer local, Brady was booked in absentia, remaining at the hospital but technically in police custody. Once he awoke and cleared by medical personnel, he would be transported to the county's Inmate Reception Center, the primary intake and release facility for male inmates in the Los Angeles County jail system, where he would be held pending trial and appointed an attorney. The feds had another facility, but LAPD took precedence over the Celebrity Slayer case.

"When is the move?"

"Soon."

"I just need more time, Larry."

"You got it, Kid."

Charlene needed the topic changed. "Where's Davidson?"

Larry swiveled in his chair. "He's hanging around here somewhere." He yelled out loud to no one in particular. "Anyone see Davidson?"

A young man in a police uniform, with red hair and a constellation of freckles over a bulky nose, almost galloped into the detective bureau of room 637. Officer Davidson, the baby-sitter cop, had been given the orders of chauffeuring the Baylors from the airport to the LAPD Headquarters on 100 West 1st Street.

"What was the mood like in the car?" Charlene asked.

"Quiet. They didn't speak one word to me or each other the whole way."

"Already starting to mourn," Larry said.

"Do you blame them?" Charlene remarked. "They probably have a lot of questions that none of us have answers to."

"Thanks, officer. Oh wait." Charlene had a thought. "Dig up everything you can on the parents. Find out if they have any outstanding debt, any enemies, or any reasons why anyone would want to hurt them."

"Sure thing."

The officer left.

Larry exhaled loudly. "We have a big day tomorrow."

"Agreed. I'd like to talk to Baylor's roommate, and her cheerleader teammates and coach."

"We also need to see her teachers, see what kind of student she was and maybe even a character reference check."

"Cal, man, is it great to see you."

Calvin was wrapped up in a large bear hug and almost lifted off the ground, which says a lot for a man who stood about six-four and tipped the scales at two-twenty. The man on the other end of the embrace out-weighed the PI, but stood a good head shorter.

Nicholas Charles, the man with two first names, was Calvin's former equipment manager with the USC Trojan football team, and also the reason why Calvin rushed to Los Angeles. Tonight, Nick wore his usual USC ball hat that covered a brown, balding head of hair. He had a round face with multiple chins and his gut forced his tucked-in golf shirt to slip out from the waistband of his track pants.

"Hey, Nick, good to see you too."

They pulled apart, and chose a booth at the USC Traditions Bar and Grill. A lot of memories came flooding back to Calvin as he had stepped into the restaurant, a lot of nights spent hanging with friends, watching the big-screen TVs, and hitting on girls. But on a Sunday night, the underground sports bar was sparsely occupied.

"I thought this place closed on Sundays." Calvin said.

"It always had been, but they are trying something new this month, some sort of special events month."

A cute waitress with a blond pony-tail, dark tan and big blue eyes approached their table with a wide smile.

"Two baskets of spicy buffalo wings and a pitcher of Trojan Amber."

The waitress nodded and skipped back to the bar, her pony-tail bouncing at the back of her head.

Calvin looked around as he slid into the booth, checking out the row of barstools, the big screen TVs, the sports memorabilia on the wall—every little detail took him back to his playing days, his time at USC.

"They never took it down."

Calvin snapped out of his flashbacks by Nick's voice. "What?"

Nick nodded towards the corner of the room, specifically a jersey hanging on the brick wall. The familiar USC cardinal and gold colored shirt, with the number twenty-one and the name Watters stitched on the back.

Calvin swallowed over a lump in his throat, and his nerves tingled.

"Price tried to get them to take it down. What an asshole."

Jordan Price, the Athletic Director at USC. He had taken over the position during Calvin's third year at college, and had been one of the main reasons for Calvin leaving school that year. There was no love lost between the two. Calvin hadn't seen Price since the former running back's departure from USC, and hadn't lost any sleep over it.

"Is Price still around?" Calvin asked. Even just mentioning his name gave Calvin a bad taste in his mouth.

"Ya, not sure why though. No one likes him and he does nothing to support our athletes. I'm pretty sure he has a hidden agenda."

"Still the same?"

"About. Working on his second divorce since starting at the school."

"I doubt he's an easy man to live with."

"Yeah, he doesn't exactly believe in the sanctity of marriage."

"He's probably starting to feel some pressure these days as well."

Nick nodded. "If he doesn't win a bowl game this year, chances are he won't be back."

Calvin was in no mood to talk about Jordan Price. The PI didn't want to bring up that part of his past, after he'd worked so hard to put it all behind him. Of course he'd thought about Price over the last five years, how could he not? If a different AD had been in place back then, who knew how Calvin's life would have turned out?

Would he have lost his scholarship, or would he have stayed, completed college, and moved on to bigger and better things?

But the world worked in mysterious ways, and fate had a different path for Calvin. Sure he had regrets, but every step Calvin had taken after college—working the Vegas streets as a leg-breaker, on the run as a primary murder suspect, trekking the Amazon rain forest to hunt down a fugitive on the run—all had been learning experiences and helped to build him up.

"So then why is my jersey still on the wall?"

"They refused to take it down. You had, still have, a lot of fans in these parts. Whether you want to acknowledge it or not, you were a God around here."

Calvin could feel his face burn.

"You can ignore it or pretend it's not true. I know that it's not your style to accept recognition or praise for what you did, you were always like that on and off the football field, but it's true. A lot of people were pissed off with how it all went down after your injury." He looked into Calvin's eyes. "You still have a lot of friends in these parts, and a lot of people who were sad to see you go. I might be your biggest fan."

Calvin knew Nick wasn't just blowing smoke, that that's really the way he felt. Calvin knew it when he played here, and he knew it after he left here. But Calvin hadn't been proud of the course his life had taken after college, and had not stayed in touch with anyone from USC. He just didn't want anyone to know how far he had fallen.

Nick's attention drew away, and Calvin turned to see that the equipment manager had spotted the waitress with their order. She set everything down on the table and Nick poured two glasses of draft beer from the pitcher.

"Can I get you anything else?" she asked Nick.

"No, I think we're good, thanks."

Then she turned towards Calvin. "Do I know you from somewhere?"

Nick snorted.

"I doubt it," Calvin said.

"You look very familiar."

"That's—"

"I'm new around here, so I doubt we know each other," Calvin cut Nick off.

The girl shrugged her slender shoulders and bounced away.

"Why didn't you tell her who you are?"

Calvin smiled. "I played five years ago. That girl looks like a freshman, so I'm pretty sure she would have no idea who I am."

"She's probably seen your picture."

"Does it really matter?"

"Whatever." Nick seemed unfazed or uncaring by any of it as he bit into a juicy chicken wing, sauce spreading across his lips and part of his cheek.

Calvin took a drink of his beer and then wiped his mouth with his hand. "So what can you tell me about the cheerleader?"

The equipment guy finished his wing by sucking the rest of the chicken from the bone and waited until he swallowed to speak. "Very little. Of course you know the routine, we had the day off today, the day after a game. We are back to practice tomorrow."

"Do you know anything about her?"

"Not really, but you know locker room talk, footballers like to discuss and share details. You should come to practice tomorrow."

Calvin pursed his lips. "I don't think that would be a good idea."

He wasn't sure what kind of name he had around campus and the football circles. Nick could say all the right things, and maybe he even gave Calvin the runaround. The former USC football star hadn't stayed in touch with anyone from the football program, so showing up at practice tomorrow could go either way.

"Her name come up at all in the room?"

He shook his head. "Don't know for sure. Like I said, I don't know anything about her, never saw her around."

"So what exactly are you saying?"

"If they were talking about her, then she's not as innocent as everyone thinks."

"What—"

"Well looky here. Ain't that a sight for sore eyes?"

Calvin turned to see his brother and Rachel standing behind him. Rachel looked around the room and stopped at Calvin's jersey.

"Detective Watters." Nick stood from his bench seat and wrapped his beefy arms around Calvin's brother, squeezing aggressively. Nicholas Charles was definitely a hugger. "How long has it been?"

"Since Calvin went to USC."

"Who's this cutie?" Nick asked, acknowledging Rachel.

Calvin stood up. "Nick, this is Rachel. Rachel, this is Nick Charles, my former equipment manager."

"Nice to meet you," Rachel said, sticking out her hand.

Instead of shaking Rachel's hand, Nick lightly grasped the end of her fingers and gently kissed the top of her hand with a delicate peck, like a regular romantic Romeo.

"Wow, what a gentleman!" Rachel said.

"Don't believe everything you see." Calvin laughed.

Nick brought his hand back as if to slap Calvin on the side of the head. "Sit down you two," Nick motioned for Joshua and Rachel to join them in the booth.

Calvin slid over to allow Rachel to sit down and Josh joined Nick on his side of the booth.

"Where's Alexis?"

Josh put up his hands. "At home with Caleb and Kayla. That's what having kids does to a social life." He smiled. "How did your interview go this afternoon?"

Calvin swung his foot under the table and struck Josh pointed-toe first in the shin. Calvin's brother winced slightly.

"Thanks for that, by the way."

Josh nodded and grinned. "My pleasure, little brother."

"So Nick," Rachel said, propping her elbows on the top of the table and leaning towards the other side of the booth. "I want all the juicy gossip on Calvin from his college days."

Nick grinned. "Oh, where do I start?"

"Hey," a voice barked out from across the room. They all turned their head towards the bar, where their waitress pointed to a framed photograph on the wall. "You're Calvin Watters."

Chapter 4

"Whoa, he's cute." Dana Dayton held the heavy bag for Charlene, but was more interested in checking out the men working out around her.

"Focus," Charlene said, as she whipped out her leg with great force, striking the bottom of the heavy bag with the shin of her right leg.

Her partner, LAPD CSI specialist Dana Dayton, let out a large breath of air and an 'oomph' sound.

"Take it easy, Char."

"We're not here to stare at boys," Charlene teased.

"Why the hell not? Look at it here. We're the only two women in a roomful of eye candy. Might as well have a look-see."

Dana had been a long-time friend of Charlene's, going through the academy together and graduating at the same time.

"Just hold the bag."

"They are watching us, so why not look back?"

"I have a pretty good idea why they are staring at us," Charlene countered, jabbing her arm straight out, her glove-covered fist thrusting the mid-part of the bag.

The lab tech, as usual, wore very little clothing to cover herself up. Dark spandex, very few strands of fabric, and a lot of skin showing. Her hair and makeup were always done, even when working out, and her oversized breasts always a water cooler conversation starter.

Though Charlene was grateful to have Dana at the kickboxing class with her, instead of being the only woman in the class, the detective wasn't misreading the situation. She knew Dana only attended for three reasons:

man-shopping, to wear the badass gloves, and friendship. She didn't have the least bit of interest in kickboxing.

Charlene signed up for totally different reasons: increase strength, confidence, coordination, and a kickass cardio workout. The high-energy routine, a combination of boxing and martial arts, burned upward of four hundred calories an hour while working her arms, chest, shoulders, core, butt, and legs.

This kickboxing class ran more intensely than a normal exercise program, and the class challenged her body in ways it was not yet used to, and hadn't been in a long while. After the Darren Brady setback, it was a long time coming back.

Dr. Gardner had suggested Charlene try it, for not just the physical benefits, but he thought it would also help Charlene mentally—a total-body, heart-pumping workout and also a pretty fantastic way to get rid of any excess tension and frustration.

"Well, you should just be happy that I agreed to attend this silly thing, when we should be out hitting dance clubs and sipping on complimentary cocktails."

"You are the only one who drinks for free. Some of us have to buy our own."

"That's because I know how to talk to people. I'm not stand-offish like some."

Charlene grunted. "No, it's because you have large breasts."

Dana winked. "Whatever."

"I thought you said you liked this class?"

"Ah, not particularly. Plus, I'm not a fan of your *carb-loading* an hour before class. I want real food."

"Gotta fuel the body properly, Dana."

"Give me a cheeseburger any day."

"I don't *need* you here, Dana."

"Yes, you do. Who else will be your sparring partner?"

"I'd just grab one of the guys."

Dana smiled crookedly. "Yeah right, like anyone would get in that ring with you after the last time. You just about broke that guy's nose."

"I barely grazed him."

"There was blood everywhere."

"He was soft. They're all wimps around here."

"Um, Char, I think that maybe you are just a tad too intense. This is not a kickboxing tournament, it's just practice."

"Sorry, Mom." Charlene rolled her eyes. Using a heavy gloved hand, she awkwardly wiped a wet strand of hair from her bangs that had matted to her sticky forehead. "Now hold on tighter, I'm going to finish hard." She tightened the MMA gloves on her hands with her teeth.

This was her favorite part of the routine, the last three-minute burnout of nonstop punching at the end. It felt like an eternity, and her arms were about to fall off, but afterwards was very rewarding. When she started learning different punches and combinations, it felt like her brain had no control over her limbs.

She fell into a routine, her series of punches included jabs, hooks, and upper cuts, mixing in front kicks, roundhouse kicks, and side-kicks. She just got into the last combination when the buzzer went off. Charlene let up, breathing heavy, sweat streaming down the sides of her face.

"Alright, it's our turn in the ring."

Dana let go of the bag as it swung back and forth, the chain, holding it up, squeaked with each sway. "I don't think so."

"What?"

"I'm done." She picked up her towel, rolled it, and slung it around the back of her neck. "I'm gonna hit the smoothie bar." She walked away, swaying her hips just right, knowing that all eyes were on her.

"Okay, guys." Charlene looked around the gym, where men were still staring at Dana walking away. "I'm gonna need a ring partner again this week."

The men in the gym all looked away. Some of the guys were Charlene's colleagues on the force, and even they refused to make eye contact.

"Come on, guys. Really?"

"Get your gear on, Taylor."

Charlene turned around to see her instructor walking towards her. He was mid-forties, had a completely bald shaven scalp, a sinewy build with muscles like ropes—a former professional fighter and certified by the International Kickboxing Federation.

She would definitely need the head gear.

Charlene traipsed into the apartment, too tired to even shrug out of her jacket. She squeezed water from her gym bottle into her mouth, staying hydrated after that workout.

Leaving the lights off, she moved through the dark, removed the phone from her hip and set it on the table, her fingers brushing up against the little plastic cylinders which were her vice, the meds calling out to her. She fell forward onto her futon bed face first. She landed on the gun in her shoulder holster and it dug into her rib cage, so she shifted slightly to relieve the discomfort.

Her hands hurt from the heavy bag, and her muscles ached from going one-on-one with the instructor. Charlene was aware that he had been easy on her, but she felt that she'd left an impression and had held her own. He could have easily wiped her off the ring canvas.

Tomorrow would be worse. Pain the next day was guaranteed. Always with her kickboxing, the soreness in her muscles hung around for about the next twenty-four hours. Lots of water and stretching would be her savior.

Her iPhone rang, the sound of the tone following the clanking of the vibrating device on top of the wooden coffee table. Charlene lifted her head, watched the phone moving around the table top for a few seconds. It stopped, but before looking away, the detective's eyes stopped at the pill bottles on the table beside the phone, the prescribed medication her psychiatrist, Dr. Gardner, had suggested she take. She stared at the vials, imagining the place she would visit when she took them, the blissful, floating paradise that had her escaping her everyday reality.

She shook her head. She'd been trying her best to limit her need to fall back into the medication. She didn't want to go back there, and there were only a few things in her life to look forward to, to keep her from going back to that place in her mind and heart. She buried her head back down into the pillow.

She eventually rolled over onto her back, the muscles in her body weary and tight. She stared into the darkness, when her phone lit up once again and the ringtone starting up. She swung her body off the futon, onto her knees, and rose to her feet. She saw her sister's name appear on the caller display function of her phone.

She pressed the green answer button and waited a few seconds while Facetime engaged and her sister's smiling face appeared on the phone screen.

"Hey Char," Jane said. Her sister's voice was full of life, full of happiness, and it made Charlene's heart warm.

They hadn't always had a close relationship. They had had their share of ups and downs (mostly downs), and Charlene hadn't been a good sister, or had even attempted to try to make things right with her family. But that was then, this is now.

Jane's calls had become more frequent over the last few weeks, since Charlene had returned to California after visiting them in Colorado. What had started out as a family holiday visit had turned into a living nightmare for not only Charlene, but her whole family.

Martina, Jane's only child and Charlene's niece and goddaughter, had been part of a serial baby-snatching ring in Denver. Charlene, as a concerned aunt and vengeful cop, had integrated herself into the investigation, against local authority's wishes, and had been part of the investigative team to bring down the kidnappers.

Charlene forced a tired smile. "Hey, Jane."

"Martina wanted to say hi."

Charlene shook her head. Her niece was less than a year old, and even though what Martina had been through, being kidnapped and held in a cabin in the mountains, would never be remembered by the baby, the whole incident had brought Charlene closer with her sister, brother-in-law and mother.

Seven babies in total taken in Denver, a case closely related to one that had occurred six years previously in Albuquerque, New Mexico. The link had led Charlene to one of the most prominent women in America, and the babies eventually found, but not after a lot of collateral damage, and a few lives lost.

But *another* really great thing had come out of that case.

"Say hi to Auntie Charlene, Martina."

Jane zoomed in on a close-up of Martina's cute, somewhat chubby face. Her blue eyes danced and her hairless head shone from a fresh bath.

Martina made some sort of gurgling sound that to Charlene, didn't sound anything like a real word.

"Hi, baby girl," Charlene answered.

At the sound of Charlene's voice, Martina became quiet, and then giggled, getting excited by moving her arms and kicking her legs. The cooing and gurgling started again, followed by some vowel sounds.

Charlene's heart leapt, and her body warmed. She sighed, already missing Martina, even though she'd just seen her a few weeks ago.

Jane's face came back on the screen. "How was your day?"

Charlene told Jane about her day, divulging little information about the case. As a cop, she had never crossed that line, put her family in a compromising position by breaking a sacred cop-code. Each case was a confidential file only for those people privy to such material.

"You didn't really get much of a break, did you?"

"Not much."

Life of a cop, always on call, no punch clock or days off. She had gone to her sister's for a holiday, but then Martina was taken, and Charlene turned from sister/family member into cop-mode, like a flick of the switch. It was in her blood, it's what she knew, and it's what she excelled at.

"Did you call Mom tonight?"

"I texted her," Charlene lied.

Her mom. A typical mother. Always worried for Charlene's safety, always checking up on her. Not because she was the baby of the family, or because Charlene lived close to home in LA; just because she was a cop, plain and simple.

Charlene's late father, Martin Taylor, retired Grade III Detective and Sergeant II on the LAPD, had been shot and killed by Darren Brady, the Celebrity Slayer. Ever since her father's death, Charlene's mother,

Brenda, had insisted Charlene call her every night when she got home, just to let her mother know she was safe.

Charlene understood the worry because she was a rare breed. She'd been a screw-up daughter for so long, the black sheep of the family, that she didn't know what else to be. She'd followed in her father's footsteps for reasons unknown to everyone, including Charlene.

She'd had a shitty relationship with the man she had respected as one of the best cops the LAPD had ever produced, but when it came to expressing their feelings, neither of them could find the words to make it right between them. Then Darren Brady took that opportunity away from Charlene, forever. She'd never have that chance to make it up to her father.

She'd worked the tough LA streets waiting for her opportunity for promotion, and after being overlooked several times, finally had that chance to take over her father's desk, and position with Detective Larry Baker.

Now it was her turn to make her mark.

"Have you heard from Matt lately?"

Just the sound of his name had Charlene's body tingling.

Matt Stone, the 'other' good thing to come from that kidnapping case in Denver. A cop. A *Fed*—that should have said it all right there.

They'd met on the job, had butted heads at first, but the more they worked together, the closer they'd gotten. The sexual tension between them was palpable. The spark was there, and although they'd been able to ignore it for a while, eventually that spark ignited, and they let their desires overcome their hesitance.

They were similar in every way—the job came first. He was motivated, driven, and a gifted investigator, a profiler with the BAU division of the FBI.

They promised to stay in touch, take it one day at a time, try the long-distance thing, but she had doubts. When would they see each other? He would always be on call as a consultant, working out of Washington but travelling the globe. She had her gig in LA, and not much time for anything else.

She hadn't seen him since leaving Denver three weeks ago, but they had spoken on the phone several times, even a few Facetime conversations so they could be face-to-face. But that was all they had, for now. Would it be enough? Only time would tell.

"It's been a few days," Charlene replied.

"Everything okay?"

"I think so."

When they spoke, it was mostly shop-talk. Matt wasn't one to reveal his emotions or feelings, but wasn't that a man thing? The conversations didn't last long, by the time they both had a minute to sit down and talk, they were either too drained from the everyday exhaustion of "the job", or on the run to another crime scene.

"Martina's starting to fidget. I'll fill her belly and then put her down."

"Sounds like a great plan. I am heading for a shower."

"Don't forget to eat, Char."

"I know, Jane."

"And you need to get lots of rest."

Charlene rolled her eyes, making sure she looked away from the screen so her sister wouldn't see it.

"Thanks, Jane."

"You need to take care of yourself, Charlene. We all care for you."

"I know you do, Jane, and I appreciate that. But I'm a big girl, I can handle it."

"Don't get mad."

"I'm not mad."

"I'm sorry. I didn't mean to—"

"It's okay, Jane. I'm gonna go grab a shower."

"Good night, Charlene."

"Good night, Jane."

Charlene shut off the phone and placed it on the table beside the pill bottles. She looked at the vials again and took a deep breath, letting out all the air in her chest. Then she headed to the bathroom.

She started the shower, turned the knobs to an accommodating temperature and removed her clothes. Her tight spandex sports bra and shorts were tough to take off, sticky on her moist skin. They finally snapped off and she let them fall to the ground.

The trip to Denver had done a few things for Charlene. With her relationship with Matt trending upward, she had regained some confidence, and started back into her routine of exercise and eating right. And the benefits of healthy living were starting to pay off as she admired herself in the mirror. Her ribcage finally started to be covered with the old muscle she once had. But she had a long road back to where she once was, before the whole Darren Brady/Celebrity Slayer ordeal. That had taken years off her life.

She stepped into the shower and lowered her head, allowing the hot water to spray on the top of her head, and run down her neck coating her shoulders and back. The warmness was refreshing, and gave her a second boost of energy, a second wind.

She massaged shampoo onto her scalp and hair when a noise from the hallway startled her. She turned and swiped her wet hand across the frosted shower glass door, leaving a streak of partial visibility. She was sure she saw the form of a person standing just inside the bathroom door.

Her body goosebumped, her hands shaky. Nowhere for her to hide. She obviously didn't have a gun in the shower. She was trapped, and in the worst possible predicament.

The person outside the shower moved towards her, gradually, almost as if trying to remain as quiet as possible.

Charlene looked around the tiny, phone-booth sized shower. Searching for anything she could use as a weapon. She grabbed the razor she used to shave her legs and held it down at her side, shielding it from the suspect's view. If that door opened, she would go for the throat with the sharp blade.

It wasn't the first time she had gone after a man's face to save her own life.

She watched the man's arm extend to the shower door handle. Then the door swung open.

Charlene steeled herself, razor blade at the ready.

When the door fully opened, Charlene came face to face with Matt…a very naked, smiling Matt.

Charlene's eyes roamed Matt's nude body, up and down, stopping at certain places to gaze admiringly. It looked like he was as excited to see her as she was to see him, maybe even more.

When she looked back up, their eyes met. They stood silent for what seemed like minutes, although it wasn't.

"Do you have room for one more?" Matt asked. His smile lusty.

Charlene didn't have to answer. Matt stepped in and closed the door. Their bodies came together—caressing, massaging—sending chills down her neck.

The detective was glad she had gotten that second wind.

Chapter 5

"Uncle Calvin!" A high-pitched, youthful voice, filled with excitement.

Calvin lay on his stomach, his cheek pressed against the pillow. He had intentionally turned away from the window where the sunlight began to filter in through the blinds, but that meant he faced the door—dangerous territory. He opened one eye and saw his six year-old nephew, Caleb, wearing Spiderman pajamas, sprinting through the open bedroom door.

"I don't think these kids ever sleep," Calvin said, rolling over on the other side to face Rachel. But her side of the bed lay empty.

"Rise and shine, sleepyhead."

Her voice yanked Calvin's head around as Rachel sauntered into the room carrying two year-old Kayla. Rachel's dirty blond hair was slightly messed, but just as stunning "au naturel" as she was all made up. She wore a pair of grey sweatpants and one of Calvin's old USC t-shirts. Kayla's curly hair was tied back in pigtails, her dimples prominent.

Calvin layered a second pillow on top of his original, fluffed it, and propped up. He gazed at Rachel, holding Kayla like a seasoned mother. All night after they had gotten home, Rachel had doted over the kids, playing games, spending time with them. She seemed right at home taking care of children, almost as if motherhood might be a natural transition for her.

"How did you sleep?" Rachel asked.

"Okay."

"I wanted to wake you up earlier, but she wouldn't let me." Caleb scrunched his nose and pointed a tiny finger at Rachel.

"She," Calvin said, sliding out of bed and lifting Caleb over his head, "saved your life."

Caleb giggled when Calvin spun him around in the air, with ease. He set the boy down carefully and felt a twinge in his surgically repaired knee.

"Are you okay?"

"What?" Calvin looked at Rachel, who gazed down at his knee.

"You made a face."

"No, I didn't."

"Yes, you did. Whenever you feel a pain in your knee, you make a face."

"I'm fine."

She scowled. "You're not fine. It's bad, I know it is. You said the doctors told you it would never have the kind of strength you once had."

"I know what they said."

"It's not like you slipped in the shower. You hurt it at football, then multiple run-ins with that Baxter guy, your trip to South America. Calvin, you've been through a lot."

"I know what happened, Rach." Calvin smiled, something he tended to do when feeling uncomfortable with Rachel's line of questioning. "Are you planning on writing my biography?"

Rachel rolled her eyes. "I'm serious. You need to take it easy. Doctor's orders."

He kissed her cheek, a quick peck to let her know everything was alright. "I'm fine."

"Men. They are intolerable. Let's go, Kayla." Rachel left the room with the two children, clearly irritated.

Calvin knelt down on the edge of the bed and rubbed at the scars on his knee. The truth was, Rachel hit it dead on about his knee—it wasn't right, and it never would be. But all of the training he had done, especially lately, had made it stable.

Calvin had no misconceptions. He knew his knee would never be like it once was. All he asked was that he could be pain free, and able to do things...not what he had done in college, but normal things everyday people were capable of doing...pain free.

Was that too much to ask for?

He performed a few fast stretches. He hadn't brought any workout gear, and his brother didn't have weights or exercise equipment, so stretching and a quick bodyweight workout would have to suffice.

His t-shirt was slightly damp when he joined the rest of the family in the kitchen, where the smell of fresh coffee and toast greeted him.

Caleb ran circles around the table, Rachel made baby sounds to Kayla, and Josh and Alexis quietly drank coffee and seemed to enjoy their new, child-free life.

"Hey, Bro, you might want to send out an APB on Rachel if Kayla goes missing."

Josh looked at Rachel, huddled over Kayla giving her full attention every minute of the morning.

"I don't know about Josh, but I might move her in as the nanny." Alexis grinned.

"Anytime," Rachel said, sincerity in her voice.

"Whoa, whoa, whoa." Calvin held his hands up defensively. "Don't I get a say in this? I might want to sleep again someday."

"Don't ever have kids then."

Alexis playfully slapped Josh's hand.

"You might want to have sex again someday too." Josh smiled.

This time, Alexis punched him hard on the arm. "Smart ass."

"Thank you for seeing us, Coach Manning."

They were seated in a tiny, comfortable office in the Lyon University Center, located on the University Park Campus at USC.

Charlene still thought about Matt from earlier that morning. She liked waking up beside him in her bed, and she also liked how he had woken her up, an "impromptu" wake-up call.

Charlene looked around the office of Daniel Manning, the head coach of the USC cheerleading team. The space was loaded with USC pictures and memorabilia, everything from gold and cardinal pom-poms to USC team sports pictures, to awards won by the cheer squad.

Manning had requested an early morning meeting with the detectives, and Charlene hoped for a little background on the victim since she'd joined the cheerleading team.

"I'm not sure how I can help you, Detectives."

Manning looked to be in his fifties. He had a thin face with brown average length hair combed back. His hair looked impressive, as if he'd spent a good deal of time with a brush and blow dryer, and then sprayed to maintain the curl and texture.

"What can you tell us about Samantha Baylor?"

The coach shook his head and looked at the ceiling. "I couldn't believe when I heard about it. She seemed like such a sweetheart. Everyone liked her."

"Not everyone," Larry chimed in.

"Touché." He rubbed his hands together. "Look, Detectives, we just have a small, coed team of eighteen members, fifteen ladies and three men. We take both graduates and undergraduates, from all years.

Because of that, we're a close group. We are a family, and support each other all the way."

"Was Baylor here on a scholarship?"

He shook his head. "We don't offer any sort of support or scholarships for our athletes. We are a club sport at USC, so we don't fall under the jurisdiction of the athletic department or any scholarship programs."

"So she was a walk-on?"

"A very late walk-on."

"What do you mean?"

"Added to our team because we had some injuries, and needed to add to our unit."

"Is that standard practice?"

"Very irregular. Normally, students are encouraged to attend live tryouts if possible, or we accept video tryouts. Usually cheerleading experience is mandatory."

"But Baylor had no experience?"

The coach put up his hands. "None."

"So why was she on this team?"

"Because she earned it. She came to a practice with her roommate, who is one of our cheerleaders, and blew our socks off. For a freshman, her tumbling skills were impressive, maybe even the best we have."

"That good?"

"I'd say, but it's not just her skill, but her ability to learn more difficult tumbling passes. She picked it up as if she'd been doing it all her life."

Charlene steepled her hands. "That couldn't have gone over well with some of the older, more experienced cheerleaders."

The coach shrugged his bulky shoulders. "I wouldn't know."

"What was her relationship like with other cheerleaders?"

"As far as I can tell, fine."

"No animosity or jealousy circulating amongst the girls?"

The coach licked his lips. "Let me tell you something about cheerleading, Detectives. I know that we get very little credit for what we do. We don't bring in the dollars like our men's sports teams. But these are competitive girls. The University of Southern California has a very proud athletic heritage. These girls represent the University at regional and national cheerleading competitions. If you look at our trophy case in the hallways, and on my wall, USC Cheer has brought numerous championship titles back home to Southern California."

"So there were problems?"

"Maybe. These girls are under a lot of pressure to compete at the highest level, and stay on this team. When it comes to collegiate cheerleading, both grades and athleticism are top priorities for our university. Our cheerleaders are some of the most involved students on campus. All members are expected to maintain a minimum 2.5 GPA, attend regular classes, and not miss our three-days-a-week practice schedule."

"You're being very vague, Coach."

"Am I?"

"Yes."

He looked at Charlene, squinting slightly. "As you can see, Detective, I'm a man, which puts me at kind of a disadvantage as a cheerleading coach, when it comes to knowing my players personally."

Charlene hadn't mentioned it, but she could tell from Larry's expression that he thought the same thing. The detective found it odd that a school would hire a male cheerleading coach. Very odd.

"I spend very little time behind the scenes, in the change room. I have one of the very best Cheer Team Advisors in the nation. Makayla Thomas is great with these girls, and she spends a lot of time with them. If you want to know anything personal, Makayla is your best bet."

Charlene scribbled the name down in her notebook.

Larry shuffled in his chair. "When is your next practice?"

"Tonight's practices have been cancelled, naturally. I'm not sure, but I'm hoping our girls will be able to handle our regular Wednesday night practice."

"Time and place?"

"Seven to ten at The Lorenzo Student Housing."

"We'd like to sit in on that practice."

The coach shook his head. "Our practices are closed to the public."

Charlene pulled back the bottom of her jacket to tuck it behind the badge attached to her waist. "We aren't exactly the public, are we?"

Manning pursed his lips. "I guess not. I'll just have to run it by the Athletic Director."

"Of course. I'll just need the names of every team member and their contact information."

They left Manning's office with very little, other than the names of the cheer members.

"Girls are competitive, and they fight over almost everything. I'm sure that Samantha Baylor slipping into a starting position on the team, without having to undergo the same kind of intense tryout the others girls worked hard for, hadn't gone unnoticed," Charlene said.

Larry nodded. "I agree. Gotta be some conflict there."

Charlene pulled out her phone and checked the time. "We still have three hours until Baylor's roommate is out of class. We can head over to

Boyle Heights for Samantha Baylor's autopsy. Webster said he'd wait for us as long as he could, because I told him about our meeting this morning."

"That's a plan."

They started walking towards their car, parked in the Jefferson Boulevard Parking Structure. Charlene spotted a Starbucks along the campus path and made a quick detour, pulling change out of her pocket.

"Want one?" she asked Larry.

"You payin'?"

Charlene hid a grin. "Don't I always?"

Detective Larry Baker was not known for being flush with his wallet. In fact, he was rumored to be the cheapest cop on the whole LAPD force.

She ordered them both a coffee and waited while the barista attended to the beverages. The Starbucks at Café 84 on the USC campus seemed brand new.

The shop was moderately filled with students clicking on iPhone, laptops and iPads, and sipping on lattes and other foamy beverages. No one gave Charlene and Larry a second glance when the detectives walked in, and Charlene wondered how many of those students were oblivious to the fact that a murder had actually occurred on their campus only two nights ago.

They received their order and left the coffee shop as a herd of chatty, giggling girls barged through the door. Larry stopped and turned to watch them as they entered, holding the door for them.

Charlene threw an elbow that landed on her partner's rib cage and he let out his breath, almost spilling his coffee.

He looked at Charlene. "What did you do that for?"

"They're a little young for you. Let's go."

They started back towards their car.

He took a sip from his white paper cup. "That's good stuff."

"Beats the vending machine back at the office." Charlene tasted hers. "So, a complete waste of time. Manning knew nothing about his team."

"I thought we'd go in there and get the juicy gossip and maybe a motive."

What the detectives had received was the exact opposite. Manning knew very little of his team members, almost as if the coach went out of his way to know as little as possible about the personal lives of the girls he led.

"You find it odd that USC has a man coaching the cheerleaders?" Charlene asked.

"Very weird." Larry looked at his notepad as they walked. "We will have to get around to speaking with this Makayla Thomas. Maybe she knows something."

e doubted it.

"... were you so late this morning?" Larry asked.

Since they were already at USC, they'd decided to hit Samantha Baylor's roommate by showing up during her course. The medical examiner promised to wait for them before proceeding with the autopsy.

After stopping in at Rory Cummings' first period class, and being told by her professor that the sophomore hadn't shown up, Charlene and Larry decided on an impromptu visit to Samantha Baylor's roommate at their living quarters.

Baylor had lived in Marks Hall, one of seven freshman residence halls on the USC campus. The building was located at 631 Child's Way, next to the university's historic Alumni House.

Marks Hall, part of the South Area Residential College, hosted a freshman community focused on the transition to college and exploring USC's First Year Experience programs. At three-stories, Marks Hall was one of the shortest of the Halls. Charlene knew that Larry, with all of his bulk, was secretly relieved that he hadn't had to climb a bunch of staircases.

A large crowd had gathered along the path as Charlene and Larry crossed campus. The building next to Marks Hall stood jam packed with students trying to get in, and others standing patiently in a line outside.

Charlene pulled over a student. He was average height, with a looped earring in his lobe and an Oakland Raiders hat set high on his head.

"What's the commotion?" Charlene asked.

"Nothing, it's always like this."

Charlene tried to look through the front window. There was a black and white sign with the letters, 'GZ' attached over the door. "What is this place?"

"Ground Zero Performance Café, a student-run entertainment venue and coffeehouse."

Charlene nodded, and she and Larry proceeded down the path towards the housing facility.

The detectives passed a group of girls playing soccer on an impressive lawn at the front of the building, reminding Charlene of the games she and her friends played when she had attended NYU. How she missed those care-free days!

Baylor's bedroom was on the third floor. They took the stairs, Larry cursing under his breath, and Charlene decided to check out the area on her way.

The first floor had two lounges: one with a piano and a TV viewing area, and a second serving as a study room. It looked comfortable and practical: everything needed for freshman students during their first year away from home.

The second and third floors were living areas with twenty-four double rooms on each floor, as well as singles sprinkled in.

They stepped out of the third floor stairwell and approached Baylor's bedroom door. As Charlene lifted her fist to bang on the outside of the door, a voice came from behind.

"Rory isn't in there."

They turned to find a slender girl in striped pajama bottoms and a stained spaghetti-strapped tank top standing across the hall, inside a partially opened bedroom door. She had long, greasy, brown hair and moist skin.

"No school today?" Larry asked.

The girl reached for her throat. "I'm sick."

"Do you know where Rory is?" Charlene asked.

"She went for a workout."

"Where's the gym?"

"In the basement."

Charlene removed her phone and called the department. "Send a CSI unit over to Samantha Baylor's room and cover it. You know what to look for."

They headed back the way they came, taking the stairs two at a time all the way down to the basement. Larry breathed hard by the time they reached the bottom step.

"She better be here," he said.

Expecting to see a dungy, cob-webbed space, Charlene was surprised to see additional amenities in a welcoming area. They took a long hallway, passing study rooms where female students quietly looked through textbooks, and a loud laundry room, where washing machines and dryers noisily tossed around clothes.

They entered a glassed-door marked, "Exercise Area", where only one student worked out: a pretty girl with a round face and brown hair pulled back into a long single ponytail. She wore tight-fitting spandex workout gear and perspiration soaked the middle of her back. She had her back to the detectives, as her arms and legs pumped hard on an elliptical. Large Bose headphones covered her ears so the girl didn't see or hear Charlene and Larry enter the room.

Charlene took in the windowless room: Stairmasters, treadmills, ellipticals and a weight machine.

The detective wondered how many girls actually used the room. As an avid, enthusiastic exercise nut, Charlene understood the kind of dedication and motivation it took to consistently workout, while juggling a fulltime school schedule, a part-time job and a social life.

"Doesn't look like she's in mourning," Larry said.

"If that's even her. Everyone mourns differently."

When her father had been murdered, Charlene's first instinct was to return to work, against everyone's wishes and orders. But that was Charlene's coping mechanism. It helped her get through tough times. Some things Charlene wanted to avoid, bottling it up, the worst way to struggle through rough patches in her life. She tried hard to overcome her instinct to turn to alcohol as a crutch.

They approached the girl, badges already out. Not wanting to startle her, Charlene stepped to the side, took a wide arc so the college sophomore could make them out.

The girl slowed to a complete stop on the elliptical, pulled off the headphones, and let them hang around her neck.

"Rory Cummings?"

She nodded. "Yes." Her voice low, weak, almost scared.

"I'm Detective Taylor, this is Detective Baker."

Larry nodded. "Can we ask you a few questions about your roommate?"

The girl gingerly stepped off the workout equipment. She grabbed a clean white towel that had been hanging over the arm of the machine and dabbed at her sweat-peppered forehead. She took a long drink from a USC Trojans water bottle.

"Do you want to do it here?" Rory asked.

Charlene shrugged her shoulders. "Sure, if that's okay with you."

The sophomore nodded and plopped down on the bench at the weight machine. She wrapped the now damp towel around her neck, overtop of the headphones. Charlene could hear the loud music echoing from the earphones since Cummings had yet to shut down her phone.

"Sam's parents came by the room this morning." Her voice quivered and her eyes welled up. "I couldn't go to school today."

"I'm sure it's hard," Charlene said.

"Is it true what they are saying? Was Samantha really murdered?"

"Who said that?"

"Everyone."

"Yes, it's true."

She brought the towel to her mouth and bit down on it, as if fighting back the urge to scream out.

"Who would hurt Samantha?"

"I don't know."

"Why would anyone want to hurt Samantha?" Charlene asked.

Cummings took a couple of deep breaths to compose herself. "I really don't know."

"Did she have any enemies? Any conflicts going on? Any reason for someone to hold a grudge against Samantha?"

She shook her head. "She hadn't been here that long. She didn't know a lot of people. I introduced her to a few of my friends but Samantha was shy, quiet. She wasn't outgoing, and didn't make friends easily."

"Who did Samantha hang out with? Was she associated with any groups? Friends? Clubs?"

Cummings swiped a strand of hair that had matted to her forehead, away from her eyes. She slid back on the bench and brought her knees up to her chest, wrapping her arms around her legs and hugging herself tightly.

"She had been recruited by a sorority. She is part of the pledge class but she still hadn't been accepted as a member."

"Which one?"

"Delta Gamma." She studied her fingernails. "I'm a member and I recommended her to the girls."

Charlene was aware that pledging a sorority involved many different activities and meetings, many of which were mandatory. For most collegiates, pledging ended up being a huge time commitment, in which you spent a lot of time with other members and pledges.

"What was her pledging period like?"

"Busy. A lot of studying and many events to attend. But she never got to the entrance exam." A tear streamed down Cummings' cheek.

"Was she overwhelmed at all by the whole process? It's a lot to take for a freshman."

Cummings shrugged. "If she was, she never mentioned it. I asked to be her big sister, to guide her through the pledging process, but it doesn't work like that. I'm only a sophomore."

"What about hazing?" It had been hanging there, the topic Charlene had really been wondering about. She had been waiting for the interviewee to mention it, but it looked like Cummings tiptoed around the issue. Always a serious topic with college sororities.

A frantic head shake. "Our sorority doesn't practice those types of unethical initiations."

Yeah, right. Of course that's what Cummings would answer, but Charlene wasn't buying it. Hazing forced pledges to participate in activities that were specifically designed to make them uncomfortable in some way, and it could sometimes lead to dangerous outcomes.

Hazing *did* still happen in some sororities, but more and more schools cracked down on it. Many colleges had zero-tolerance hazing policies and also used other methods to prevent it, such as student hotlines to notify the school of hazing violations.

Cummings must have seen the doubt in Charlene's face, because she added quickly, "We have a strong anti-hazing process. Instead of forcing girls to do things together, our pledge moms create fun events for the girls that make them naturally want to be together."

"Listen, Ms. Cummings," Charlene said. "This is a murder investigation, your friend's murder. This isn't exactly the time to worry about getting your sorority girlfriends in trouble."

"I know that," she answered, a little too quickly.

"Was Sam going to be accepted into the sorority?"

Cummings looked down into her lap, her hands still shaky and moving constantly. She must have known the detectives watched her because she froze her hands and looked up at the cops. "I doubt it."

"Why not," Larry asked.

Cummings swallowed. "Sam wouldn't agree to do some of the things they asked her to do."

"Like what?"

"Does it matter?"

"Maybe."

She sighed audibly and stood up, moving across the room. The weight room door opened and a young red-headed woman with freckles and baggy sweat clothes came in. Larry flashed his badge and she obediently turned around and left without saying anything.

When Charlene turned back towards Cummings, the sophomore student had sat back down. Tears filled her eyes.

"It was so stupid. But some girls, when they get in that situation, are so worried about pleasing the sisters that they literally do anything they need to do without asking questions."

"So what did they want Samantha to do?"

"One of the first acts of the process is for each pledge to lie blindfolded on a table while brothers from a fraternity write on their body what they think are her physical flaws. But Sam refused to go through with it."

"How did the head sisters take that?"

"Not well."

"You better give us their names."

As Larry wrote down the names of the sorority heads, he asked, "What about meals? Where did she eat? Who did she eat with?"

"All residents have a required full meal plan. We usually ate in the cafeteria together. To be honest, most of our time was devoted to cheering. We had school, a few friends, and cheer."

Charlene remembered her first year at NYU. What a whirlwind. The college life had agreed with the detective, maybe a little too much. She had never been able to grasp the rails, slow her life down since. Go, go, go, with no time to waste.

NYU, the college life, had changed Charlene. Maybe it was being away from home, across the country, away from the shadow of her old-school father who seemed to put his work ahead of his family. He was as hard as nails when it came to Charlene and her lifestyle.

But whatever it was, she just let it all out, let it all go.

The detective wondered if these girls, Samantha Baylor and Rory Cummings, had been on that same road, or had they found a way to control their urges, the social temptations that drew newbies in? Had they managed to orient to the college life so that they could fit in and get by?

"Were you with Samantha on Saturday night?"

Cummings' head snapped up. If she'd been playing poker, her opponent would have gone all in. She did not have a first-class poker face.

"Where were you?" Charlene asked, before Cummings had a chance to backpedal.

"At the football game. We both cheered that night."

"What about after the game?"

She hesitated, as if looking for a lie. "The fans stormed the field, as they do after every win. We usually get separated and lost in the crowd, but we met up in the change room afterwards."

"Okay, what about after that? Where did you guys go after the game?"

Her hands fidgeted, rubbing, and twiddling fingers. Her body language suggested defiance. What was she hiding and why? Why was she so stressed, squirmy, nervous?

"We went to an after-party at a frat house. Most of the players usually go there, and it's always the biggest and best party after a Trojan win."

"How long were you there for? Was Samantha with anyone?"

"Actually, once we got there, we went our separate ways. I didn't see her all night."

This could have been a lie. Why would they ditch each other, if they were as close as they say? They were roommates and sorority sisters. But nothing in Cummings' body language told Charlene she lied.

"Who was she with?"

Cummings shrugged her shoulders. "Not sure."

"Was she seeing anyone?"

"Nothing serious."

"Anything non-serious?"

"She did have an on-again, off-again thing going with a guy."

"So on-again or off-again at the time she was murdered?" Charlene asked harshly, tired of the run around from this college sophomore.

"I'm not sure."

"Who's the guy?"

"His name is Mark Simon. He's on the football team. But they weren't together recently."

Charlene and Larry looked at each other.

"Did you find Samantha acting strange recently? Maybe not herself? Anything different?"

"She had been sick the last couple of school days. She missed her morning classes three days in a row. She mentioned she came down with a bug."

Charlene would have to look into that.

"Thank you, Ms. Cummings. We'll be in touch. And you might want to stay away from your room for a while, we have some people coming over to examine and explore."

"Police?"

"Yes."

Larry and Charlene headed for the stairs.

"Should we go see this guy?" Larry asked.

Charlene shook her head. "Webster is waiting for us."

Chapter 6

The smells hadn't changed, and the only physical changes were the names on the white plates overtop the stalls.

Calvin stood in the middle of the room, directly over the 'SC' stitching on the red carpeted floor. He ran his fingers over the inspirational words on the four pillars in the middle of the room, teams of the past, championship teams, teams he'd played on, football gods and legends.

A few new player photographs, but his own still hadn't made the locker room wall. Calvin doubted it ever would, not after how he had gone out.

The lounge furniture had been upgraded—new leather recliners and foot rests, double big-screen TVs—first class, top of the line all the way.

Calvin sat down at one of the stalls in the middle of the room and closed his eyes. He breathed in deeply, the scenes coming back. He missed that feeling, the adrenaline rush of epinephrine zipping through his veins. He was ready to go to war again with his teammates.

"Take you back?"

Calvin opened his eyes as Nick walked into the room. He had his hands jammed into his pockets, and a wide smile.

"Thanks for letting me in. Takes me back for sure."

Calvin placed his hands on his knees and pushed himself up into a standing position. Although the stalls remained empty, since equipment was already packed for transportation to the practice facility, and the uniforms were being washed, Calvin could picture the atmosphere he longed to be a part of again.

"Should we go out onto the field?"

Calvin nodded, followed the overweight equipment manager out of the room and entered the hallway: a walk Calvin had done dozens of times before, but this time, it was totally different.

The first thing the former running back noticed was the silence. Usually dozens of steel spikes crunched concrete as the team walked in unison, preparing for battle. They chanted, screaming words of inspiration, pumping each other up and getting in the "tiger" mode. Now, Calvin's dress shoes clicked on the cement, echoing in the empty corridor.

As he neared the exit, eyeing the green grass and stadium pews in the distance, his vision blurred, and his ears twitched, picking up the imaginary sounds of eighty-four thousand screaming USC fans.

His reality set in when instead of football referees and scantily dressed cheerleaders to greet him, Calvin noticed the police tape and fingerprint powder dusted across the fine needles of field grass.

The crime scene was still intact. Calvin approached the area where the footprints merged and where Samantha Baylor's body had been discovered. The PI wondered which footprints had already been on the scene before the LAPD had trampled the grounds.

The PI surveyed the footprints: multiple sets of different sizes, all going in different directions to and from where the body had lain. The depth and size of the shoe soles also told Calvin that each print was owned by male bodies, some much heavier than others.

"How many exits and entrances around the stadium?" Calvin asked.

"Lots," Nick responded. "What are you thinking?"

"Nothing."

Other than the footprints, there wasn't much for Calvin to find. Unfortunately, the scene had already been processed, the LAPD investigators had already confiscated every piece of evidence found at the scene.

Remnants of a police investigation remained—crime scene barricade tape, extinguished flares, numbered evidence marking tents, placards, evidence identifiers and measuring devices—as this scene was still closed to the public, and it would be for some time. Calvin wondered if the field would even be prepared for the Trojans' next game.

Since Calvin had been working a lot with Detective Dale Dayton and the LVMPD, the PI understood that crime scene investigation was a massive undertaking. 'Processing a crime scene' was a long, tedious process that involved purposeful documentation and the collection of physical evidence.

The area had been chalked out, spray painted, and dusted. There wasn't much for Calvin to do there, that hadn't already been taken care of by the local cops.

"Oh my God. Calvin?"

He turned around to find a black woman in her fifties, with long dark Whoopi Goldberg-like dreadlocks and prescription sunglasses. She pressed a button and then put away her phone.

Calvin immediately recognized her. "Tiana?"

The older woman got up on her tiptoes and wrapped her arms around Calvin's neck softly, squeezing him. "It's so good to see you."

"How have you been?"

Calvin had met Tiana Washington as a freshman. Tiana worked as a security guard at the LA Memorial Coliseum, where the USC football team played all of their home games, and Calvin had spent a lot of time at the stadium.

Calvin remembered Tiana as a friendly woman with a kind soul. She had been a single mother of two boys, a nine year old and five year old, with whom Calvin had autographed a team jersey. They were cute kids and Tiana did all she could for them, worked all hours for little pay and made sure to be there for them when they needed her. They meant everything to her.

"I've been good, still bustin' my hump at this job." She revealed crooked teeth. "How 'bout you?'

He nodded. "Good. I'm a private investigator in Vegas."

"Vegas," she squealed. She elbowed him in the ribs. "Look at you."

"How are the boys?"

She grinned, a motherly-pride smile. "Growin' like bad weeds. Elijah still has your shirt."

"I'm glad."

She looked sad. "Why didn't you stay in touch after you left us?"

Calvin let out his breath. "I wasn't exactly proud of where I ended up. It wasn't the life I had envisioned for myself, and I didn't want to bring anyone down with me."

"We were really sad to see you go, the boys missed saying goodbye."

"I know. I'm sorry."

"Oh well, you're back now. What are you doing here?"

"I'm actually investigating the murder of that cheerleader."

It looked as if Washington took a baby step back, or had Calvin just imagined that? She did hold her breath slightly and let out a tiny gasp.

"That poor girl. It's a damn shame."

"Were you working that night?"

"Sure was." Her phone beeped and she took it back out to look at it.

"Is it important?"

She waved him off and returned the phone to her jacket pocket. "Just the boys."

"Did you see anything that night?"

"Nothing. Listen, Calvin, I better get back to work or the boss will have a fit if he sees me here talking to you."

"Do you mind if I stop by the house sometime to see the boys?"

What he really wanted to do was get Tiana alone and question her about that night at the Coliseum. He was sure, as a security guard, she would have seen something suspicious, even if she wouldn't want to share it with the cops.

"The boys would like that. You remember the address?"

"You bet."

"Bye, Calvin. See you soon."

He turned back to Nick. "So why did you call me in for this?"

"Just seemed like the right thing to do. I knew you worked as a PI, your brother LAPD, but we don't exactly trust the cops around here. You are one of us, or at least you were one of us. This could cause a shit-storm for this school, and we knew that you would do what was best for USC, and keep things tightly under wraps. You won't run this school through the mud."

"With all due respect, Nick, a girl was murdered here. I'm going to find out who killed her, and I don't care who is involved, school related or not."

The equipment guy nodded his head, his flabby double-chin bouncing with it.

Calvin took one last look around. "Let's go."

"Have you thought any more about coming to practice this afternoon?"

Calvin exhaled. "Yes, I have thought about it."

The Los Angeles County Department of Medical Examiner-Coroner was located on North Mission Road, less than a twenty minute drive from USC. Larry took the CA-110 to West Exposition Boulevard to avoid the congestion.

Lloyd Webster hovered over the dead body, which had been stripped and placed on a steel gurney, when Charlene and Larry entered the processing area. Since Webster was well into his sixties, had been with the Medical Examiner-Coroner (ME-C) Forensic Science Unit for over thirty years, he no longer performed field work, so he had not been at the scene. Instead, he remained in the labs and conducted the in-house analysis.

Webster was a master at conducting comprehensive scientific investigations into the cause and manner of any sudden, suspicious or violent death occurring in Los Angeles County. The Laboratory performed analysis in four distinct forensic disciplines: Drug Chemistry, Toolmark Analysis in biological specimens, Toxicology, and Trace Evidence.

Webster had thick white-gray hair parted to the right and black-frame glasses. His white lab coat was unbuttoned and his long tie dangled lazily off his neck. He looked up when the detectives walked in.

"This one yours?"

Charlene nodded. The chemical odors of ammonia and formaldehyde watered her eyes.

"My notes and photos are on the counter."

Larry went and stood beside the body as Charlene crossed the room to where the photographs had been scattered across the counter top. She placed a finger on top and flipped through the glossy pictures, looking over Webster's notes in the process. Some photos had been from the crime scene and others from Baylor in the lab, both before and after she'd been cleaned up.

Charlene was more than confident in Webster's ability—preserving the body, taking photographs and being meticulous in his scrutiny of the corpse. He was a by-the-book, old school examiner, and consistently ran through every step outlined, knowing that his job determined what happened. Missing one minor blood clot or one small internal hemorrhage could spell the difference between the autopsy determining a cause of death or it being ruled "undetermined".

"Shall we get started?" Webster asked, looking directly at Charlene. "I've already broken the rigor mortis in her arms and legs."

She nodded slightly, placed the photos back on the metal counter top, and returned to the side of the gurney. Now that rigor mortis had been broken, Webster could manipulate Baylor's body into different positions for examining purposes.

Samantha Baylor lay completely naked, her clothes cut off her body with scissors. She'd already been cleaned, weighed and her body measured. The skin on her body smooth and tight. She had small breasts and a mole underneath the left one. She was short and thin, but muscular, as she'd needed to be for cheerleading.

Webster set a black voice recorder down on the gurney beside the body, to assist in recording notes from his examination.

Baylor had a dark neck contusion by a handprint.

"As you can see, there is distinct bruising around the victim's throat, multiple layers which hadn't come out before, but are now starting to color." The ME noted any abrasions, bruises, cuts and damage to the skin. "Her windpipe has been crushed, from human hands."

Even with a woman as petite as Samantha Baylor, that would take significant strength.

Then, using his gloved hands, Webster looked under the hair and inspected Baylor's scalp. He checked under her fingernails for foreign bodies which might be the product of a struggle. Any external clue might be critical in reconstructing the cause of death, particularly if foul play was suspected, which it was.

"Look here." Webster placed four fingers, two on either side of a set of strands of hair and pulled them apart. "There had been blood matted to her hair, so now that she is cleaned up, we can see it clearer."

Charlene leaned over the body and located a sizeable scalp wound, both a bump and a cut at the victim's hairline.

"This would have caused significant head trauma. It happened pre-mortem, but not long before."

"Is that what killed her?"

The ME shook his head. "It would have made a serious impact from the blow, maybe a concussion and probably dazed her, but it is not the cause of death."

"What caused the head contusion?"

"We can't identify that yet."

A block had been placed under the back of the body, causing the limbs to fall away and raised the chest upwards, to make it easier to cut open. Webster removed a small scalpel from his coat pocket and made a large "Y" shaped incision from both shoulders, meeting in the sternum, then straight down to the pubic bone.

Even though Charlene had stood in on an autopsy in the past, it wasn't something she enjoyed watching, and looked away. Samantha Baylor, so young, so full of youthful vigor, being cut open and examined after a wrongful death.

"What about samples?" Charlene asked the ME.

"I've already handed over all samples: blood, stomach contents, intestinal contents, the works for analysis. It's in my notes."

This would indicate whether Baylor had ingested any poisons, drugs or even alcohol—all which could be relevant, depending on the circumstances, for building a picture of the precise cause of death.

Charlene turned away from the surgical work and went back to the clipboard on the counter. This time, she read through it carefully, doing her best to ignore the sounds and smells coming from the body behind her. Sample trace had been initially taken—lipstick, fingernail scrapings, and a clip of pubic hair.

She scrolled down when she stopped, her blood buzzing. She turned back towards the examiner. "Traces of semen found inside the victim?"

The ME looked up and squinted at her. "Yes, inside the vagina. It's been swabbed and sent to the lab. Also signs of sexual activity prior to death."

"Was she raped?"

"Not likely, but we couldn't rule out sexual assault. So we immediately performed a rape sequence: wet mount slide, vaginal swabs, cervical swabs, and a vaginal wash. No signs of bruising or stretching inside or around the vagina. Looks like consensual."

Charlene turned back to the notes, following her finger as she read. "Oh, boy."

Webster's voice tugged Charlene's head back up.

"What is it?" Larry asked.

The ME wiped some sweat from his upper lip with the front of his gloved hand. "Looks like our victim was pregnant."

Charlene half-sprinted to the body. "What?"

"How far along was she?" Larry asked.

"Not far along at all, maybe three or four weeks, but definitely pregnant."

"Are you sure?"

Webster looked at Charlene as if insulted.

Charlene said to Larry, "This girl has just gone from the model student and child who isn't interested in boys, according to her parents, to a pregnant freshman with traces of sperm inside her."

"She's definitely not the Virgin Mary," Larry said.

Charlene turned back to the medical examiner. "So what's your final analysis? Do we have a COD on the victim?"

"Definitely asphyxiation. But there appears to be no post-mortem damage."

That feeling came back.

As Calvin stepped onto the sideline at the Howard Jones Field, the Trojans' practice facility, his blood started pumping. The former running back standout began bouncing on the balls of his feet.

The current roster of players was already out on the field going through their routine. It was a Monday afternoon practice, and Calvin couldn't help but remember the Monday practices, where your body still hurt, muscles still tight, from the pounding the players took in a Saturday game.

Monday's practices included light drills, no pads, as players and coaches ran through game plan plays for the week in preparation of Saturday's contest. Calvin hadn't looked at the team's schedule, so he had no idea who or where the Trojans played on the upcoming Saturday.

Nick made eye contact with him from the opposite sideline and came hustling over, speed walking, like a duck, as quickly as a man his size could move without incurring a cardiac arrest. If Calvin had hoped to remain under the radar, those dreams were squashed with Nick's dramatic welcome. As the equipment manager moved across the field, the groups of players huddled in units all stopped talking and stared at the burly equipment manager.

When they saw Calvin, a few pointed, and mumbled words to each other.

Could they possibly know who Calvin was? It had been five years since he had donned the USC cardinal red and gold jersey, which meant that not one player on the current roster had been a teammate of Calvin's. They couldn't possibly know who he was. Could they?

"How subtle," Calvin said, as Nick reached him. The man sweated heavily and his shirt had grown damp. They bumped fists.

The equipment manager looked around, noticing for the first time most of the players looked his way. "I told most of them you were coming."

"What? Why?"

Nick chuckled. "These guys could learn something from you."

"You shouldn't have done that, Nick."

He waved his hand at Calvin. "Come on, you're a hero around here. Let me introduce you to some of the guys."

"No, I'm fine right here."

"Heads up!"

A shout from behind them turned Calvin's head, just in time to see a tight-spiraled football hurdling towards them. The large black man stuck out his arm, and reeled in the ball, catching the laser beam throw brilliantly, almost nonchalantly. He pulled the ball into his body, tucking it under his arm instinctively, as if ready to take a hit.

Nick grinned. "You still got it. Like you haven't missed a beat. Man, is Ryan off today. I don't think he's hit one target all practice. He just headed back into the dressing room to get retaped."

"The kid has a lot to deal with. Everyone's expectations of him are through the roof. Maybe the pressure is getting to him."

"It didn't get to you. You had that same pressure when you played here, to be the best every single game."

"Everyone handles pressure differently."

Calvin massaged the pigskin, brought it to his nose and smelled in the new leather. He closed his eyes and reminisced for a moment.

"Excuse me."

The PI opened his eyes and turned around. A young black man with a Denzel Washington crew cut and big cheek dimples held a shy look on his face as he jogged towards them.

He held out his hands. "Nice catch. Not sure what Ryno was aiming for."

Calvin flipped him the ball but the boy didn't move, just stared at them.

"What is it, Brandon?" Nick asked.

He looked at Calvin. "Are you Calvin Watters?" There was a slight nervous stutter in his voice.

"Yes," Calvin said.

"Sorry, Brandon," Nick said. "Calvin Watters, this is Brandon Harris. Brandon is one of our running backs."

"I'm only a backup," Harris said shyly, looking down towards the ground.

"For now," Calvin said. "I'm sure you'll be a starter soon."

Harris looked at Calvin sincerely. "Thanks."

"That it, Brandon?" Nick tried to usher the player away.

Brandon ignored the equipment manager. "My dad said he watched you play. You were the best running back to ever play at USC. He said no one even close to you." The kid had a guileless face.

"Thanks, Brandon. Tell your father I appreciate those kind words."

"He's been watching USC football for a long time, and so proud when I made the team."

"Good for you, Son. I'm sure he's extremely proud of you. Your hard work paid off."

Harris beamed.

"That it, Brandon?" Nick asked again. "You better get back to the scrum or the coach will have your hide."

As if on cue, one of the coaches yelled. "Harris, bring that ball back."

The young man nodded and turned away.

"Hang on, Brandon." Calvin tugged at the boy's jersey, turning him around. "Did you know the girl who died?"

He nodded slightly. "Not personally, but I saw her around at parties and stuff."

"Did you see her hanging with any of your teammates?"

He looked at Calvin with uncertainty on his face. "I don't want to get anyone in trouble, Sir."

Calvin shook his head. "Not at all. I just wondered if anyone on the team might know her a little better so I could find out more about her."

"I think she dated Mark for a while, but I believe they broke up."

"Mark?"

"Mark Simon."

"Perfect, I'll ask Mark about her. You better get back."

"Right. It was nice meeting you, Sir."

He turned and trotted back to the huddle. When he entered the scrum, a few of his teammates spoke to him and looked at Calvin, as if asking about the old black man on the sidelines.

"Seems like a stand-up guy. What's his story? Scholarship?"

Nick snorted. "Hardly. Walk-on, from a wealthy family."

"Really?" Calvin wasn't the kind to stereotype, but because of the life he grew up in, in and out of foster homes and on the streets, he had a knack for picking out the wealthy people, those who grew up with a silver spoon in their mouth. It always came out in the way they moved, confident and cocky, more than those who grew up on the streets and had to fight and claw for everything.

"Mega rich. His parents live in Baldwin Hills."

Baldwin Hills in south Los Angeles was one of the wealthiest majority-African American areas in the United States, the African American Beverly Hills.

"He's a good kid," Nick said. "But lacks football confidence. He'll never get into a game though."

"Why's that?"

"You haven't been following the team, have you?"

Calvin felt his face burn. "No."

In fact he *had* been following the team. He'd followed them every year since his dismissal. But he wasn't going to admit that.

"Our starting RB is one of the best in the country. He might even break some of your old records this year."

"Is that right?" Of course he knew that as well.

"Yep. But he's one cocky bastard though. Hard to listen to."

"So which one is Mark Simon?" Calvin asked, changing the subject.

Nick looked around the field and pointed to a thick-necked, baby-faced white kid with short brown hair. "He's one of our back-up linebackers from Arkansas."

A handsome kid, but not one that would have stood out from the pack. Calvin knew that being a back-up on any college team was tough sledding, you took the punishment all season long from the first-stringers and received none of the glory from game day victories. You played for the love of the game and the hope of someday having your number called and making the starting lineup on Saturday. Sometimes hope was just a frail thread to cling to.

"Thanks."

Chapter 7

"A lot of testosterone wafting in the air," Charlene said, pretending to sniff with her nose to the sky.

"It's a college football practice, what did you expect?" Larry answered.

Charlene and Larry stood on the sidelines as the USC Trojan football team walked through their "no-pads" practice. A whistle blew, a loud shrieking sound, and the players gathered in a huddle around the head coach. Some players knelt down on one knee while others stood in the background. Their attention seemed to be drawn to the locker room corridor, where a player emerged, walking towards the huddled team.

A good looking kid, actually gorgeous—long blond hair, flowing locks blowing in the California breeze, and a perfectly shaped, sharp nose. He had narrow shoulders and a dark tan—like someone who had just come from the beach, more like a surfer than a football player. The only player to wear a gold jersey, and he had a cocky saunter, as if he knew he was "the man".

"Look what the cat dragged in," Larry said.

"Ryan Turner, USC golden-boy," Charlene answered. "I guess the coach doesn't mind waiting for a Heisman-trophy candidate and USC's best shot at winning a national championship this season."

Everyone stopped, the coach pausing from addressing the team, as they all turned to watch the star-quarterback saunter lazily into the pack. They gave him high-fives, the coaches patted his backside, as he knelt at the front of the group, the coach restarting his speech.

"Did you see the size of the poster for Turner at the Coliseum? It's almost like a shrine for the kid when you enter the stadium," Larry asked.

"I saw it, how could I not? The whole season is riding on that kid's shoulders, and it looks like he is eating up the spotlight. That's a lot of pressure for a college kid to take on."

"Doesn't seem to be bothering him."

Charlene watched the crowd, recognizing the jubilant faces of young men excited to play the game they loved. They were in their glory, playing football for one of the best programs in the nation, undefeated and looking forward to a potential national championship. It didn't look like anything could slow down the high-speed Trojan train running over every team in their way.

Except maybe a murder.

Charlene wondered how many of the players even knew that a girl had been killed on their home stadium field after their last game. The detective was sure that news had spread, and she questioned how much that ate at these players, or if any of them had been involved.

Her gaze shifted around the small outside field, where dozen of coaches and training staff worked meticulously to make sure the players were well pampered and taken care of, everything from athletic training to water bottle filling to taping up injuries. She understood the undertaking in running an NCAA football team, and the amount of support it took to keep it going. The USC football program amassed a lot of money for the school.

Her eyes stopped and locked on a well-dressed, squarely built black man with a shining shaved scalp. He wore a tight-fitting long-sleeved V-neck and his arms bulged against the sleeves. The guy's even-toned face looked too old to be an injured player, although definitely in the kind of shape it took to play college or professional ball. He stood on the sideline at the far side of the field speaking with one of the USC trainers.

"I know that guy," Charlene said.

"What guy?" Larry said, looking at Charlene.

The detective thought she had said it under her breath, hadn't realized she had spoken the words out loud. She pointed across the field to where Larry followed the direction of her finger.

"Looks like a player," Larry said. "Probably injured."

Charlene shook her head. "Too well dressed, and his face is too mature. Man, he's good looking though."

"If you like the type," Larry remarked.

"What, tall, dark, handsome and built like a Mack truck?"

Larry pursed his lips. "Women. I thought you had a boyfriend?"

Charlene snorted, and then she had it. "That's Calvin Watters."

"The former running back? You sure?"

She nodded. "Positive. I used to watch him play and my dad talked about him all the time."

"Hell, everyone around here talked about him. A god in these parts."

"He's good looking."

"Easy, Taylor, stop drooling. I heard he went from breaking football records at USC to breaking knee caps in Vegas." Larry laughed at his own joke.

"I'm sure his life and situation are a little more complicated than that."

"Isn't his brother LAPD?"

"Ya, he's a detective with Central. Isn't Watters a PI now?"

"I think I heard that. He was involved in that whole ordeal in Vegas, the murder case that made national news. What's he doing here?"

"Let's go find out."

"You sure you can handle that? Would you like a paper bag to breathe into?"

Charlene rolled her eyes and walked away, leaving her partner behind and heading across the middle of the field, towards where Calvin Watters stood. A loud whistle drew her attention. When she turned, she saw a group of players running towards her. They stopped abruptly on the whistle.

"Ma'am," one of the coaches yelled at her. "Would you mind getting off the field?"

Charlene looked around and noticed that she stood in the middle of the field, smack dab in the center of where the team ran through drills. She backtracked to the sideline, slightly embarrassed.

Larry smiled a wide grin. "Nice goin', Taylor. Why don't we walk around?"

She didn't look at her partner, feeling the burn on her cheeks. "Up yours, Larry."

Calvin saw them coming. He'd been working alongside cops for so long now that he spotted these two plain-clothed detectives from the other side of the football field. They didn't even have to badge him.

"Looks like we have company," Nick said, nodding towards the two cops heading their way.

"Calvin Watters?" The woman in the lead.

"Yes, Ma'am." He shook her hand. Calvin noted she had lively blue eyes.

"I'm Detective Taylor, this is my partner, Detective Baker."

Just who his brother had said. Calvin shook the man's hand. "Nice to meet you."

"You're a long way from Vegas. Visiting your old stomping grounds?"

Curt, to the point. Although a masculine jab, little warmth covered her face.

"You could say that." Calvin still wasn't ready to tell these detectives that he was working the murder investigation. Even though he would eventually need their help, and hope to get their cooperation in the material they had, he wasn't sure he could trust them, yet. His brother had vouched for both of them. "This is Nick Charles."

Nick shook hands with the detectives.

"We know your brother," Taylor said.

"Don't hold that against me." Calvin shook his head at the corny joke.

"He's a good cop, a good man," Larry said.

"You think the team has what it takes this year?" Charlene asked. "Their running game is strong. Not as strong as when you played, but pretty good." She smiled at Calvin, this time warmer, and kind of cute. "And Turner has a cannon that will open up both the passing and running game. The defense has its weaknesses, they can't stop the run and their secondary is hurting, but I think they can score enough points to win."

Calvin looked at the female detective, sure that his face registered surprise. She knew her ball, impressive. She was attractive, medium height for a woman, who looked like she spent time on a treadmill. Her blue eyes shifted inquisitively, and danced when serious. He wondered if her looks took away from her ability, if the male cops took her seriously or just saw her as another blond Californian. She probably had to prove herself every day, and that impressed Calvin even more.

"Mr. Charles."

The group and the moment were interrupted by a husky voice behind them. They turned and saw a large, wide-shouldered white guy in a light tan, tailored suit with the collar up, marching towards them. His black hair held neatly in place with gel, and a scowl lined his square face. He had a large, crooked nose even on a wide face, which held tinted glasses.

"Mr. Price. How are you, sir?" Nick swallowed loudly.

The fuming, solidly-built man dismantled the huddle, almost knocking over Detective Taylor as he broke through the human shield to reach the equipment manager. He checked an expensive watch visible because the man's sleeves were rolled up crisply.

"What is he doing here?" The man nodded crossly towards Calvin, a baleful look to send a message. "These practices are closed to the public."

Calvin said nothing, but could feel his jaw muscles tightening and relaxing. He looked at the man, whose face had turned a bright red, as if from too much sun, and the vein on his forehead pulsated. The PI threw the man an awkward smile and winked, knowing that it would only infuriate him more.

"Sir, with all due respect, Calvin isn't exactly public. He used to be one of us."

"The key words there, Mr. Charles, 'used to be'. He is no longer one of us, and not welcome here. He doesn't even live in LA anymore."

"Sir, Calvin is now a private investigator. I thought he could help us find out what happened to the girl. Since he used to be USC, I thought he might have our school in his best interests."

Calvin took a side glance at the detectives. Taylor looked at the ground, but something in her face told him that the reason for his presence at the field had registered long ago. She looked as if she wasn't impressed with the sudden news blurted out by Nick. Damn, he should have kept his mouth shut.

Calvin looked back at Price, who now salivated at the mouth. "He is no longer USC, and has no affiliation to this school." He looked at the detectives. "I'm sure the police are more than capable of conducting this investigation. Please make sure Mr. Watters finds the exit. If he needs a police escort, so be it."

"Yes, sir."

Price turned away but then promptly turned back, pinning them with a glare. "You're a JAG now, Watters, and don't forget that. Get used to it."

With that, he spun on his heels and stomped away. They watched him leave the premises.

Taylor turned back to Nick. "Who was that?"

Nick's face had turned a bright red and sweat trickled down the sides of his pudgy cheeks. "Athletic Director, Jordan Price. Sorry about that. He's under a lot of pressure this season."

Charlene asked, "More than usual? Why's that?"

Nick wiped the perspiration with his hand. "He'll never have a team this strong again. Rumor has it that Ryan will enter the draft and turn pro next year, so we will rebuild with a rookie quarterback. It's now or never for Price."

"He used to play for the Trojans, didn't he?" Larry asked.

Nick nodded. "Back in the eighties, starting linebacker and mean as a pit bull."

"Looks like he's kept himself in pretty good shape," Larry said.

"And still as mean as a pit bull," Charlene added.

"He should be. He spends basically all day, every day in the gym working out."

Taylor looked at Calvin and grinned. "He seems to like you."

Calvin shrugged nonchalantly.

"I guess having your nose broken will do that," Nick butted in.

Taylor's eyes widened when she looked at Calvin. There was something in the back of her eyes that sparkled, something that told Calvin she wasn't surprised, or concerned. "You broke *that* nose?"

Calvin shrugged again. He was ready for a police escort out of the stadium, but neither of the cops seemed to be moving towards him.

"What did Price mean when he called you a JAG?"

"Just Another Guy," Calvin answered.

Even though true, Calvin still had trouble coming to terms with it. He no longer turned heads when entering a room, no longer the 'rock star' in everyone's eyes.

Taylor put on a pair of dark sunglasses. "So now that we know why you're really here, just stay out of our way, Calvin."

He tried to read her face, but nothing told Calvin that the detective bluffed. Getting information from her might be trickier that the PI had anticipated. This one would take more finesse than aggression, which Calvin was perfectly capable of, turning on the charm when needed. The female detective looked like she had a hard shell, and would be a tough nut to crack.

The detectives walked away, and Nick and Calvin watched them leave. Calvin was still impressed with the shape the detective kept herself in.

She had a take-no-shit attitude and seemed to let nothing faze her, and she didn't seem to take orders from anyone, even someone as high up as Jordan Price. This case might be fun to work, and more challenging with an uncooperative cop working against Calvin.

The deck was stacked against him, but the PI knew that those cards could instantly change hands.

Chapter 8

At the family table, a warm sensation flooded over Calvin. He and Rachel were young and single. They had no children and, although a healthy-living couple, neither of them had a passion for cooking. They got by, ate out mostly, and occasionally made something at their apartment, something simple like pasta.

Sitting there, in an actual dining room, surrounded by the closeness of his brother's family, gave the PI a fuzzy, family-feeling. One he had never experienced before.

Calvin grew up in foster homes. After his mother passed away, Calvin, at the age of thirteen, never had a real family to call his own. He never experienced the family dinners, sitting down with loved ones, sharing stories and talking about his day.

As he watched his brother and sister-in-law, hovering over and organizing their children for supper, Calvin envied his brother, and the life Josh had built for himself. He was older than Calvin, hadn't suffered the same impact when their single mother had died. Josh had been old enough to take care of himself, while Calvin struggled through the foster care system. Calvin couldn't help but wonder what life would be like had his mother lived, and not succumbed to the cancer that had taken over her body and left her less than eighty pounds of frailty.

He looked over at Rachel across from him. She too watched the family of four getting settled. He could see in her eyes, the hope that had always been there. He knew Rachel wanted a family of her own someday. Could he provide that for her? Could he be a father? Not just a father, but a dad, a great dad—one who was there for his kids, who would protect them, stick around through the good times and bad?

Not like Calvin's own father, who had left his family after Calvin's birth. The PI never really knew the man, had met him a couple of times when Calvin had hit the big time at USC, when he thought it would be in his best interest to be a part of Calvin's life. But the star running back wanted nothing of it, and had sent the man on his way.

In Calvin's mind, he only had one parent, a single woman who worked two jobs to support her boys, both mother and father to her children. And that woman had helped make Calvin the man he was today. Calvin also had a priest, Father Mac, to thank for making him who he was.

"Everything okay?"

Calvin snapped out of his trance by Alexis' voice. She and Josh had seated themselves at the ends of the table, and the food spread out.

Calvin sniffed the air. "Looks and smells great."

"I got myself a good one." Joshua chuckled.

"Help yourself."

They served their plates, Calvin loading up on meat and potatoes. The roast beef was tender and the mashed potatoes smooth and creamy. The kids quietly ate, and made a mess of food on the floor, their food trays and their faces.

To Calvin, the night and atmosphere were perfect.

"How was your day?" Josh asked.

Calvin looked at his brother. "I met your Detective Taylor."

"What did you think of her?"

"Kind of intense."

"I'd say. Her colleagues call her Chip behind her back. She has a lot of issues she's dealing with—being a woman in law enforcement, the death of her father, and being nearly killed not long ago."

Calvin knew that every time his brother spoke about police work: cases, colleagues, etc., Josh probably violated department procedures. But that was a family thing, helping each other out whenever they could. It hadn't always been like that.

"She seems to have a lot going on, but looks like she's coping."

"She's tough, and will eat you alive if you're not careful."

Calvin grinned. "I'll tread lightly."

"She's fair, resourceful and very good at her job. She might actually be an ally if you work the angle correctly."

"She's kind of cute, too," Alexis blurted out.

They all looked down at the end of the table at her.

She shrugged. "What? I'm just saying, I saw her picture in the paper after she solved that big case with the guy killing all the actors."

"Did you find anything out, yet?" Rachel asked Calvin.

"I have a couple of leads, but nothing concrete yet. It will take some time. I know this school and this football program, it's like one big family."

Josh said, "I'm sure they're not exactly welcoming you with open arms."

"I still have a few friends in the program."

"Have you seen Price yet?"

"Just ran in to him today."

"How did that go?"

"About how you would expect."

Joshua ran his hand through his hair. "Yikes. What's on the slate for tomorrow?"

Calvin swallowed a mouth full of potatoes and then said, "I'm going to speak with a few players, see if I can find out more about the victim. I think she hung around the team, maybe even dated one of the players. Seems like a good place to start. Then I might talk with some of Baylor's cheerleader teammates. There's a lot of options out there."

"Just be careful, little bro. If you need anything from me, let me know."

Calvin nodded and took a bite. They ate in silence for a while, his brother's words echoing in his thoughts.

Calvin was no longer welcomed at USC, no longer the golden boy, poster child surrounded by screaming fans. Although he still had a few friends involved with the team, he was virtually an outsider, and would not receive the cooperation that he once might have.

The PI was well aware of the close knit family community of the USC Trojan football team. They didn't welcome people into their circle too often, so he would have to finesse his way where possible, until it was time to ram his way, as he had done years ago in a red and gold jersey—first-and-goal on the Coliseum football field.

But he knew he had the upper-hand over the LAPD. The football program hated cops, and did their best to keep them out of their dirty laundry. Calvin might be able to squeeze in more than Taylor, or at least break the barrier, so that meant the detective might need Calvin more than he needed her.

He could play that angle.

"What do you want to do tomorrow, Rachel?" Alexis' voice startled Calvin.

Rachel shrugged her slender shoulders. "It doesn't matter."

"How about some retail therapy?"

Rachel looked at Calvin who raised his hands in an 'up to you' motion. She looked back at Alexis and nodded. "Okay."

He kind of felt bad. He had spent very little time with Rachel since arriving in LA, but she knew, he had told her outright, that he was in the city to work. It wasn't a vacation, but she had been persistent to join the trip.

Calvin also worried that Rachel would be a distraction while he worked this complicated, important case. But she had been true to her word. She had stayed out of the way and allowed Calvin the room and space to work on his own. She hadn't whined or complained, and Calvin was grateful that Alexis didn't work and had time to spend with Rachel. They seemed to be getting along splendidly.

Perfect. Rachel would be busy for the day, and Calvin could spend time investigating.

"Uncle Calvin?"

The PI turned to face the small, fragile voice coming from his nephew. "What's up, Caleb?"

"Will you watch a movie with me tonight?"

How could he resist that? "You betcha, buddy."

It looked as if he already had his night planned out. He saw Rachel secretly smiling from the corner of her mouth. She definitely enjoyed this.

"More wine?"

He already poured it before she had time to answer.

She watched the smooth red wine leave the bottle and empty into her glass. Then Matt corked the bottle.

She had never been a 'wine drinker'. But her boyfriend had casually introduced it to her and she eventually acquired a taste. When he sat back down, she stared across the table at him. He was handsome, short black hair, but messed slightly since he'd just gotten out of the shower. He had a strong, chiseled jaw line and blue eyes that had drawn in Charlene the first time she'd looked into them.

He just did something to her, totally out of character for Charlene. She acted like an immature school girl around him, giddy, happy to see him. She blamed some of that on the fact that they rarely spent time together because of their busy work schedules. He was confident and good at his job. He loved shop-talk, breaking down cases they both worked on, and was, to Charlene, as sexy as hell.

Plus, her family loved Matt.

She took a sip of wine and let it linger in her mouth before swallowing. She sniffed the air, the garlic hanging at the back of her nostrils, taking in the dinner that Matt had prepared for them. He had outdone himself once again with the Pasta Carbonara.

"What did you do today?" she asked. "Other than this." She spread her arms out across the table.

"A little of nothing. Had a couple of calls with Washington, went to the gym, got some groceries. You had absolutely nothing in the fridge."

So goes the life of a single LAPD detective working on the fly. Charlene didn't usually take the time to eat a solid, healthy meal, let alone grocery shop, much to the chagrin of her ever-concerned mother.

"Oh, except beer," he added.

Oops. She had to change the topic of conversation. It wasn't going in the direction she wanted.

"Wow." she grinned. "That's not like you. Actually relaxing for a change." Working the case in Denver, Charlene learned that Matt was hot-wired and an energy bug.

He smiled. "It felt pretty good."

"Well, don't get used to it. I'll have chores for tomorrow."

He would only be around for a couple of more days, so she didn't want to get too comfortable with his being here, because it would make saying goodbye that much harder. She'd like to spend more time with him, but duty, this new case, called for her attention. And it wasn't like her to ask for time off. She'd had enough of that lately.

"How'd it go today?"

She nodded and ran a finger through her hair. "Some interesting findings. The victim was pregnant."

"Whoa, that'll open some doors. Who's kid?"

"No idea, yet. We tried to get to the boyfriend after practice today but got turned down, because he's being ordered representation." She hesitated, then added. "I met a very interesting character today."

"Oh ya?"

"Ever hear of Calvin Watters?"

"The football player?"

"Former football player."

"I thought he landed in Vegas?"

"He did. He works as a PI there now."

"Oh, boy."

"What?"

"You and PIs."

"What do you mean?" But she knew exactly what he meant.

"Remember in Denver when I took you to meet my friend?"

Her voice cracked. "Harold Linden."

Linden, a PI in Denver working the same case as Charlene and Matt, had found evidence against suspects who killed him in cold blood before he'd had the chance to tell anyone. Luckily, he had left behind some proof for Charlene and Matt to nail the guilty suspects.

"Yep, you told me all about your thoughts on private investigators."

"Can't a girl change her mind?"

"Yes, she can, and she does often." His eyebrows bounced. "Sometimes they don't even know what they want or like."

She pursed her lips. "Touché."

"So what did you think of Watters?"

"First impression: Not well liked around the football team anymore."

"Really? I remember reading an article about him in Sports Illustrated, the toast of the town back in the day."

"Things have changed. My gut tells me he's smart, and probably his attention to detail, precise. He doesn't beat around the bush and is a straight shooter."

"Might be a competent resource for you. Someone once close to the inside."

"I don't think I'll draw that card just yet. But I will keep it in the back of my mind."

"So you'll use him." He squinted his eyes slightly, giving her his 'evil' eye, but with a twinkle in it. "Like you used me in Denver."

She couldn't deny the fact that she had manipulated her way into the case in Denver, even though Matt had been completely against it. Her first instinct was to use Matt for information, to get close to the case, and she had won. But she'd also learned that he was told to babysit her by his superiors.

Strange to think how far the two of them had come since that time, when they had butted heads and competed for top dog status. In the end Matt had relented, and brought her into the FBI's trusted circle of friends. She owed him for that.

She smiled seductively. "Men are too easy."

"I am a sucker for a good lookin' chick with a thong and shoulder holster."

She threw a dinner roll at him and he ducked to avoid it. It missed him and hit the wall behind Matt's head, rolling back across the wood panel flooring under the table. He bent to pick it up, and amusingly broke it apart and took a bite.

"So where do you go from here?" he asked, his mouth full of partially chewed bread.

"I think the more important question is, where do you go from here?"

Charlene knew that Matt talked about her case, but she was more concerned about where he would be flying off to when he left LA. What was wrong with her? Here he stood, her dream man, a great guy, who took time off to be with her, and all she could think about was how little time she had with him.

"Don't change the subject. What about your case?"

She had never been quick to trust people and share facts about a case with them. When her niece had been kidnapped, Charlene refused to share knowledge of the case even with her own sister.

The detective had spent a lot of long hours with her dad, sharing details, going over cases. He had been the only person she had ever trusted enough to talk about work with. But Matt diligently worked his way into her little circle of trust.

"You don't trust many people, do you?" he asked.

"That's not true."

"Yes it is. You're a tough egg and want to do everything on your own. I read your file, remember?"

She looked at him hard, and his stare relented. She sighed loudly. "Larry and I have a few people targeted tomorrow. After speaking with the victim's roommate, I think I need to speak with members of the sorority where she had pledged. I also think it's time to ruffle some feathers with the football team. I've let them stew long enough."

"Ah yes, that take-no-shit Charlene Taylor I read about. Time for the bulldog to go to work."

She picked up another bun and faked another throw at him. "I also want to speak with the stadium security guards. A murder like that couldn't have gone unnoticed under their watchful eye."

"True. Someone should have seen or heard something."

"Okay. You still haven't answered my question. Where are you heading from here and when will you be back."

Matt winked. "Miss me already?"

She rolled her eyes. "Hardly." Even though her heart fluttered.

"I got a call about a job in Seattle. They want me out there in a couple of days."

"A couple of days?"

He raised his hands in mock surrender. "Best I can do."

Her lips curled at the corners. "Then we will have to make the most of the time we do have."

Book II

A Running Start

Chapter 9

"Late again," Larry huffed, as Charlene got out of her car and tucked in her shirt. "That's twice this week already, not like you. I'm starting to think you're moonlighting on me."

"Sorry." She gasped, out of breath catching up to her partner, who had already started moving up the walkway towards a large brick building with multiple white pillars holding up an overhang.

The words Delta Gamma were fastened high up on the white front paneling and the sorority's symbols hung on a sign over the white, double-wide French-door front entrance. Dozens of freshly-cleaned windows lined the front of the historic, two-story building.

Charlene pressed the buzzer at the side of the door and heard a loud chime ring inside the building. The sounds of giggles and running feet thumped towards the door.

"Doesn't sound like they're mourning their sister, does it?" Larry asked.

"Baylor wasn't technically part of the sorority yet, just in training and only a pledge."

The door opened and a young, attractive blond woman, half naked except for a black crop top and extremely short cut-off jeans, where the pockets and threads hung down under the homemade cut, greeted them with a smile.

Charlene already had her wallet out and flipped it open to the badge.

"Oh," the girl groaned. She shut the door on them.

Charlene looked at Larry and the heavy-set detective shrugged his bulky shoulders. They heard more giggling, some whispering and more footsteps. Charlene raised her hand to rap on the door when it opened quickly.

This time a short, thin, dark-complexioned brunette, with luxurious hair—long outward curls with one side tucked behind her ear—stared at them.

"Can I help you?" she said.

"I'm Detective Taylor, this is Detective Baker. We'd like to speak with you about Samantha Baylor."

"Sure."

She opened the door wide, turned her back to the detectives and moved further into the front entrance.

"Would you like my sunglasses to cover those roaming eye balls?" Charlene whispered to Larry.

"Up yours, Taylor."

They went in and found a group of girls, at least half a dozen, huddled around the front room, all quiet and staring at the LAPD detectives. It included women of different height, weight, hair color and race. There certainly was no discrimination with this sorority.

But still they stared: some sat, some stood, but all became motionless and speechless. Larry swayed on the heels of his feet nervously, looking completely uncomfortable.

On the drive over, Charlene had gone through her notebook and read the names that Rory Cummings had given her, so the detective was prepared heading in.

"Emma Moore and Mia Davidson," Charlene stated matter-of-factly.

No one moved, no one stepped forward, but each girl looked around the room at each other. Charlene noticed most sets of eyes staring at the petite, beautiful brunette who had answered the door the second time.

Charlene looked at her, but the head sorority sister wouldn't make eye contact.

"I'm Emma."

A lazy southern accent turned Charlene's head to the curving wrought-iron staircase, where a Barbie-like dishwater-blond woman, with heavily applied make-up and tight tanned skin had started descending the staircase, but stopped halfway down.

"Ms. Moore. We hoped to ask you some questions about Samantha Baylor."

The woman continued down the stairs and approached them. "Why of course." She snaked her arm around the brunette. "Mia and I would be happy to answer any questions you have. Isn't that right, Mia?"

Davidson still didn't look up from the floor, but nodded meekly. Then Moore added, "But Samantha wasn't yet part of our sorority."

"Yes, we are aware, but I think you can help steer our investigation."

The sorority sister grinned, a fake, showgirl smile. There was no doubt to Charlene that Emma Moore had probably been a pageant girl growing up, and by the look of her, had probably won her fair share of them.

Last night, before leaving the office, Charlene and Larry had talked about how they would proceed with the interviewing of these two ladies. Since working together, Larry and Charlene had realized that their most effective method of interrogation techniques included separating the parties involved: Larry taking one interviewee and Charlene the other. Then they would regroup after and compare notes.

"Can we do it here?" Moore asked. She was obviously the leader, as not one other person in the room had yet to speak. It looked like a Stepford Wives sorority to Charlene.

"I don't see why not," Larry said. The detectives had also discussed this, always more beneficial to allow the interviewee to remain in the friendly confines of their normal, everyday surroundings.

"Ms. Davidson," Larry said. "Would you do me the honor of accompanying me for a walk outside?"

A great maneuver on Larry's part. It was never a good idea for a male, especially one in an authoritative position, to be shut into a room alone with a female. Any kind of accusation could arise from that. Plus, Larry didn't look at all comfortable inside the sorority house.

Davidson looked to Moore, who gave the sister a perceptible nod. "Sure," Davidson replied.

"I'll wait outside if you want to put something on," Larry turned away.

"I'm good like this," Davidson answered.

Larry paused and Charlene chuckled. The sixtyish, old-school detective, with two adult children of his own, still wasn't accustomed to the skimpy garments that today's youth donned.

Larry breathed in deeply. "Okie dokie."

They met upstairs, in an area known as the Anchor Room, filled with comfortable, cozy couches, large flat screen TVs, expensive decorative wall accessories and trendy, up-to-date table fixtures.

Charlene sat down on a three-cushion couch and rested her satchel on a brass coffee table. Moore poured herself a glass of ice water from an antique carafe, and chose a square-shaped, cushioned back chair placed across from the detective. Charlene thought it a good distance to keep the sorority sister relaxed, but at bay.

Charlene already had her pen and pad out by the time Moore made eye contact.

"So how well did you know Samantha Baylor?" Charlene asked.

"Not well. We always have so many pledges that it's difficult for me, or any of us to get to know them until they're fully sworn in, if they make it that far."

"What kind of pledge was Ms. Baylor?"

"What do you mean?"

"Was she going to make the cut?"

"We hadn't decided that yet."

"Did she pass all of your tests?"

"What tests?"

She was good, cool and calm under pressure, but after that last question, Charlene had seen a slight shift in posture, unnoticeable to the untrained eye, but the detective had caught it immediately. She was trained to read faces.

"Ms. Moore, I'm sure your sorority runs these girls through a series of tests, to make sure they make the grade, worthy to be associated with the Delta Gamma name?"

She leaned back in her seat, as if composing herself. "Of course we need to make sure these girls are up to our standards, but we hardly test them."

She said it so nonchalantly without looking Charlene directly in the eye, the detective knew it to be a lie.

Charlene switched directions.

"Look, I don't care about what kinds of things you make the girls do. I'm here about a murder, a murder of one of your pledges. If you aren't going to answer my questions, I'm sure one of those girls down there, once I get them back to my precinct, will open up to me. What do you think they will say?"

Moore's nose wrinkled slightly. Normally, it wouldn't give Charlene a second thought, but it was the third time it had happened in the last two minutes, a definite nervous tic.

Now to pull out the big guns.

"I was told by one of your sisters that you didn't like Samantha."

Moore squinted her eyes. "I barely knew her."

"We were told that she wouldn't agree to some of your, let's say, unethical practices."

Now she stood up. "I don't know who you spoke with, but I can assure you that this sorority runs everything by the book and we have the utmost care and consideration for our sisters."

Charlene folded up her notepad, and tucked it in her jacket. "You leave me no choice. I'm going to have to pull in each and every one of your members, one at a time, and interview them. That means we will be opening up a new investigation into this sorority. Thank you for your time, Ms. Moore." Charlene stood up.

"Wait."

Bingo. Charlene turned around and waited.

"Samantha was probably going to be a part of our sorority."

"Really? I was under the impression that she wasn't."

"Who told you that?"

"A very reliable source."

"Well, Mia and I are the *only* ones to make that decision. We have final say on everything that happens in this house."

"Did anyone in this house, that you know of, have a problem with Samantha Baylor?"

"Not that I know of. Samantha seemed like a really sweet girl, and I know for a fact that she really wanted to be a part of this sorority."

"What makes you say that?"

"Let's just say she was willing to go above and beyond."

Charlene let that sink in. The detective wasn't sure what to think, as she seemed to be getting misdirected from everyone involved in this case. Half of the people thought that Baylor was a saint, and the other half have confirmed her to be a sinner. It seemed that no one really knew her at all.

Baylor's parents didn't know their daughter was pregnant, hell they didn't even know she had a boyfriend. Samantha's roommate said she was shy and quiet, wouldn't agree to the sorority's terms, but now Emma Moore talked about Baylor doing whatever it took to make the team.

"So then you felt that Samantha Baylor was Delta Gamma material?"

"Absolutely."

"Thanks for meeting with me, Mr. Adams."

The overweight black man turned towards Calvin. He got up from the bench and shook the PI's hand.

"Calvin, I'm not your teacher anymore. You can call me Leonard."

"Sorry, force of habit."

"You always were gracious and polite, especially for being 'Calvin Watters', big man on campus."

Adams was in his early sixties, had a fuzzy salt and pepper afro with a matching beard. His oversized, black-framed glasses took up most of his face. He'd taught Calvin economics, and they'd formed a friendship because Adams was one of the only teachers to take Calvin seriously, and not treat him like a Trojan football star.

Calvin caught a break when he'd seen Mr. Adams' name on Samantha Baylor's course workload, which he'd procured from one of his contacts inside the administration building. And Rachel didn't think he could sweet talk.

"Thanks for seeing me."

Adams nodded and sat back down. He looked out into the throng of students walking the paths. "I have a few minutes between classes. I couldn't believe when I heard from you. It's been a long time. I always wondered about you."

"Sorry I didn't stay in touch."

"No need to apologize. I didn't like the way the school handled your situation."

"Thanks."

"How's your knee?"

"It's okay."

He scratched his beard and said, "I always felt you got a raw deal."

"You teach Samantha Baylor," a statement more than a question.

Adams nodded, but he looked off into the distance. "So that's what this is about?"

"I'm investigating her murder."

"So it was a murder?"

"Looks that way."

A few seconds of silence passed. "Who are you working for?"

"Private contractor. I'm a PI now."

"You were always an intelligent guy, Calvin. I knew it, I saw it. Your brain functioned differently, and everyone underestimated you. They only saw the football player, I saw much more. Who hired you?"

"The team."

Adams huffed. "There's no way you're working for Jordan Price."

"Nick asked me to look into it."

"You have Trojan blood flowing through you, Calvin."

"That's not gonna muddy my vision."

"You sure?"

Calvin nodded.

"Samantha registered for my freshman economics class," he said grimly.

"What can you tell me about her?"

"Sweet girl, shy, sat at the front of the class. Inquisitive, craved knowledge."

"What kind of student was she?"

"Remember, this is a small sample size I'm working with. We haven't been in school long this semester."

"Anything you can tell me would be great."

"Exceptional student...at the start."

"What happened?"

"Not sure. She started missing some classes, showed up late for others. When she did attend, she seemed distracted, unfocused."

"How so?"

"Like I said, she always sat at the front of my class, so when she was absent, I noticed. She also was very inquisitive—always raising her hand to ask or answer a question. But she stopped doing that."

"Did you notice any physical changes? Maybe bruises or marks on her face or body?"

He shook his head. "Not that I noticed."

Calvin shifted from foot to foot. "Did she ever say anything to you?"

"To me? Of course not. I'm just the teacher. I thought about reaching out, but hesitated. I guess I should have."

Adams dropped his head, staring down at the ground.

Calvin put a hand on the man's large back. He could feel Adam's shaking slightly. "It's not your fault, Leonard."

When he lifted his head, his cheeks looked wet. He wiped them with the palm of his hand. "But I got worried, because she had so much potential."

"When did this transformation take place?"

Adams shrugged his wide shoulders. "A few weeks ago, maybe. Hard to say. We have so many students to worry about, but the problem is we have to treat them like adults, when really, they are still kids."

"Who did she hang around with? Were there any students in your class you noticed her getting friendly with?"

"Like I said, a shy girl. She kept to herself most of the time, and I didn't notice any particular students coming or going with her. I never saw her outside of class so I couldn't say for sure who her chums were."

"Did you mention your concerns to anyone else, other than those teachers?"

He shook his head, and then checked his watch, an old Rolex that looked like an antique. "Sorry, Calvin, but I have another class in a few minutes."

Calvin stuck out his hand. "Thanks again for seeing me, Mr. Adams."

Adams shook his hand, but his grip wasn't as firm or strong as when they'd first met earlier. "Calvin, what did I tell you to call me?"

"Right, sorry."

Larry looked busy in his car, parked in front of Charlene's, outside the sorority house. He had his reading bifocals perched on the end of his nose as he flipped through his notepad. He looked over at his partner when she opened the passenger door and slid in.

"How was your walk?" she asked.

"Quiet."

"Davidson didn't give you anything?"

"Less than nothing. Almost as if she was afraid to say anything. She kept looking back at the house."

"Moore was the exact opposite, she's definitely running the show. She quickly defended the integrity of the sorority. She said that Baylor was going to be pledged."

"Really?" Larry looked at her over his reading glasses. "I thought Baylor's roommate said that Samantha wasn't going to make it. The head girls didn't think she was right for the family."

Charlene nodded, biting on her bottom lip, as she thought.

"What kind of vibe did you get from Moore?" Larry asked.

"I think she's hiding something, but I don't know if it has anything to do with Baylor or the murder. She's very protective of these girls and the sorority. She's a leader, and will do anything to make sure Delta Gamma is taken care of."

"So who do we believe?"

"Someone is trying to throw us off the scent. Is Rory Cummings serious about her sisters not liking Baylor, or is she trying to point a finger at them, sending us towards them and away from someone else?"

He chewed on one arm of his reading glasses. "Is Moore lying? Because Cummings seemed sincere to me."

"I think—"

Larry's cellphone, an old-school flip-phone, rattled in the middle console coffee-cup holder, indicating a call.

"Hold that thought." He answered. "Baker here…..yes, sir." He hung up and turned to Charlene. "Let's go."

"Where?"

"The precinct."

"What's the rush."

"Someone just turned himself in for the cheerleader murder."

Chapter 10

Calvin steered the rental car down the one-way of a seedier, LA neighborhood, located in Westlake North. He had been in the area once before, years ago, but now every house looked similar. He checked the address he had jotted down on the front cover of the sports section of the newspaper.

He had spent time in worse places, a lot of time on the streets, hanging out with street sleaze. Hell, Calvin had been street sleaze himself.

He pulled up to the curbside of a rundown home that was well past its 'better days'. He grabbed the package he'd brought from the passenger seat and got out of the car. The slam of his door echoed in the quiet, empty neighborhood.

The house had been stripped of its splendor. The once white fish-scale exterior siding was fading and stained yellow, and the bars over the single-paned windows had started to rust. Calvin swung open the gate door with a creak, and followed a pathway that had once been solid concrete, now cracked with weeds springing from the openings. The rest of the lawn was buried in dead grass.

The PI placed a hand on the railing as he climbed the steps, but it wobbled and almost caved in, the loose floor-boards creaking. The bright front door looked like a fresh coat of paint had just been applied. He felt the door to make sure it wasn't damp before he knocked.

The door sprung open with enthusiasm and a young, African-American boy, with a shaved head and sunglasses much too wide for his face, looked up at Calvin.

"Who are you?" the boy asked.

"I'm Calvin, your mommy's friend. Who are you?"

"Jeremiah."

Calvin took a step back. "Whoa. The last time I saw you, you were just a baby. How old are you now, seven?"

"Eight."

"Jay, who is it?" Tiana Washington appeared from the back and smiled as she approached the open door. "Calvin."

The Coliseum security guard stepped past her son and hugged Calvin, the PI wrapping his big arms around the woman. A noise inside the house startled them, as they detached from the embrace.

Another boy stepped out onto the front porch. The boy could have been Jeremiah's twin, the shaved head and similar facial features, but much taller than his younger brother.

Calvin looked at the boy, and the boy looked back. They stayed that way for seconds, sharing a moment, staring as if in recognition.

"Is this Elijah?"

Her eyes gleamed. "It sure is. Did the jersey give it away?"

Elijah wore a pair of faded jeans with the knees worn out. Over his slender upper body, the boy had on an old, stained, red, gold and white number twenty-one USC jersey.

"He's gotten so tall," Calvin pointed out.

"Well, it's been almost six years. Turn around, E," Tiana demanded.

The boy shuffled his feet and turned around to show Calvin the number twenty-one, with the letters W-A-T-T-E-R-S ironed on the back. The lettering had started to fade and peel off. Calvin's black-sharpie signature was still legible.

"I can't believe he still wears that. It's a lot smaller on him now than I remember back then." The short sleeves went down to about Elijah's elbows and it was skin tight, despite the fact that the boy was rail thin. "Nice jersey, young man."

Calvin held out his hand. Elijah flashed a crooked-tooth grin, ran and jumped to give Calvin a high-five.

Tiana looked at Calvin. "You're kidding, right? He rarely takes it off. I have to wrestle with him on Sundays just to be able to run it through the wash once in a while." She turned to her sons. "Okay, boys, let's head off to school."

Elijah, Tiana's oldest son, pulled an electronic device out of his school bag and plugged in earbuds. He maneuvered it until satisfied, and then tucked it away.

"Go on, boys."

Elijah and Jeremiah skipped down the steps, their lunchboxes rattling at their sides. "Bye, Mom, luv ya!"

"Wow, a phone already, at his age," Calvin remarked.

Tiana snickered. "Hardly, I can't afford that. That's my old phone. He uses it as an iPod, so it's synced to mine. Free of charge."

When the boys disappeared around the corner of the house, Calvin held up his package. "Wine?"

Tiana winked. "You certainly know how to make an appearance. Come on in, Calvin."

He followed her inside. The house hadn't changed much since the last time Calvin had been there. Back when he'd been a student at USC, Calvin had been invited to Elijah's birthday party as a surprise for the boy. Of course, the running back couldn't resist accepting the offer, just to see the smile on the boy's face, and maybe make his day and life a little more fulfilling.

Calvin had been the star, the toast-of-the-town, and when Tiana had mentioned to him that he was Elijah's favorite player, Calvin had shown up at the house for Elijah's sixth birthday, with an authentic, Calvin Watters USC number twenty-one jersey.

As a single mother, working fulltime and trying to raise two young boys, it was easy to see that Tiana tried her best to keep up with the house work. With no extra money for a nanny, no close relatives to move in and help out, Tiana was on her own.

The smell of toasted waffles and maple syrup wafted through the air as Calvin entered the house. The thick beige carpeted floors had been recently vacuumed, although partially covered by boys' clothes, sneakers, game controllers and a half-constructed Lego building set. The evidence laid to rest by a pair of young, healthy, active boys on the run.

The inside of the house was filled with old but well maintained furniture. The coffee table had been wiped clean, and the only remnants were an empty Gatorade bottle, a bag of Skittles scattered over the wood, and two unlit scented candles. A stack of USC Football game program guides lined the bottom of the table.

A desk pushed up against the wall held an open laptop, looking new. The screen saver displayed a picture of Calvin, in full USC Trojan gear—an action picture taken during one of his games against the Oklahoma Sooners. It looked as if Calvin ran in for a touchdown.

Shafts of sunshine burst through the gap in the heavy velvet curtains, casting a dim light across the room, and Tiana zipped them open with one quick jerk. The refrigerator started to hum loudly and they both looked towards the kitchen.

"It's old, it does that."

Calvin nodded and sat down on a couch cushion. The couch and love seat were strategically placed to face a small, old-style television set turned off.

"How about a drink?" Tiana asked.

Calvin shook his head. "No, thanks. Please, sit down."

She removed the phone from her pants' pocket and set it on the table, before sitting down on a rounded, floral-patterned chair. Calvin knew that Tiana probably ran on fumes. She had just finished a 12 hour shift at the coliseum, and then raced home to get her kids ready for school.

"Your mother-in-law still watch the boys?"

Tiana nodded. "She's a saint. I don't know what I would do without her."

"We all need family. They are the backbone to living a happy life. The fact that your mother-in-law is willing to take the boys every night when you work is a sign of her love, and the person you are."

"She probably feels a little guilty that her son ran off and deserted his kids."

"Ever hear from him?"

She shook her head. "Nah. The boys have stopped asking about him."

"They look like handsome young men. You seem to be doing a great job as both mother and father."

Her eyes moistened slightly. "Thank you, Calvin. I'm trying my best."

Living without a father, not easy, Calvin thought. But better to have a loving mother and no father, than a dead-beat one hanging around.

"They will be just fine."

Silence ensued, the quietness not bothering either of them. Calvin glanced around the room. The original wallpaper still clung to one wall, and the antique cream-colored paint in another corner curled up from age.

"Go ahead."

Tiana's voice startled him. He looked at her. "Go ahead with what?"

"Ask me."

"Ask you?"

"I know you're here about the murder. Word spreads quickly in our little school. When Calvin Watters comes back to campus, after the way it ended, people talk. I know that you are investigating that cheerleader's murder."

Calvin leaned back, his large girth and weight settling into the soft cushions. "Were you working that night?"

"Of course, I work almost every night."

"Did you hear or see anything?"

She pursed her lips. "Nothing."

"What about Wayne?"

Wayne Parker was the senior security guard at the coliseum. He worked with Tiana on most nights. The man was in his seventies, and didn't see or hear well, but with budgets and today's discrimination laws, he kept wanting to work. It wasn't like any sort of crime happened around the stadium...until now.

Tiana snorted. "Wayne wouldn't hear a dump truck driving through the empty coliseum hallways."

Calvin rubbed the stubble on his chin. "So, no sign of anyone entering or exiting the building?"

"Not on our watch. We performed our regular rounds, but there is never anything to witness."

"How many naps did Wayne take that night?"

Tiana grinned and said, "You remember him."

"Ya, he means well. So I know that you do most of the rounds and you are the eyes and ears. Are you sure that nothing out of the ordinary happened? Maybe something to draw your attention away from the stadium corridors."

"Calvin, I didn't see anyone go in or out of that building. I swear."

Tiana's phone vibrated on the wooden coffee table, rattling around. She picked it up and checked the screen, and then set it back down.

He hesitated a few seconds to see if she would answer the text. "Still no cameras inside the stadium, correct?"

"Correct. They'd never had a need for it before. There are cameras outside and in the stadium lobbies, but nothing inside on the field itself. Maybe that will change now."

"Did you know the cheerleader?"

"No, never met her."

"Has anyone around the stadium, workers, or anyone else connected with the program, been acting strange recently?"

"I haven't noticed anything."

"The doors were all locked up tightly?"

"Except the team entrance."

"Oh ya, game night. The team doors stay unlocked so that coaches can stay late into the night to review game film."

Tiana adjusted some books that lay flat on the table. Calvin picked up on the evasive maneuver.

"No locks were found damaged, so the back doors had been used. I'm not sure how else to answer it."

She looked back up at Calvin after a few seconds had passed. "You think so?"

"There's no other option. Someone had to have a way in, and a way out. Unless those other doors had been left unlocked."

"Sorry I can't be more help, Calvin."

"This him?"

Charlene and Larry stood on the other side of a one-way glass, staring at the guy who allegedly killed Samantha Baylor.

"He says so," said Ronald Dunbar, Captain III and Commanding Officer of the Robbery-Homicide Division of the Detective Bureau. Dunbar was thick-necked and balding, a wily former detective and someone Charlene respected. The detective could smell the stink of smoke from her captain, who let on he had quit long ago.

They watched a short, scrawny, nerdy-looking kid, with blue-dyed, gelled-up spiked hair. The boy seemed young, and acne pelted his baby-faced skin.

"Who are we looking at?"

"His name is Lewis Mahoney. He's a freshman at USC, studying engineering. From a wealthy family in Fresno, only child, straight 'A' student."

Charlene scanned the suspect's very short CV. "Does he have a history with Baylor?"

"He hasn't been questioned yet. We've been holding him for you. This is your case."

Charlene turned to Larry. "Let's go."

They took the thin file from their boss and entered the room. Up close, Mahoney didn't look old enough to even carry a driver's license. The kid fidgeted nervously, shifted in his seat and swallowed hard.

Charlene smacked the folder on the table top and sat down. Larry remained standing, hovering over Mahoney, who sat, and came to Larry's belt buckle. The size of Larry standing over anyone intimidated most men, but because Mahoney was so tiny, young, and had just confessed to a homicide, the detective's shadow loomed that much larger.

Charlene stood up, removed her suit jacket and hung it over the back of the chair. She unbuttoned her cuffs and rolled up her sleeves.

"Do you want a drink?" she asked.

Mahoney shook his head.

The detective sat back down. "Would you like an attorney, Mr. Mahoney?"

Another head shake.

Charlene looked at Larry who shrugged. She peered back at Mahoney. He wouldn't make eye contact with the detectives. He stared at the table, statue-still.

"So you killed Samantha Baylor?" Charlene blurted out.

The suspect nodded. Still no eye contact or any kind of reaction. The boy looked almost tranquilized, like he'd been drugged or hypnotized. Charlene wondered if a drug test had been administered to Mahoney. His eyes didn't look glazed-over or bloodshot.

Charlene inhaled deeply and blew air from her cheeks. "Why did you do it?"

Mahoney finally looked up and sneered. Charlene didn't think the facial expression fit on the young man's face.

"The bitch was a tease."

Charlene didn't know Mahoney, had never met the kid or even heard of him so far in the early stages of her investigation. From everyone she had spoken with: Mr. and Mrs. Baylor, sorority sisters, and the roommate, not one person mentioned Mahoney's name. Samantha Baylor's parents didn't even know of any man in their daughter's life.

"Did you have a relationship with her?" Charlene wasn't one to judge, but Mahoney didn't seem like the type of guy Baylor would keep company with.

"Nah. She led me on, but wouldn't go through with it."

"How did you do it?"

"Uh?" The question caught Mahoney off guard. He paled, his mouth curling into an "o" shape, and perspiration peppered the skin over his upper lip.

"How did you kill Samantha Baylor?"

His eye-balls rolled up and to the right, which sometimes meant the person searched for an answer. "With my bare hands." He held out his small, fragile-looking hands. His skin was soft, as if moisturized, tenderer than Charlene's.

"Smother her? Choke her? Hit her over the head?"

"I did what needed to be done." He looked frustrated, like he hadn't been prepared for the line of questioning.

"So which is it?" Charlene persisted, like the bulldog she'd been rumored to be in her work mode.

He leaned back in his seat and crossed his arms. "I want my attorney." His eyes refocused on the table top and he refused to look back up. "Now."

"He doesn't fit."

Charlene and Larry sat back at their desks. Mahoney met with his attorney, some rich trial lawyer hired by Mahoney's wealthy parents. They were also on the way from Fresno.

"I agree." Larry wiped a bead of sweat above his right eyebrow.

"Killers always know exactly what the cops know, but Mahoney doesn't even know how she died. He's lying."

"Why?"

"Protect someone?"

"We need to hit the streets with this. Put Mahoney's name out there and his picture in front of people close with Baylor. We need to find out if he had any contact or if he's even in her social circles."

"Let's polygraph him."

"His attorney would never allow it."

"Let's talk to him, tell him that we think his client is innocent and a polygraph will prove that."

"You're cute, Kid. You think an attorney would believe we think a suspect, who turned himself in for murder, is innocent? What if we're wrong? What if Mahoney did do it? He would just be incriminating himself even more. A lawyer would have a field day with that."

Charlene leaned back in her chair, which swiveled with her momentum. It made no sense. Why would Mahoney admit to something he didn't do, something as huge as a murder? Who could he possibly care that much about to protect?

They'd already put a search warrant request in for Mahoney's dorm room. The kid had nothing on him when he'd come in: no phone, wallet or ID. There was no vehicle registered to his name in the DMV files, and he didn't even have a license, so all of that stuff had to be somewhere.

"Look who just came in," Larry said.

Charlene turned and glanced over her shoulder, just catching the back of a very expensive Armani suit jacket.

"The sharks smell blood," Charlene replied. As if on cue, her desk phone rang and she picked it up before it sounded a second time.

"Detective Taylor, do you and detective Baker have time to come into my office?"

Her boss sounded very diplomatic and polite, which wasn't Captain Dunbar's style at all. He was a Bronx kid, grew up a tough street punk, with the facial scars and healed over broken bones to show for it.

"Sure thing, Cap."

She hung up the phone and they treaded across the room to the captain's office, located at the corner of the Detective Bureau in the new LAPD Administrative building. The detectives entered without waiting for an invitation.

Instead of smelling like the captain's second hand smoke, usual for more than a few of Charlene's visit, a pleasant odor wafted through the air. The man in the Armani suit, sipping on a double espresso, didn't bother getting up from his place on the captain's old leather couch.

"District Attorney Clark wants a word before you head out." The captain crushed on some ice. He'd been trying to quit smoking, and that was just one of his latest tricks to eliminate 'the crave'.

To say that Jeffrey Clark was mildly attractive would be the understatement of the year. The man was drop-dead gorgeous—slick black hair perfectly styled, clean-shaven gleaming skin, mesmerizing hazel eyes, and strong, square facial features. He attracted women by the droves, but Charlene wasn't the type of girl to capitulate to his charm.

He wore only the most expensive clothing, and had a steady stream of women draped on his arm for every high-end social event in the city.

JC wasn't a fan favorite amongst LAPD cops, because he was full of himself and a straight shooter, sometimes brutally honest. Charlene didn't think either way of the man; she hadn't been on the detective force long enough to have yet butted heads. Although she thought Clark attractive, she wasn't in his charm. She found the DA a little too cute, too clean-cut and not as rugged as she liked.

The DA's expensive cologne reached Charlene's nostrils and made her slightly light-headed. He leaned back, completely relaxed, sunken deep into the cushions, his cuffs rolled up and silk suspenders tight over his shoulders. Clark smoothed out his charcoal tie.

"Lewis Mahoney," the DA said.

"Just met him," Larry replied. "We are in dialogue with the suspect."

Most of the younger cops on the force grew intimidated by Clark's "larger-than-life" status, and the confident swagger he approached every case with. But Larry, the wily, experienced investigator, saw right through Clark's bullshit.

"He confessed."

"Yes, he did," Charlene said. "But we have nothing on him."

"Confession factors?"

"None."

"Really?" Clark's eyebrows arched. "Length of interrogation?"

"Short."

"Prolonged?"

"Nope."

"Time of day?"

"Morning."

"Psychological makeup of the suspect?"

"That could be a problem. He could plead diminished capacity."

Charlene knew that there were always factors to consider when a suspect confessed during an interrogation, and how those detectives had handled the line of questioning, both physically and emotionally. None of that applied in this case because Mahoney had just walked into the department and confessed.

Clark rubbed his smooth, freshly shaven cheek-skin. "I want this clean. Why would he confess?"

"Not sure. Maybe we should have Dr. Gardner speak with him."

Gardner was the LAPD psychiatrist and a consultant on many of the high-profile cases. He also had weekly meetings with Charlene to help give her an outlet, be a bit of a sounding board for Charlene and her difficulties.

Clark said, "Let's not let Mahoney's mental state interfere with this just yet. He has no alibi, and we have no alternate suspect or alternate theory."

"What's the theory on Mahoney?" Charlene snapped back. "No motive, no opportunity. We have no evidence on or around the body, and no evidence that Mahoney even had any kind of prior relationship with the victim."

"Then that is your priority. Find me something on Mahoney. This is your opening, take it and run with it."

Charlene was ever aware that the DA had a master's in criminology from USC, so he knew the school well, and this case probably meant a little more to him on a personal level.

She bit on the side of her tongue. "Yes, Sir."

They reconvened back at their desks.

"That was pleasant," Charlene said.

"Wasn't it, though? His usual high and almighty bullshit. Should we get to work on Mahoney?"

Charlene shook her head. "Not yet. Let's pursue the lead we said we would."

"That's my girl. Just like your old man. Hunches and instinct. Intuition should never be ignored."

Charlene's eyes moistened. "My father used to tell me that." At times, Larry was so much like her old man that it felt as if he was actually still around when they had their talks. Cop talk was all they really had, and all she had to cling to.

Larry said, "Clark isn't gonna call the shots on our investigation."

"Not yet, anyway." The negativity of Mahoney's guilt was growing. He had none of the answers that told the detective he was guilty of this crime.

Even though Charlene knew they could tap-dance around Clark's instructions for a day or maybe two at the most, eventually they would have to go at that suspect. But for now, she had other areas of interest to track.

"Did you get any contact information from Calvin Watters?" Larry asked.

"No, why?"

"He's a game-changer."

"What do you mean?"

"Former student, former player, still a lot of contacts at that school and in this city. He might still have the equivalent of street cred with the power elite around USC. Could be a reliable source for us."

"What makes you think he would work with us? I doubt a PI, especially with all that Watters has been through in his life, trusts cops enough to work with them."

"His brother is one, and he's worked closely with Vegas cops in the past. I don't know if Watters is the one with trust issues."

"What's that supposed to mean?"

Larry pursed his lips, and shook his head. He had a shit-eating-grin spread across his face.

She knew what he meant. It was no secret how the men in her department, throughout the whole LAPD, thought of Charlene's attitude. She wasn't the easiest cop to get along with, and didn't easily delegate, share, or trust others. But she was working on that—a slow, painfully long process.

"Just call his brother and get Calvin's number. Once we have that, let's go talk to the security guards. Their shift will be starting soon."

Chapter 11

Calvin stood outside the Lambda Chi Alpha fraternity house, the heavy stereo beats coming from inside rattling the window panes. The former USC student had attended a few parties at the frat house, after games. Lambda Chi Alpha had the reputation of throwing the biggest and best parties, especially after a Trojan win.

As he approached the front door, the sounds, although a different style than when he'd attended school, took him back.

In Calvin's playing days, the big football running back listened to hard stuff, the "pump-up" music of old that got his blood pumping and the adrenaline flowing. Today's college kids listened to more rap or pop, top 40 type music. Calvin knew that music tastes solidified with age. Music wasn't what it used to be.

He rapped heavily on the outside of the door and waited. The music from inside didn't stop, but it lowered in volume. Calvin wondered if the frat was used to complaints from neighboring buildings, and expecting another visit to request the music be turned down.

The door opened and Calvin came face to face, as in eye to eye, and Calvin stood well over six feet, with a large, much younger black kid. The college student was thick, not well-built but heavy-set none-the-less. He must have toppled the scales at three bills.

The frat guy said nothing, but stared at Calvin. Calvin nodded, sure the young man intimidated anyone who came to the door, and probably on call in case neighbors came over to complain about the noise. Calvin wasn't exactly the "intimidated" type.

Before Calvin could speak, a voice came from the back.

"Who is it, Meat?"

The student, who filled the full door frame with his width, turned and yelled back. "Some dude." His voice was a deep baritone.

"Ask him what he wants."

He turned back towards Calvin, still not smiling. "What do you want?" He crossed his arms, playing the role.

"Relax, Chief. I'm just here to talk."

"Talk about what?"

"The party."

The big guy asked, "Huh? You a cop?"

"Do I look like a cop?"

"Who is it, Meat?" A good looking, short white guy, or maybe who just looked short beside 'Meat', squeezed through between the guard and the doorframe. "Who are you?"

"Calvin Watters."

The kid's eyes opened wider. "No way. You shittin' me?"

Calvin put his hands up.

"Come in, please." He turned. "Meat, get out of the way."

They all entered the frat house. The kid who invited Calvin inside turned down the speakers and rounded up the Lambda Chi Alpha brothers scattered throughout the house. The front room was large enough to host a small gathering, but equipped to throw one hell of a college party—pool table, dart board, stereo and gaming systems. A bar in the corner had a dozen shot glasses turned over and a shelf on the wall lined with a variety of empty liquor bottles, looking like a nice collection had started. A tapped keg stood on a table in the corner, surrounded by a row of red solo cups.

Once they gathered, the leader, animated and excited, pointed at Calvin. "Do you guys know who this is? We are in the presence of greatness."

No one answered, as Calvin expected. The PI was surprised that any of these students, who wouldn't have been around when Calvin attended USC, would even be familiar with his name.

"This is Calvin Watters, former USC great. The running back from hell. He could run through you or around you. This guy is the football LeBron James of USC. He holds more USC records than any other football player. He is like a God."

The guy went a bit overboard, but Calvin's chest swelled slightly. He looked around the room, studied the young men sitting and listening, and none of them seemed very impressed. They didn't look all that interested.

"How do you know so much about me?" Calvin asked.

"My dad used to talk about you all the time."

Now it made sense. Calvin had reached that stage in his life where it was now college students' parents who knew about the former running back. It crushed the ego just a bit.

"So why are you here?" One of the guys sitting on the couch asked. He wiped his hands on his pant legs nervously.

"I'm here to ask you guys about the party the other night."

The room grew quiet, the boys all looking around at each other.

Calvin added, "I heard that Lambda Chi Alpha throws the wildest parties."

The leader nodded and chose the arm of a couch. "You heard right." He was a good-looking kid, short hair and pale skin. He had a 'rich' air to him.

"I heard that this is the place to be."

The guys in the room seemed to relax a little, and leaned back in their seats, almost as if they let out the breath they'd been holding in.

"Let's just say that Lambda Chi Alpha knows how to party." They started high-fiving each other.

"I heard that." Calvin waited for the back-slapping to quiet down. "How about we talk about the last party you guys had, after Saturday night's game."

The room again fell silent. The boys all looked towards the leader.

"Now why you wanna do that?" He snorted and looked at his buddies. "You a cop now or something?"

They laughed, but a nervous, unsure kind of uncomfortable chuckle.

"Actually, I'm a private investigator, now. I'm looking into the murder of Samantha Baylor. Did any of you guys know her?"

Now the leader stood up. "Whoa, whoa, whoa, what you tryin' to do, here?" Meat also stood up and stared at Calvin.

Calvin looked at the bodyguard and then back to the leader. "First, you better tell your guard dog to sit back down."

The leader motioned for the big guy to retake his seat on the couch, and then he said, "So what's the deal?"

"I'm not here to cause any problems. I just thought you might rather talk to me than the police."

"Cops?"

"Yep, the cops. They have their sights set directly on this fraternity, and they *will* be coming."

"He's bluffing," Meat said.

"Am I?" Calvin asked.

The leader had lost his cocky attitude. "So if we talk to you, we won't have to talk to them?"

"Probably not." A complete lie, but they didn't know that.

The head of the fraternity scratched his head and seemed to be studying his brothers. "What do you want to know?" he said, barely above a whisper.

"Was Samantha Baylor here?"

"For a little while."

"Who was she here with?"

"She was a cheerleader, who do you think she hung out with?" The attitude returned.

"Football team?"

"Well done." The leader did all the talking, the only one answering the questions.

"Anyone in particular?"

"Not this time," one of the other students, a young-looking kid with straight hair, glasses and acne, spoke up.

"What do you mean, not this time?"

The boy looked at the leader.

"You have my permission to speak," Calvin said.

"She used to date one of the players, but recently broke up."

"Which one?"

"Mark Simon."

Confirmed. "When did they break up?"

"Not long ago."

"Why?"

The boy was about to speak when the leader stood back up. "Look, we have nothing to say that can help. Nothing happened here."

"I'll be the judge of that." Calvin looked back at the boy on the couch, who had now sunk into the cushions, as if wanting to disappear. "Why did they break up?"

Again, the leader cut off Calvin's line of questioning. "We don't know that. We don't hang out with football players, girlfriends, or the cheerleaders. Why don't you ask them?"

Now the big guy, the bodyguard stood up and flexed his fists.

Calvin stared at the boy, using his 'collector' voice and body language. "Sit down, Meat, or that's all that will be left of you."

The kid obediently descended without comment.

"Did you see Baylor leave the party?" Calvin asked.

"Yes, she left early, almost immediately after she got here."

"Did she leave with anyone?"

"I don't think so." He looked around the room as if for confirmation from his fraternity brothers, and they all shook their heads.

"Anything peculiar about the night?"

"Nope." Tiny smirk. "Kick-ass party just like every other weekend."

They had the car radio set on KFWB 980 LA News Radio Station just to hear of any mention of the murder or Mahoney. Charlene knew that there had been certain moments in history where the LAPD had leaked information about certain cases, and it was not uncommon for some young cop to take a bribe or have a slip of the lip. The media also had a tendency to make up their own information if they couldn't get any from the police. But she didn't hear any mention of her case on the news talk show.

She turned down the radio. "So what can you tell me about this boyfriend, Mark Simon?" Charlene asked.

She steered the bureau car towards the John McKay Center at USC, where the football team held video meetings ahead of their evening practice.

Mahoney's attorney wouldn't let the detectives speak with the suspect/alleged murderer, until the boy's parents were present, indicating that vital information existed that they weren't yet privy to. The Mahoneys flew in from Fresno via private jet.

The detectives allowed it as long as Mahoney was kept in custody until they could properly interrogate him after they'd run some background on him. Charlene still didn't believe Mahoney had done what he'd said he'd done, but she still wasn't sure why he would lie about it.

"Boyfriend? Are you sure we can call him that?" He snorted. "We haven't gotten a straight answer from anyone, on again off again, not really seeing anyone. Who knows how close they were."

"He's the best lead we have, so we might as well work on it."

Larry had on his reading glasses. "Big old country boy. Emphasis on big. From Orland, made the Trojans as a walk-on last season. He is a second-string linebacker, average grades, nothing flashy. His parents are farmers, has a younger sister still in high school."

Orland was a small city in Glenn County, in the Sacramento Valley, in the northern part of the California Central Valley.

Charlene had one hand on the wheel, and her other elbow propped on the door to the open window. "So basically someone who stayed under the radar his whole life."

"Maybe."

Parking was light at the MacKay Center since only the football team used the three-floor facility at that moment, so they found a spot near the front of the building and headed inside. They hadn't called ahead, hoping the element of surprise would suffice, so no media teams could prep Simon, but Charlene was sure they had already spoken to him, since his girlfriend, or former girlfriend, was a murder victim. They wouldn't be turned back twice.

They entered a reception area where a short blond girl with pigtails and a wide smile greeted them. They made their request and were told that the football team was currently locked behind doors on the second floor.

"I'm sure my badge will unlock some doors. Just direct us to the stairs."

"Or elevator,' Larry added.

Larry cursed and heaved as they walked the one flight of stairs up to the landing. They opened the door and entered the impressive 25,000 square foot second floor. They passed a vast outdoor patio that overlooked the USC campus.

The first room they came to looked to be a coach's office. An overweight black man, with a bald head, shaved tight to the scalp, and a magnum mustache, hustled out and cut off their path.

"Can I help you? This is a restricted area for football student-athletes only."

Charlene already had her badge clipped to her belt, so she nonchalantly tucked the bottom of her suit jacket to the side to reveal it.

"We're here to speak with Mark Simon."

The coach, one of the dozens of assistants on a football roster, nodded. "Right this way."

He turned on his heels and walked down the hall. Charlene had to hustle to keep up as the coach double timed it. The detective wondered what the rush was.

He stopped at a door at the far end and knocked lightly on the outside. He waited a couple of seconds and opened the door to the meeting room. It was pitch black, and a video displayed on a large, cinema-sized screen in a state-of-the-art video production facility.

"Coach?"

"What is it?" A hard, crusty voice came out of the darkness. Then the light turned on.

"The police are here to see Mark."

"Right."

The assistant coach turned to face the detectives. "Just a moment."

A few seconds later, Simon exited the players' room, head down, pale skinned, crew-cut hairdo.

"Is there a room we can use?" Charlene asked the coach.

"Sure."

He led them to an empty room and turned on the light. "This okay?"

"Fine, thank you."

It was the size of a dorm room. Several chairs surrounded a long pine table and a couple of lamps sat unplugged in the corner. It looked like a room never used.

Charlene removed her jacket and laid it across the table. "Have a seat, Mark."

"You need me?" the coach asked Simon.

The boy shook his head. When the coach left, the linebacker sat down at the table on one side, and the detectives went to the other side.

Simon had yet to make eye contact with the cops. Charlene waited, holding out for Simon to look up at them.

When he finally lifted his head, his cheeks reddened and his eyes were droopy and sad looking. Gone was that laid-back, country boy demeanor.

"I assume you know why we're here?" Larry asked.

Simon nodded his sober face once. "I was told not to say anything without my lawyer."

Larry said, "We're just chatting."

"We've been getting mixed messages, Mark," Charlene said. "Were you dating Samantha Baylor?"

"Kind of," he said absently.

Charlene looked at Larry. "What does that mean?"

"We had broken up. But we were trying to work things out."

"Why did you break up?"

As Simon started to answer, the door opened and a black-haired woman, with a subtle underflip hairstyle and an expensive suit strode into the room and dropped a briefcase on the table.

"I'd like to have a moment with my client, please."

"Who are you?"

"I'll only need a few minutes," she said, without looking at Charlene.

Chapter 12

Calvin realized that he could only keep Rachel cooped up in his brother's house for so long. Eventually, she would want to get out, see the town, and do something fun. Plus, he wanted to get her away from his sister-in-law, before Alexis started whispering in her ear about marriage and kids. Not that Calvin was against any of that; he just wasn't ready.

So Calvin, biting his tongue and putting the investigation aside for a couple of hours, performed his boyfriend duties and took Rachel sightseeing in downtown LA, which to the big man was a crowd-frenzy nightmare.

He felt like a tourist again, but he was anything but. Calvin had spent three glorious years in this city, rubbing elbows with the local celebrities who frequented the downtown sites. He showed Rachel around with a hint of pride—understanding that at one time, LA had been *his* city.

They touched all of the hot spots: Venice Beach, Hollywood, museums, and Rodeo Drive—window shopping only, and watching his girlfriend gasp when the latest Hollywood celebrity exited the boutiques.

They even went joy riding down Mulholland Drive, the road of classic make-out points, Hollywood chase scenes and scenic splendor. They stopped at only a few overlooks, and although it took less than an hour, to the PI, it felt like a lot longer.

When Rachel mentioned Disney, Calvin knew it was time to get her home.

Understanding his girlfriend's feelings of helplessness because she wasn't able to aide Calvin in the investigation, he asked her if she would check Facebook, Twitter, & other platforms for mention of the murder. An important job, and no telling what was being said on social media.

Feeling that Rachel was content, and would be willing to allow Calvin a few more days of freedom to work on the investigation, he dropped her at Joshua's house and took off.

Time to get back to the investigation.

They reconvened in the conference room twenty minutes later. Charlene wasn't certain what the attorney had said to Simon, but she was sure the woman wasn't telling her client to willingly cooperate with the investigation. That *never* happened.

They introduced themselves to Michelle Gallant when they re-entered the room. Gallant acted as the senior representative for all USC student-athletes. Charlene remembered some of the more memorable characters to play athletics at USC, and the detective was sure Gallant had some stories to tell from those Trojan players.

Calvin Watters, perhaps…

The detectives sat down across from Gallant and Simon. "Do you mind if we continue where we left off?" Charlene asked sarcastically.

"By all means," Gallant replied. There was no smile behind her eyes—all business.

"Before interrupted," she glanced at Gallant, who remained stone-like. "You were telling us about your relationship with Ms. Baylor. Can you please expand on that?"

Simon looked at his representative, who gave him a curt nod.

"I met Sam at a party."

"Where?"

"One of the fraternities."

"When?"

"First couple of weeks of school."

"Go on."

He licked his lips. "She was sweet, shy, and cute. We talked, and kind of hit it off. I asked her for her number, and after some persistence, she gave it to me."

"Were you seeing anyone at that time?"

"What? No."

Quick answer, defensive. Gallant put her hand gently on Simon's wrist.

"Did you call her right away?"

"I think the next day." He grinned, but then must have realized the inappropriateness of a smile. "I don't meet a lot of girls."

"Please," Charlene cut him off. "You're a football player with the USC Trojans."

"I'm not a starter, or a star. I'm not popular like some of the other guys. It felt good to have a girl interested in me."

"So you started seeing each other. Have you had any other girlfriends at USC before Ms. Baylor?"

"No."

"None?"

"Not one."

Charlene didn't think Simon lied. She had thought this case could be a rage of jealousy, maybe a former lover or girlfriend, but a pretty far stretch for a college student to commit a murder over a relationship. But the detective *had* seen it before.

"So when did things go south?"

"Huh?"

"When did you break up," Larry interjected.

Simon stared grimly at Charlene and said, "Maybe three weeks ago."

"Did you see her at the party on Saturday night?"

He looked at the attorney who again nodded.

"Yes."

"Did you speak with Ms. Baylor at the party?" Larry asked.

Another glance at his lawyer. "Yes."

"Did you do more than just talk?" Charlene's voice level rose a bit.

"What? I didn't kill her." The boy's face paled, and he looked terrified.

"Mark," Gallant said. "They didn't ask that." She looked at Charlene. "Can you please reword the question?"

"Sure," Charlene said to the woman seated across from her. She looked the second-string linebacker right in the eye. "Did you have intercourse with Samantha Baylor on the night of her murder?"

Now Simon started to tremble. It looked like he was going to break down entirely and weep right at the table. His body shivered.

"Yes, but—"

"Detectives," Gallant stood up. "I think we are done, for now."

"You really don't think your client is getting away that easily, do you?"

"My client has an important practice starting in a few minutes and needs to go."

"More important than finding the person who killed his girlfriend?"

Gallant didn't take the bait. "Ex-girlfriend. We know our obligation to this investigation and we are more than willing to cooperate and meet you down at your office for further questioning."

"Thank you for your cooperation."

Again, Gallant didn't bite at Charlene's sarcasm. "Can you meet with us tomorrow?"

"Absolutely," Larry answered.

Gallant looked at Simon. "Let's go, Mark. I will take you to practice."

"I'm sure we'll see you there as well, Mark." Charlene said, staring at Simon, and ignoring Gallant's gaze of steel.

As Gallant passed Charlene, she stopped and stood face to face with her. "You know, Detective, you are coming really close to harassing my client. With your past, you might want to be more careful." She spun on her heels and, with Simon at her side, headed for the door.

"Oh, Ms. Gallant, when you come downtown tomorrow, you can also bring a sperm sample from your client."

They both turned, Gallant unsmiling and Simon looking confused. "What?" he said.

"Did you know she was pregnant, Mark?"

"What?" He looked totally taken off guard, and it did not seem like an act.

"Let's go, Mark." Gallant pulled her client out of the room.

"Did you see that?" Charlene turned to Larry.

"Looked genuine."

"Do you really think Simon had no idea that Samantha Baylor was pregnant?"

"Man, just like old times."

Calvin stood on the sidelines at Howard Jones Field, the sights and sounds taking the former running back to his past, nothing had changed—coaches barking out orders, players grunting and yelling encouragement, and shoulder pads ramming against each other.

"Tuesday, always my favorite practice day," he mumbled.

"You always were nuts," Nick replied, with a smile.

Calvin's muscles tensed as he followed the Trojans running through their play book. Tuesday and Wednesday practices ran in full pads, full drills like any typical football practice. The difference was that on Tuesday, your muscles were still a little sore and tight from Saturday's game, and the burn was the perfect release.

"Looks like our cop friends are back." Nick pointed across the field into the bleachers where detectives Taylor and Baker talked and pointed at players.

"Have they interviewed any of the players yet?"

"They met with Mark Simon this afternoon, pulled him right out of meetings."

"Sounds like Taylor's style, from what I've heard about her. She won't tiptoe around anyone. I bet the coach just loved that."

"He wasn't impressed."

He watched Taylor but said, "What did they learn?"

"Nothing much, I expect. Michelle swooped down and saved him, as per USC tradition."

Michelle Gallant, Calvin knew the woman, the name well, although he had never had to call upon her services, but the PI had many a teammate who had required her valuable negotiation skills in and out of the courtroom.

A sharp whistle blew from the head coach signifying a drink break for the players, as the team slowed down and departed the field to hit the drink table on the sidelines.

"You wanna meet Mark?" Nick asked Calvin.

Calvin nodded, and followed Nick across the field to the opposite sidelines, where the players huddled around the trainers and water guys. Calvin figured he could get more from Simon than the cops ever would.

"Mr. Watters?"

Calvin couldn't remember the last time someone called him Mr. Watters, if they ever had. Brandon Harris jogged towards him. The back-up running back had his helmet off and held it in his hands, his short black hair wet and dripping with perspiration, his face streaked with sweat tracks.

"Hey. Brandon. Looking good out there."

The young man smiled shyly. "Thanks."

"So what's up?"

"I told my father that I met you. He sounded pretty excited." The boy looked down at the ground, which was ripped up by steel cleats. "I wonder if you might consider showing me a few things."

"What did you have in mind?" Calvin asked.

"Anything that can make me better, quicker, shiftier. I'm not sure. I just know that I want to give myself the best possible chance to improve and be a starter someday."

Calvin wasn't sure if this was the boy's decision, or if his father had put him up to it, but the former RB didn't have to think long. "I'd be happy to. Go grab a football."

"Cool." The boy spun quickly, and excitedly jogged over to a bag of footballs on the ground. He rummaged through it and pulled one out, then sprinted back and handed it over to Calvin.

When Calvin took the ball, squeezed it and tucked it under his arm, his nerve endings tingled—as if his natural adrenaline switched on as soon as the ball found his hands. He could almost hear the USC crowd chanting his name. The ball, nestled into his side, just felt so right.

Calvin looked up and realized that he must have looked pretty silly, lost in his past, reliving his youth and the success he had accomplished.

"Okay, show me how you hold the ball and get in an athlete's stance," Calvin said.

The kid grabbed the ball, tucked it away and bent his knees.

Calvin circled the running back, looking at his stance and checking significant points. "The stiff arm is a running back's best friend. If done effectively, it can be a lethal weapon in preventing an opponent from tackling you. I'll show you three different ways you can use a stiff arm to keep defenders at a distance."

The boy, intense, looked ready, eager to listen and learn.

"Wait for the defender to get within arm's length of you. As he gets close, he will reach his arms out to try to tackle you. Strike his upper facemask with the palm of your hand. Hit through the facemask, extending your arm to prevent him from being able to grab you." Calvin ran him through it slowly, showing the technique multiple times, then let the boy try it on him. "Don't grab his facemask. Be sure not to break stride. Got it?"

He nodded. "I think so."

"Good. Number two." Calvin bent his knees, getting as low to the ground as he could, which wasn't easy for someone who stood 6'5". "You'll want to make sure you're lower than the defender, and he needs to be around two feet from you. Bend your elbow down, and strike under the defender's facemask, pushing it up toward the sky." Calvin performed the move so swiftly and with so much force that he almost knocked the young man over. Calvin grabbed him to straighten him up. "Sorry. Remember, don't grab. Use the push-off to create separation from the defender. He can't tackle what he can't see."

They ran through it a few times, and the Trojan back-up RB picked it up quickly.

"What about the third one?"

Calvin smiled at the boy's youthful enthusiasm. "Okay, number three. When the defender comes in to tackle you, use his momentum against him by pushing his helmet or body away from you in the same direction he is going. Gather your feet and prepare to cross face past his body."

Calvin showed the move, which he had made famous amongst the US college ranks.

"Well, well, well. What do we have here?"

Calvin heard the voice, and even though he knew the speaker wasn't talking outright to him, the pitch and volume told the PI that someone acknowledged him, even though he didn't recognize the voice.

Calvin and Brandon turned, where a group of four players huddled ten feet away, staring at them. The "ring leader" was a dark-skinned guy with a cardinal red bandana and two gold front teeth. He wore jersey number twenty-one.

"Looks like we have a has-been teaching a never-will-be," the leader spouted, with a snort. His posse all laughed along with him.

"Give us a break, Isaiah," Brandon said, turning back to Calvin.

Isaiah Watson, Calvin thought, the running back believed to have the abilities to break all of Calvin's USC and NCAA records this season and over the next two years. The kid was said to have it all: speed, skill and agility. He stood just barely six feet, still above the average height for an NFL running back, his retro afro made him seem taller. That was why Calvin had been such a phenomenon: a man his size to move like he could.

While football was known as a sport looking for the biggest, baddest players around at that particular position, that doesn't always mean height when talking running backs. You don't normally want the player to stand too tall in the backfield because it makes him easier for the defensive players to find. Shorter players can 'hide' behind the taller offensive linemen. You also want to have a low center of gravity, makes it easier to get underneath the pads of defenders looking to make a tackle.

Shorter players equaled shorter legs, which meant shorter strides and an ability to change directions quicker than a taller back. Again, Calvin went against the norm and proved all those statistics and facts wrong.

Watson was lean, but with a thick lower half, which probably meant he had no trouble breaking arm tackles when running through the box, and the upper-body strength to not bounce off defenders, and have his momentum disrupted so easily. But Watson was said to be 'more quick than powerful', and well under two hundred pounds.

"No, seriously, Mr. Watters, sir, please show me what to do," Watson mocked. His gold teeth shining, having fun at Calvin's expense, making his cronies laugh.

Brandon looked back at Calvin. "Forget it. I better get back to practice."

Calvin handed the football back to Harris. "Sure thing, Kid. Good luck to you."

"Thanks again, Mr. Watters."

"Call me Calvin."

"Oh, first name basis. You guys gonna kiss on your first date?" Watson laughed long and hard at his latest joke.

"Fuck off, Isaiah. From what my dad told me, Calvin would have buried you on the field."

"Easy, kid," Calvin whispered to Harris.

Watson grinned. "Really? He's a big ole boy for sure, but can he move like this?"

Watson shuffled his feet and dodged back and forth with incredible quickness. His feet were like sticks of dynamite, exploding up and down off the turf.

"You've seen the record books," Harris countered. "He has the USC record for the forty."

"We both know I would have broken that this year if I hadn't stumbled off the start."

Harris lifted his hands in the air as if in an 'oh well' move. Watson looked pissed off, the smile had vanished from his face and he no longer laughed. His eyes narrowed, a half-squint, throwing daggers at Calvin and Harris.

"Let's do it, then," Watson said. He held an amused expression on his face.

"What?" Calvin said.

"Let's set it up, once practice ends."

"Whoa." Calvin held up his hands. "I'm not here to race, fellas."

Watson blew air through his clenched lips. "I knew it, punk."

Calvin teasingly looked at himself, his high-end, name-brand dress clothes. "Do I look like a punk to you?"

"I'm not sure what you look like to me, maybe a poser?"

Calvin took a step forward and then stopped himself. He took a deep breath. "Look, guys, I'm not here for this. I'm just here to do my job and move on."

Watson looked at Brandon Harris. "Better find a new hero, back-up."

"You're just lucky Calvin isn't dressed for it, or your mouth wouldn't be flapping its gums."

"I'm sure Nicky here can find something to fit on that old man's body. Right, Nicky?"

Nick Charles had been standing listening the whole time, staring from Watson to Calvin, back and forth as the conversation went on—as if in a trance.

"Nicky," Watson repeated, this time a little louder.

Nick snapped out of it and looked towards the starting USC running back as he asked the question again. "Think you can get some clothes for this chump, so I can show him how today's running backs move?"

"Huh…" He looked at Calvin.

Calvin looked at Nick, then at Watson, and then back at Nick. He nodded slightly.

"Huh, ya, sure," Nick said.

Chapter 13

"This should be interesting," Larry said, through drags on his cigarette. He stood behind Charlene, with one foot up on the bench where Charlene sat.

Charlene looked up from her notepad for the first time since they'd reached the first row bleachers at the Howard Jones Field. There looked to be turmoil of some sort, a group of guys huddled at midfield, not far from where she and Larry sat. They were close enough to hear what was said, but Charlene hadn't been paying any attention to them, as the detective was too focused on going over what she heard in their afternoon interviews, or what they hadn't heard, to be more truthful.

Mark Simon seemed as if ready to give them some answers, until the USC attorney came to pull him out of the fire. After that, Simon closed his mouth. Charlene knew that he would eventually make his way to her office for questioning, but now he would be prepped and on his lawyer's short leash.

What threw off the detective was the genuine expression on Simon's face when told about Baylor's pregnancy.

The stadium security guards gave them mostly unhelpful answers. They added nothing to the investigation. The man, Wayne Parker, was in his seventies, and although in excellent physical condition for a senior, he neared retirement and probably didn't put the effort into his work that he had when he'd first started over forty years ago.

The other security guard, Tiana Washington, stumped Charlene. A woman in her forties, who seemed competent and intelligent, gave them very little to go on, as if almost going out of her way to avoid answering their questions. Vague and indecisive in everything she said, Charlene just couldn't read the woman.

"What's going on?" Charlene asked, standing up to get a closer look at the individuals on the field.

"Looks like we have a turf war." Larry propped his big shoe on the railing.

"What about?" Charlene just now noticed who stood in the middle.

"Looks like the new alpha dog is calling out the old alpha dog."

"Really?"

"Isaiah Watson has just challenged Watters to a race. I can't believe Watters accepted."

"He's a former athlete, Larry. Those competitive juices never stop flowing."

"I got twenty bucks on Watson."

"I'll take that bet?"

His face twisted in confusion. "Really?"

"Absolutely."

"You don't look like a sucker, Taylor."

Charlene winked. "My boyfriend would disagree."

"You know what I meant." Larry's face reddened slightly. "I'll be happy to take your money."

"I'll take my chances."

"You do realize that Watters hasn't probably run a race since the arthroscopic surgeries that ended his career, right?"

"Look at his body, Larry. He hasn't been sitting around eating potato chips."

"Lifting a few dumbbells isn't the same as what these college athletes go through. Plus Watters is quite a bit older, out of practice and let's face it, past his prime."

"Watters has been through hell and back since leaving college. You and I have both followed the work he did with the LVMPD."

"Yes, that knee has taken a beating. He might even hurt himself in this race. Watson is a machine, and will dismantle him."

She could feel her heart speeding up. "We'll see."

"It's basically strength versus speed."

"Watters had his own speed in his day."

"Exactly, in his day. If we compared Watters in his prime and Watson now, the most important physical skill set a running back can have is quickness. Advantage Watson."

"You don't have to be a burner to be an effective running back. Watters was fast in the open field, not as quick. But he'd shown himself to be quick enough that, combined with his size and strength, dominant."

Larry cleared his throat. "Watson is more quick than fast, not as fast as Watters in the open field, even I'll admit that. A running back needs to be able to get through a hole as soon as possible."

"Whether he then has the open-field speed to not get caught from behind is another thing, which Watters had. He was special because he possessed that speed along with the strength and physical stature to take hits running up the middle and still drive forward."

"I'm not arguing Watters was great, but every fact and verb you used to describe the former running back was done so in the past tense. Remember that."

"Watters would have been the perfect NFL running back because he possessed enough muscle-mass and strength that he could withstand hits from linebackers meeting him in the hole, and still find ways to fall forward." The voice came from behind them, so the detectives turned around and found an elderly gentleman, with thinning white hair, a bulbous nose holding up a pair of bifocals, and a buttoned-down long sleeve shirt, despite the heat. "That's extremely difficult to consistently do by running backs under two-hundred pounds."

"And who are you, Sir?" Charlene asked.

"USC's biggest fan. I've been watching games for over fifty years. Since OJ was a freshman. Calvin Watters was the best football player to ever wear the cardinal red and gold...hands down."

"You know, you don't have to do this." Nick Charles handed Calvin a pile of folded clothing: shorts, t-shirt, socks and even steel cleats of his size.

"I know." Calvin took the clothes and placed them on the bench beside him. He started to remove the work garments he had worn to the practice.

They sat in a small change room down the hall from the football team's dressing room. A row of brown lockers lined the wall behind Calvin and a full line of blue bathroom stalls faced him. Sinks and mirrors on his left and the showers, with plastic curtains, to his right.

"I'm not gonna lie to you, Calvin. Watson is an asshole, but he's fast, with greasy speed. I've never seen anyone quicker with that first step, and I watched you play for almost three full seasons."

"So I've heard."

"You were a great player, Calvin, maybe the best I've ever seen. And I've seen some dandies come through this college." There was a warning in his voice.

"What's your point, Nick?"

"You're no longer a young man."

Calvin's neck muscles tightened. "I'm more aware of that every day."

"How's your knee?"

"It'll hold up."

The truth was, Calvin wasn't sure if or how his knee would handle the wear and tear, the impact and intensity this short, quick burst speed race would have on his ACL. He'd torn it multiple times, and many surgeries hadn't been able to save his career. But he had worked hard over the years, despite all of those setbacks, but it had been a while, since his final showdown with Baxter, since he'd truly tested it.

Despite his wounds, Calvin worked out intensively because he never knew when he'd need his knee to be as strong as possible and prepared.

If Rachel knew he was doing this, she would be furious. What his girlfriend didn't know wouldn't hurt her.

"Are you sure?"

Calvin finally looked up at his former trainer after tying his second shoe. The short, overweight man, who had been a good friend to Calvin during his USC days, held a concerned look on his face.

Calvin stood up and slapped the trainer on the back, a loud smack echoing in the empty change room.

"Relax, Nick. You worry too much." Calvin adjusted his shorts. "Let's do this."

When they stepped outside and onto the freshly cut grass, it was as if a hush fell over the crowd, both the players and coaches. They all watched Calvin as he followed behind Nick, making his way towards where Watson and a few other players waited.

Calvin felt like a prize fighter making his way towards the ring, following behind his manager. An old fighter, getting ready to defend his title against a much younger, stronger, better opponent. The weight of the world on his shoulders.

Sweat filtered down his backbone from both the heat of the sun and the situation.

"You know, you have nothing to prove," Nick whispered.

"Ya, I know."

"You set that record a long time ago. This is 2020."

Calvin thought of Nick's words as he made his way to the starting line in the end zone. He really had nothing to prove, and really nothing to lose from this race. If he lost, no one really cared because he was a washed-up nobody, a has-been who no longer played. But if he won, then Isaiah Watson would be a laughing stock. So in that sense, all of the pressure parked on Watson.

Nick kept glancing around the field nervously.

"Nick," Calvin said. "Relax."

"I'm making sure Price isn't here."

"Why?"

"Are you kidding? If he sees you racing his starting running back, he would go crazy. He has a lot at stake this season."

Watson had removed his upper-body equipment, helmet, jersey and shoulder pads, and only had his lower body USC gear on. He wore a tight black shirt with cut off sleeves, revealing arms embroidered with tattoos.

"I'm surprised you showed." Watson snorted. The sun reflected off his gold teeth and slightly blinded Calvin. "The coaches have set up the forty yard dash for us. You up for that?"

Calvin looked down at the forty yard line, where a coach stood beside an orange cone. It looked a lot further away than he remembered, but it had been over five years since he'd run it. He knew that Watson was quick off the hop, and Calvin doubted he could keep up with that first step.

"How about a sixty yarder?" Calvin offered.

"Ooh, the old man's got balls." He looked down the football field and yelled. "Coach, set up sixty!"

The coach nodded, picked up the orange cone and moved farther down the field another twenty yards.

"I don't know, Gramps. Can you even see that far?" He snorted another laugh. "I don't know CPR. Think you can handle it?"

"We'll soon find out."

"You know, you can still back out of this," Nick whispered in Calvin's ears. "Don't let your pride get you in trouble."

"I'm too old for pride, Nicky," Calvin said, without looking at his former trainer. His eyes now locked on the goal, the target—the coach at the end of the line. "You better move out of the way."

Nick took three steps back.

The two sidelines were completely bare now, as everyone had moved closer to the constructed race track. They lined the sides, players and coaches from starting line to finish line. IPhones came out to record soon-to-be YouTube videos ready to go viral within seconds of the contest ending.

Calvin looked around, at the attention this had garnered. He knew this race wouldn't be just between him and Watson. It wouldn't just be witnessed by the dozens of people at Howard Jones field.

This would be seen by millions across the world—players, coaches, fans, scouts, analysts, front office employees—people who made the important decisions, and people who determined what the future held for any aspiring professional football player.

The sun's heat burned down on them. Perspiration leaked down the side of his face and the shirt Nick had given him was already damp and sticking to his upper body.

People in attendance started clapping and making noise, whistling and starting their recordings. For an instant, only a brief moment, Calvin felt light-headed and a little dizzy. He shook it off and prepared, getting down in his take-off stance.

The grass was warm on his palms, and smelled freshly cut.

Then, he cleared his mind. The noise disappeared. His peripheral vision blurred, and then blanked completely, as if a pair of blinders had been thrown over his head. No sounds at all, just the silence, and the sight of the coach at the end of the finish line.

His adrenaline surged.

Calvin gritted his teeth, and dug the toes of his cleats into the soft turf. He placed his fingertips on the ground in front of him, leaning forward, the tips of his fingers whitening from the shift in his weight, readying his momentum to blast out of his stance at the word.

One of the coaches raised his hands beside Calvin. "Ready..... set......go!"

Both men took off, quick starts, but Watson just a fraction of a second quicker out of the gate. Calvin was impressed with the running back's quickness, like a rabbit escaping its hole.

Calvin stole a quick glance to his right, at his opponent. Watson pumped his legs hard, his arms churning in stride. Once Calvin got six steps in, he gained speed, accelerating, his arms and legs now working as a team in unison, pumping collectively as one. He knew he gained ground on Watson, who looked to be slowing at about the half-way point.

Calvin felt no pain, no exhaustion. Sweat soaked through his shirt but his muscles felt strong, powerful strokes, with no signs of tiring. The PI overtook Watson with about twenty yards to go.

He stole another glance. Watson's face was tight, stressed, his neck wire-taught. His biceps bulged, the veins prominent. The vein in the young man's temple throbbed, and he looked a little broken. Like he knew defeat was upon him.

Charlene stood beside Larry, as Calvin Watters attempted to take down a much younger, more physically active and hardcore footballer. It was evident to Charlene that Watters still had that edge that separated the good athletes from the great ones. He had the drive, that need to "be the best", and not let anyone stand in his way.

She placed her weight on the outer edges of her feet.

When Watters overtook Watson with about twenty yards to go, Charlene let out a silent squeal, which attracted a quick glance from her partner. She looked down and realized that she'd been clutching the front row railing, and her hands now white-knuckled from gripping the metal bar so tightly.

But with ten yards to go, Watson had a sudden surge and Watters seemed to lose pace, in what looked like a photo-finish, something only found in the Kentucky Derby. Charlene let out the breath that she hadn't known she held in.

"Looks like your man lost," Larry pointed out, the relief audible in his voice.

"Looks that way," Charlene said, hiding a smile.

When the race ended, and the runners finally slowed their momentum and cadence, everyone turned to the coach who had been standing at the finish line, waiting for his final assessment and to declare a winner.

Watson bent over slightly, hands gripping the bottom of his shorts. Watters stood erect, face to the sky, greedily gulping in breaths of air. Both racers panted, perspiring, and slowly started to make their way back, walking towards the finish line. Watters limped noticeably.

The assistant coach put his hands in the air, and said, "Watson."

The gathered crowd erupted. His teammates ran to where Watson stood, handing out high-fives, fancy teamwork handshakes, and they even attempted to put Watson up on their shoulders.

The atmosphere on the field electric, as if a giant had been slain on that day.

When the crowd dispersed, Nick Charles and Brandon Harris walked towards Watters, who squatted and rested his elbows on his thighs, breathing hard while watching the USC Trojans carry on around their starting RB. Charles and Harris put their hand on the PIs back. But to Charlene, Watters didn't seem the least bit disappointed. He rose and shook Harris' hand.

When the huddled teammates around Watson disbanded, Watson made his way towards Watters. The starting running back for the USC Trojans looked to limp slightly as he walked. Watters lifted his head and saw the college kid heading towards him. He stopped, hands on hips, and waited.

The two men came together, and Watson stretched out his arm towards Watters. They shook hands, and then the two running backs, the current and the former, exchanged words, what looked like pleasantries to Charlene.

What had they said?

After a final nod, Watters turned away, and with Nick Charles at his side, walked off the field and entered the complex, heading towards the change rooms.

Charlene stepped off the first row of the bleachers and moved across the field.

"What about my money?" Larry's voice shot out from the distance.

"It was a hell of a race," Nick said, as Calvin buttoned up the last of his shirt buttons.

"Yep," Calvin replied. He was still wet, from a combination of sweat from the race, shower water and moisture in the air, but the adrenaline from the race ebbed.

"I thought you had him."

"Close one." Calvin's knee throbbed.

"Oh well."

Calvin exhaled. "We'll get over it."

Nick returned the smile. "I guess we will. The Calvin I knew never would have."

"That Calvin has matured, finally."

Nick picked up Calvin's dirty laundry from the bench and tucked it into a bag, pulling the draw-string tight. He flung it over his shoulder. "I'll wait for you outside."

Calvin stood up, putting more pressure on his good knee to save the weak one. He had one foot up on the wooden bench putting on his socks when the equipment trainer left the room. He heard Nick speaking with someone when he opened the door, and then the door closing.

As Calvin tied his shoes, the sound of heals on linoleum clicked towards him. He heard a voice before seeing anyone.

"You cost me twenty bucks."

Detective Charlene Taylor leaned her back against the concrete-bricked wall, one foot up flat against the stone, and her knee bent.

"Sorry about that." He smirked. "The safe money was on Watson." He went back to tying his shoes.

"Why did you let up?"

Calvin looked back up, his hands still in the middle of tying a knot. "What?"

"You pulled up near the finish line. You let that kid off the hook."

"Hardly."

She blew air out of her nose. "Oh please. You had that kid beat. Why did you do it?"

Calvin stood up and attached his wrist buttons. He tightened his tie and shot his cuffs. "I don't know what you're talking about. He's a twenty year-old in his prime."

"Alright, if that's the story you want to stick with. But I know what you did out there."

"Whatever you say, Detective. And this is the men's room." He smiled, and then slipped past her and out.

He tried not to limp in front of her, and could hear her following him.

"What did Watson say to you afterwards?"

"Just guy talk."

She snickered. "That's it?"

"Yep."

"Okay."

"What do you want, Detective." Calvin spotted Taylor's partner, Detective Baker, standing at the end of the hall.

"I thought we could talk."

Calvin shook his head, but said, "About what?"

"The case."

Those two words stopped Calvin in mid-stride. He turned around and cocked his head, trying to get a read from the detective. There was one of two reasons an LAPD detective would want help from a PI: one, they had gained absolutely no traction on the case, or two, they worried that Calvin knew more than they did.

Either way, he held all the cards here.

"What did you have in mind?" he asked.

"Our office?"

"I thought somewhere a little less….serious. You guys eat yet?"

Taylor pursed her lips. "Nope."

"How about the Naughty Pig at 6pm?"

Chapter 14

If there was one street in all of LA that symbolized the city lifestyle, it was Sunset Strip Boulevard. The Naughty Pig, formerly known as West Hollywood's Lazer Kat, had traded in their disco theme for a more sports oriented fan base. Although the legendary dance floor still existed, the main attraction was now the sports playing on the TVs—the sports bar vibe.

Calvin and Rachel walked into a crowded restaurant, the sounds and smells bringing Calvin back to a past life: back when the only worries were where the next keg party would be, and what team would draft him first overall in the NFL draft. Talk about a lifetime ago.

They passed the 'wait to be seated' sign and approached a short hostess with shoulder length brown hair, who bounced on her heels as she moved.

"You'll have to wait to be seated, sir," she said, her blue eyes smiling.

Calvin stretched his neck and saw Detective Taylor at a booth, facing the door. She lifted a finger in the air to acknowledge the PI.

"We're with them."

They passed the waitress and advanced towards the booth. Taylor was partially blocked by the expanse of her partner's shoulders and the width of his back, as Detective Baker sat across the booth from Taylor, his back turned to Calvin.

They stepped up to the side of the table, Calvin in the lead and Rachel cowering timidly behind the large black man.

"Detectives," Calvin initiated contact. "This is Rachel. Rachel, this is Detectives Taylor and Baker, the cops I told you about."

Rachel shook their hands.

"Please, allow me." With a deep inhale, Baker sucked in his gut and struggled to squeeze from his side of the booth. Once out, he straightened the tucked in dress shirt from his waistband. "You guys take this side. I know my partner can never get enough of me."

Rachel smiled. "Thank you."

Calvin and Rachel slid into the booth. The PI tried not to grimace as he bent, his throbbing knee aching to the bone. He hid it from Rachel. "You guys order yet?" he asked.

"Just drinks."

"This place change much?" Taylor asked.

Calvin looked around. "Everyone seems a lot younger."

"That could be one way of looking at it," Baker replied.

Calvin shrugged. "Cup's always half full. I'm not getting older, everyone else is getting younger."

A red-headed waitress, with curls and dark lipstick, set down a pair of mugs in front of the detectives. She poured some fancy European beer for Baker, which caught Calvin totally off guard. Baker didn't look like an import-beer drinking kind of guy, not that there was any kind of stereo-type for that.

The sweating glass on the table in front of Detective Taylor held a clear liquid fizz, with bubbles rising from the bottom to the top. A slice of lime cut through the rim of the glass. Calvin wondered what a tough female cop like Taylor drank on her down time.

"Tonic water," Taylor said.

Calvin looked up from the glass and saw the detective staring at him. "What?"

"You stared at my glass. Probably thinking about what I drank."

Calvin wondered what his face looked like at that exact moment. His brother had told him about Taylor's drinking problem. Was she conscientious about it? Was she in recovery, trying to kick her habit? Did she know that Calvin already knew about her reckless lifestyle, and tried to prove to him that she turned it around? He doubted that.

Josh had told Calvin stories about how Taylor's drinking had torn her family apart, and had caused more than one problem in both her personal and professional lives.

"What can I get ya?" The waitress smacked on gum and blew a bubble.

"Rachel?" Calvin asked.

"I'll have what he's having." Rachel acknowledged Detective Baker, as he sipped on his drink and left a semi-circle of foam above his upper lip. He wiped it with his sleeve.

"Just a water for me," Calvin said.

"I'll be back for your food orders."

When the waitress left, Calvin turned towards the detectives. "So, why did you want to see me?"

"I didn't realize there'd be a civilian present," Taylor said. "I'm not comfortable discussing a case in front of a civilian."

Calvin pressed his bottom lip up over his top and nodded. "No problem. We don't have to share information." He looked at Rachel. "Let's go."

Rachel held a confused look on her face, but began to slide backwards from the booth. They both stood up and turned away from the detectives.

"Hold on."

Calvin stopped, but it hadn't been Taylor's voice, Baker had called them back. The PI turned around and saw Baker whispering in Taylor's ear. She wasn't smiling, or even looked like she was giving an inch to her senior partner.

Finally she nodded and looked up at Calvin. "Sit back down."

They retook their seats at the side of the booth, just as the waitress set down their drinks in front of them. They ordered their food quickly, hurrying the waitress off.

"So what do you know?" Taylor asked immediately.

"So are we sharing information then?"

Taylor looked to be chewing at the inside of her mouth so hard that Calvin thought she would draw blood. It seemed like all she could take to squeak out one word between her clenched lips. "Yes."

Calvin relaxed into the padded backing. "So why do you need me?"

"We had a confession today," Baker said.

Calvin nodded. "I heard."

"Your brother's keeping you abreast of the situation, I see."

Calvin grinned.

"Now our boss wants us to go at this kid with everything we have," Taylor added.

"Did he do it?"

Taylor shook her head. "I doubt it."

"Then why confess?"

"Not sure, exactly. Could be a mental illness. But our captain and the DA seem to think he's perfect, and want us to come up with something. So that is what we'll be doing all day tomorrow, trying to nail down motive and opportunity. And of course some sort of evidence."

Calvin nodded. "You mean other than the confession?"

Taylor cocked her head. "Touché."

"What do you want from me?" Calvin asked.

Baker said, "Everything else."

"That all?" Calvin said sarcastically.

Taylor arched her eyebrows. "Can't handle it?"

Calvin thought about it. The proposal, working with LAPD, made sense for both sides. Multiple lines of investigation sped everything up, and branched it out.

Taylor took a drink. "The security guards won't give us much."

"They might not know much."

"That's true, but hard to believe they saw nothing all night. I know that you already have a connection with her."

It was Calvin's turn to drink. "How do you know that?"

"I'm a cop. It's my job to know."

"We saw her son with an autographed Calvin Watters jersey on," Baker said.

Calvin hesitated, but something in the way Taylor looked at him instantly told the PI she could be trusted. "I met with Tiana Washington today."

"And?"

"She's definitely hiding something. She isn't herself."

Taylor nodded. "I also think it's kind of funny that no one knows more about our victim. Samantha Baylor had a roommate, was a member on the cheering squad, a straight "A" student, and her religious parents' golden child. And yet no one seems to know anything about her."

Calvin said, "Tomorrow is Wednesday."

"What does that mean?"

"Cheer practice. I have an 'in' I can work."

"Good. Use that. Someone must know something."

"What about the boyfriend?" Calvin asked.

Baker pulled out a pack of cigarettes and placed it on the table. "We are still waiting to hear from his lawyer, but he's not going anywhere."

"I need to use the bathroom," Taylor announced, lightly shoving her partner's large bulk, forcing him from the booth.

"I'll come too," Rachel said.

Calvin could have sworn he saw Detective Taylor mutter under her breath, but he couldn't be certain. When the ladies left, silence engulfed the men at the table.

Baker sipped at his beverage.

"Some partner you have there, Detective," Calvin said.

Baker blinked. "She doesn't usually make a great first impression."

"First impressions are overrated. Just ask anyone who ever met Ted Bundy."

Baker raised his glass to toast Calvin.

"She seems hesitant to work with me," Calvin said.

Baker snorted. "You don't know the half of it."

"What does that mean?"

"She called Vegas right after we left you at the field, talked to some Detective Dayton out there."

Calvin grinned. Dale. His best friend and probably the person Calvin trusted the most in Sin City. He'd formed a meaningful bond with the Vegas detective working alongside him to help solve one of the city's biggest and most notable homicide investigations the bright-lighted strip had ever seen. They were now like brothers.

Calvin didn't even blink, not an ounce concerned about what Dale had said about him. This showed Calvin just how cautious, meticulous, and untrusting Taylor really was.

"Obviously he said all the right things."

"He must have, because my partner doesn't trust too many people. She hates PIs."

"Hate is a pretty strong word." The female voice came from behind them.

The women had returned and snuck up on them.

Baker looked at his partner. "Would you like me to use your exact quote then?"

"Maybe not," Taylor said.

The waitress returned with their meals, and the four ate in silence.

Taylor wiped her mouth with a napkin. "As soon as I can, I will meet you at the stadium tomorrow night for the cheerleading practice."

Calvin swallowed, and then said, "Cheer practices are held at The Lorenzo Student Housing."

"No promises I'll make it on time, but I'll do my best. You have my cell number, right?"

Calvin nodded.

Taylor called the waitress for the bill, as her partner started checking his pockets.

"Damn, Taylor, I forgot my wallet," Baker said.

The detective rolled her eyes. "Shocker." She looked at Calvin. "You staying for another drink?"

"I heard that there's a vigil tonight at USC for Samantha Baylor. I'm going to swing by to check it out."

"Really?" Taylor looked at her partner. "We should hit that."

Baker nodded, while he stuffed the last of his burger in his mouth.

"What about dancing?" Rachel said.

Calvin looked at the detectives. "I promised Rachel we would go out to a club tonight. Part of the LA dance scene." He turned towards his girlfriend. "We will, I promise. But I have to do this first."

"Wow, so many people," Rachel said.

Definitely an understatement. Community members had gathered for a candlelight vigil for Samantha Baylor, after Baylor's death had become known to students on campus. The vigil had been organized by Baylor's cheerleading squad, in conjunction with Delta Gamma.

Hordes of students filled the area: holding hands, singing songs, raising lit candles over their heads. Calvin wondered how many in attendance actually had a prior relationship with Baylor, or even knew of the freshman cheerleader.

They'd parked next to the detectives, a definite benefit to being with cops since they had access to any parking spot on campus. The four of them had pushed their way through the crowd, getting as close to the center of the mourning as they could.

The newly appointed Dean of Religious Life began the vigil with a moment of silence for Baylor, and then spoke into a mic. "We gather here to remember Samantha Baylor...."

"Those are Baylor's parents." Detective Taylor pointed to a handsome couple, well dressed and made up.

The Baylors stood at the front of the row, closest to pictures of the murder victim that had been pinned up.

Calvin nudged the detective. "I think that's Mark Simon."

"Yes it is," Taylor acknowledged. "And that's Rory Cummings he's with, Baylor's roommate."

"Interesting. They seem close."

"Yes they do."

Simon and Cummings hugged, leaning on one another, supporting each other through the ceremony. If Calvin didn't know any better, or didn't know either of these individuals, he would have thought them to be a couple.

"Let's split up," Taylor said.

"What are we looking for?" Calvin asked.

"Anything. Talk to some people, find out what's being said." She turned to Baker. "Try not to stick out."

Calvin snaked his way through the crowd, feeling Rachel's hand gripping his shirt to keep up and not lose him. Very little chatter amongst the mob of students, mostly weeping and low humming of songs.

The PI kept his eyes on the front of the ceremony. There had been a number of candlelight vigils conducted at USC, always for fallen students. USC knew how to take care of their own, and the services were always professional and tasteful. Even the students knew to be respectful and courteous.

The next speech came from the Vice President of Student Affairs. "She is in our spirit, in our community."

Calvin's eyes moved constantly, always on alert, looking for anything out, anything off. Was someone hanging around who shouldn't be, reacting to the proceedings in a manner not appropriate for the moment?

"These poor students." Rachel tugged on the back of his shirt, turning Calvin around. "How will they cope and move on, especially those close to Samantha?"

Rachel knew about loss. Calvin ever aware of her past, aware that Rachel had had to overcome a lot herself, and could probably relate to many of the students in attendance. She'd been abused by a stepfather who'd pushed her away, onto the Vegas streets living a life as a streetwalker, trying to get by and do whatever it took to survive.

"USC has all sorts of strategies in place for this kind of thing. Grieving students have access to the care they need. Students can contact the Engemann Student Health Center to reach counselors, and staff members can contact the Center for Work and Family Life."

"How do you know all this?"

When Calvin's father had attempted to connect with the running back after never having met the man before, Calvin had gone through some emotional turmoil. He'd reached out for support, even though none of his friends, classmates or teammates had known about it. It wasn't a time he liked to think about. In the end, he didn't want any part of his father or his dad's ideas.

But he'd also seen it with teammates, those who'd lost loved ones. Every university had their own system in place, but the 'Trojans Care for Trojans' program, which allowed students and staff members concerned about their colleagues to anonymously submit online forms to bring those experiencing personal difficulties to the attention of USC Support & Advocacy, was second to none in the country.

"There will be a lot of students looking for support."

"The best support students have in times of tragedy is each other."

Calvin stopped when handed a journal. He looked up at the student who had passed it to him, realizing that multiple journals were being passed around during the vigil, so that students and staff could write messages to Baylor's family, inking their sentiments. He gave it to a young woman with red-rimmed eyes.

The VP of Student Affairs ended her speech with, "If you need help, ask."

"Did all of these people really know Samantha Baylor?" Rachel asked.

"No," Calvin said. "Most are curious, or just want to be a part of it. The majority have good intentions, but I would think that some are just here for social media attention. This is, after all, 2020."

Next to speak stood a woman who Calvin hadn't seen or even thought about for years. The Associate Dean of Religious Life, Paula Collins, stood before the gathered crowd and extended her arms out wide. A hush fell over the mob.

"You all know me," Collins began. "In addition to Counseling Services, our University has more than fifty religious and spiritual leaders representing most faiths and worldviews, who could serve as someone for those in need of anyone to speak with. We are here for you."

"Who are you going to talk to?" Rachel asked.

"No one."

"No one? I thought detective Taylor said—"

"This isn't the time or place, Rachel. These people are in mourning. It wouldn't be right to question them here. We have time for that."

Calvin craned his neck to look around, but saw no sign of Taylor or her partner. There was no way to pick anyone out of this crowd. Had they left? Had they thought the same thing as he and given up their pursuit?

Rachel looked at him, a mix of desperation and hope in her eyes. "Dancing?"

"Sure, why not."

He waited to hear Rachel's deep, steady breathing. Once the soft moans escaped her mouth, the PI slipped out from under the covers. He quietly pulled two bottles from his duffel bag and tiptoed out of the room.

Calvin proceeded to the kitchen, hobbling. He removed a couple of painkillers from one vial, and two anti-inflammatories from the other, and swallowed them. He kept the lights off, removed two bags of frozen vegetables from the freezer, and then went into the living room. He twisted on the standing lamp and gingerly sat down on the sofa.

He checked his phone.

Calvin realized that for best results, he should have iced his knee immediately after the race, but that had not been a possibility.

He sat against the arm of the couch and raised his leg onto the back of the couch, elevating his knee above his heart. Next, he performed an ice massage with the frozen bag. He applied it directly to his knee, and then moved it around frequently.

After twenty minutes, he set the bag on the coffee table. He would apply it again in about thirty minutes. But he had some time to kill.

He pulled out his notepad and flipped through the pages he'd added today. He heard footsteps in the hall and looked up.

His brother stepped into the living room. "I saw the light. Couldn't sleep?"

Calvin shrugged.

His brother's eyes wandered to the coffee table, to the melting bag of vegetables. "Uh-oh," he said.

Calvin put a finger to his lips. "Rachel doesn't need to know."

Calvin swung his leg onto the coffee table so his brother could sit down on the couch.

"How bad is it?" Josh asked.

"You know, not as bad as I thought. I've been training it pretty hard over the years so maybe that's helping."

"Is that from the dancing?

"Totally worth it. I owed it to Rachel, since she's been craving a night out with just the two of us since we landed in LA."

"Or is it from the race?"

Calvin's head snapped up. "You know about that?"

Josh smiled. "News travels quickly. Apparently Watson posted a story on Instagram about it, how he had taken down the legendary Calvin Watters."

Calvin shook his head. "Guess I'm not Superman anymore."

Josh held his gaze for some time, and then said, "I've never known you to lose at anything."

"Age is catching up to me."

Josh smirked. "Ya right."

"What is that supposed to mean?"

"I know you better than you think."

"And?"

Josh shook his head. "Never mind." He glanced at the notepad in Calvin's hands. "How's the investigation going?"

"Like trying to swim with a giant rock tied around my neck."

"That well, huh?"

"Taylor and Baker have asked me to join forces."

"Interesting."

"They are chasing leads on a suspect, but I am going to follow a different direction."

"Any ideas?"

"Hunches."

"Sometimes those can work out."

"Sometimes. What are you doing up?"

Josh shrugged. "Making sure you're alright."

"You know, I'm your younger brother, but I'm not a kid any more."

"You'll always be my little bro. I still want to take care of you, like I *should* have done back then."

"You have nothing to apologize for. You had your own thing going on, and a pretty bright future to think about."

"I still don't like how it all went down." He curled up his fists. "You in and out of foster homes."

"Hey, I survived. It only made me stronger."

Josh shook his head emphatically. "It's just not right."

Calvin placed a hand on his brother's back and felt Josh shake. "Everything turned out perfectly."

Josh turned to face Calvin. "That's all because of you. Most boys that age, under those conditions, wouldn't have lasted a day. I owe you for what I put you through."

"You don't owe me anything, Josh."

"I have a lot of missed time to make up for, and I plan on doing that."

Then Josh caught Calvin off guard when he leaned in for a hug, and wrapped his arms around Calvin. The PI squeezed back.

"I love you, Calvin."

"I love you too, Josh."

Chapter 15

Calvin blinked awake on Wednesday morning, his knee stiff, but surprising not the bone-throbbing pain he'd expected.

He reached over but Rachel wasn't there. She'd always been an early riser, so the noise of the kids playing so early in the morning hadn't bothered her at all. In Calvin's previous occupation, Vegas collector, AKA "leg-breaker", he hadn't punched a clock, and most of his jobs were handled late at night, so he'd had the opportunity of sleeping in every day. Even now as a PI, his own boss, punctuality at the office was not a necessity.

He flung the sheet off his body and over to Rachel's side of the bed. His knee was red, and only slightly swollen.

He would always have to rely on painkillers, exercise and stretching. But the biggest concern for everyone close to Calvin in his life, was that despite the doctors' warnings: cautioning him to always be vigilant with everything he did, err on the side of caution when it came to participating in sports or extra-curricular activities, making extra sure not to overextend or do anything that could jeopardize his ability to even keep walking, Calvin continued to push the limits.

He rolled into a seated position on the edge of the bed and set his feet on the floor. He pushed down, putting pressure on the ball of his foot, testing out the soreness of his knee.

Workable.

Calvin adjusted his boxer shorts and picked up a t-shirt off the floor, pulling it over his naked upper body. Using his hands, he pushed himself into a standing position, keeping weight off his bad knee, for now.

It always took a few minutes and a few reps to stretch out and feel flexible and stronger.

He hobbled around the end of the bed and stood in the middle of the room. He kicked away a cluster of clothes on the floor to give himself enough room to move, pushing them under the bed.

The PI took a deep breath, and then started a series of stretches and exercises that had been handed down to him by a group of physiotherapists, shared by some of the best in the industry.

Most people who had never had a knee injury before would be surprised to know that getting more flexible in large muscles such as hamstrings, hip flexors and quadriceps could help ease knee pain.

Calvin stayed focused when he did his morning workout regimen. He made sure his spine remained stable, unchanged, while he performed exercises.

As he started his final exercise, single leg squats, Calvin became aware of someone at the door. He turned around to find his six year-old nephew, Caleb, standing just outside the room watching Calvin's every move. Caleb's big brown eyes stared widely.

"You wanna try, big guy?" Calvin asked.

The boy nodded shyly.

Calvin waved his nephew in. "Come on."

The boy gingerly stepped inside the room.

"Stand here." Calvin placed his giant hands around the boy's slender shoulders and directed him into place beside the former football player, between Calvin and the bed. "Just do what I do."

Calvin lifted his right foot off the floor and performed a squat with his left leg, bending down almost low enough where he could touch the ground with his hand. When Caleb lifted his leg and started his squat, the boy teetered and leaned, then falling over and hitting his side against the bed.

Calvin picked his nephew up. "You okay?"

Caleb nodded. "I want to try again."

"Okay."

This time, Caleb extended his arms, as if pretending to be an airplane, and was able to steady himself enough to go part way down and all the way back up.

"Way to go, buddy!" Calvin hollered. He and Caleb high-fived. "Should we keep going?"

The boy nodded, and this time added a smile.

A few minutes later, Calvin heard a giggle behind him. No mistaking whose giggle it belonged to. He closed his eyes, because Calvin knew what came next.

"Oh, that is so cute," Rachel said in a high-pitched voice. "Stay there, I'm going to get my phone."

"No, not the phone." Calvin slumped his shoulders. She always had to get the phone.

Rachel returned less than a minute later. "Okay, do it again and I will take a picture."

"Rachel, really?"

"My followers will love it."

"Why does everything have to go on social media?"

"Every time I post your picture, I get a lot more likes."

Charlene woke up and checked her phone. She could hear Matt's steady breathing and knew that he still slept, what seemed like a peaceful, easy sleep. The bed sheet was tucked under his arms, the hair on his bare chest rising and falling with each breath.

Matt was the reason why Charlene's sleeps had been much, much better.

She quietly slipped out of the bed, careful not to wake him, and grabbed a clean pair of Matt's boxers on her way to the bathroom. She took one last glimpse at Matt sleeping, before closing the door quietly.

She pulled the boxers over her naked body and rolled down the waistband until they fit snuggly.

The detective stood at the sink and swiped strands of hair away from her face. She let it grow longer, the dirty-blond locks reaching down below her shoulders. Although more demanding to maintain, she liked the idea of having more options with it. She looked in the mirror, and for the first time in a long time, Charlene liked what she saw, the reflection no longer scaring her. The shadows under her eyes were lighter.

It wasn't so long ago that Charlene had valid reasons to avoid mirrors. Her skin ghostly pale, and not because of lack of sunshine in the Golden State. She had formed large, dark circular rings around her eyes, from both a lack of sleep and an increase in stress. She had stopped eating, losing significant weight, her clothes hung loosely off her. At one point, as bad as it sounded, Charlene couldn't see a light at the end of the tunnel, thought that there would be no getting back.

She opened the vanity drawer for her toothbrush, and one of her pill bottles rolled to the front of the drawer. She stared at it, swaying back and forth on its side, as if taunting her.

She pulled it out and shook it, a few pills left. She read the prescription, her name clearly printed on the outside, prescribed by Dr. Edward Gardner, LAPD psychiatrist. Charlene shook her head, unbelieving that she had been so dependent on the little pills.

Charlene straightened her back. Her ribcage no longer prominent. She put on weight, good weight, running and exercising again, things she had always been accustomed to doing in her professional career as a police officer. She had missed that feeling of the tightness and soreness in her muscles, and a body that burned after a workout.

It felt good to be back.

It wasn't just her physical looks that had changed, but her overall outlook on life and her ability to cope. Emotional instability had been something the detective had had to overcome, and even though still not all the way back, she liked the road to recovery she took one step at a time.

Had she exorcised her demons? Not totally, but she liked where she was at in her life. A combination of things helped Charlene recover and mend.

She had her family back. The relationship between Charlene and her sister and mother had never been stronger. For years, Charlene had been the black sheep, the screw-up daughter who frustrated her entire family: the wild lifestyle and the untapped potential she drank away. The detective had to admit that the mental stress her family had endured during the kidnapping of Martina, Charlene's niece, and bringing that case to a head successfully, had brought her whole family closer together.

Her weekly visits with Dr. Gardner had been a healing experience. Even though Charlene had been against the department-appointed psychiatric evaluation, it had allowed the detective to unburden herself and remove that dead weight that her father's death had created. She had now come to the realization that her relationship with her father could never be resolved.

And Matt. Charlene was never the kind to fall head-over-heels for a guy. She liked to be in control, she liked relationships to run on her terms. But she had to admit, she was smitten...not that she would ever confess that to anyone, let alone Matt. She liked the upper-hand. But Matt had a calming effect on Charlene, one that reflected her new attitude.

Last night's vigil hadn't garnered any leads. Everyone who the detective had expected to be there had been—very grim, very sad. It was one of those moments that no one ever wanted to be a part of, a victim leaving this world much too young, way before her time. Everyone in attendance felt it last night. The whole scene reminded Charlene of her father's funeral, not so long ago. Even though Martin Taylor had been much older than Samantha Baylor, it hadn't been any easier to swallow.

The few people Charlene had spoken to last night hadn't known Baylor. They'd admitted they'd just 'followed the crowd'. The detective didn't dare get in-between Baylor's close friends and family at last night's service. Although hungry for a solution, that would have been in poor taste.

The bathroom door opened and Matt stood in the doorway, wearing nothing but a smile and a towel cinched around his waist, showing off his tight gut.

She looked away, into the mirror and tried not to smile. "Sorry, ocupado."

"You mean you won't share?"

He stepped into the bathroom, and moved in behind her. Matt wrapped his arms around her waist and she could feel his warm breath on the back of her neck. Her skin prickled with heat.

"Do you want me to go with you to see him?"

She should never have told Matt that Darren Brady, AKA the Celebrity Slayer, had wanted to meet with her.

"No. This is something I will have to do myself."

"Sure?"

"Yes."

"I'll stay if you need me."

"I know."

Silence lingered.

"I can't believe you're leaving today." Charlene pouted her lips playfully.

"That's the job."

"I know, but it's not fair. You just got here."

He rubbed his jaw against the back of her neck, his scruff scratching lightly. "You're never here anyway. And now you have this new case that consumes your life."

"I'm sorry. When I get into work mode, I just kind of forget everything else around me. I have a tendency to automatically reject things not concerned with the current case I'm working. It's just the way I'm wired."

He moved his head towards the side of her face. "I think it's one of your most attractive qualities," he whispered into her ear.

"One of them?"

He smiled, looking her body up and down. "Well..."

Charlene laughed.

"You'll get more work done with me gone, anyway."

"That's true. You *are* a distraction."

He cupped her breasts in his hands and kissed her hair and the back of her neck. The nerves of her spine and shoulder blades quivered.

She knew it wouldn't always be like this. They were new, just starting to date. Like most couples in a new relationship, they couldn't keep their hands off each other, the sex exhilarating and frequent, exciting all the time.

But the newness would wear off. Eventually they would grow apart, become distant. At least that was Charlene's experience. Or was that just her?

"You know, I still have two hours before I need to be at the airport."

She could feel his hardness behind her, through the terry cloth fabric of the towel, and his breathing accelerated. "Oh, really?"

His lips moved down to the top of her shoulder, covering it with kisses, and then spun Charlene around, cupping the angle of her jaw to kiss her hard on the lips. With his muscular arms, Matt gripped her buttocks and lifted her up onto the edge of the basin vanity. Charlene wrapped her legs around his waist and let him take her away.

She pulled away and grinned slyly. "Two hours, huh?"

He smiled back. "Yep."

"There's so much that can be done in two hours."

"What's first on the agenda, boss?" Charlene slapped a twenty dollar bill on Larry's keyboard before dropping down at her desk.

She set a Styrofoam cup of black coffee in front of her partner, who had the sports page open and was skimming over his reading glasses. She was ever aware of her tardiness this morning and all week, and her partner's unsaid disapproval. She'd just come from dropping Matt off at the LA International Airport.

What most people didn't know was that detective work consisted of routine.

"Thank you." He grabbed the money and shoved it into his pocket. "I was in an hour ago," Larry said, without looking up at her. "You usually always beat me in." He glanced in her direction. "But not this week."

"Been busy."

"Uh-huh."

She wouldn't make excuses, and certainly didn't want Larry to think she'd gone soft by letting a guy dictate her schedule and have her "off" her game. Charlene admitted that Matt was a distraction when here, but now gone, it was time to get serious.

Larry closed the paper and tossed a stapled file onto her desk.

"What's that?" she asked.

"Davidson's background check on Samantha Baylor's parents. I read it this morning before you came in."

Charlene grabbed the papers and leaned back in her seat, rifling through them. "Anything interesting?"

"Nothing. In fact, pretty boring—no debt, no enemies, no one with any reason to see harm to them."

"On paper, anyway."

Larry nodded. "If we want the dirt, we'll have to dig deeper."

Davidson had done a thorough job, using the Baylors' social security numbers to look into their lives—employment, bank accounts, credit cards—the works.

"I think we can both agree that Baylor's parents aren't a priority here. If need be, we can delve deeper later on."

Larry opened the newspaper back up, and grunted his approval. Keeping his eyes on the newspaper, he said, "Nothing useful pulled from Baylor's room. They hacked into her laptop but she only did school work on it."

She removed the lid on her coffee and blew on the top. "What about her phone?"

"Still hasn't been recovered."

"Wonder if the killer took it."

"Why?"

"Maybe she had messages on it from the killer. Maybe they had connected before, talked about meeting each other. I don't know. Any chance we can get a hold of the phone provider and see if we can dig something up?"

"I'll look into it." Larry wrote in his notepad.

Charlene asked, "What did you think of our meeting with Watters?"

"I think we can trust him."

"He seems on board alright."

"I don't think he knows enough about the case yet to determine if Lewis Mahoney killed Baylor as he said he did. I think he wants to look at all of the options."

Charlene took a sip and let the caffeine work its way through her body. "From what Detective Dayton told me, Watters is thorough and leaves no stone unturned. He's also smart, and still has a few connections in this town."

"I'm a little worried about his legacy at USC though."

She set down her coffee. "What do you mean?"

"I think that Watters is no longer welcomed in some circles. There seem to be a few of the 'upper echelon' who aren't interested in having him around."

"You mean like the AD?" Charlene thought about the verbal abuse Price had handed down to Watters on the day she'd first met him at the practice facility. He had been intentionally offensive, and Watters had not taken the bait. That had shown great restraint.

"I forgot to ask you what Watters had said when you confronted him about throwing that race."

Charlene looked at her partner. "You saw that?"

Larry nodded.

"And you're still going to take my money?"

Larry shrugged. "A bet's a bet."

"Watters denied it, as I thought he would. But the tone in his voice proved otherwise. It showed me the kind of man he is, to let a cocky punk beat him and have his moment of glory. Watters seems humble, and no glory hound."

"Jordan Price seems to have a hate on for him."

"Didn't Watters break the AD's nose?"

"That's the rumor."

"What's Price's story, anyway?"

Larry folded up the paper and put it down. "Played USC ball in the nineties. He took over as AD in Watters' junior year. After Watters hurt his knee and told he'd never play ball again, some dispute ensued over his scholarship eligibility. The AD ruled against Watters keeping his scholarship, which meant the RB was out of school, since he couldn't afford tuition."

"That's pretty low."

"Next thing you know, meeting is adjourned, and people say Price is seen leaving the building with a bloody rag held against his nose. Two days later, he has matching raccoon eyes to go with it."

"I don't blame Watters if he did slug him." She pushed the button to wake her computer. "Have we heard from Mahoney's attorney?"

"Apparently Mahoney is going through a psych eval. today. Once we get those results, we'll talk to Clark to see how he wants us to proceed. We'll probably need our own psych eval. on him."

"We still need to talk to him."

"We'll get our shot, but we have to be ready. That's today's job, get everything we can on Mahoney."

She logged onto the internet. "I still don't like him for this."

"I know you don't, so you'll like this." Larry twisted around, which looked like a challenge considering his large girth, and grabbed a see-through evidence bag that had been sealed and tagged. Inside the bag hung a plastic vial with a white liquid substance. "Mark Simon's sperm sample, delivered this morning."

"Really?" Charlene bounced forward in her chair, out of her seat and grabbed the bag out of Larry's hand. "Gallant came through?"

"Yeah. The USC counsel came in here first thing this morning, a smug look on her face as she handed it over."

"Since you brought him up, I did some research and thought of something. Let's pretend for a second that Mahoney didn't do it. With the ME's analysis that COD was asphyxiation, we can't rule out 'Breath Play'."

"Breath Play? What's that?"

"Erotic asphyxiation, intentional restriction of oxygen to the brain for sexual arousal."

Larry shifted in his seat. "How did you exactly research that, Taylor?"

She grinned devilishly. "None of your business."

"You're right, I don't want to know. You think this might be a crime of passion?"

"I don't know, but I don't think we can rule it out just yet."

"Good point. We can't rule anything or anyone out, yet."

"Let's get that sperm sample over to Dana and see what it tells us."

She and Dana Davis had joined the LAPD the same year, went through training at the police academy together. Dana had spent her first two LAPD years as a patrol officer, but when time to choose a specialty, Dana landed on the CSI team. Now, the only work time Charlene got to spend with Dana was when the detective had evidence for Dana's special task unit in the Trace Evidence Lab.

The Los Angeles Forensic Science Center Crime Laboratory, located in the Hertzberg-Davis Forensic Science Center at California State University, was designed to hold both the Los Angeles Police Department's Scientific Investigation Division and the Los Angeles County Sheriff's Department Scientific Services Bureau—the largest local full-service crime laboratory facility in the United States.

The building was built to be an impressive site. With room for approximately four hundred staff members, evidence from approximately 140,000 criminal cases was submitted for analysis annually by both agencies.

She'd called ahead so Dana was waiting in the parking lot for Charlene and Larry, as he turned off State University Drive. If a name ever suited anyone, it was Dana Davis'. They called her "Double D" around the LAPD, and it wasn't just because of her initials. Dana had told Charlene that *they* had been high school graduation gifts from her parents.

Dana waved to them. Her white lab coat fully unbuttoned revealed a skin-tight white t-shirt tucked into a pair of skinny cargo pants, augmenting her voluptuous upper body.

When Larry pulled the car to a stop in front of the building, Dana placed her hands on the bottom window frame and leaned forward, the lapels of her lab coat opening wider.

"Hey, Char," Dana said cheerfully. Then turned her voice into a more seductive tone. "Hi, Larry."

Larry leaned back in his seat and pulled at the shirt collar around his neck. He sweated above his upper lip. "Hello, Dana."

Dana looked at Charlene and they both laughed at each other. Dana's blond hair was tied up and she wore dark, rimless sunglasses.

"I heard your man's in town," Dana said. "When can I meet Mr. Wonderful?"

Larry looked at Charlene. "So that's why you've been late every morning this week."

"Morning sex, Larry," Dana replied. "The best kind there is."

Larry's face reddened.

"He's already gone," Charlene said.

Dana pursed her lips and said, "Damn. Come and gone, just like that. I'm not sure this guy even exists."

Charlene grinned. "Oh, he's real."

"What did you bring me this morning?"

Charlene held up the bag. "Sperm."

"Larry, you shouldn't have. My boyfriend will be so jealous."

Larry swiped at a droplet of perspiration running down the side of his face.

"Dana," Charlene warned. "Be nice."

"Larry knows I love him. I'm just playing around."

The forensic specialist reached inside the car and across the seat, coming very close to brushing up against Larry, which Charlene thought would make her partner's week. She grabbed the bag and then pulled back and out of the vehicle.

"It's tagged," Larry whispered, as if short of breath.

"Thanks, Dana. Talk later."

They pulled out of the lot and headed towards USC.

Chapter 16

Calvin sat on a bench he hadn't been on in over five years, on the south side of campus. He couldn't count the number of times he'd waited in this exact position for a friend, teammate, or girl, seated outside the USC Leventhal School of Accounting.

Calvin had majored in Business Administration during his three plus years at USC, in the USC Marshall School of Business, connected to the Accounting building, so he knew the building inside and out.

Brandon Harris was an accounting major and, from the looks of his class schedule which Calvin had acquired from a reluctant administrative assistant, had a morning financial accounting class. The class ended soon, and Calvin didn't want to miss Harris leaving the building.

The PI had zeroed in on Harris for a number of reasons. The first, and most obvious, being that Harris looked up to Calvin, almost worshipped him. And Calvin actually liked the young up-and-comer.

Number two, Harris didn't seem to run in any team cliques. For anyone who had never been a part of a team, they missed out. Calvin knew the feeling well. To be a part of a team was to be a part of a family. You became brothers. That created a special bond.

Calvin wanted to protect Harris by meeting with him outside of practice schedule time, away from his teammates, who might not take too kindly to Harris talking to Calvin. Calvin just hoped that none of Harris' teammates took the same class and would be in a group.

"Hi."

Calvin turned to find a cute, brown-eyed girl with big dimples and frizzy hair. The stranger had settled onto the bench beside him without making a sound. Calvin looked back towards the door but didn't see any sign of movement.

He looked at the girl at his side. "Hi."

"Are you waiting for someone?"

"Is it that obvious?"

She smiled back, and the dimples on her cheeks opened even wider. "Kind of. Do you mind if I sit here?"

"Not at all. Should be wide enough for the two of us."

She giggled playfully. The girl looked to be about seventeen or eighteen, and had similar features to Samantha Baylor, the murder victim.

"Are you a senior?" she asked.

He hid a smile. "Um, not exactly."

The doors to the building opened and the quiet business college sector of USC erupted as hordes of students flowed out. Calvin's eyes darted, picking out faces and hair. It wouldn't be easy with so many teenagers talking, some running, many sipping coffee, and all going in different directions.

"Junior?" the girl asked.

Calvin ignored the girl and studied the faces as they moved in unison, heads bobbing, giggling, loud chatter, students with bright futures and filled with hope. Then, Calvin spotted Harris, in the middle of the pack, speaking with a much shorter, red-headed female student.

"Sorry, I have to go." Calvin bounced to his feet and took off in a fast walk.

"Wait…" He heard the girl's pleas but her voice trailed off as he distanced himself from the bench.

The backup RB made a right onto a paved path and disappeared again in the throng of students going in both directions to and from class.

Calvin caught up with Harris as the student turned onto the Trousdale Parkway. Harris moved hastily and Calvin tried to keep up, always weary not to over-extend his knee.

"Brandon," Calvin called out.

Harris turned around at the sound of his name. "Calvin?" He sounded surprised. "What are you doing here?"

Calvin slowed his pace as he neared the USC running back. "Can we talk?"

"Sure." He looked down at his companion. "Sorry, Laura, can I call you later?"

"Okay."

The girl walked away.

"Sorry," Calvin said. "I hope I didn't interrupt anything?"

Harris grinned. "Nah, just a classmate, for now, anyway."

"Gotcha. How about I buy you a coffee to make up for blocking you?"

They huddled in a small coffee spot called the Literatea, located in the Nazarian Pavilion off the Trousdale Parkway. The small café was a more sophisticated coffee house than the traditional Starbucks, with wide cushioned, comfortable lounge chairs corresponding with booth benches. The room was stocked with hardback, second hand books, and students lined up, selecting healthy 'grab and go' items to complete their college day, and make their study hours more productive.

Nineties music played overhead as Calvin ordered himself a regular black coffee and Harris ordered something called a "nitro" coffee, the café's specialty. Calvin paid and they tucked themselves into a corner booth, where no one gave them a second look.

They sat across from each other, Calvin focusing on the outside, looking through the large front window. A student pulled a bike from of a rack-full, and put a helmet on his head.

"How's practice going?" Calvin said, breaking the silence.

Harris brought the coffee to his lips and sipped at his beverage. "You know, a little weird these days with everything going on."

"You guys going to be ready for Saturday?"

"I hope so."

Calvin blew on the top of his coffee and took a sip. "Look, Brandon, I know the brotherhood. I totally understand that things that happen inside the circle of trust amongst teammates stays there, but I could really use some insight from you."

Harris wiggled in his seat. "What are you looking for, Calvin?"

"I'm not exactly sure. How well did you know Samantha Baylor?"

Harris' eyes shifted quickly, looking around the café. Calvin was aware that even the whisper of her name around parts of the USC campus would turn heads and get people talking.

"No one knows we're talking," Calvin reassured the running back.

"I saw her around."

"Where?"

"Parties, practices, games. You know, she dated Mark for a while, so she attended team functions, and she cheered. As USC athletes, we kind of interact with them often."

"Wait a minute. You said dated. Does that mean they were no longer a couple?"

"I think they tried to work things out."

"So they were at the party together?"

"Kind of."

"Explain that."

Harris took a full sized gulp of coffee. "They broke up a few weeks ago."

"Why?"

The RB shrugged his shoulders. "They got in a big fight at a party. Samantha ran out crying. Everyone saw; it was like an explosion."

"What was the fight about?"

Harris said, "I don't know. Not sure anyone knows. Mark definitely wasn't talking about it but he seemed pretty pissed off about something."

Calvin jotted this down in his notepad. "What happened that night after she left?"

"Not sure, we just went back to partying. It wasn't exactly an uncommon event, a breakup at a party. Once everyone starts drinking, anything can happen."

"So no one talked about it the next day?"

"Not really."

"So last Saturday night, they were back together?"

"Kind of. They didn't show up together. Sam came with her roommate, but she and Mark hung out and seemed to get along once they met up."

"And they definitely left together?"

"I'm pretty sure, but I wasn't really paying any attention."

"What kind of person was Samantha Baylor?"

Again, Harris looked around the café. "Sweet. Innocent. Maybe a bit immature and naïve."

"How's that?"

Harris licked his lips. "I just got the feeling, from watching her interact with some of the guys, that she could be easily persuaded." He emphasized the word 'persuaded'.

"Did you ever see any of the other guys *persuade* her?"

From his experience working the Vegas streets, much of Calvin's job depended on his ability to collect payments for his boss. But there was more to 'collecting' than people thought. To an outsider, it just looked to be about breaking bones and administering punishment and torture. But Calvin had been well trained, and had also picked up things on his own.

The PI had become a human lie detector. He had learned the telltale signs, could read body language and knew when someone wasn't being completely honest. At that moment, Harris' eyes shifted, and his breathing quickened slightly.

"Not that I could tell," he whispered.

"Nothing going on with any other guys?"

A swallow, his Adam's apple bobbed. "Not on the team."

"Any guy at all?"

"Not that I know of."

Calvin didn't push Harris. If the kid wanted to tell him, then he would. The PI had to keep it casual, let Harris think that it was just friendly conversation.

"Your father come to many games?" Calvin asked, steering the conversation away from the case.

Harris smiled proudly. "Every home game, and some road games."

"Must be nice to have that kind of support."

"It's great. I think he just shows up in hopes that I will someday get to play at least one snap."

"How does that look?"

"You've seen Watson move. What do you think?"

Calvin nodded. He knew what he would do had he been the coach.

"Sorry I can't help your investigation more, Calvin."

Calvin wasn't surprised that Harris knew he conducted the investigation into Samantha Baylor's death. "Look, Brandon, the last thing I want to do is break your teammates' trust. But has there been any locker-room talk since the murder? Or even talk about Samantha Baylor before that?"

Calvin knew all too well some of the things that players discussed inside a sports team's locker-room. Especially with college boys, hormones in full throttle, testosterone at their highest levels.

Harris' smile reached his eyes. "You know the guys when they get together, the things they say. You can't believe half of it."

"Anything about Baylor?"

"No, sir." No hesitation.

It took them over an hour to get to Harris Hall, one of the two North Residential College buildings, where Mahoney's dorm room was situated. They'd arrived early to the Campus Safety office, and then were redirected to the USC Housing Services Office, in order to show the search warrant and gain access to the suspect's room. Eventually, after all of the hoops had been jumped through, they were finally escorted to Harris Hall, located next to the university's historic alumni house.

A group of male students were engaged in a game of touch football on a sizeable green lawn right at the front of the building. A pair of female students tossed a Frisbee, blocking the front entrance. The garden plaza seated a number of students on benches: listening to music, on phones, and chatting.

When they entered the front door of the three-storied, classic-style college residence hall, Charlene and Larry breathed easier with the building's air-conditioning unit running full throttle.

Charlene flipped her sunglasses to the top of her head. "We got it from here," she said to the campus escort, a short Hispanic man with dark curly hair hidden underneath a cardinal red USC ball hat.

Once the security guy left, the detectives entered the main floor. There were no bedrooms on the first floor, strictly the lounge area for students, as well as study rooms. The viewing room, a large thousand square-foot area, had a black piano with an empty bench in the corner, and a group of students huddled around a giant big screen colored TV.

"Let's pull some of these guys after we look at Mahoney's room. See what their take is of the kid."

The second and third floors were the living areas, with twenty-four double rooms on each level. Mahoney's room was on the second floor, so they took the stairs.

Students were encouraged to decorate their own rooms, to their own tastes. Charlene and Larry had yet to meet Mahoney's roommate, so they stopped outside his door and knocked. They weren't about to yell out their intentions as cops, but realized their presence hadn't gone unnoticed.

A blackboard hung on the outside of Mahoney's door with the words, "Go Away", poorly scribbled in white chalk.

When no one answered, the detectives tried the doorknob. Locked.

Using the key they'd received from the housing office, the detectives ignored the sign's advice and let themselves in.

The detectives walked into a room that looked like two separate worlds. The room divided almost evenly with twins of everything: single beds, chest-of-drawers, study desks and small closets. But that's where the similarities ended.

"Which side do you think is Mahoney's?" Larry asked.

One side looked like the typical male-college dorm room, or what you would expect to find: clothes scattered inside-out on the floor and unmade bed, magazines strewn on the nightstand, a gaming system and computer on the desk, with multiple controllers and head-mics hanging down. It looked like someone hurriedly left without worrying about picking up. No personal items on desks or nightstand, but only one thing hanging on the wall—a half-naked poster of Cardi B.

The other side of the room lay completely spotless, not one stitch of clothing or even one item misplaced on the floor. The bed stayed perfectly made, pulled tight with marine-like sheet corners. Clothes had been folded neatly on top of the dresser and books placed in a row, in order from smallest to biggest, on the night stand. The computer looked like it had been freshly wiped, and centered perfectly on the desk with school textbooks and a digital alarm clock. A dark bookcase was completely jammed with hardback titles, books lining up in alphabetical order of author's names, both fiction and nonfiction.

But the side wall beside Mahoney's bed was a totally different story, covered in USC memorabilia, almost like a shrine to the Trojan football team. Everything from team and individual player posters, to banners, to a giant foam hand and fingers.

Charlene approached the wall. "Whoa, talk about an obsession."

"An unhealthy one," Larry answered.

They snapped on gloves and started with Mahoney's side of the room. Charlene went through the lone desk drawer, neatly placed and departmentalized in sections. Very few items existed: USC football season tickets, school supplies, a change jar and an empty USC money clip. She opened up the laptop and turned it on.

"Password protected," she said. "We'll have to take it back and let the tech guys at it."

Charlene removed her phone and punched in a number. "This is Detective Taylor, badge number 198107, requesting a CSI team." She gave the address and dorm number. She clicked off and looked at Larry. "We need to find some sort of connection between Samantha Baylor and Lewis Mahoney. Something that puts her here in the dorm room physically: a hair follicle, skin flint, fingernail clipping. Or something that connects her emotionally: an email, text message, or private message."

Larry rummaged through Mahoney's clothes hanging in the closet, when a noise behind them at the door turned their heads. A young-looking Asian kid stood just inside the doorway, staring at them. He had a square face, spiked hair, and bad acne.

"Who are you? What are you doing? That's not your stuff. Don't move, I know karate." He got into a fighter's stance and pulled out his phone. "I'm calling the police."

Charlene stepped forward and pulled back the bottom of her jacket, wrapping it around the badge clipped to her belt at the front of her waist. "Don't bother, Mr. Chang."

The kid hesitated, and grudgingly put his phone away. "How do you know my name?"

"Edward Chang, right?"

He nodded. "What are you doing here? Where's Lewis?"

Nothing had been released yet, in the news, about Lewis Mahoney's confession and his alleged murdering of Samantha Baylor. Word hadn't spread, the LAPD doing a surprisingly good job of keeping it hushed.

There was still nothing to support the theory that Mahoney killed Baylor—no motive, no opportunity, no proof or evidence.

"Shut the door, Edward." Charlene tried to make her voice and facial expression show Chang the seriousness of the moment, and one that needed to be handled with severity.

Chang wiped his hands on his pant legs, nervously. He looked out into the hallway before shutting the door.

The detective had to tiptoe around this interview. They didn't want people to know about the confession, but she needed to get Chang's take on his roommate. This was a critical character witness, someone who would have spent a lot of time with Mahoney and would have seen him at his most vulnerable.

"Did something happen to Lewis?" Chang asked, worry on his face.

"Do you know this woman?" Larry flashed a picture of Samantha Baylor in her cheerleading uniform.

"Is that the cheerleader who was killed?"

The detective didn't answer, but Charlene used her eyes to keep the atmosphere in the room somber.

"Her name is Samantha Baylor," Charlene finally said.

"That is her. Why do you want to know that?"

"Have you seen her before?"

He shook his head and said, "No, why would I?"

"Did Lewis know her?"

"How would I know?"

"Has she ever been in this room?"

"What?" Chang looked genuinely confused. "Why would she—" Chang's eyes lit up, as if something clicked. "Did Lewis kill that cheerleader? Is that why you are here, going through his clothes? Is he in jail? Is that where he's been?"

"Answer the question," Larry said. The detective didn't raise his voice. Charlene had rarely seen her partner express an emotion openly, but the tone of his voice shook Chang, and the student paled slightly.

"I don't think so. I mean…I've never seen her here." Chang dropped on the edge of his messy bed, on top of the clothes, looking clearly shaken.

"Were they seeing each other?"

Chang covered a snort-laugh.

"What's so funny?"

"You think Lewis dated that cheerleader?"

Charlene looked at Larry and then back to Chang. She asked, "Why is that so absurd?"

"I'm not even sure Lewis likes girls. I've never seen him with one or even talk about any. Lewis kept to himself most of the time. He went to games by himself, he studied alone, he ate in his room, and never got any calls from anyone other than his parents."

"So you're sure you've never seen this girl around here or with Lewis?"

"Oh, I'm more than sure. A girl like that," he pointed at the picture in Charlene's hand. "Would never be caught dead—" He realized the word that had just slipped out of his mouth and stopped himself. "I'm sorry. I mean she would never hang out with people like Lewis and me."

Charlene didn't have to question him further on this. She knew exactly what he meant. There would always be cliques in college, the cool kids and the outcasts, jocks and nerds, sorority and fraternity, all sorts of groups.

"Did you see Lewis on Saturday night?" Larry asked.

"So he did kill that girl?"

"Focus!" Charlene snapped.

"Sorry. Umm, Saturday night. Yeah right, hardly."

"Why's that?"

"That's game night."

"So?"

Chang pointed a finger towards Lewis Mahoney's wall, the shrine of USC Trojan memorabilia. "Lewis is impossible to be around on a game night."

Charlene picked up a USC football bobble head from the desk. "And why would that be?"

"Well, as you can see, he's kind of a die hard. He lives and breathes that team. I've never seen anyone go above and beyond for a team. I'm talking about face and body painting, spending tons of money on stuff as you can see. He worships those players."

"What about after the game?"

"Nope."

Larry asked, "When did you see him again after that night?"

Chang shrugged his shoulders. "He was in his bed when I woke up the next morning."

"Who was home first?"

"Me. I didn't hear him come home. I'm kind of a deep sleeper."

So Mahoney had no alibi, yet. That didn't help Charlene's notion that Mahoney hadn't killed Baylor and only covered for someone.

Larry handed Chang his card. "If you think of anything else, give us a call."

Chapter 17

The red brick building with the bright red front door loomed largely at the end of the path. Calvin stood back and stared, aware of its history.

He wasn't part of the scene, but well aware of what might go on behind those closed doors. In the midst of the chaos of sorority life, it was not uncommon for conflict between girls to run rampant. Drama and gossip often seemed to go hand in hand with the pledging process. While getting to know the current members created an atmosphere of sisterhood, it didn't always go as expected.

"You goin' in there, dude?" A kid with a heavy looking backpack asked as he walked by Calvin. "Good luck with that."

Calvin walked up to the door and used the brass knocker. He could hear loud talking and giggling on the other side of the door.

It opened to a round-faced, slightly overweight redhead. "Oh, hi there," she said, batting what looked to be extended eyelashes. She wore extremely short shorts that displayed tawny, cellulite legs.

"Hi."

"Can I help you?"

He lightened his voice. "I'm here to see Emma Moore."

The girl looked disappointed. "Oh, of course you are."

"Excuse me?"

"Nothing, come on in." Her shoulders slouched and her body language relaxed. She stepped to the side to allow Calvin entrance. "I'll go get her. Just wait here."

"Thanks."

Calvin waited just inside the door. He looked around. Oh, how he had dreamed of gaining access to the building seven or eight years ago. From the doorway, he could see through to the end of the building: the symbol of an anchor painted on long, dark hardwood flooring that led to a spiral staircase at the end of the hall.

The same redhead appeared out of a side room, led by a stunning blond girl with flawless tanned skin, who moved with a straight-up posture—someone used to getting what she wanted.

"Julia, you're right. He is cute." She flashed a beauty contest smile and held out her hand. "I'm Emma Moore. What can I do you for, sir?"

Calvin wasn't sure if the girl expected him to kiss her hand or not, but she certainly wasn't royalty to him, so he just shook it. Her fine-boned hand felt small and fragile in his grip.

"I'm Calvin Watters. I'm a former student here."

"Football player, right?" the redhead asked.

"Yes."

"I thought I recognized you." She turned to her leader. "He raced Isaiah yesterday. Everyone has been talking about it."

"Really?" Moore seemed to dissect him with her eyes. "Who won?"

"Isaiah," the redhead answered.

"Yes, he's a quick one."

"I wondered if we could speak," Calvin said.

"I'd be happy to, Mr.—" She hesitated, as if searching for the answer. Like she had already forgotten his name.

He said, "Watters."

"Right. Mr. Watters."

Calvin was sure that Ms. Blondie had purposely forgotten his name, to try to prove that she led the charge in this meeting. Fine with him.

"My room, then?" she asked, as if testing him.

"The meeting room will be fine."

She pouted her lips teasingly. "Pity. You'd find out more in my bedroom."

He ignored her sassy remark and followed her through the front room and down a hallway. The other sorority members seemed to stare at Calvin as he moved through the house, and the PI wondered how many men actually made it in and through that front door.

Moore opened the side door, flicked on a light switch, and waved him inside. He wasn't sure he wanted to turn his back on Moore, because Calvin wasn't sure where Moore's hands would end up when he turned around. But he entered and waited for her.

Moore stepped inside and shut the door. "Have a seat." She gestured to a group of short mahogany tables pushed together to form one long conference-like table, surrounded by dozens of wooden chairs with patterned-white cushioned seats.

Calvin sat down and Moore had the audacity to lean back and half-sit on top of the table beside him. Then she crossed her legs one over the other and started playing with the strap on what looked to be very expensive shoes.

Moore looked as if life had been easy for her: perfectly manicured nails, flawless complexion, and an artificial tan.

She dropped her foot to the ground. "What would you like to know?"

"Samantha Baylor."

"Poor girl. I liked her."

"Really?"

"Yes. She would have been a perfect Delta Gamma candidate. Just what we look for in a pledge."

Not what Calvin had expected. "Did she obey all your rules?"

"Sure."

"Did she do as asked?"

"Yes."

"Did you see her on Saturday night?"

Moore shifted in her seat. "Are you a cop? Because you never showed me a badge, and I'm pretty sure you're not. Who sent you here?"

"Why do you think someone sent me?"

"Why do you want to know about Samantha?"

"I'm curious like everyone else."

She squinted at him, her eyes growing small, scrutinizing. She stood up and flattened out her pleated skirt. "Want a drink?"

"No."

"Suit yourself." She approached a cupboard that turned out to be a well-stocked liquor cabinet. Moore poured herself a drink, added ice and took a small sip.

"Not very ladylike to be drinking this early in the morning."

Moore put her arms out in a 'who gives a shit' gesture. "This is college, right?"

Calvin nodded. "So did you see Samantha Baylor on Saturday night after the game?"

"She attended the party." Another gulp, this time a healthy portion of booze.

"Did you see her leave?"

"I don't think so."

Calvin twisted his lips and said, "Either you did or you didn't."

"I guess I didn't."

Moore seemed to be loosening up. Maybe she would let her guard down. Time to try another route.

"Did you happen to see the fight between her and her boyfriend a little while back?"

Another drink. "Everyone saw and heard that fight."

"What was it about?"

Moore half-smiled, her eyes starting to glaze over slightly. It looked to Calvin that Moore probably didn't drink frequently, and was a light-weight when it came to holding her liquor.

"Let's just say that Mark is the jealous type."

Calvin asked, "Was Baylor cheating on Simon?"

"I wouldn't say cheating, as in ongoing."

"So she cheated?"

"So the rumor goes."

"How goes the rumor?"

"Not exactly sure if she slept with anyone."

"What the hell does that mean?"

"It means, Mark found some texts on her phone. I doubt Samantha would have cheated on him. She would never have gone through with it."

From the police reports and speaking with the detectives, Baylor's phone had never been recovered.

"Do you know who else it involved?"

Moore moved closer to Calvin, squeezing between him and the table. Calvin rolled back on his chair.

"No clue," she whispered, so close to Calvin's face that he could smell the alcohol on her breath.

"So what did Baylor say, exactly, during this fight?"

"I can't remember." She leaned into Calvin, almost falling on him. "Why don't you watch it for yourself? Everyone recorded it, it's all over the internet."

Time to move on. Moore was tipsy, and Calvin wasn't sure he could believe anything more that came out of her mouth. He also didn't want to have Moore's fingerprints all over his clothes.

"Okay, I gotta go."

Her head snapped up. "What? Already? We are just getting started."

He let himself out of the room, and found half a dozen girls staring at him. He wondered how many of them had been standing right outside the door during his meeting. He retraced his steps to the front door, hearing the conference door open and close behind him.

"Thanks for stopping by, Mr. Watters," Moore said, sounding very much like she had miraculously sobered up within minutes. Had she played Calvin back there?

Calvin turned to see Moore smiling at him. She raised her hand, her pinkie to her mouth and thumb to the ear. She mouthed, 'call me'.

The redhead came to her side. "Did Bridgette send him here?"

Moore looked at the redhead with daggers in her eyes.

"Bridgette?" Calvin asked.

Moore repeated, "Thanks for stopping by, Mr. Watters."

"Thanks for your time, Ms.—" He hesitated, as if forgetting.

She ground her teeth. "Very funny."

The door slammed in his face.

"Bridgette? Bridgette who?" Larry had his glasses perched on the end of his nose and stared blankly at his computer screen. He kept one hand on his mouse.

"He didn't say." Charlene scrolled down on her screen.

"Well then how are we supposed to find one girl named Bridgette out of a school with over forty-thousand students? Maybe she isn't even a student anymore."

"Calvin and I both believe she is currently a student."

Larry looked over at her. "Oh really? Since when are you two on the same page?"

"From what Calvin said, the sisters of Delta Gamma assumed that Calvin had spoken to this Bridgette girl. So that tells us that Bridgette is more than likely still a student there, and has some kind of ties to the sorority. And if that's the case, then she could have some insight into Samantha Baylor."

He clicked the mouse button. "Okay, I'm in the school student directory. Looks like there are twenty-six Bridgettes. Do we know how it's spelled?"

"No, Calvin just heard the name. How many different ways are there to spell it?"

Larry squinted his eyes and counted out loud. "Six."

"Great," Charlene said sarcastically. "Forget that. Log onto the Delta Gamma website and let's scroll through the sisters from each year."

"Good thinking."

Larry did as requested and arrowed over to the student lists. "Three last year."

"Okay, check this year's list and see which one of them is no longer there."

"I'm not just another pretty face, Taylor." He clicked his mouse button a couple of times. "Got it, Bridgette Acres."

"Okay, let's find out her contact info and class schedule. We need to speak with her."

"That might take a search warrant or at least some high-level permission, because that would go against their privacy policies. Let's get Calvin on that."

"Perfect. We'll see him at the practice, we can tell him then."

"What are you two working on?"

Charlene looked up and saw Captain Dunbar staring down at her. She could also smell his tobacco stained clothes.

"The cheerleader case, sir."

"Anything yet on Mahoney?"

Charlene always found it amazing how commanding officers could keep track of everything going on in their divisions, no matter the number of cases on the go. But that made the chiefs special, and a cut above the grade, the qualities that helped them achieve those promotions.

"Not yet, sir," Larry said. "From what we saw in Mahoney's dorm room, no sign that he and Baylor had any prior connection or contact. The techs are hacking into his computer to run through it."

Charlene added, "We are still waiting for DNA samples. CSI has pulled fingerprints, gone through the shower drains, brushes, and anything else where Baylor could have left any kind of transfer for us to connect some dots."

Dunbar scratched the three-day stubble on his face. Stress-sweat stains soaked through his shirt. "Did you hear from Gardner yet?"

"Not yet."

Charlene swiveled completely around in her chair to face her captain. "We spoke with Baylor's teachers again, flashed around Mahoney's picture. No one remembers seeing her with him, and they don't share any classes together. Honestly, chief, we are running on dead-ends with this Baylor-Mahoney theory."

"Well, the kid confessed to murdering her, so it isn't exactly a theory, now is it?"

Dunbar didn't talk down to Charlene, but every time his deep-throated tone rose slightly, it felt like a harsh-rebuke, like a slap on the hand from a seasoned veteran investigator to a rookie detective.

"We'll find something, boss," Larry butted in, as if sensing some tension.

Charlene exhaled, thankful for the interruption.

As the chief walked away, Charlene's cellphone rang. The detective checked caller ID. "It's Gardner."

It wasn't a 'good' thing that Charlene had Dr. Edward Gardner's cell number already saved in her phone. Most cops could shrug it off as working with the LAPD lead criminal psychologist, but Charlene had a much closer, more intimate relationship with the doctor. She was Gardner's patient, and had been meeting with him regularly for appointments.

She clicked on. "Detective Taylor."

"Good afternoon, Detective Taylor, this is Dr. Edward Gardner."

The first name probably wasn't necessary. "Did you speak with our suspect, Doctor?"

"Yes I did, Detective. Very interesting."

"What did you find out?"

"Lewis Mahoney is unique, and an interesting piece of work. Do you have time to meet either now or this evening?"

"Sorry, Doc, I'm up to my eyeballs with this case."

The doctor snorted air out through his nose. "Oh yes, the ever-busy LAPD detective. I know the kind well."

"Ask him if our guy is loony-tunes," Larry said.

Charlene shushed Larry with a wave of her hand. "Would it be possible to give me a quick assessment over the phone, Dr. Gardner?"

She knew it wasn't Gardner's style. Everything with him was long and drawn out, very serious. He liked people to know how intelligent he was.

That was more Larry's style, to use terms like: loony-tunes, loose marbles, or cards short of a full deck.

"From our initial interview, I'd say my preliminary assessment of Lewis Mahoney is that the man suffers from paranoid fantasies."

"Did he do it or not?"

"Perhaps. I believe he might think he did it?"

"So is he lying or not?"

"I don't think he's lying, I think he believes he did it."

"Is he capable of that?"

"Doubtful. Mahoney isn't violent. There is a lot more to him though. I will leave a full-written report on your desk in the morning."

"Thanks, Doc." She hung up.

"So?" Larry asked.

"I think we need to find ourselves a new suspect."

"So what are we doing here," Larry asked. "This is Wednesday, that means the last intense team practice in full pads before Saturday's game. This is an important session. Big game coming up."

"We are running a homicide investigation, Larry. I'm certainly not worrying about upsetting any football players preparing for a game." Charlene chewed hard on a stick of gum, a nice change.

"What are we hoping to find out here, tonight?"

"I'm sure by now news of Mahoney's confession has surfaced. So I'm hoping that the real murderer is starting to feel comfortable, cozy, and maybe even confident enough to let his guard down."

"Here? Tonight?"

Charlene shrugged her shoulders. "Who knows?"

A whistle sounded, breaking their conversation. They turned towards the field, where dozens of young men in uniforms jogged towards the head coach who stood in the middle of the field. They huddled around him, some kneeling down on one knee, others standing behind the kneelers. No matter how they entered the circle, every set of eyes were on the coach. He had their full attention, and it showed Charlene the respect the head man warranted.

Charlene's eyes wandered the field and stadium. So many people took part in a football program that it was difficult to keep track of everyone—forty-five starting players, and that didn't include second and third stringers and all of the personnel involved off the field, from coaches to team management.

Although Charlene could not overhear the coach's words, she knew he had a reputation as a player's coach—a motivator who could read his players and knew all of the right buttons to press to get the most out of each individual player.

When the huddle broke, the players ended practice with a cheer, a chant of grunts. Then they turned and started jogging towards the dressing room, steel cleats clicking on the concrete, along with excited chatter.

"I'm going to talk to some players and see if anything is circulating," Larry said. He turned and shuffled off, blending into the groups of players headed toward the locker room. Larry was a big man, and even *he* had to look up when speaking to some of the players, especially members of the offensive line.

Charlene put her foot up on the bench, and started tying her flat-soled lace-up shoes when she heard the gravel on the ground behind her crunching under steel cleats. She could sense the presence of someone standing behind her.

"Consider this your two-minute warning....before I ask you out," said a New England accented voice.

Charlene stopped tying her shoe in mid-lace. It was one of the cheesiest pick-up lines she had ever heard, and it made her want to swing around to see who would have delivered such a lame phrase.

She finished tying and turned around. The detective first saw the gold, number nine short-sleeved jersey showing off corded, veined forearms. When she looked up, she gazed into the hazel eyes of a young-looking, blond kid with a cute, cocky smile and a surfer-tanned face. She'd seen the face many times splattered all over the city: billboards, posters, bus signs.

"Ryan Turner," Charlene said, in almost a whisper.

The kid brushed away wet strands of blond hair from his face. "That's me."

Although they had a key running back, Ryan Turner was USC's one-shot to a championship this season. The offense centered around him. The program's future, the whole season rested on this young man's shoulders. He was a shoe in for a Heisman trophy, expected to break not only school records, but also college records, and a guaranteed first round draft choice to the NFL, when ready to leave school and pursue that path.

"Has that line worked on many girls?"

He grinned. "Is it that bad?"

She had to hand it to the boy, he had guts. Cute, with sharp-angular features, but maybe a little too cute for his own good. He had a cocky, almost adolescent quality to him.

Charlene drew back the bottom right side of her jacket, and tucked it in behind the butt of her revolver lodged in the hip holster. Not only did it reveal her sidearm, but it also showed off the detective's badge attached to her belt.

Turner looked down and his eyes changed. He intentionally averted his gaze away from the gold badge and gun, and put his hands up. "Too bad."

He turned and walked away. The detective stole a glance at the QB from behind, checking out his scrawny buttocks hugged tightly in the shiny polyester spandex-like football pants.

Charlene was about to call him back when her partner came out of the changing facility.

"Just got off the phone with the Cap. Mahoney's parents want to meet with us."

"About what?"

"No idea. But it should be interesting."

"But I want to talk to a few people involved with this team."

"Not worth it."

"What do you mean?"

"Every player I spoke with told me that they'd been instructed not to talk to the police."

Chapter 18

As a PI, working alone for the first time since before college, Calvin appreciated the solitude. On his own he had no one to rely on, and no one else to blame when things didn't go the way he had planned. He was his own boss, made his own hours, and his own decisions. This was more his style.

The Lorenzo Student Housing area brought the ultimate college living experience, only affordable for the wealthier USC students (definitely not Calvin). Lorenzo, an upscale student housing community located within University Park Campus Patrol Area, was a half-mile from the USC campus.

It stood directly adjacent to the Expo Line, which allowed students to travel from Lorenzo to anywhere in LA in no time—the Fashion District, the Grammy Museum, the Staples Center, or the Santa Monica Pier.

Calvin had to use some of his charm to work his way through the secured electronic-access on all doors. All it took was a smile and a nod, and a young woman walking out held the door for him. Why couldn't it have been this easy five years ago as a student?

If you thought the enormity of the outside three-building unit impressed, the inside and amenities blew the mind: fully-furnished student housing apartments, professional sand volleyball court, two indoor basketball courts, virtual gaming and video arcade room, karaoke room, community lounges rooftop sundecks, two gyms, sixteen-seat conference center, four resort-style swimming pools, five rooftop sundecks, four libraries with computer labs and study rooms, a rock climbing wall, and running track and cardio room.

Calvin stood back from the action, ever aware that word had probably spread of his involvement in the case, and although he had yet to speak to any of Baylor's cheerleading teammates, he wasn't sure if any of them recognized him. And even if they didn't, Makayla would surely balk at his presence at a cheerleading practice.

The men and women on the cheer team, in modest practice attire, displayed impressive talent—the way they moved, flipped, jumped and danced—showed both extreme physical strength and synchronized rhythm.

People who questioned the intensity and competitiveness of college cheerleading needed to sit-in on one of their practices—three nights a week, three hours in length, and that was on non-game or competition weeks.

The image of the twirling girls and flashing pompoms took Calvin back to game days, where the cheerleaders, and the fans, went crazy every time he scored. He pictured Makayla's supple body as she had made up a special cheer, for Calvin's touchdowns, that left the crowd breathless.

He waited until the coach blew the final whistle to end practice. When he stepped out from the shadows of the bleachers, female heads turned towards him. A few smiled at him, some smirked, and others looked very surprised.

Calvin guessed they weren't accustomed to spectators during practices, or maybe people even prohibited from entering and watching, but when Calvin started walking towards them, they all stopped and stared.

"It's okay, girls," Makayla yelled. "He's with me. So hands off." She winked at Calvin.

The girls continued to pick up their things—towels, water bottles, pompoms and extra garments—and headed to the change rooms to shower up.

Calvin returned Makayla's smile and approached the assistant coach. She walked towards him, boots clicking sharply.

"Hey, sexy," she said.

Makayla was dressed in a pair of extremely short, frayed denim shorts and a white USC crop-top, probably one size too small. The belly-shirt exposed her naval-piercing.

"Hi," Calvin said shyly. "Are Charlotte Rooney & Alicia Williamson at practice tonight?"

"Yes," Makayla said suspiciously.

"Is everything okay, Ms. Thomas?"

Calvin nodded in acknowledgement towards the coach, who held a concerned expression. Manning hadn't been the cheerleading coach when Calvin attended school but, although he didn't know him, Calvin had heard that Manning was very protective towards his players—as a coach should be.

"Yes, Coach Manning. He's a friend of mine."

"Calvin Watters," the coach said.

Calvin was surprised the coach knew him. "Yes, sir."

"I remember when you wore the colors as a member of the Trojans. You were a hell of a player."

"Thank you, sir."

They shook hands and the coach turned to Makayla. "See you Saturday."

"Have a good one, Coach."

The man left.

"Let me go get them," Makayla said in almost a whisper.

Calvin knew it to be a sensitive topic at a tough time for the team. They had just lost a team member, and Calvin had been a part of a team before so knew it felt like losing a family member. He had to tread lightly, and be aware and sensitive of the girls' emotions.

It wouldn't be an easy interview. He pulled out his phone, used as a recorder, and thought about how to proceed.

Makayla returned with two girls, still dressed in their practice clothing.

"Calvin Watters, this is Alicia and Charlotte."

The girls forced a smile, and one of them smacked on gum, looking completely bored.

Rooney, a sophomore, had a soft face full of pimples, blonde hair pulled into pigtails, and designer sunglasses sitting on the top of her head. Williamson, a third year junior, had furtive violet-blue eyes, and brown hair pinned tightly.

No point in beating around the bush. "Hello, ladies. I'm investigating Samantha Baylor's murder."

"We know."

"You do?"

Rooney said, "The whole campus knows. Everyone is talking about how the great Calvin Watters has come home to find a killer."

Calvin licked his lips. "Can I ask you some questions?"

"I guess so," Williamson said, after adding a slow eye-roll.

"What did you guys do Saturday night?"

Rooney shook her head. "Absolutely nothing."

"You weren't at the game?"

"No," Williamson said. "We weren't cheering that night because Samantha and another girl took our place."

"How did that make you feel?"

"Well, she was a freshman, who had never cheered before."

Rooney butted in. "How would that make you feel?"

Calvin thought about it. "Pissed off."

"Exactly," Williamson said without hesitation. "It wasn't fair."

"But Samantha was real good," Rooney added. "She deserved to be there."

Williamson sighed audibly. "So we were mad, it doesn't mean we killed anyone."

"Did you go to the party after the game?"

The girls looked at each other.

"Tell the truth, girls," Makayla said, acting like a strict mother hen.

"Yes," the girls said in unison.

Makayla nodded. "I heard them talking about it in the dressing room."

The cheerleaders looked at Makayla and sneered.

Calvin prompted them back on course. "Did you see Samantha at the party?"

"Of course. We didn't cheer that night, but we were still part of the team. We still hung out and partied together."

"Did you see her leave?"

"I never noticed," Rooney said.

"Me neither," said Williamson.

"So you never saw her again after the party?"

They looked at each other. "No. We didn't."

"What time did you guys leave the party?"

They both shrugged their shoulders.

"Who were you with when you left?"

Their faces flushed. They looked at each other.

"Girls," Makayla said.

"Boys," Williamson said. "Just a couple of boys."

"Which boys? Football players?"

The girls reddened. Judgmental or not, it was none of Calvin's business who the girls went home with, but the guys' names as alibis crossed the girls off a list of potential suspects, because as of now, everyone at that party was a suspect.

"Isaiah and Cameron."

Calvin knew Isaiah Watson. The Cameron the girls were referring to must have been Cameron Roberts, a defensive tackle. Because Calvin had been following the team, following USC football ever since he'd been shunned by the program, he knew most of the starters by name.

"I have to ask this, girls. When did you two say goodbye to the guys?"

They breathed in a few times, swallowed hard, teetered back and forth on the balls of their feet, looking totally uncomfortable, almost embarrassed.

"What you say to me doesn't leave this conversation. I know you don't know me so you can't know if I'm sincere, but I promise you. You have my word."

Makayla said, "He can be trusted, girls. I vouch for him."

Calvin added, "I need to know for alibis."

The girls jerked their head towards Calvin. "Are we suspects? Are Isaiah and Cameron suspects?"

"Honestly, girls, everyone at that party is a suspect."

"But I thought Lewis admitted to doing it? He's nuts and it seems like something he would do."

"You know Lewis Mahoney?"

Rooney nodded. "Anyone connected to the football team knows Lewis. He's addicted to the program."

Calvin rubbed the skin on his face. "Really?"

"Oh yeah, absolutely. He gives his heart and soul to the team. But there's something not right about him."

"Did you see him at the party?"

Williamson shook her head. "He never came inside. He's extremely shy and keeps to himself. He doesn't like crowds, but he usually hangs around."

"Was he outside the party?"

"I think I saw him standing out there. I can't be certain though," Rooney said.

"He's usually always there, though, standing and watching from the path. The football players try to get him to come in, but he never does," Williamson added.

"Well, not all of them. Some of them are assholes to him," Rooney countered.

"I still need to investigate all possibilities," Calvin said. He wrote as fast as they spoke. "So, back to my original question: what time did you guys say goodnight to the boys?"

Williamson looked at Calvin, a sly grin tugged at the corners of her mouth. "The next morning."

When the girls left, in his peripheral vision, Calvin saw Makayla's head jerk around towards him.

"How about a night cap?" she asked.

When Charlene and her partner walked into the LAPD Detective Bureau in room 637, it felt as if a hush fell over the cops. Of course, Charlene knew that it hadn't, but nonetheless, a strange feeling swept over her when she walked into the building at 100 West First Street. This was her home every day, where she worked, the place she was accustomed to.

Now, being summoned to the office by the parents of a murder suspect, a new sensation overcame her. Tonight felt like she stood on enemy territory. Why would parents of a murder suspect want to meet the lead detectives on the case, right here at the detective bureau?

"You ever see anything like this?" Charlene asked Larry.

"Nope."

The fact that her partner had never been through a meeting like this, with over thirty years on the force and hundreds of cases, said something.

Lewis Mahoney's parents, along with their attorney, awaited the detectives in a back room in the detective bureau. Charlene walked into the room with the feeling of heading into a bear trap.

What kind of bomb were these people about to drop. Why didn't they want Charlene's captain and the DA present? Were they going to try to cut some sort of deal, off the record?

Charlene still believed in Mahoney's innocence. So far, there had been nothing found in Mahoney's phone or computer on Samantha Baylor. Absolutely no indication that Mahoney knew Baylor, let alone dated her. All of this news only helped to confirm Charlene's theory of Mahoney's innocence.

"Thank you for coming, Detectives," the attorney said, glancing over her bifocals.

Sarah Schmidt, the prototypical attorney to the rich, looked as if she had been at it for a long time. Her black hair was streaked with gray, and she was dressed to the nines in an expensive-looking, well-cut pantsuit in a conservative navy color.

Although recently divorced, Mahoney's parents, both mother and father, sandwiched the attorney. They didn't look at each other, but at least they handled themselves in a civilized manner and could be in the same room together.

Melissa White, who now went by her maiden name, had a lipless mouth and dirty-blond hair, cut in a bob. Charlene noticed that Aaron Mahoney, Lewis' father, still wore a wedding band on his left hand. He had a coarse five-o'clock shadow on his face, and small, deep-set eyes.

From their file, Charlene knew that the Mahoneys had money. The detectives sat down, Charlene still having said nothing. She and Larry had agreed to remain stone-faced, and wait for the Mahoneys to play their hand. Obviously this meeting had been well rehearsed in advance, and the Mahoneys probably told what they could and couldn't say.

"When can we speak to your client?" Larry asked.

"Lewis has had a long day," Melissa White responded in a disembodied voice. "He's had to work with two psychologists so he's very tired."

"Lewis isn't well," Aaron Mahoney spoke up.

It looked as if the Mahoneys' attorney had given the parents the green light to speak, something Charlene hadn't seen much. Normally the lawyer handled the conversation and allowed the odd comment from clients.

"How's that?" Charlene asked, even though she already had Dr. Gardiner's initial assessment.

"He hasn't been well for some time. We've known that." She strained her neck to stare at her ex-husband. "But *we* chose to ignore it and look the other way. *We* thought that Lewis might outgrow his problems." She looked down into her lap. "But I guess *we* were wrong."

The detective gazed back and forth between Mahoney's mother and father. They refused to look at each other, and Charlene could see the animosity that had torn them apart. Was Lewis the reason for his parents' separation? Had having a child with mental health issues created a wedge between them?

Without saying anything, the attorney slid a document across the table at the detectives. Charlene picked it up.

"That is a doctor's report from three years ago. Lewis Mahoney, diagnosed with delusional disorder." Charlene read the evaluation as the attorney continued to speak. "Delusional disorder is generally a rare mental illness in which the patient presents delusions, but with no accompanying prominent hallucinations, thought disorder, or mood disorder." She sounded like she was quoting someone.

Schmidt was good, and well prepared for this meeting, unlike Charlene and Larry. The detectives still hadn't received Gardiner's written, complete evaluation, so they were caught off-guard with this.

"We thought going off to college would mature Lewis, and help him outgrow this. Our doctor said he was at no risk to himself or anyone else," White said.

Schmidt continued with her citation. "Delusions can be fixed false beliefs that involve situations that could potentially occur in real life. Apart from their delusions, people with delusional disorder may continue to socialize and function in a normal manner and their behavior does not necessarily seem odd."

Charlene put the paper back down on the desk.

"So you sent a troubled kid away to school, all by himself?" Larry asked.

"Lewis has never shown any violence towards anyone, ever. He's a gentle, well behaved kid who sometimes daydreams," the father's voice held a defensive tone. "We would never risk Lewis' or anyone else's health."

Melissa White pulled her chair in closer to the table, and it made a scraping noise on the floor. "We made sure to place Lewis in a safe, comfortable environment. We made arrangement for him to stay at Harris Hall for a reason. The males and females are in different sections, every floor has a laundry room, the study rooms and television lounges on each floor offer both quiet reading space and an excellent place to meet with friends, all residents have a required full meal plan. We thought this to be the best path to encourage Lewis' success at school."

Charlene hadn't overlooked that both Lewis Mahoney and Samantha Baylor were USC freshmen. Seven freshmen residence halls existed, so always a chance that Mahoney and Baylor crossed paths in their residence. But Baylor had stayed at Marks Hall, on the south side of USC, and Mahoney lived in residency on the north side, proving even further that they probably had no contact prior to Baylor's death.

"Lewis had signed a waiver to avoid counsel," Charlene said.

"Detective." Schmidt pursed her lips. "That paper you just read clearly indicates that Lewis Mahoney is not of sound mind to make his own legal decisions."

Charlene sighed. "So what have you gotten out of your client that can help us clear him? So far, nothing you have told us eliminates him as a suspect. We have an eye witness report that puts Lewis at the party, in the vicinity of Samantha Baylor only hours before her murder."

"I think Lewis is covering for someone," Aaron spoke up.

He must have caught his counsel off guard, because both Melissa White and Sarah Schmidt looked at him with confusion in their eyes.

"Did he tell you that?" Larry asked.

"Not in so many words."

"Hang on, Aaron." Schmidt had placed a small hand on Mr. Mahoney's forearm to stop him from speaking. "Maybe we should discuss what you may or may not have heard."

Mahoney pulled his arm away from the attorney's grasp. "Lewis is no killer. He would never have done this."

It was against every police unwritten rule, and even though Larry had discouraged her from coming forward, she had to take a chance. "I agree."

Now everyone stared at Charlene. The parents both had gaped mouths.

"Taylor," Larry whispered.

Charlene ignored her partner. "I don't think Lewis did it either, but there is no evidence yet that shows us he didn't."

"Let's be honest, Detective. There's no evidence that says he did it, either."

"Except his confession."

Schmidt leaned back in her chair and smoothed out her jacket.

Charlene nodded. "Mr. Mahoney, tell us what you believe."

He looked at his attorney tentatively, and Schmidt gave a slight nod, as if to say, 'tread carefully.'

"I truly believe that Lewis saw something, and believes that he is involved somehow."

"Do you have proof of this?"

He shook his head. "No. But the way Lewis spoke with me, not so much in his words, but in his tone and manner. Lewis and I communicate frequently and we've been through a lot."

"And I've been an absentee mother?" White's voice had a harsh edge to it.

"Stop." Charlene stood up. "I don't care about your relationship. What you do on your own time is none of my business. Let's stay focused on your son, and this case."

Both parents leaned back in their chairs from the rebuke, as if taken aback.

Charlene plopped back down and spoke to Aaron, while staring at Melissa. "Go on, Mr. Mahoney."

"Lewis has always had this thing, where he sees something happen and believes that he is involved somehow. And he's very protective. When he really cares about something or someone, he will do anything for them. Lewis might very well believe he killed that girl, because he saw something, maybe even the murder itself."

"I can get it out of him, Detective," Melissa White said.

Even though the detective should have been ecstatic with this statement, now Charlene worried. This case had grown personal between Mahoney's parents, and there could be a pissing match between the two that would cloud everyone's judgment, and cover-up the truth. Both parents blamed each other for their son's problems.

"We need a sperm sample from Lewis."

"What? Why?" Schmidt demanded.

"Samantha Baylor had sexual intercourse shortly before her death. If Lewis' sperm doesn't match what we pulled from Baylor, then that will make Lewis' guilt that much less likely."

White stood up. "This is absurd."

Charlene shrugged her shoulders and stood up as well. "Okay. That's fine. We need to talk to Lewis then, and soon. Enough of this bullshit."

Now Larry stood up. "Whoa, whoa, let's all calm down." He looked at the attorney. "Have your client prepped to speak with us tomorrow."

Schmidt stood up, now only Aaron Mahoney remained seated. "We'll have him ready for you tomorrow, and we'll have your semen sample. Please, sit back down."

Chapter 19

Calvin checked the clock on his phone. He should have been going home to Rachel, since she'd texted three times in the last ten minutes wondering where he was. But she knew coming here that the majority of his time would be wrapped up in investigating this murder. He had pleaded with her to stay in Vegas, but she needed to get out of the city and deserved a break of her own.

So he found himself back at the Los Angeles Memorial Coliseum, home of the Trojans. Something bothered the PI about the whole scene, the details of the homicide investigation. Calvin couldn't help but wonder how nobody, not one person, had seen or heard anything from that night, when two security guards had been on duty, and surveillance surrounded the venue.

All the tapes were clean and the guards both admitted to seeing nothing.

Standing at the back of the building, at the player's entrance, Calvin turned and looked around. It was late in the evening, starting to darken, and nobody else was around. He stood alone, other than a security camera looking down at him.

Calvin entered the coliseum via the players' and coaches' entrance. Every team personnel knew that these doors remained unlocked well into the night, so that coaches and players could stay late to finish up any game preparation needed.

Once inside, he walked through the empty halls, the only glow given off by dim-bulbed florescent night lights. Strolling the darkened lobbies, the PI had his iPhone flashlight illuminated, flashing it out in front of him.

It was eerily quiet. Calvin had never been in the stadium this late at night. He was more accustomed to the stadium on game day, when there wasn't an empty seat in the house, the halls streamed with bodies, and snack area lined with hungry patrons. The stands filled with enthusiastic and energetic fans.

He scanned the walls with his light. A large, billboard-sized poster of Ryan Turner, the USC golden-boy, clung to the concrete-blocked wall. The Trojan football program depended on Turner this season. An athletic director's dream—young, handsome, talented, and a Californian. He had a bright future....if he could stay healthy.

After about fifteen minutes of walking, Calvin looked around. He still had yet to see either of the security guards. He was aware that the aging Wayne Parker, who had spent years on the rounds, practically laid up in the office. But where was Tiana? How often did she make her rounds?

At the next entrance, Calvin slipped out of the lobby hallway and moved towards the seating area. When he exited the short hall, it opened up into the inside of the stadium. He was on the first level at the Olympic Arches, Peristyle and Court of Honor end, with a full view of the playing field.

He just stood and gazed, basking in the beauty of the stadium field. An impressive sight.

He reached the aisle at the end of his row of seats and took the stairs down towards the field. He easily scissor-stepped over the bottom guard rail that separated the first row of seats from the field, and hit the field grass in the home team's end zone.

Calvin walked across the soft, freshly-mowed Bermuda grass. It wasn't completely dark, but he still flashed his light as he moved, not sure exactly what he was looking for, until he reached the twenty-yard line on the opponent's side of the field.

The area covering the twenty-yard line into an opposing team's end zone was known as the Red Zone, deemed the most important area in football, and when a team got the ball within twenty yards of scoring, it became a dangerous place. Defenses tightened up, pressure intensified and gaps shrunk.

Teams expected to score, and the best teams in football always had the best "red zone offense" efficiency.

Calvin, being the US military history buff, understood that the term "Red Zone" had originated in the military for an area particularly dangerous, an area within firing range of the enemy that had no cover.

He flashed his light around the exact spot where Samantha Baylor's body had been discovered. Partial remnants of an investigation remained, with a few police markers still visible. But the area had been somewhat cleaned up, since nothing more of use had been recovered, and a football game would be played there in a few days.

With a major NCAA football program involved, all red tape, bureaucratic bullshit got expedited.

Multiple footprints ran to and from the body location, but the majority of them, the most trampled area, went from the body towards where the USC team entered from the dressing room to the playing field. So that seemed like the most logical direction to head.

Using his light as a guide, the former Trojan tried his best to step lightly towards the entrance, to avoid most of the implanted footprints already on the ground. Calvin noticed nothing unusual or out of place as he reached the concrete section of the walkway.

Night had fallen, blackening out the vicinity. Unless the murderer had a light, Calvin couldn't see someone unfamiliar with the area able to move freely in the dark. The stadium offered no lighting on the football field itself, giving anyone a difficult time to move about. Most people today, since everyone owned cellphones, had access to lighting.

But a light would have been picked up or seen by someone, wouldn't it have?

As Calvin moved into the concrete hallway that led to the Trojan dressing room, the PI's light picked up a dark spot on the wall at about his shoulder level. In the light of day, the lighter color difference would never have been picked up. Now pitch black, Calvin's light beaming a shadow on the wall, the discernible shade change was noticeable, albeit only slightly.

The circle of light grew larger as Calvin approached the wall. It was miniscule, almost more of a short smear, but a definite stain, darkish rouge in color. He held the light right up to it, but the blot had dried up.

Blood? Could have been, right color, but nothing certain. Even if it was, it could have belonged to anyone, put there at any time. It could have been an angry football player who punched the wall. There are a number of ways and a number of people who could have left it there, if anything at all. Maybe just dirt.

Calvin would have to call it in and get some sort of forensic team here to test it. He pulled out his phone, looked up Detective Taylor's contact information from his list, and dialed her number. The call went straight to voice mail.

"Detective Taylor, this is Calvin Watters. I think I found something at the Coliseum. Could be nothing, but could be something. Call me back." He hung up.

Calvin got down on his knees and shone the light close to the concrete floor, looking for a droplet that would help prove his theory that the smear on the wall was actually blood.

After methodically searching the floor for ten minutes, Calvin determined that if indeed blood, it hadn't belonged to anyone going towards the players' dressing room. So, he changed directions and searched in the location heading back out towards the field.

After another exhaustive and lengthy search, Calvin found no blood spatter or drops on the concrete or grass heading out towards the body. There could be a number of explanations for this, one of them being that the injury had just been a scratch, therefore no blood would be leaking.

Also, the grass had been mowed so if blood was on the grass blades, it would have been eliminated.

Discouraged, the PI treaded back out towards the lobby. As he exited the Bermuda-grassed end zone, a noise attracted his attention. Something or someone snuck around inside the lobby area. Was someone watching him? Following him?

Paranoia sunk in. After everything he had been through the last few years, his radar twitched.

He quickened his pace towards the sound, his light shining out. As he rounded the corner, he walked right into a small, slender woman. She released a breath of air and fell to the ground. Calvin shined his light on her.

"Tiana?"

"Calvin?" She shielded her eyes from Calvin's bright iPhone light. "Is that you?"

"Yes."

"I thought I heard something."

Calvin shone his light to the ground to avoid her eyes and helped her back up to her feet.

"What are you doing here?" she asked.

"Investigating."

"Still? I thought someone confessed to that murder?"

"He did. But there is still no evidence against him."

She breathed hard through her nose. "You mean his confession isn't enough?"

"Not always."

"How did you get in here?"

"I came in through the coach's entrance."

She chuckled. "Figured as much."

"You know about that?"

She swatted her hand at him. "I know you boys been usin' that entrance for years."

Leave it to Tiana to let the players slide a bit.

"I think I found something important."

"Really? What? Where?"

"I'm not sure yet, but it looks like blood."

"Where?"

Calvin said, "Back there, in the hallway leading from the field to my old dressing room."

"Really?"

"Yes."

"Can I go check it out?"

Even though Tiana worked as a security guard, she saw herself as some sort of cop.

"Sure, go ahead."

Tiana left him and headed towards where Calvin told her.

He took a couple of deep breaths, his heartbeat starting to slow. He hadn't realized that Tiana had startled him, and his breathing just now returned to normal. Or maybe it was from the excitement of finding some potential evidence that the LAPD had missed.

Calvin started moving towards the exit when he heard a clatter behind him. As he turned, something hard came down on the top of his head. The room moved, and shadows appeared before him.

He took a step forward and wobbled. He grew lightheaded and dizzy, a ringing in his ears increasing.

It took his brain a few seconds to register, a brief delay in his response. "Wait—" his speech slurred.

His knees started to buckle, and he collapsed into unconsciousness.

Charlene punched off her phone and put it away. The hallways were black at the Coliseum, so the detective had her Maglite out.

She'd just listened to Calvin's message, something about possibly finding something connected to the case. She'd have been here earlier if Mahoney's parents hadn't wanted her to stay, to plead their case about their son's state of mind, and his *obvious* mental illness.

Either Mahoney's parents and lawyer tried to cover up for the kid, or they felt exactly the same way as Charlene felt. Mahoney was innocent, and either covered for someone or was totally delusional. Either way, he couldn't have done it, but the LAPD still hadn't found anything to prove his innocence, or confirm anyone else's guilt.

She scoured the hallway walls. Watters' phone message was vague, and told Charlene nothing about where in the Coliseum he waited, or what he thought he had discovered. Charlene didn't like PIs, and even though Watters' reputation preceded him, Charlene still wasn't quick to trust him.

She had entered at Gate Thirty-one, by the 'Court of Honor', so if Watters strolled on the other side of the stadium, it could take twenty minutes to find him. She pulled her phone back out and, as she moved gradually towards the playing field, dialed Watters' number. The heels from her shoes clanked on the freshly cleaned concrete floor.

When the dial tone rang in her ear, Charlene was sure she heard a phone ring in the distance, the vibration echoing throughout the empty hallway. The detective followed the sound, a random ringtone, but the sound matched perfectly to the tone in Charlene's ear. She let it ring three more times before it forwarded to voice mail.

She rounded the corner at Gate Twenty-eight, and saw a form in the shadows about forty yards away. It was tough to make out anything in the darkness, and when Charlene raised her light and shone it towards the images, it looked like someone hovering over a body.

"Hey!" Charlene yelled.

The figure moved, as if looking towards Charlene. The detective proceeded towards the person. Something fell to the floor, clanking loudly on the concrete. It sounded like something metal. The dark form turned and took off in the opposite direction.

"Wait!" Charlene screamed.

She picked up her pace, rushing towards where the person had been, light still out shining in front of her. The lump on the floor turned out to be a large body, unmoving. Charlene rolled him over and shone the light towards his face.

Calvin Watters. His eyes remained closed and a metal pipe lay on the floor beside Calvin's head.

"Shit!"

She knelt down next to the PI, and shook his shoulder lightly. "Calvin," she said.

No response. She chewed on her lower lip.

Charlene placed her index and middle finger on the side of Calvin's neck, in the soft hollow area just beside his windpipe. It took some time for her to find the pulse, moving her fingers around a bit, but it was definitely there. Breathing, but unconscious.

The hit to the head must have caused trauma to Calvin's brain. She used her watch to count seconds, count how many beats she felt in a minute.

Calvin's breath stirred slow and deep.

She touched the PI's shaved scalp and felt a sticky wetness, blood already leaking from the gash on his head caused by the impact from the steel bar.

Charlene looked around the empty corridor. The detective understood the LAPD foot pursuit policy. Officers had to be mindful that immediate apprehension of a suspect was rarely more important than the safety of the public and department members.

The fact that Calvin was injured and Charlene alone, were reasons enough to not continue a foot pursuit.

"Oh, my God!"

The voice spun Charlene around, drawing her gun from her holster. It was outstretched and aimed, finger tight on the trigger. Someone ran towards them.

"Freeze," Charlene said.

The person slowed, but did not stop, now moving at a walker's pace.

"What happened to Calvin?"

Charlene recognized the female voice. She shone the light up into her face. Tiana Washington, the head of security from the Coliseum.

"Do you have a phone?"

Washington nodded.

"Stay here with him, and call nine-one-one," Charlene ordered, hearing the urgency in her voice.

"Where are you going?"

But the detective had already stood up and raced towards where the person had vanished, now almost three minutes ago. The person had a huge head start, and the chances of Charlene catching him or her, slim.

She stopped and listened, hoping for footfalls in the empty corridor—nothing. Charlene remained at a standstill. The detective had to make a guess as to which way the suspect ran. Did he leave, or was he in hiding, somewhere inside the coliseum.

Charlene could hear her own pounding heartbeat.

She exited the Coliseum at Gate Nineteen, and ran out towards Exposition Park Drive. There were no signs of any vehicles or traffic. The parking lots bare. If the guy had a car parked there, then he was long gone.

Exposition Drive made a 'U' turn completely around the Coliseum, and ran both ends into Bill Robertson Lane.

The detective stepped out into the middle of the roadway and spun around, checking both directions. No sign of anyone.

She dropped her arm and gun to her side and made her way back to Calvin, calling for an ambulance on her cellphone as she moved.

Book III

From the Grave

Chapter 20

When she opened her eyes at the crack of dawn, the grogginess settled in. She blinked half a dozen times to clear her thoughts. Charlene shifted her head on her pillow switching sides, looking at the empty spot on the futon that Matt had filled only yesterday.

The first morning this week waking up without Matt beside her. It's not as if she was accustomed to waking up beside men, not since her last boyfriend, Andy, had left her life.

Most of Charlene's adult life had been filled with men coming and going, never staying long, only lingering enough to get what they wanted, and what Charlene wanted. Most men left that same night. That's just how Charlene had wanted it, liked it—no obligations, no expectation, no unhappy endings.

But this was different.

Hell, it had only been four days, three nights spent together. He comes and goes, but in a different manner than all those other guys.

Charlene admitted that there had been a time in her life when she appreciated the reckless, carefree lifestyle. It was fun, but she also knew that there would come a time when it would be time to grow up.

Her family hadn't agreed with the way Charlene had lived her life.

Aware that a life of an on-the-run LAPD detective would be hectic, and makes it almost impossible to manage any kind of personal or social life, Charlene accepted that, and had always dreamed of following in her dad's footsteps.

Children, a family of her own, was something that the detective had never imagined for herself. That was her sister Jane's role, who loved being a wife and mother, and who excelled at both.

It wasn't as if Charlene hadn't had a maternal role model to follow. Brenda Taylor had been an exceptional mother figure to both Jane and Charlene. It was a father that Charlene never had. But the younger daughter admitted to herself that she was as much to blame for that as her busy, overworked LAPD detective father.

Martin Taylor had Charlene in his forties, probably hadn't expected any more children, or maybe didn't even want them. He had his career to focus on, and he was a damn good cop, maybe one of the best ever to don the dark blue uniform, and LAPD badge.

Old school to the bone. He didn't believe that Charlene, or any woman, should carry herself as his daughter had. Charlene's mother played the role of house-wife to perfection: suppers ready, house tidied, doting over her tired, stressed-out husband.

But this was 2020, and that wasn't Charlene Taylor. The detective rolled onto her back and stared at the ceiling.

Her dad. They'd had only two things in common: the Dodgers and being cops. And after all these years, Charlene still had a passion and love for both.

She rolled off the futon and on to her knees, then stood up to multiple cracking sounds from her knees. Reaching her hands to the ceiling, Charlene stretched out her spine. She arched her back, her spaghetti-strapped pajama shirt riding up to reveal her naval piercing—another souvenir from a night of binge drinking with her friends.

Tattoos and piercings were more things that drove her father nuts, and her body displayed both.

She rummaged through the dirty-clothes hamper in the bathroom, finding her running clothes in the covered up bottom. It had been almost a week since Charlene followed her morning routine, a challenging jog through the city streets. She had been getting her extra-curricular morning fitness exercise in other ways, when Matt had been around.

She slipped into her workout garments and left her apartment, skipping down the steps of her building to the parking lot. There, she performed a quick stretch to warm-up, plugged her iPhone buds into her ears, cranked up the tunes and took off in a light trot.

Charlene had been running for years. It had started as a morning routine in college, where she'd learned that excessive sweating could cure a hangover. It eliminated headaches and got her mind set and prepared for a heavy workload of school courses.

She kept the routine alive long after college for different reasons, even though she still suffered from hangovers and morning nausea.

Two important factors for the workout:

One, Charlene loved to push herself. She had always been a self-motivated, self-driven woman. She had always had a need to prove herself to everyone else, the doubters, and the naysayers. She held a grudge against those who said she 'couldn't', it only drove her harder, and increased her desire to succeed.

The second reason was that now, the jogs helped her process everything going on around her.

There was never an 'off' moment for a detective—no punch-out clock, or time to sit back and enjoy the ride. It was constant, case after case, always on call and on the go. Charlene had cop blood running through her. Born with the gene, she couldn't just turn off a switch and let it go. The detective could never shut down, cases ran through her mind in a constant loop.

So now, jogging, meant time for thinking—run scenarios in her head, go through the suspect inventory, catalog evidence, and anything else pertaining to the investigation. To get her head straight for another day in detective-land.

Today, it was all about the Cheerleader Case—Samantha Baylor's murder.

Lewis Mahoney couldn't be guilty. Charlene was sure of that. He had a history of mental illness, delusional, but everything in his file told the detective that the first year USC student was incapable of murder.

Nothing in Mahoney's computer or phone suggested he had any kind of relationship with Baylor. Mahoney's roommate admitted the same. He had to be covering for someone.

Charlene expected to get lab results back today from Mark Simon's semen sample. The boyfriend was always the first suspect, and in this case, plausible. Simon was seen at the post-game party with Baylor. They had been broken up weeks ago, but seemed to be on the mend and had worked through the rough patch. What motive did Simon have to kill his girlfriend?

What motive did anyone have to murder a freshman cheerleader? Who felt threatened enough to do that?

As for enemies: cheer teams were competitive. Girls who grew up around it would give anything to be a part of a cheerleading team, especially one as high-end as USC. Girls worked their whole lives for that opportunity. They gave scholarships for that kind of commitment.

Charlotte Rooney and Alicia Williamson had lost their starting spots on the team to Samantha Baylor. Baylor was a first year cheerleader, with no experience, and someone who hadn't given her time and life to the sport. Hard feelings? Maybe. Hatred so deep that a murder would be committed? Doubtful.

Sororities have always been a high-stakes game. Each sorority fought year after year against each other for the newest, most eligible freshmen recruits. Samantha Baylor would have been a high draft choice: straight 'A' student, beautiful, part of the USC cheer squad.

There had been many rumors about sororities using objectionable techniques to attract eligible members, and even worse tactics for initiation. Anything goes when it came to rookie initiations, placing the girls in uncomfortable, embarrassing situations, to downright nasty forms of hazing.

Emma Moore and Mia Davidson, the two ladies in charge of the USC branch of Delta Gamma, were very high on themselves, and very protective of their sorority. There was absolutely no proof that Samantha Baylor had been exposed to any form of hazing exercises, and everyone who had been spoken to stated that Baylor was a shoo-in to become a sister. So what would be the motivation to kill her? Jealousy? Of what?

One of today's major tasks was to find Bridgette Acres, the girl who had quit the Delta Gamma team. What was she hiding from, and what made her leave the organization?

Once Charlene turned off West Maryland Street onto South Lucas Avenue, she picked up the pace of her run, needing the perspiration and increased heart rate, the morning sun warm on her back. Her new route turned down West Fourth Street and passed by the Children's Home Society of California.

The sight reminded Charlene of an old case she had worked, and continued to follow-up on.

Ever since Charlene had made friends with seven year-old Lauren Schwartz, a possible abuse victim, the detective had made it a mission to look into different living arrangements for the young girl. Charlene had yet to find evidence against Lauren's scumbag stepfather, but the detective wouldn't rest until she got Lauren out of her destructive household. The detective had a soft spot for the seven year-old.

South Bixel Street signaled to Charlene that she had hit the halfway point through her run, and time to turn it up even more. She gained speed, weaving around people crowding the sidewalk. Her breathing grew heavier, sweat dripping into her eyes.

Take your mind off the burning chest and lungs—back to the case.

There was still no evidence to point in any one direction. No suspect stood out. Charlene had never been a part of an investigation that had taken so long for something pertinent to turn up, unusual. It had been four days since Baylor's body had been discovered.

Something had to give.

Her mind wandered to last night, the medics and police showing up at the Coliseum. Charlene had confiscated the metal pipe used on Calvin, who had been out cold. Paramedics rushed him to the hospital.

But Calvin Watters was tough, and Charlene had no doubt he would bounce back. But who had been behind that unprovoked attack?

His eyelids felt heavy as he tried to open them. A buzzing in the base of his skull prickled, and his brain felt on fire. When his eyes finally fully opened, Calvin gazed at the square-tiled ceiling.

The lighting dimmed. Where was he and how had he gotten there?

"He's awake."

The voice startled Calvin, the noise piercing his ear drums. He turned his head painfully and saw Rachel rushing towards him. Behind Rachel stood his brother, Josh, looking tired, and a little bit concerned.

"Oh my God, baby. Are you okay?" Rachel ran to his bedside and kissed his forehead lightly.

"Ya, I'm fine." Calvin barely recognized his own voice—small, low.

He attempted to sit up but his temple throbbed, and sweat bubbled on his scalp. He fell back down onto the hospital bed.

"Whoa, take it easy, bro." Calvin's brother now at his side, placing a protective hand on his shoulder. "You've had a rough night."

Calvin tried to sit up again, and this time, with his brother's strong arm, he wriggled into an upright position.

"What happened?" Calvin asked.

"I was hoping you'd tell us."

Rachel's face showed worry. They'd been through a lot, and Calvin knew that his life, his occupation, would always carry some sort of consequences and possible trauma.

He rubbed his eyes. "I can't remember. How did I get here?"

"Detective Taylor."

Calvin looked at his brother. "What?"

"She phoned for an ambulance, and then she called me," Josh said. "Told me that she found you on the floor at the Coliseum. You got hit on the head. Do you remember anything?"

Calvin blinked his eyes shut, squeezing them hard, trying to recall anything from last night—his mind foggy.

Something had happened, but his memory lapsed in and out, coming back in snapshot images. He'd been hit, something hard over his head.

"Did they find the guy who hit me?"

Josh grimaced. "No. He took off. What do you remember from before the incident?"

Calvin shook his head. "I can't." He rested his head back on the pillow, reaching for any kind of memory. "It's not there."

Josh asked, "What were you doing at the Coliseum?"

Calvin rubbed his forehead, squeezing his temples, his brain foggy. He recalled walking through the deserted hallways. But what had happened next?

The room door opened, a beam of light flashing in through the crack, stinging Calvin's retinas. He squinted, lifted his hands to shield his eyes, a black image coming towards him out of the shadows.

"Mr. Watters, I'm Dr. Tomlinson."

The doctor, standing the same height as Rachel because of a stoop in his posture, had small regular features.

"Hey, Doc."

He flipped a couple of pages on his clipboard. "You took quite a shot." He looked at Josh. "Do we know what he was hit with?"

"Metal pipe."

"Ouch."

Calvin touched his scalp again, the point where most of the pain centered around. He felt a bandage wrap, and a bump the size of a golf ball. At least the nurses hadn't had to shave his already bald head. Just brushing his fingers over the wound shot needles of pain through him.

He knew he had grimaced when the doctor said, "Don't touch, it's still very tender. You have severe head trauma. We did a CT scan but there doesn't seem to be any permanent damage to the brain. A little bit of swelling which should reduce with time and rest."

"It hurts like hell," Calvin said.

"It will, for a while. We'll feed you some medication for the pain." He pulled out a tiny light and flashed it at Calvin.

"Whoa, Doc. That stings."

"Sorry." He lowered the light. "Your eyes are still dilated. You've suffered a concussion, and we will have to monitor the symptoms carefully."

"When can I leave?"

"We'd like you to stay for observation."

Calvin shook his head quickly, but it felt like his brain rolled around inside his skull. He closed his eyes. "I got a case to work."

"Mr. Watters, you're lucky to be alive. That metal pipe could have caused a lot more damage than what we've found. There are no exact sciences with traumatic brain injuries. It's not like a broken bone."

"Is he going to be alright, Doctor?" Rachel's shaky voice asked.

"I'm fine," Calvin said.

"Most people usually recover fully after a concussion, but as I said, there are no guarantees."

"What are the side effects, Doc?" Josh asked.

"Effects are usually temporary, but can include headaches and problems with concentration, memory, balance and coordination."

Josh grinned. "He's never been that coordinated to begin with."

"Up yours," Calvin said, attempting again to sit up by himself. This time he was able to, although the pressure in his head swelled. "I'm fine."

"He can't remember what happened?"

"Amnesia surrounding the traumatic event is common."

Rachel sniffled. "What can we do for him?"

"His brain needs rest. In the early stages of recovery get plenty of sleep at night, and rest during the day. To rest your brain you need to reduce the demands you make of it."

"I said I'm fine," Calvin's voice rose a decibel, and the others in the room looked at him. Rachel's eyes opened wide. "Sorry."

"Calvin." Rachel leaned over him and put her hand on his shoulder.

The strong scent of her perfume hit his nostrils, a sensation flooding him. "I'm gonna be sick."

Rachel grabbed a waste basket from beside his bed table and gave it to him. Calvin vomited into the can, dry heaving what little contents remained in his stomach. His temples throbbed.

"I'll have the nurse bring in some medication for you. You need rest, Mr. Watters. That's the most important thing right now."

But Calvin didn't have time to rest.

Charlene reached the office feeling refreshed from her morning jog. Indications that the case was actually moving forward sat piled on her desk, in the form of completed files from the designated teams working the investigation: forensics, medical examiner, crime scene investigators, and street cops.

Larry leaned back in his seat munching on a glazed donut, watching her silently. She removed her jacket and threw it on the back of the chair. Sitting down, she rolled up to her desk and turned on the computer.

An evidence bag lay on the detective's desk containing the steel bar from the coliseum. The bag had been labeled with the case number, date, time and details of where it was found.

"No fingerprints found," Larry said, without looking towards Charlene.

"What do you know, Larry?"

"What makes you think I know something?"

"Because you have that smug look on your face every time you find out something before me."

"You know me so well, Taylor."

The female detective tapped on the keyboard to sign in and logged into the internet. Larry opened up the top file, the forensic report.

"Dana dropped this off last night."

"I bet you wish you had been here to greet her."

"I think she wishes I had been here."

Charlene snorted. "Yes, I'm sure of that."

"The semen found inside Samantha Baylor matched Mark Simon's sample."

Charlene pursed her lips, unimpressed. "I think we assumed that. He admitted to having sexual relations with her on the night of her murder."

"He's sterile."

Her fingers stopped, hovering over the keyboard. She turned towards her partner. "What?"

"Simon is sterile."

"Jesus." Had Charlene been holding a mug of coffee, it would've been on the floor.

"I guess Ms. Bible Belt wasn't so innocent after all."

"So that means it wasn't his baby inside Samantha Baylor."

Larry shook his head. "Nope."

She leaned back in her chair, bending it back as far as it went. "Someone else got her pregnant."

"Yep."

The detective bit on the inside of her cheek. "Give me the case file."

He handed it to her. Charlene flipped through the pages, the investigative report which showed procedures, interviews, and all of their findings, to date. Then she double-checked and compared it with the medical examiner's notes.

"According to the ME, Baylor was three to four weeks pregnant." She spoke to no one in particular, but out loud.

Larry swiveled in his chair and rolled over to Charlene's desk with a single leg-thrust. "Yeah."

She flipped pages. "The alleged fight and breakup between Baylor and Simon happened three to four weeks ago. Simon said they worked things out, getting back together, when she was murdered."

"Go on."

"What if someone took advantage of that breakup, when in her most vulnerable state? What if she got pregnant from that one sexual encounter?"

"Hold on, there was no indication that Baylor dated anyone else. Of everyone we interviewed, Baylor's roommate, friends, classmates and team members, not one person mentioned anything about Baylor being with anyone other than Mark Simon."

"What if the conception was a one-time thing? What if it actually happened that night, when Baylor had been drinking and argued with her boyfriend?"

"That's an interesting theory."

Charlene snapped back, "But possible."

"But not probable."

"Why not?"

Larry tugged lightly on his lower lip, seeming to be in thought. "This just opens up our suspect list."

"I think we can agree that Lewis Mahoney is not our murderer?"

Her partner nodded.

"So what now?"

He sighed. "Let's go over the suspects we have. Who has the most to lose? Motive? Opportunity?"

"Mark Simon, the on again, off again, boyfriend. He admitted to having sexual intercourse with Baylor on the night in question, but said goodbye to her prior to her time of death."

"He went home to bed, so no alibi to corroborate his story."

"Do you think he found out she was carrying someone else's baby and snapped?"

"Maybe."

"But from his facial expression and body language, when we mentioned her pregnancy, it seemed like he had no idea."

"True, it looked legit."

"There is absolutely no evidence to support Lewis Mahoney as our murderer. None. Zero."

"Except his confession."

Charlene shook her head. "That still floors me."

"Sorority girls...weak. Nothing says they held any ill-will towards Baylor."

"Cheerleaders were bitter, but not to the point of killing their teammate."

"I agree. Plenty of suspicion, but no probable cause. So back to the drawing board."

"What about that sorority sister dropout? What was her name?"

He checked the report. "Bridgette Acres."

"Yeah, let's try to find her today and check out her story."

"We should also find out who else attended that party where Baylor and Simon broke up. Who else knew about it that night?"

Charlene winked. "Not bad, partner."

"This old dog still has a few good days left."

She smiled. "Maybe I won't have to put you down after all. But let's go check on Calvin, first."

Chapter 21

"How are you feeling?"

"I'm fine, Rachel."

She'd been asking him that same question every ten minutes for the last hour, and Calvin felt a little helpless. Every time he tried to move, his head swam. He couldn't concentrate, and his clumsiness bothered him.

The PI had no stamina when it came to walking around the room. Frequent trips back to bed, to sit down on the edge and catch his breath. He couldn't believe how that one shot had taken so much out of him.

Surprisingly, in all of his years of playing football, high school and then college, a full-contact sport with all of its physical punishment, Calvin had not once sustained a concussion.

Not that there had been any kind of protocol back then, like in the game today. So even if he had had a concussion, he would have been required to play through it, suck it up, and go on. The whole 'concussion' issue had just started to become headline news.

"Let's try again," Rachel said. She took Calvin by the arm.

He pulled it away from her. "I can do it by myself."

He stood up with a grimace, and staggered slightly. Rachel gripped his bicep with her small hand. Again, he jerked his arm away from her grasp, but this time, he felt regret at his treatment of his girlfriend.

"I'm sorry."

"It's okay," Rachel said. Her eyes held compassion. "The doctor said that you wouldn't be yourself for a while."

He moved around the room, slowly. He could see the signs in his physical state as much as his mental state, but tried to ignore them. His reflexes had slowed, his thoughts confused. Calvin felt fatigued all the time. The lights had to remain dimmed because the brightness brought an increase in the pain in his temples.

The door opened, and he and Rachel turned towards it. He recognized the man and woman who walked in, but their names eluded him.

"Hey, Calvin," the woman said.

Calvin hesitated. "Hey."

"How are you feeling?" the man said.

Calvin nodded, looking from the woman to the man. "Okay, thanks."

"Do you remember anything?" Again, the woman.

"No."

"I tried to run the guy down, but I guess I've lost a step in my old age." She raised her hands in defense.

The detective he'd been working with, the one who found him. But what was her name again?

"Detective Taylor," Rachel said. "Thank you so much for finding Calvin and calling us."

That was it. Taylor.

"Of course. It's good seeing you again." Rachel shook hands with Taylor and her partner. The detective looked at Calvin. "Larry and I just wanted to check in."

"Did you see who did this to me?" Calvin asked.

Taylor shook her head. "Definitely a man. But it was too dark. I didn't get an ID, anything like height or size."

Calvin tried to register information, but his brain just didn't cooperate.

The detective looked at him strangely. "You called my cell and left a message. You said you'd found something. Do you remember?"

A nauseating pain buzzed in the base of his skull. The detective's words floated, as if hearing them under water. Her voice, a ghostly sound with a dreamlike quality.

Rachel cut in and said, "We were just about to leave the room and walk around. Would you guys like to join us?"

"Sure."

They left the room. Calvin felt like a child—a toddler who needed someone watching him constantly as they strolled through the hospital hallways. He could hear voices surrounding him, but their words weren't registering, as it took his entire focus and concentration to walk a straight line, moving one foot after the other.

"Calvin—"

"Huh?"

He turned and noticed the female detective speaking to him. What was her name again?

"Mark Simon isn't the father of Samantha Baylor's child."

Many names. Names that he should recognize. "Interesting," was all he could manage. He wanted to sound smart, sound like he knew what he was talking about. But it would be difficult to fake.

"That widens the investigation," the male cop said.

"We can use your help whenever you're ready."

Taylor. That was it. Detective Taylor.

"I'm ready," he replied.

Rachel stepped in between them. "No, you're not."

"Yes, I am."

"I agree with her, Calvin," Taylor said. "You don't look too good. You need rest. The doctor said that it might take some time."

"I'll be okay. Just some memory lapses. But I'll be back and ready in no time." But from their facial expressions and silence, no one listening seemed to believe him.

"Lewis Mahoney is out as a suspect," Taylor said. "There is nothing on him, and our last string of hope is to get something out of him about what he *does* know about the murder. He'll walk soon; we don't have enough to keep him. If he's admitted into a psyche ward, nothing he tells us will stand-up in court."

"So we start back at square one," Baker added. "We look at everyone."

"That includes everyone at that party." Taylor had her hands on her hips, looking at Calvin with a saddened expression.

"Party?" Rachel said.

Taylor shot a look at Rachel, as if to say a civilian shouldn't be overhearing their cop-talk.

Rachel acted as if she didn't notice the detective's signal. "Calvin asked me to check social media for anything about Samantha Baylor."

"I did?" Calvin didn't remember ever having that conversation with his girlfriend.

"Yes, you did."

"Did you find anything?" Now Taylor acted as if she had no problem with Rachel butting into their conversation.

"There is a video on YouTube."

"Of what?"

"A college party. The video of Samantha Baylor and her boyfriend breaking up."

"Jesus." Taylor turned to her partner. "We knew that a video existed somewhere, but we hadn't had time to follow up on it. Rachel, you just saved us some work."

"I can show you on my iPad back in the room."

"Let's go."

Excitement surged through Charlene. Finally, maybe something positive in this case. For four days they'd been treading water, looking for anything to follow, or direct their investigation.

Now she followed behind Rachel, almost pushing the girl along, hoping to rush her back to the hospital room where, hopefully, evidence awaited.

She glanced behind her and saw Calvin lagging, as if having trouble keeping up. He moved gingerly, almost calculating his every action. He looked dazed, out of sorts. That knock on his head had taken its toll on the big man. Charlene wondered how much more help Calvin would be in this investigation.

A few paces from the room, Charlene stepped in front of Rachel and pushed open the door, holding it for the petite blond. The air was thick, staler inside.

Rachel entered and let the door close. She went over to where her jacket was bundled up on the top cushion of a corner chair. Lifting the jacket, she picked up a black iPad. Seconds later, the room door reopened and Calvin walked in, gripping Larry's shoulder for support.

"He okay?" Charlene asked.

Larry gave her a look.

"I'm fine," Watters said. He was perspiring and breathing hard, plunkering down on the edge of the bed.

"Here it is," Rachel said, flipping the tablet to face Charlene and handing it over.

A video had been uploaded to YouTube. The title underneath the video read, 'Party Fight', published over three weeks ago, only hours after the fight had actually taken place. Someone had decided to instantly get the video up and embarrass anyone involved.

The description of the video was vague, 'Who wants to see a college breakup?'

No names were mentioned. It had received thousands of hits, over six thousand likes, nine point eight thousand 'thumbs down'. Hundreds of comments had been posted.

Charlene scrolled through them, checking to see if she recognized any names. But the majority of comments were anonymous.

"Who uploaded the video?" Charlene asked.

Rachel shook her head. "I clicked on the publisher but no hits or page came up on it. So either this was the publisher's first and only video to upload, or someone tried to remain unknown."

Charlene touched the 'play' icon and raised the volume to its highest level. Other than Calvin still seated on the bed, they all huddled around the detective who held the screen in her hands.

The picture showed Samantha Baylor in the kitchen, drinking, talking and laughing with a group of friends. The music blasted, multiple conversations with loud chatter, but nothing could be made out. Something happened off screen, because the crowd all looked in the same direction when Mark Simon entered the screen. He pointed a finger at Baylor and approached her. The girls around Baylor looked horrified as they scampered away. The video zoomed in on the confrontation.

"Teenagers are always prepared now with those phones. Nothing gets missed," Charlene mentioned.

The gang in the kitchen stood back and witnessed Simon go off on Baylor. The music being so loud, made it impossible to make out Simon's words, but his face reddened and his jaw clenched. His lips moved rapidly.

Baylor took the harsh rebuke, recoiling without saying a word or putting up a fight. There were tears in her eyes when she ran off. The camera followed her all the way to the front door, and then cut off abruptly.

"Send this link to my email." Charlene handed the tablet back to Rachel, along with her business card.

While Rachel did that, Charlene glanced over at Calvin on the bed. He was lying down on his back, with his eyes closed. His chest heaved up and down, and it looked like he had fallen asleep. The detective felt a dark chill as emotions swirled, thinking of the PI on the concrete floor at the Coliseum last night.

She turned to Larry. "Let's take this back to our tech guys. I'm sure they can find out who posted the video. Maybe they can block out the music in the background and bring up voices in the foreground, maybe let us hear what Simon had said to Baylor."

"It doesn't help us determine who Baylor was with that night. I only saw her talking to a group of girls." He grinned. "Doubt any of them knocked her up."

"No, but it gives us some witnesses at the party. And if we can find out who posted this video, we can talk to them about what they remember from that night. Maybe they even followed Samantha Baylor out of there."

"What about him?" Larry asked, nodding towards Watters.

"He needs more rest. Calvin, we'll come back later and get you caught up."

But the PI didn't move.

"Done," Rachel said.

"Great, thanks. Let's go, Larry." She stopped at the door, holding it open for her partner and looking back at Rachel. "Take care of him. We'll be back."

"Let's see what we can do here," said Marcus Cross, systems analyst with the LAPD. Cross looked to be in his late thirties, wore Harry Potter glasses, and had two days of stubble on his face.

The LAPD Technical Investigation Division was located at C. Erwin Piper Technical Center on Ramirez Street, only a five minute drive from the detective bureau on West First Street, but over a forty minute drive, fighting traffic, from the hospital where they had visited Watters.

The Technical Laboratory, comprised of four specialized units, provided support services to investigative personnel in the department— the Latent Print Unit, the Photographic Unit, the Polygraph Unit, and the Electronics Unit.

They stood in front of a table covered with multiple screens and keyboards, as Cross went to work. Charlene didn't know the first thing about computer hacking, and she wasn't interested in how Cross got the job done, just in what he found out. Charlene had plugged in the YouTube link and had turned the computer over to Cross.

"Looks like our YouTube poster is anonymous. YouTube only requires an email to create an account and post videos, and they can choose to keep the email from being public."

"We know that, but can you find out who it is?" Larry asked. He seemed to be growing impatient with all of the running around they did, and Charlene couldn't blame him. This case had them running in circles, and they weren't really following clues, just grasping at straws.

"The video has been edited and definitely cut off when posted."

"What do you mean?" Charlene asked.

"You see this?" The tech pointed to the monitor. "The video has an extension and was recorded to last longer. Looks like whoever posted this is an amateur and just cared about the section we watched."

"Why would they cut it off?"

The tech shrugged his narrow shoulders. "Laziness. Just easier to post the shorter video. And it wouldn't take as long to upload. Maybe our poster was in a hurry to get it up and visible for people. Amazing how many hits it's received."

"Someone wanted to embarrass Baylor and Simon."

He punched a few keys, dragged the mouse around the screen and clicked buttons. His fingers tapped quickly.

"Whoever it is either has never used or posted on YouTube before, or has posted under a different identification."

"What else do you know?"

"No followers. The person filled out the registration form with very little information, and it looks like a fake name and address. The email account they used was created the same day as the video posted. They have not been active on the site since. Whoever it is wants to remain hidden."

"Keep working on it," Charlene said.

"Let me check the server. It's possible to remain anonymous unless the Youtuber makes their email public, and then maybe we can trace the email. I guess I'll have to hack Youtube."

"You can do that?"

The tech rolled his eyes, as if insulted by Charlene's question.

As he performed his expert analysis, Charlene's mind wandered to Calvin Watters. Who she saw this morning was not the same man she'd met a few days ago, who took down a twenty-year old star running back in a race, and who seemed confident and sure of himself. He looked far from the man who held the University of Southern California in the palm of his hand.

Watters looked frail, fragile. He seemed unsure, and Charlene knew that a concussion, depending on its severity, could cause a lot of damage. All he could do was rest and hope everything returned to normal, whatever that normal would be. But she knew one thing for sure, the detective couldn't count on Watters' help with this case anymore.

The detective's phone rang. She recognized her mother's number. She walked away from the group and left the room. When she entered the hallway, she clicked on her phone.

"Hi, Mom."

"Hi, honey." The sound of her mother's voice always made Charlene smile—such a calming, soothing voice. "Where are you?"

"I'm at work. What's wrong?"

"Nothing. I just haven't seen you in a few days."

"Sorry, Mom. I started a new case, so I haven't been home much."

"I heard that Matt was in town."

Charlene hesitated. "How did you know that?"

"Little birdies." She could hear the smile in her mom's voice.

Charlene's family adored Matt, and for good reason. The FBI agent had been instrumental in finding Charlene's niece, Martina, when the baby had been kidnapped in Denver. If it hadn't been for Matt and Charlene working together as partners, Martina might never have been recovered, and the kidnappers never exposed.

"I wish you would have brought him by for a visit."

"Sorry, Mom. He was only here for a few days. I didn't even know he was coming and I barely saw him myself because of work."

"When can I see you again?"

"I promise to come by soon."

A long silence on the line ensued. Charlene couldn't even hear her mother breathing, and wondered if she had hung up.

"What's wrong, Mom?"

"You know, it will be your father's one year anniversary soon."

Charlene tensed, the phone feeling heavy in her hand. Had it already been one year since his murder? It only seemed like last week she had received the news that his body had been found in his car off Sunset Boulevard.

"Charlene, are you there?"

Her mother's voice broke her focus. "Yes Mom. I'm here."

"Well, I'll let you get back to work. Bye, honey."

"Bye, Mom."

She hung up, still thinking about her dad. He had been one of the best detectives to ever don an LAPD badge. She hoped to one day be mentioned with the same respect as her father's name amongst LAPD brass. He will forever be remembered as a meticulous investigator, with a high rate of success.

The door opened beside her and Larry poked his head out. "We might have found something."

"We?" Charlene laughed to herself. The only thing her partner could do on a computer was play solitaire.

"Just get in here," he snapped.

Cross had the computer turned towards them and said, "I'm not sure if this helps, but I have somewhat of an ID."

"Already? That was fast."

"I'm not just another pretty face." He snorted at his own joke. There was nothing 'pretty' about his face.

"Who is it?"

"Don't have a first name, just initials."

"Who?"

"RJ Cummings."

Charlene looked at Larry. "Baylor's roommate?"

"Rory Cummings."

"Could be. That's interesting. Why would Baylor's roommate post that video and embarrass Samantha?"

"I'm not sure," Larry said. "Let's go find out."

"Check Cummings' timetable and see what class she has right now. I want to nail that backstabber before she has a chance to prepare."

Chapter 22

"Cummings is in a Project Management class."

They stood outside the Bovard College, sticking out like ink drops on a blank page, amongst the casual-clad college students milling about them. Larry wore black sunglasses, and Charlene could just imagine his eyeballs bouncing around with all of the young women passing them by.

So much of this case had been wasted in traveling back and forth across the city.

"Why do you think Cummings posted that video?" Larry asked.

"No idea. When we talked to her, she seemed to really like Baylor. Even the cheer coach said they were inseparable. Baylor had pledged into Cummings' sorority, they attended parties together, and according to Baylor's parents, they were best friends."

"That's messed up. What's wrong with girls?"

"Oh, we can be catty when we want to be."

"I'll never figure you women out."

"Don't even try, Larry. There she is."

Larry turned to gaze where Charlene pointed at the front door to the building.

"That's not her."

Charlene had already started walking towards Cummings. "Yes it is, she's just dyed her hair a different color."

Charlene stopped. She grabbed Larry's sleeve as he passed her and pulled him back.

"What are you doing?" He had a confused look spread across his face.

"Look."

Charlene nudged her head at Cummings, who had stopped about twenty yards from the front of the building she had just exited. The sophomore looked at her phone, smiled, and texted something using both thumbs.

When Cummings looked up from her phone, a guy emerged from the gathered crowd and wrapped his arms around her. They embraced, in what Charlene deemed more than just a friendly acquaintance. It had a romantic element to it.

"Fuck," Larry stammered. "Is that—"

"Yep. Mark Simon."

"Baylor's ex?"

"Same one. Let's go."

Charlene moved towards the two students, feeling a rush. Her adrenaline pumped. She could hear Larry hustling to keep up.

"Ms. Cummings," Charlene said, interrupting the conversation she had with Simon.

The students looked at Charlene, as all the blood drained from their faces.

"Detective Taylor, right?" One of those statements from Cummings with a tone telling Charlene that the sophomore student had been unprepared for any kind of confrontation.

"Yes."

"Ms. Cummings," Larry said. "We have some questions to ask you."

"I better leave," Simon said. He looked from Cummings to the detectives, and swayed on the balls of his feet.

"About Samantha?" Cummings gazed toward Simon and held his stare.

"Yes." Charlene turned to Simon. "And I think you should stay, Mark."

She looked back at Charlene. "Did you find something? Do you know who killed her?"

"Not yet, but we're hoping you could help by answering some questions."

"I have class," Simon said. His breathing quickened.

Larry stepped forward. "You're staying."

"Why did you post that YouTube video?" Charlene didn't waste time with the formal interview questions.

This was the baseline interrogation method, focusing on both visual and speech-related cues. The idea with this method was to compare an interviewee's verbal and non-verbal responses during informal conversation before the interview, with the responses during the actual interview.

"What?"

Cummings looked completely shaken and off guard. Her fingers trembled, skin paled even more. She looked from Charlene to Larry, and back to Charlene.

"The video of Mark and Samantha breaking up at the frat party. You posted it to YouTube and it got shared all over social media."

Simon's head jerked back, eyeballing Cummings. "You posted that?"

Her gaze met Simon's, then turned back to the detectives. "I...uh—"

"You knew what that would do to everyone involved," Charlene cut her off. The detective could feel her heartbeat speed up.

Simon repeated, "You posted that, Rory?" His voice trembled.

"I...uh—," she stuttered.

A tear snuck from Cummings' left eye and slipped down her cheek. She swiped at it with the front of her hand.

"Why did you do that, Rory?" Simon asked.

Cummings turned completely towards Simon, color flowing into her cheeks, and took his hand. It was as if the detectives had vanished. "Stupid thing to do, I know. I was angry, and a little drunk."

Simon yanked his hand away from Cummings. "I can't believe you would do that. Sam was your best friend."

"Mark, I made a mistake. I tried to take it down but by that time it was all over the place. Everyone had shared it and I couldn't remove it."

"You knew it would hurt Sam."

Charlene and Larry stood back and let the scene play out.

"I know, and I think that's what I wanted. Sam had everything and didn't even care about it. It came so easily to her, so naturally. She had it all and it wasn't fair."

"Why didn't you just tell us how you felt?"

"I should have. I know that now. I was stupid, Mark. I'm sorry."

Simon turned and walked away, without another word. Cummings stood motionless, staring at the football linebacker, watching him leave, maybe from her life for good.

Larry took a step towards Simon but Charlene put her arm out to block him. "Let him go."

The detective gave Cummings a full minute to recover, and compose herself. When she finally turned towards the detectives, as if acknowledging them for the first time, Charlene stepped towards her.

She lowered and softened her voice, as much as she could. "We need to know about that night, Rory."

It wasn't one of Charlene's normal tactics, but she knew that certain times called for sensitivity. She worked as a heart-on-her-sleeve detective but knew that sometimes raw emotion was a detriment to obtaining information.

Cummings took a deep breath. "I'd rather forget that night."

"That's too bad," Larry said.

"You hurt people, Rory. You need to face your mistakes and accept responsibility for your actions."

"It was only social media."

"This is 2020. Social media is everything for a lot of people, especially college students. They live and breathe through how many friends and followers they can attract. That's why people count the 'likes' on their posts, and go back ten times to check it. They wonder if they did something wrong if their count isn't high, and they're traumatized if they're 'unfriended' or 'unfollowed'."

Cummings bowed her head, staring at the ground. She sniffed loudly, holding in tears, and her body shook.

"Are you ready to answer some questions?" Larry asked.

Cummings nodded.

"We saw the short clip of your video, Rory," Charlene said. "We saw everyone there from the footage, but we need to know who else was there."

"Mostly just the football team and the fraternity brothers."

"Was Lewis Mahoney there?"

She shook her head. "I don't remember seeing him. But he never came inside. Too shy."

"You ever see him hanging out with Samantha?"

"No."

"Did you see Samantha that night after the fight?"

Head shake.

"The next morning?"

Cummings licked her lips. "I was sleeping when she got home and left in the morning before she woke up."

"Did you talk to her about that night?"

"No."

"You were her friend. Why wouldn't you speak with her about such a traumatic event?"

"I waited for her to bring it up, but Samantha was a very private person. She didn't like to talk about personal things. So I let it go."

"Did you know she was pregnant?"

Cummings' head jolted up at the detectives. "What?"

"Samantha was pregnant."

"Oh my God."

"The baby died with her."

Now Cummings broke down fully—bent over at the waist, large, loud sobs. Students walking by looked towards them but no one stopped to ask if they could help, or came over to comfort her.

"Put the phone away."

Charlene took out her badge and flashed it towards a pair of preppy-looking boys who had stopped and began recording the episode with their phones. Once they saw the detective badge, they shuttled away.

Charlene put a hand on Cummings' back. "We'd like to see the complete video you took from that night. Do you still have it?"

Cummings nodded.

"It's on my laptop."

Cummings unlocked her dorm room door and let the detectives in. The right side of the room, Samantha Baylor's side, had been completely cleaned out.

Cummings must have seen Charlene looking there, because she said, "Sam's parents came and took everything yesterday."

Not completely everything. The LAPD still had all of Baylor's things that they had confiscated, things that had been absolutely no help to the police—computer, books—nothing held any kind of significance to Baylor's murder or her murderer.

"It's over here."

The computer rested on the desk, closed, surrounded by Cummings' personal items. The sophomore flipped it open and booted it up.

Charlene looked around the room. Only a few days ago, when the detective had first entered the room to investigate Baylor's death, the room had a happy vibe to it, like female college students lived there, and had decorated it with their own personal styles and tastes. Now the room seemed empty, almost sad. As if Samantha Baylor's life had been taken, so had the life from the room. Cummings had done nothing to it, no changes or updates, since the death.

Once Cummings had logged on, she clicked her way through a few icons and into her saved iPhone account. She scrolled through numerous pictures and into her videos. She tapped on an unnamed one, only identified by the date the video had been taken. Charlene recognized the date as the same night of the frat party and break-up.

"Play it," Charlene ordered.

They watched the same video as they'd seen at Calvin Watters' hospital room, the one Rachel had found on the internet. Only this one clearer, and longer.

The first twelve seconds contained a selfie video of Cummings smiling into the camera, followed by pointless chatter from attendees in the room. The camera lens swayed and wobbled as the holder, Cummings, left the main room and entered the kitchen to where a group of people, mainly football players, hung out.

"Watch this," Cummings whispered on camera.

"Stop it there," Charlene barked.

Cummings pressed the pause button and looked at Charlene.

"Did you know they were about to break up?" Charlene asked.

The soft tone had left the detective's voice. She leaned in close, face to face with Cummings. Charlene bent over into the sophomore's personal space as the student sat at her computer desk.

Cummings backed away instinctively. "What? No."

"Why did you say that?"

"I don't know."

"Did you set it up?" Larry asked.

Cummings hesitated, obvious to the detectives.

"What did you do?" Charlene said.

"I never meant for anything to happen."

"What did you do?" Charlene repeated, this time her voice more stern.

Cummings took a deep breath. "I told Mark that Samantha texted other guys."

Larry shook his head. "Jesus. Was that true?"

"Not exactly."

Charlene asked, "How exact was it?"

"She talked about other guys all the time. How cute they were, or nice. How she would like to get to know them."

"Why would you do that?" Larry asked.

"You liked Mark, didn't you?" Charlene jumped in.

She swiped bangs out of her face. "Samantha didn't appreciate him. He is so sweet and treated her like a princess. Just because he didn't play in games, Samantha took him for granted. She always talked about the stars of the team."

"Like who?"

"All of them."

"Some friend you were." Charlene turned back to the computer monitor. "Continue."

The video started at the exact start of the video the detectives had watched earlier in the day. The link Rachel had found on the internet.

The exact same sequence of events transpired as they'd seen before, but when Charlene checked the timer clock at the bottom of the video, she saw that it lasted longer than what had been shown on YouTube.

Charlene waited it out. "Why did you clip the video when you uploaded it to the internet?"

"It takes a lot more time to upload a longer video, and I didn't want to be on it."

"That's why the anonymous posting," Larry said, putting it together. "This is where it ended on the YouTube site."

The video lasted another six seconds. They saw Samantha Baylor run from the room and people standing around staring at each other, as if no one knew what to say or do.

Then movement in the bottom corner of the screen caught Charlene's eye before the video promptly ended.

"Go back," Charlene instructed.

They reviewed the video, but this time Charlene focused on the bottom of the screen, at the left hand corner of the monitor. The detective waited for the end, knowing that she would only have a half of a second window to catch it.

"There." She pointed.

"Where?" Larry asked.

"Play the last five seconds of the video. Watch here, at the bottom." Charlene held her finger on the screen, to where she wanted them to watch.

Just before the video ended, less than a second before to be exact, someone moved towards the opening where the kitchen connected with the main room, as if following Samantha Baylor out. It could have been coincidental, but as everyone else in the room was frozen in shock, someone reacted immediately and lunged for the exit.

"Who was that?" Charlene asked.

"I'm not sure," Cummings replied.

"Think. Look harder."

Cummings watched it again. This time the whole video, but the person they sought had been standing near the kitchen entrance/exit, so not visible in the rest of the video, only becoming partially visible when the camera followed Baylor all the way to the kitchen exit.

The detectives stood up and faced each other.

"Definitely a male," Larry said.

Cummings quietly watched, repeating the video. Totally focused.

"I think it's Ryan Turner."

The statement turned the detectives. Now they both leaned over Cummings' shoulders to look at the computer screen themselves.

"What?" Larry's voice had changed.

Cummings repeated, "I think it's Ryan."

"The USC starting quarterback?"

"There's only one Ryan Turner at USC, Larry," Charlene said.

The detective knew that this discovery had just changed the course of the investigation, and would ruffle some feathers...which wasn't out of the detective's comfort zone. She had absolutely no problem with it.

Charlene straightened up and turned towards Larry. "This should be interesting."

"We better talk to the captain first."

"Nah, we're good."

"Taylor," Larry's voice hardened. "We need to talk to Dunbar."

"How about we go to Mahoney right away? See what his lawyer says?"

"Okay, but before we draw attention to Turner, we talk to the cap and Clark."

"Fine. Make the call."

He could feel the sweat beads peppering his scalp. Calvin bent over, back extended, arms dangling below his waist. His head swelled as the pressure of blood flowing to it made his temples throb.

The PI blinked twice, the tears stinging his already red eyes. He focused on his shoes, on the laces, but even attempting to tie up his sneakers sent a rush of nausea and waves of dizziness into his skull. Even the simplest of tasks seemed like an impossible mountain to climb these days.

Calvin noticed Rachel's feet shuffle towards his bed, and then heard the cracking of her knees as she bent at his side.

"Let me help you."

"I got it." He swatted away her hand.

"Stubborn," she mumbled, getting up and moving back to the side of the room. "Do you want me to go get something for lunch, instead of having hospital food again?"

"I gotta get out of here."

He tried to rise quickly, quicker than he should have and staggered. His arm shot out, reaching for the bed, grasping the bed rail. He steadied himself and hoped that Rachel hadn't seen his sudden attack of wooziness.

"Go?" Rachel said. "You can't even tie your own shoes."

Calvin looked down and confirmed her remark, his shoes still weren't tied. *Damn.*

"Just lie back down," Rachel said.

"I need to go, Rachel."

"What for?"

"I have an investigation. People are depending on me."

"The doctor said you need rest."

"No one knows my body better than me, and I say that I'm good to go."

He let go of the bed railing and stood erect, straightening and trying his best to look solid on his feet. If Rachel sensed he was any less than a hundred percent, she would fight him every step of the way.

He knew that he was far from okay, but Calvin had been able to push pain aside and play through it in college. He'd had a high tolerance for pain, but this felt different. This wasn't physical pain...his brain wasn't functioning normally.

"Lie back down." Rachel hurried to his side and took him by the shoulders to guide him onto the bed. Calvin shrugged her off with a shake of his shoulders.

"I'm f—"

A sudden urge to vomit took control and he rushed to the bathroom. The quick, rapid movement brought upon a dizzy spell, mixed with the queasiness sent spasms throughout Calvin's muscles. He dry-heaved hard into the toilet, his stomach clenching, his eye balls bulging. He could feel the veins in his neck pulsating.

When he looked up, Rachel stood at the doorway, fear slashed across her face. He had seen that look before, when they'd been hunted by Derek Baxter, a lethal ex-marine without equal, out for revenge against Calvin, after the PI had blown off the marine's leg. Calvin had always had the strength to make Rachel believe in him, to protect Rachel and let her know that he would never let anything happen to her. Now the shoe was on the other foot.

"Now will you lie down?"

He nodded and retreated to the bed. He shook off his untied shoes and lay back on the bed, on his back facing the ceiling. He closed his eyes and a snapshot image appeared—a blood splatter.

His eyes shot open.

"I saw something last night."

"What?" Rachel leaned on the bed beside him. She placed a cool hand on his forehead. "You're burning up."

"Blood."

"Blood?"

"Yes. At the football field."

Her voice sounded distant. "Whereabouts?"

He heard the sink tap running. "I can't remember, but it was on a wall somewhere."

"Whose blood?"

"I don't know that either. Maybe that girl's, what's her name?"

"Samantha Baylor?"

He felt a cold, wet cloth laid on his forehead. It felt good. "Yes. Her."

He'd always shared investigation information with Rachel, because she possessed street smarts, and was quick on her feet.

The door opened and Calvin's doctor walked in. "How are you feeling now?"

"Not well," Rachel replied, before Calvin had a chance to say anything. Had she really answered quickly, or did Calvin's brain just take longer to register a response?

The doctor said, "Some symptoms may appear right away, while others may not show up for days or weeks after the concussion. Sometimes the injury makes it hard for people to recognize or to admit that they are having problems. The signs of concussion can be subtle."

"I think he's ready to admit that there's a problem," Rachel said to the doctor.

Their conversation continued but their voices trailed away.

The doctor approached the bed and removed a light. He took the cloth off Calvin and held open his eyes.

Calvin swiped at the light. "Jesus, doc. Put that way."

"Light still bothering you?"

"Yes. What does my scan show?" Calvin asked.

"Concussions are typically associated with grossly normal structural neuroimaging studies. In other words, unlike other injuries, concussions are usually injuries no one sees and, contrary to popular belief, don't show up on most MRI exams or CT scans."

"So why did we do it?"

"The CT scan evaluates the types of bleeding or swelling of the brain during the first twenty-four to forty-eight hours after the injury. Although there is no bleeding in the brain to worry about, we did find a slight hairline skull fracture."

"So what does that mean?" Rachel asked worriedly.

"Nothing much we can do. It just takes rest and relaxation, no stimulus to the brain for some time."

"Great," Calvin said, closing his eyes again.

Calvin could overhear Rachel and the doctor exchange words but he couldn't hear well enough and wasn't computing the information. He lay back and let his mind wander, let his thoughts flow freely.

He heard the door shut.

"What can I do?" Rachel asked.

"Call the detective."

Chapter 23

"Thank you for seeing us, Lewis."

Charlene was surprised at how quickly Mahoney's attorney had agreed to meet with the detectives, as if the lawyer had been awaiting a call, and jumped at the opportunity. Why was that?

It had taken them very little time to assemble, which told Charlene that Sarah Schmidt had been spending most of her time with Mahoney, and that her retainer had probably run out long ago in the Mahoney's endless supply of "old" money.

"Has something new come up in your investigation?" the lawyer asked.

The tiny interrogation room in the west wing of the building was full. Around the table sat Lewis Mahoney, Mahoney's parents and his attorney. Charlene and Larry joined them.

The Los Angeles Sheriff's Department patrolled four thousand square miles, and oversaw the largest jail system in America. Its eight jail facilities held an average of seventeen thousand men and women, more than the fifteen thousand inmates held in all sixty-three county jails in New York state. All but one of Los Angeles County's facilities was overcrowded, and the system as a whole had thirty-eight percent more prisoners than meant to house.

So when Mahoney's attorney lobbied for Lewis to be detained in the Southern California Hospital at Van Nuys for further assessment, because he wasn't a flight risk, the officials gladly complied, especially since Mahoney's parents had offered to foot the bill.

Jails were locally operated, and held people serving short sentences or deemed too dangerous to release while they awaited trial. Overcrowding in Los Angeles County jails had long been a problem.

Larry started, "We found—"

"Who are you protecting, Lewis?" Charlene interrupted.

Sarah Schmidt, the high-priced attorney pursed her lips. It was obvious to the detectives that Schmidt hadn't been able to get anything, no matter how much badgering she had done, from her client. Mahoney planned to take his secret to his grave with him, whether that meant going down for Samantha Baylor's murder or not. He was not thinking clearly.

The thickness of the silence engulfed the air in the stuffy room.

"Ryan Turner."

They turned to face Mahoney's mother, the person who had spoken the words. She stayed stone-faced, worry lines wrinkling a face that had seen recent Botox treatments, but had aged since Charlene had last seen her.

Everyone at the table seemed genuinely surprised by the words.

"Melissa?" Aaron Mahoney, Lewis' father and Melissa White's ex-husband, said in shock.

"Momma!" Mahoney screamed, as if his world had been shattered. "You promised me you wouldn't say anything."

"This has gone on long enough, Lewis. You could go to jail. And for what?"

Mahoney pouted his lips. "He's the best, Momma."

"He doesn't even like you, Lewis. Those boys just use you."

It was as if only two people existed in the room. Everyone else frozen, silent. Charlene's skin prickled.

No one knew what to say. A tense silence hung in the air.

Charlene looked at Larry. They had a hunch that Turner had gone after Baylor that night after the fight at the party, but it was only that, a hunch. Having Mahoney admit covering for Turner without the detectives mentioning the name, gave more validity to the admission. But how did this news all connect?

Time for some answers, finally.

"Did you see Ryan Turner kill Samantha Baylor?" Larry asked.

Mahoney shook his head. "No."

"Did you kill Samantha Baylor?"

Mahoney looked at his mother. She closed her eyes and nodded for him to tell the truth.

"No," he said.

"What did you see that night, Lewis?" Charlene asked.

Mahoney hesitated. He looked at his attorney. Schmidt nodded. He then looked at his mom, who stared back at him with a glare. Lewis Mahoney never once looked at his father. Charlene always aware, that even though she had shared a special, unspoken bond with her father, it was always the same-sex parent who wielded the most influence in a child's life, who they looked up to and emulated.

"Did you see Ryan Turner with Samantha Baylor on the night of her murder?"

He nodded slightly.

"Were they at the Coliseum?"

Mahoney closed his eyes. "I followed them there. They walked from the party."

"What else did you see?"

Mahoney rubbed his temples as if fighting a pain. "They stood in the back parking lot, where team busses always drop off the players. They talked."

"About what?"

"I don't know. I hid in some bushes. Ryan caught me following him once, and he got mad. He told me never to do that again."

Larry had his notepad. "What time was this at?"

"I don't know, ten or eleven maybe."

"So what did you see?"

"They just talked. And then they went inside."

"How did they seem?"

"What do you mean?"

Charlene specified, "Was Samantha sad?"

He shook his head. "I don't think so. She smiled and laughed. She seemed happy."

"Did you follow them inside?"

"No way."

Charlene felt her shoulders slump.

Larry asked, "What happened next?"

"I waited for a while and then Ryan came back out."

"Was he alone?"

"Yes."

"How long was he in there for?"

"Maybe five minutes."

"Then what did he do?"

"I followed him back to the party."

"Did Samantha Baylor ever make it to that party?"

Mahoney shook his head.

"Did you ever see her come back out of the Coliseum?"

Another head shake. "But I left with Ryan."

Larry leaned over and whispered into Charlene's ear. "Forget it."

"I think I have another idea," she said to Larry. She leaned back and perked straight up, facing the table. She could smell Mahoney's body odor. He probably hadn't washed since confessing. "This isn't the first time you saw Ryan and Samantha together, is it?"

Charlene remembered that almost everyone she'd interviewed on campus admitted that Lewis would hide outside of the frat parties and watch the action, but he would never go in. Chances were, he saw something from that other night.

"No, it isn't."

She could see Larry looking at her. "When did you see them together before."

"It was a few weeks back. I saw them leave a party together."

"Where did they go?"

"Back to Ryan's apartment."

"How long did she stay?" Charlene asked, but she already knew the answer.

Mahoney hesitated, but then said, "All night."

He heard the vibration of his phone on the bedside table before the actual ringtone. Calvin twisted his neck to the side, looking over as it pulsated on the wood, moving around in circles, as if taunting him.

He sprang forward into a sitting position. The sudden, quick shift in position dazed him slightly, the light-headedness had his brain swimming. He brought his hand to his eyes instinctively and immediately regretted the decision, because he knew that Rachel was watching him.

"You okay, Calvin? I'll get it for you," she said.

"No," he said, a little too snappishly. "Sorry, Rachel. I'm okay, I can answer it." He reached across and pulled the phone off the table. "Hello."

"Cal?"

He recognized the voice of his good friend, detective Dale Dayton of the Las Vegas Metropolitan Police department.

"Hey, Dale. What's up?"

"Just checking in on you."

"What do you mean?"

"I heard you got a nasty bump on the head."

Calvin glanced over at Rachel who sat quietly on a hospital chair working on a crossword puzzle, refusing to make eye contact with him. "Oh really?"

"Rachel called me, she seems concerned. Said she's never seen you out of it like this. And she has been with you through some pretty rough shit."

Calvin had never been one to trust cops, even with his brother on the force.

He and Dale had first met back when Calvin was wanted in connection to the murder of a prominent casino owner in Vegas. Dale had been one of the only people who had believed in Calvin's innocence. Dale showed Calvin he could be trusted, and they'd instantly started up a friendship.

"How are you feeling?" Dale asked.

"I've been better, but I think I'm coming around."

"You'd better be careful, Calvin. Your body has sustained a lot of serious injuries over the last few years, and not just anybody can walk away unscathed. Some of these things can have lasting effects and need to be monitored before it's too late."

"I know, I know. This isn't like any normal injury I've had before. It's not something I can just ice down or operate on. All I can do is wait and hope, and not being in control of my own situation is something I'm not used to."

"You've never been very good at delegating, or letting other people help you. That's always been your job, to take care of everyone else."

Calvin could sense the smile in Dale's voice.

"Any word on North?" the PI asked.

"Not yet, but it isn't from a lack of looking. Jimmy has his ear to the ground, and he's stretching his underground contacts to the max."

Detective Jimmy Mason was Dale's partner, and another person Calvin trusted with his life, even though Calvin's relationship with Jimmy didn't run as deeply as it did with Dale, ever since the whole Baxter ordeal started, which seemed like so long ago.

Jackson North remained on a nationwide manhunt search list. North, a former US marine, was part of a 'hitman for hire' program created by a group of former military elite who called themselves the Seven Deadly Sins. North and his best friend, Derek Baxter, had spearheaded the money-making scheme.

When Calvin killed Baxter a short while ago, government officials warned them that once North found out about Baxter's death, the former spotter would be out to avenge his friend's murder. So far, there had been no signs of North, but Calvin knew, as he had when Baxter hunted them, that anyone connected to Calvin was in grave danger and not safe anywhere.

Calvin leaned down with the phone clutched to his ear. "How long do you think it will take for news of Baxter to reach North?"

Calvin tried his best not to sound worried, because Rachel listened in, and she'd already put her life on the line multiple times since starting a 'real' relationship with Calvin. It got to the point where Calvin wasn't sure if it was safe for Rachel to be with him anymore. He could only protect her, and keep her out of harm's way, for so long. At some point, he had to think about her and her best interests, even though he loved Rachel like he had never loved a woman before.

"No idea. No one seems to know that answer, because no one has any idea where North is even hanging out. But you'll be the first to know when Jimmy or I hear anything."

"I know, thanks for looking out for me."

"You know you don't need to thank me for that." A long pause ensued. "You still working with Detective Taylor?"

"I think so. But she's really running on her own right now, until I can get back on my feet."

"From what I hear, that's the way she likes it. Be careful with her, Calvin. There are a lot of rumors circulating about her."

"Like what?"

Calvin was aware that cops were cops, no matter what city they worked out of. Like one family, looking out for each other, and news travelled quickly in their small circles of law enforcement.

"She's a loose cannon, and a risk to everyone around her. She lives on the edge, and she doesn't care who gets in her way."

"What are you saying, Dale?"

"She's unpredictable and hanging by a thread. Get some rest, Calvin."

"Taylor, wait up."

She could hear Larry rushing behind her, trying to catch up, gasping for air, his smoker's lungs heaving and taking in air. But Charlene moved with a mission.

"Shouldn't we talk about this?"

Normally a twenty-five minute drive from the Southern California Hospital at Van Nuys to the detective bureau on West First Street, and that's without the after-work, heavy LA traffic which they would now have to fight on Route 101. They'd spent a good deal of time in the vehicle, more time wasted than Charlene would have liked. But that was part of the job.

"Talk about what, Larry? We have a new suspect, and that investigative direction needs to be followed."

"It's Ryan Turner."

"I don't care if it's the pope, and you shouldn't either."

Charlene had learned early how the game worked, but the detective wasn't exactly the kind of woman to follow the rules. In LA, like any city, untouchables existed when it came to advancing your career—amongst those athletes and celebrities.

Larry knew how to play it, and that's why he had been succeeding in LA for thirty years. Charlene wasn't an ass-kisser, and had never expected to get ahead by playing the game and not ruffling feathers. That wasn't her style, never had been, and she wasn't about to start...for anyone.

"I'm just saying that you need to learn a few things about being a detective in LA. It's not all about how hard you can push back. You need to learn not to go at everything with a battering ram."

She twitched her nose. "That's what I've got you for, partner."

"What do you plan on saying to the captain?"

"Maybe he can lead or at least direct us."

They took the elevator to the sixth floor of the Los Angeles Police Administration Building and made their way to the detective bureau in room 637. The captain stood outside his office, pacing back and forth, chewing on an unlit cigarette. He remained the only one left in the office, as the lights were shut off and everyone else had gone home for the day.

It had taken a lot of coaxing from upper management to talk Dunbar into not smoking any more in the building, even though it had been twenty years since California became the first state to ban smoking in bars and other public places. Dunbar hadn't been quick to comply.

"What is it, Taylor? I should be at home with my family."

"I know it's late, sir, but we need to talk about this case."

"Clark is on his way."

"What do we need the DA for? I just want to talk about our investigation strategy."

But Charlene knew that the minute she mentioned Ryan Turner's name on the phone with her captain, that he'd be terrified about a backlash from USC, and would be on the horn to Clark, seeking the district attorney's approval. Even though Charlene understood the complications and the significance of her actions and findings, she still wasn't afraid of the consequences.

They didn't have to wait long. Within minutes, Jeffrey Clark strode through the door, a briefcase in one hand and his cellphone in the other, a half-snarl on his face as he sent a text to someone. They waited in the captain's office as Clark entered and dropped down on the couch.

He put away his phone. "You've got ten minutes, Detective. I have reservations at Urasawa."

Urasawa, on North Rodeo Drive, was one of the most expensive sushi restaurants in America. Without a doubt one of the most celebrated restaurants in LA. Normally reservations were booked months in advance, Clark had probably made one call earlier in the day.

"We want blood samples from Ryan Turner."

Charlene handed the paperwork over to Clark. She had filled it out in the car, on their lengthy drive back to the department. Clark took the papers, placed a pair of expensive reading glasses over his eyes, and scanned them over.

"What do you hope to find?"

"Samantha Baylor was pregnant."

"You think it's Turner's?"

"Maybe."

Clark removed the reading glasses and chewed on the end. "You want me to go to a judge with 'maybe'?"

"There's more."

"Go on."

"After Larry and I found out that Mark Simon couldn't conceive children, we knew that we might never find out who fathered Baylor's child. So I called Lloyd Webster to see what we could do."

Clark knew that Webster worked as the LAPD medical examiner, so no need to point that out to the DA.

Clark asked, "What did Webster say?"

"He said that blood tests are becoming available that can determine paternity of an unborn fetus."

Clark partially sat up. "Really?"

Charlene continued. "All that's required is a blood sample from at least one of the possible fathers."

"How reliable are these new tests?"

"Very. We just need blood samples from both the mother and the father. We already have Baylor's blood sample on file."

Clark grew quiet, then he said, "What do you have on Turner to warrant this kind of transaction?"

Larry said, "We have an eye witness who saw Baylor leaving a party with Turner, go back to his house and spend the night there. According to our calculations, it would have been right around the time that Samantha Baylor got pregnant."

"Who is your eye witness?"

Charlene hesitated, and looked at Larry. She knew that her story lost a lot of traction at this point, in the eyes of the DA. Her witness list was thin.

"Lewis Mahoney."

Clark's head shot up from the paperwork. The DA heaved. "Mahoney?"

"Yes." She realized her voice lacked confidence.

Clark slid up on the couch. "Detective, isn't Mahoney the guy who you, Detective Taylor, wanted to administer a psych evaluation after he had confessed to Samantha Baylor's murder?"

She exhaled loudly. "Yes, sir."

Air escaped through the DA's pursed lips. He got up and crossed the room, looking out the window at the parking structure on the ground.

He clenched the papers in his hand. "Turner's attorney would wipe his ass with this request. What do you hope to gain from this?"

"Turner could be the father of Baylor's unborn child."

"You think he murdered Baylor because he got her pregnant?"

"People have killed for less," Larry said.

This spun him around, he looked at them. "Really?"

Charlene said, "I don't know what I think. All I know for sure is that according to all of our accounts, reports indicate that Ryan Turner may have been the last person to see Samantha Baylor alive. And that's something we should move on, despite who he is."

She knew she struck a nerve with her last remark. The DA didn't like to be told what to do, and he didn't want people thinking that someone else called the shots, or that he tiptoed around the city, not wanting to piss anyone off. District Attorney Jeffrey Clark was a man of action, and stood for something in LA. Charlene hoped that she could play on his emotions with this demand.

Clark pulled out his phone and pressed a button, probably checking the time to make sure he wasn't late for his reservation. He looked at the captain, and then at the detectives, who had remained seated.

Charlene challenged his stare.

He looked directly at Charlene. "How solidly are you standing behind this hunch, Detective?"

"With everything I've got," she replied.

He looked at Larry. "What about you, Detective Baker? You're the senior agent here."

Charlene knew full well it had nothing to do with being the senior agent. Clark wasn't the first asshole to discount Charlene because of her gender. The DA looked at Larry for a male perspective, and had more respect for him because of it.

Larry remained stone-faced. "I'm with her."

"Yes, that seems to be the attitude of a lot of Americans these days."

Charlene smiled at the line, a jab at the state of today's US government. She could trust Larry. He always had her back no matter what she decided to do.

Larry had been her father's best friend, a pallbearer at his funeral, and ever since then they'd been partnered together. He'd almost been like a father-figure, taking her under his wing. Whether out of guilt or respect, she had never asked. But she appreciated having a partner who would go to bat for her.

"I'll find a judge to sign off on this. But, Detective, remember who you're dealing with here. I know you. You won't care who you cross, or think twice about your future in this city."

Chapter 24

As Charlene jogged down South Lucas Avenue, she made a mental checklist of the day's schedule.

The first thing she needed to do was check in on Calvin Watters. The detective would have liked nothing more than to have Calvin by her side today. Not only did the PI possess obvious muscle, but he'd also been said to have a high IQ, and Charlene would like to see that on display. Plus, he had USC contacts and knew how to work an angle.

But an eighty percent Watters was no good to her. She needed him at his best, at peak performance. Charlene hoped that the rest yesterday at the hospital had been enough to turn him around, maybe jog his memory and make him a worthwhile ally.

What were the odds that the DA had found a judge to sign off on the papers to pull a blood sample from Ryan Turner? But what if the baby wasn't Turner's?

The all-American, Heisman quarterback could be one of a number of candidates. Could the detective really pull blood samples from everyone at that party? If she did that, she would be a joke, a laughing stock. But Charlene's gut told her that Turner was a key to the answers.

As Charlene weaved in and out of pedestrians heading to work on this early Friday morning, she thought about who benefitted the most from Samantha Baylor's death. Who had the most to lose if the cheerleader lived?

The detective could find no motive for this murder. Charlene thought about the various reasons she'd run across for murder, from years of working in law enforcement: revenge, frustration, hate.

But from all of the interviews that both Calvin and Charlene had conducted, no one showed any ill-will towards Samantha Baylor. No one hated the freshman, or even held a grudge against her.

The Emma Moore interview didn't sit well with Charlene. The head of the sorority where Baylor had pledged seemed to be hiding something, and the detective didn't trust her. Today, Charlene wanted to find and speak with Bridgette Acres, the girl who had quit the Delta Gamma sorority.

Money and greed were also motives. Baylor didn't have money, or the kind of money to warrant a murder. She wasn't worth anything in terms of life insurance.

When it comes to sex and jealousy, there were no signs of sexual abuse. Was Mark Simon bitter that someone had impregnated his girlfriend? Did he even know? Had Rory Cummings been jealous of Baylor's relationship with Mark Simon, because it looked like the roommate now moved in on Simon? She hadn't waited long once Baylor was out of the picture.

Those two remained at the top of Charlene's suspect list.

A personal vendetta always motivated criminals. Charlotte Rooney and Alicia Williamson had lost their starting jobs on the USC cheerleading squad because of Baylor. Enough to kill for? Doubtful.

As Charlene jogged by a local bakery, the sugary smells tickled her nostrils. Focus.

Charlene didn't see this case as having a political factor. Baylor didn't have many friends, wasn't outgoing or one to speak out about things like politics and religion. She didn't make friends easily, but she also didn't do anything to upset or disgruntle classmates, teammates, or acquaintances.

No signs that Baylor abused drugs. Nothing showed up in any tox. reports. She didn't even smoke or drink excessively, so narcotics weren't a factor.

Having exhausted every system available to US law enforcement agencies, Charlene found nothing to indicate that Baylor's murder was part of a serial case. Had the killer committed other crimes? Did he or she have a history?

Everything in Charlene's grasp, from the suspects to the evidence to the hearsay, came down to one word—weak. No one stood out as someone with enough hate or reason to commit a murder, to take a life and risk imprisonment for life.

The last reason why people commit murders, in Charlene's estimation, one that had been gnawing at the back of the detective's mind since the onset of this case—to keep a secret.

What did Samantha Baylor have and who did she have it on? What did the freshman cheerleader know…what secret did she take to her grave?

The music on Charlene's earbuds paused, and a half second later her ringtone commenced. She eased into a trot, and removed the phone from her running pouch.

Since becoming a detective, Charlene had her office phone programmed so all incoming calls rerouted to her cellphone.

She slowed her breathing and answered the call. "Hello."

"Detective Taylor, it's Officer Berry. I was told to call you. There's been a murder."

The last thing Charlene needed right now was another case. The Cheerleader Case, as her colleagues had been calling it around the office, already ate up all of her time. But so goes the life of an LAPD detective: too many murders, too few detectives on the force.

"What's the address?"

"The corner of Anderson and Sixth."

Charlene stopped moving completely. "Wait, that's Central. Let them handle it." Her plate was already overflowing, and she didn't need another murder on top of that.

"The Central Bureau called me to find you."

"Why?"

"I'm not sure, but they said the victim's name is Tiana Washington."

Calvin rested on the edge of the hospital bed. It was as if the world was spinning out of control around him. He felt no head pain, no effects from the concussion symptoms. Maybe only the meds his doctor had prescribed, taking over his body? Was this real?

As he stared at the floor, voices spoke out in the room around him, but the words were strewed, nothing made sense. The conversation with the people in the room was like senseless chatter. When he closed his eyes, Tiana's image appeared in his vision—her smiling face, the fun she had with her boys.

How could this have happened? A young, single mother who hadn't done anything to anyone. Life was so unfair, so cruel.

The door to the room opened, and everyone turned their attention towards it. Detective Taylor stepped inside.

"Have you heard?" she said.

Her hair dangled, still wet from a morning shower, her blond strands curling under her jaw line and gumming to her cheeks. Her shirt was untucked and it looked as if the detective had dressed hurriedly this morning.

Calvin's eyes met the detective's. He nodded. "Josh just told me."

Calvin finally noticed that the voices in the room belonged to his brother and Rachel. He thought they'd left, but they still stood there, after Joshua had told him about Tiana's murder. Rachel's eyes were red and wet. Even though she had never met the victim, Calvin had talked about Tiana, and Rachel knew how much she had meant to the PI, the former running back who had grown close to not just Tiana, but anyone involved with the Trojans back then.

Rachel's hair was messed and her clothes wrinkled from sleeping all night in the chair next to Calvin's bed. She rubbed the back of her neck, which probably twisted full of kinks and knots from the awkward sleeping position.

"I'm sorry, Calvin," the detective said. She approached the bed.

"Is it connected?" he asked, looking her in the eye, hoping to read any kind of reaction. His years working on the streets as a collector had made him somewhat of a pro at reading facial expressions and body language.

It had to be connected. What were the odds? It couldn't be a coincidence. Tiana had been a security guard at the Coliseum.

"I don't know. I haven't been to the crime scene yet."

"What do you know?" Josh asked.

"Were you the one who told them to call me?"

Joshua nodded. "When I got the call, I thought it seemed suspicious."

"On my way here, I called the detective who had been originally assigned to the case." She removed her phone and lit it up. She read. "The body was found in her home."

"Who found it?"

"Her mother-in-law."

"Jesus." Calvin shook his head. "Poor Flora."

Taylor asked, "You know her?"

"Met her a few times. She takes care of Tiana's kids when she works."

"Ya, the mother-in-law said that Tiana always picks the kids up after her shift, but never showed up this morning. She wasn't answering her phone, so she brought the kids home to get ready for school and found Tiana on the floor."

Calvin shook his head. "The boys will be devastated. She's the only parent they know."

"Why would she be at home? Any idea why she would have gone there instead of picking up the boys?"

Calvin massaged his temples. His mind swam, vision slightly blurry. He stood up carefully. "She always went home to prepare their breakfast first. Then she would pick them up so that they could get organized for school."

Taylor's voice softened. "How are you feeling?"

"Better."

"No, you're not," Rachel said.

He looked at her out of the corner of his eye. "Yes I am, Rachel."

Taylor said, "I hoped you'd come to the house with me. Since you've been there before and you know the victim, you might see something out of place.

"I don't think that's a good idea." Rachel's face showed signs of worry.

"I'm fine, Rachel. I've gotten plenty of rest and I've had no symptoms for the last twelve hours."

That Rachel knew about, anyway.

"It's your call," Taylor said.

"I'm good."

"I'll go see the doctor and fill out the release forms," Detective Taylor said, and rushed from the room.

Taylor seemed to have the same kind of drive and determination as Calvin's buddy. Dale was a devoted and dedicated, hard-driving detective. Detective Taylor seemed just as motivated and gritty as Dale, which meant she and Calvin would team perfectly together.

"Are you sure you're up for this, Calvin?" Josh asked.

Calvin looked at his brother, and then at Rachel, who stood behind Josh, refusing to make eye contact. He had seen that mood before. Rachel wasn't getting her way, and had given up trying to change Calvin's hard-headed line of thinking.

He stood up. "I'm ready."

"I'm not just talking about your concussion, which is serious enough. But this is Tiana. I know how close you two were."

Josh put a hand on Calvin's shoulder.

"Let's do it."

Taylor stormed back into the room. "We're good to go. The doctor signed off."

"Calvin can't drive," Rachel said.

"That's okay, he can come with me. My partner is meeting us at the house."

Calvin turned towards Josh. "Can you take Rachel back to your house?"

Rachel stepped out in front of Josh. "No."

"Rachel, yes. You're exhausted. You've been by my side and up for two nights. You've had no sleep, and I'm worried about you."

"I'm worried about you."

He took Rachel's hand. "Rachel, I love you, and I need you to take care of yourself, first. I'll be fine. Go back and sleep in a real bed. Spend the day with Alexis and the kids. I'll be back later."

She pursed her lips. "Fine."

Calvin prepared for a moment of rebuttal, but when it didn't come, he looked at the detective. "Let's go."

The vehicles parked outside Tiana's house, when Calvin and the detective eased up to the barricade, indicated the importance of the scene. Police tape blocked off the entrance, EMTs, both uniformed and plain-clothed officers milled in and out of the front door.

Evidence Response Team members were busy unpacking their vans, while tech crews performed duties on the outside yard. Calvin was certain that scores of professionals conducted the same dealings inside.

Taylor jumped from the vehicle even before the car had come to a complete stop. "Let's go."

She slammed the door and bolted for the front yard, flashing her credentials and weaving around various professionals, a woman on a mission.

Calvin eased out of the vehicle, grabbing the top of the door frame to lift himself into a standing position outside of the unmarked cruiser. The pain from the knock on his head started to ebb back, but Calvin would never mention a word of it to anyone.

He shut the door and looked around the scene. The air hung sticky and hot. Dark sunglasses protected his fragile vision.

A chain of observers had parked themselves outside of the police tape, trying their best to rubber-neck a glimpse of the action taking place inside or outside of the residence. Phones flew out, pictures and videos would soon hit social media and go viral.

Calvin turned back and started for the house, heading for Detective Taylor, who had stopped to speak with a big burly man Calvin recognized as the detective's partner. They grouped in a triangle with another man, who was dressed like a casual, undercover cop. Calvin had seen his share of cops, and they all carried themselves in a certain manner.

The guy was short, even shorter than Taylor, with shoulder length curly black hair and dark, Latin-toned skin.

Taylor waved to Calvin. "Calvin, come here."

The PI approached them, aware that some of the others on the job had stopped to look directly at him.

"Calvin, this is Detective Rodriguez, head of the Gang Related Crimes Division."

Calvin shook his hand.

The man smiled. "Calvin Watters, I remember watching you play ball."

"Is this gang related?" Calvin asked.

"I just told Detective Taylor, I don't think so."

"Neither do we," Taylor said. "I'll take over from here. Thanks for your help, Detective."

Rodriguez nodded. "It's all yours, but I'm gonna run it through GRIT anyway, just to be sure."

"GRIT?" Calvin asked.

"LAPD's Gang Related Information Tracking," Taylor answered.

Rodriguez nodded and left them.

The detective looked at Calvin. "You ready for this?"

Calvin nodded.

A row of orange cones blocked vehicles from parking too close to the crime scene. They headed towards the house and made their way up the walk. An officer stood outside the front door, almost as if directing traffic.

The cop had a young, boyish face and brown bangs almost covering his eyes. "Hey, you're Calvin Watters."

Calvin smiled slightly.

The cop acknowledged Detective Baker. "I was the first one here, sir. The crime scene is intact, Detective. Nothing has been moved. I roped off the scene, called it in, and the coroner has already pronounced death. Forensics is inside now gathering evidence."

The kid looked eager to please.

"Actually, I'm a detective also," Taylor said sarcastically. She looked pissed that the male officer only spoke directly to Baker.

Calvin figured that Taylor was used to the male-chauvinism in this male-dominated industry she had chosen to pursue. He was growing accustomed to her unwavering intensity.

"Oh, sorry." The kid's cheeks colored slightly.

"Who's on the scene, sheriff or highway patrol?" Taylor asked.

"Central Division was, but they handed it over. We waited for you."

"I want a seal placed on the house. Let's look at everyone living within a two mile radius."

"I thought this was a gang killing?"

"Just do it." Taylor's voice had hardened.

"Yes, ma'am." The cop scooted away, almost happy to get out of there.

Taylor nodded at Calvin. "Let's go in."

Calvin followed behind. As he stepped inside, he closed his eyes and tried to bring up images of the last time he'd been there.

He noticed the cluttered floor first. Tiana had usually kept a relatively tidy house. But the place had been trashed. Whoever had been there had gone through everything, looking for something.

"Did you do this?" Calvin asked.

Baker shook his head. "Not the cops. It was like this when they got here."

Calvin looked around. "Whatever they were looking for, they didn't find it."

"How do you know?" Taylor asked him.

They strolled through the house. "The whole house is trashed. When you find what you're looking for, you stop and leave."

"Maybe they found it at the end."

"Maybe." But Calvin doubted it. He had performed his share of house searches, looking for money owed by degenerate gamblers.

Tiana lay on the floor in front of the same couch where Calvin had been, only a few days ago, having a drink with Tiana. Her body remained in an awkward position, on her back, her legs and arms extended. Her face showed signs of shock.

Calvin bent down closer to the security guard, settling on his haunches.

"No damage on the locks," Taylor said. Calvin was pretty sure she spoke directly to him now.

"The doors were probably unlocked," he said. "She would have been in the kitchen preparing breakfast."

"Maybe she knew the killer and invited him in?"

Calvin got up. "Or her. Anyone can fire a gun."

They stood over Tiana, and Calvin intentionally looked away. He glanced around the room that had been torn apart from top to bottom. If his memory and mind worked properly, he didn't notice anything out of place....except.

A fifty-inch, flat-screen color TV, the focal point of the room, sat on an old, scratched, paint-chipped coffee table.

"That looks new," Calvin said.

"And expensive," the detective responded.

"Did she have that last time you were here?" Baker asked.

"I'm not sure, but I don't think so." He looked around and his eyes stopped at an empty desk against the wall. "I think there used to be a computer on that desk."

"Laptop or desk top?"

Calvin squinted his eyes, fighting off a headache. "Laptop, I think."

Taylor walked over to the desk and knelt down. She picked something up and showed it to them, the end of a computer plug in. "Gone."

"Does she have her phone on her?" Calvin asked. "She was attached to that phone."

Taylor grabbed the shirt-sleeve of an officer passing by. "Anything found on the body?"

"No ma'am."

"Any electronics found at all?"

"Nothing yet, Detective."

"Call the station and organize a GPS trace on Washington's cellphone."

Calvin didn't say anything, but he was impressed with Taylor's quick thinking.

"I'll find the ME," Baker said, and walked away.

Taylor asked, "Anything else out of place, Calvin?"

He looked at Taylor who wasn't looking back at him. She stared off, as if in thought, maybe thinking of next steps.

"I don't think so. I wasn't here for long, only in this room, and, to be honest, my memory isn't one hundred percent. Maybe we should speak with Elijah."

"Who's Elijah?"

"Tiana's oldest son."

"Good idea. He might notice something."

"I don't see any electronics at all: phones, computers, iPods, iPads? The kids each have their own devices. Maybe in other rooms."

"Or maybe whoever was here, wanted those devices."

Calvin massaged his temple to slow down the throb. "Tiana wasn't herself."

"How so?"

"She just seemed off. She was usually a happy, upbeat person, but the last couple of days, during my interaction with her anyway, she seemed on edge, checking her phone every few minutes."

"Maybe we can call the phone company, get a readout of every text she had received, and a list of the phone log."

"Can that be done?"

"Not sure."

"ME said she died of a single gunshot to the chest. Not sure the caliber yet." Baker returned with a young man about six feet tall, black hair neatly parted and glasses. A pretty blonde followed behind them.

"No sign of a struggle," the ME said. "From the depth of the bullet, I'd say the killer stood about eight feet away, but of course that's a guess. We'll learn more when we get her back and clean her up."

"Hey, Char," the blonde said. She smiled, revealing a gap between her two upper front teeth.

"Dana, this is Calvin Watters."

"Pleasure," she said to Calvin as they shook hands. Calvin took a second glance, swearing the lady batted her eyelashes at him, but he was still a little groggy, so he could have been totally wrong.

"Down, girl," Taylor said. She looked at Calvin. "Dana is one of our lab rats."

"Forensic Investigator," Davis corrected the detective.

"I'm glad you're here, Dana." Taylor moved to the body and bent down over it. "The victim has some sort of transfer on her pants."

The forensic expert knelt down beside Taylor and scooped the evidence off the pants and into a baggie. "Looks like grass and dirt. I'll take it back and have it analyzed."

"What are you thinking?" Baker asked, looking at his partner.

Taylor was biting the outside of her lip, and Calvin picked up on what the detective was thinking. "Bermuda grass," he said.

They all looked at him.

"Exactly," Taylor replied.

"What does that mean?" Baker asked, a look of confusion on his face.

"The Los Angeles Memorial Coliseum turf is made of real grass, Bermuda grass to be precise."

"Well, she was an employee of the Coliseum. She might have just gotten some on her at work."

"She could have," Taylor said.

"You're thinking a groundskeeper?'

Taylor shrugged her slender shoulders. "Just brainstorming here. They were the first to find Baylor."

"The first witness is always the first suspect," Baker mumbled.

"Any electronics found in the house, Dana?" Taylor asked.

"Not yet, which is strange considering children lived here."

"Mind if I look around?" Calvin asked.

"Go ahead," Taylor said, and then turned away to speak with her colleagues.

Calvin left the cops, and headed for the hallway which led to the bedrooms. The house was tiny, a single floor bungalow of about a thousand square feet. It had never been upgraded, still the same shag carpet and what looked like the original paint job.

The walls were decorated with family pictures and kids' art projects. Youth trophies and race ribbons displayed on homemade shelves. Obvious that Tiana had been proud of her boys' achievements.

Every room had been overturned: furniture, appliances, closets and dressers unloaded and strewn everywhere. The killer had been looking for something, and it didn't look like a usual robbery.

Every square inch of the house had been tossed, not just the usual hiding places like underwear drawers and freezers, where a typical thug burglar would look. Calvin hypothesized that this wasn't just some random act of violence—this was a preplanned murder that had to be connected to the Samantha Baylor case. And Calvin wondered if Detective Taylor felt the same way.

The walls in Elijah's room were plastered with sports memorabilia, from both USC football and other LA sports teams: Dodgers, Kings, Lakers, Raiders and Rams. This kid seemed to have an addiction to sports. Calvin's poster stood front and center in the middle of the wall, much larger in size than the others. He had signed it, years ago.

He moved to Tiana's room, which contained the same mess as the rest of the house. He didn't notice anything significant, and he didn't want to get in the way of the professionals in the house. He could always come back later, with or without the detectives.

"You ready?"

He looked up and saw Detective Taylor standing at the bedroom doorway.

"We are heading over to the Coliseum. You coming?" she said.

He arched his eyebrows. "Groundskeeper?"

"Worth a shot."

Chapter 25

"You still have a lot of pictures up around these hallways," Taylor said.

They walked through the Coliseum, examining the walls. Baker's heavy breathing sounded loud in the empty corridors.

Calvin said, "Ya, but it looked like I've passed the torch. Turner has more posters up, and much bigger ones."

"He is the new golden boy for sure."

"I still say he'll never be a pro," Baker chimed in.

"Why didn't you turn pro, Calvin?" Taylor asked. "You must have had the opportunity after your junior year."

It happened more and more these days, collegiate athletes leaving school early for the contracts that awaited at the pro levels.

Calvin swallowed hard. "I chose to stay here."

"Come on," Taylor insisted. "Those millions of dollars weren't calling you?"

"I made a promise to my mother. She'd always wanted me to get an education. I guess I didn't keep that promise either."

They walked in an awkward silence. Their footfalls making the only noise.

Baker caught up and walked stride in stride with them. "You ever think of going back? It's never too late."

Calvin nodded. "I've thought about it. Maybe when the time is right."

They reached the end of the hallway and stepped out into the sunlight, looking down on the field, where the groundskeepers worked: spreading turf, making final preparations for tomorrow's game day—a crew of roughly twenty groundskeepers working, mostly in the cardinal and gold end-zones.

Lawn mowers rode one last time over the perfectly manicured field, where tomorrow it would be ripped up by two-hundred pound angry men in steel cleats. That smell of freshly cut grass filled the air.

"They say the heat allows grass to grow more." He wasn't sure why he said it as he looked out onto the field.

Taylor didn't answer.

Final touch-ups were being made with hand-painted rollers, which kept the paint out of the soil layer of the turf and limited the paint to the blade of the grass. Because of this, paint could be easily removed for other sporting events taking place at the Coliseum, like the NFL Los Angeles Rams football games, who shared the same venue.

About thirty big floor fans were strategically placed around the field so the paint would dry quickly.

They walked by a USC wall-of-fame and an extra-large photo of the athletic director, Jordan Price, splattered front and center. Price wore an expensive suit with a high collar, and a cocky grin.

Calvin noticed Taylor take a second glance at the picture, and knew what she thought. It was no secret around the USC campus of the feud that had existed between Calvin and Price, and the detective had witnessed the coldness between the two, first-hand.

"So what's the story between you and Price, anyway?"

Very few people knew what really happened that night. Calvin had never told anyone and chances were, Price wasn't bragging too much about it either.

"Let's just say, we didn't see eye to eye on Price's decision to discontinue my scholarship."

Even after all of these years, Calvin still wasn't ready to fully divulge the facts of the meeting.

"Sounds like a dick move, if you ask me."

Calvin just grunted.

They reached the base of the field and Taylor waved to one of the groundskeepers, a dark-colored Hispanic man with sun-spotted skin.

As the worker walked towards them, Taylor said, "This is Francisco Sierra, the groundskeeper who found Samantha Baylor."

Calvin didn't recognize the man, but there was no way for the former running back to know all of the people who worked at USC, especially those he rarely ran in to.

"Detective?" Sierra's accent sounded thick.

"Good morning, Mr. Sierra. Where were you last night?"

The question caught Sierra off guard. Calvin loved Taylor's direct approach. No beating around the bush, straight to the point.

"At home with my family."

That could be verified.

"Do you know Tiana Washington?" Baker asked.

Sierra nodded. "Of course, very nice lady."

"She was murdered this morning."

Sierra's face tightened. His forehead was peppered with sweat pellets from working on the field all morning in the hot sun.

"Oh no." The man brought a hand to his face, looking visibly shaken. Then looked back at the detectives. "You think I did it?"

Baker said, "Just asking questions."

"Why would I kill Tiana?"

Taylor crossed her arms. "Maybe to cover something up."

"The cheerleader?"

No one answered Sierra.

"Why would I kill that cheerleader?"

He had a point. Calvin saw no good reason for the groundskeeper to kill Samantha Baylor, and the PI doubted the detectives had any good reason for the groundskeeper to do it either.

"Did you talk often with Tiana?"

He shook his head. "Not often."

Taylor removed a pad from her jacket. "When was the last time?"

"Couple of days ago."

"What did you talk about? Did she seem off?"

"Not as talkative. She usually talked so much that I had to tell her I had to get back to work. But on this day, she seemed distracted, just some small talk and then she moved on."

Sierra had noticed the changes in Tiana, as Calvin had.

"Would she have any reason to be on the field during her job?"

"Not really."

"Thank you, Mr. Sierra."

The groundskeeper nodded and returned to his work, moving slower than before.

Calvin looked around the field and when his eyes hovered over the team locker room hallway entrance, a thought tugged at his brain.

"Since Sierra noticed Washington seemed off, as you did, it's safe to say that something was on her mind. What's wrong?" Taylor said.

Calvin looked up and saw the two detectives staring at him, Taylor looking concerned.

"I'm not sure. I think I'm remembering something from the night I took the shot."

"What is it?"

Calvin struggled to bring back the memory. He left the detectives standing in the middle of the field. He started speed-walking towards the field team entrance, finally hearing the detectives jogging to keep up behind him.

He kept walking straight off the field and into the empty hallway, as if in a trance, being pulled in that direction. The concrete floor gleamed, the walls covered with player photos. Calvin wasn't sure what he was looking for, but something in his unconscious had drawn him into the hallway.

He stopped and looked around. "There."

He remembered—the tiny specks of blood spatter on the wall.

"What is it?" Taylor asked.

"Blood," Baker said. He took a deep puff of a cigarette and turned his head to blow smoke through his nose. "CSI didn't work inside towards the dressing rooms so they wouldn't have spotted it."

Taylor started moving towards the wall and turned to speak over her shoulder. "I doubt they would have spotted this anyway. Call it in."

Detective Baker pulled out his phone and walked away, bringing it to his ear and covering his other ear with his free hand.

"Nice job," Taylor said to Calvin.

"Thanks."

Calvin swiped the back of his hand across his forehead and noticed that he was sweating heavily. He stabbed at the wall to steady himself, and then lowered down onto a long wooden bench welded to the wall.

"You okay?"

"Fine."

Baker came back. "They're sending a team over here to collect. Also, the soil analysis came back, definitely Bermuda grass, good call."

"Thanks." Taylor took the compliment as if she wasn't accustomed to receiving them.

Baker continued, "I also sent a car over to Sierra's house to speak with the family and neighbors. I don't think he is our murderer though."

"Me neither," Calvin said.

"Have to make sure, though," Taylor added.

Calvin's temples throbbed. "How long will your team take to get here?"

Baker threw out what was left of the butt of his cigarette. "We have some time, but we should be here when they arrive."

"What now?"

Taylor sat down beside Calvin. "Let's stay on campus, and go see Bridgette Acres."

"Who's that?" Calvin asked.

Taylor eyed Calvin, and the PI felt as if under a microscope. "The Bridgette name you gave us when you interviewed the sorority girls."

Calvin had no idea what she was talking about.

"You don't remember, do you?"

"No, sorry."

"Bridgette Acres was a member of the Delta Gamma sorority. She quit the sorority for some reason, and I'd like to find out why. I don't like those girls, and I think they are guilty of something."

Calvin looked back at the detective. "You think Baylor died because of a sorority dispute?"

"I still have no idea why she was murdered."

The PI couldn't recall ever speaking with sorority girls, but if Taylor said he had given them Bridgette's name, so be it. But the PI remained more than just a little frustrated, and had trouble living with the idea that many of his memories had been lost, and might never be retrieved again. Calvin was always the one in control, but now he had to ride the coattails of a female detective who seemed to have a chip on her shoulder.

How long would she let him hang around?

Charlene watched Watters through the rear-view mirror as he squirmed in the backseat. Although the large PI was black, he had paled slightly since they'd left the Coliseum. They had thought about walking, Charlene had suggested it, but Larry voted for taking the unmarked, and from the look of Calvin's face, he might need a break.

"Maybe you should wait here in the car," she said.

"I'm fine," Calvin replied.

But the grimace on his face told another story.

After moving out of the historic Delta Gamma sorority house, Bridgette Acres had moved into a small, one-bedroom apartment on campus at the Cale and Irani Residential College.

Even though they didn't have a parking permit, they parked a block and a half away from the building, at the USC Shrine Structure, which irritated Larry. The parking lot was designated for those students living in the Cale and Irani building.

They got out of the car and Charlene noticed Watters grab the roof of the vehicle to steady himself, even though he tried to hide it. The detective knew the type, worked with many of them.

The male ego was a fragile thing, and men didn't like to be seen as vulnerable or weak, the testosterone running through them that sometimes made their brains make decisions that their bodies weren't ready to accommodate.

"Still don't know why we had to park so far away," Larry grumbled, as they walked towards the building, the hot sun burning down on them.

Larry still dressed in his nineties style clothing, even though he had put on about thirty pounds since those days. His tweed jacket was unforgiving in the heat of the California sunlight, and Charlene knew that his shirt would be full of sweat stains by the time he made it to Bridgette Acre's room. Charlene had tried to talk him into some new fashion, but he was too hard headed to oblige.

The Cale and Irani Residential College was a five-story edifice designed in the Collegiate Gothic brick and stone architectural style. The first floor was devoted to common areas and facilities and the student apartments appeared on the upper floors. The second floor had a large courtyard.

When they stepped into the building lobby and the fresh air-conditioning hit them, Charlene heard Larry sigh. They stopped and flashed their badges at the Customer Service Center devoted to assisting residents, located on the first floor beside a FedEx Mail Center, before making their way to floor three.

Bridgette Acres answered the door on the first knock—a petite, pretty African-American girl with high cheekbones and hair too tightly braided. Charlene saw similar features between Acres and Samantha Baylor. Acres looked like a girl who didn't smile often.

"Good morning, Ms. Acres." Charlene showed her badge. "May we come in?"

"What's this about?" Acres brought her hand to her face.

"We promise not to take up much of your time."

Acres stepped aside slightly and cracked open the door a few more inches to allow them to squeeze inside. Acres lived alone. The apartment area was spacious for a single person, with a very modern look.

"We can sit over here," Acres said, pointing to a sitting area at the end of the large room they had entered.

They chose an L-shaped, mustard-colored couch, the only piece of furniture in this part of the room. Because of the shoulder span of both Larry and Calvin, there was very little space left for Charlene and Acres on the sofa. Larry immediately unbuttoned his collar.

Charlene sat next to Calvin, who seemed uncomfortable. A drop of sweat rolled down the side of his face and his breathing had gotten slightly louder, almost labored. Charlene worried he might not last the interview.

"So what's this about?" Acres asked, sitting cross-legged, campfire style.

Charlene slipped her phone in her pocket. "Delta Gamma."

The sophomore shifted in her seat. Charlene wasn't sure if the sudden uncomfortable transfer came from the conversation topic, or the lack of space on the couch.

"What about them?"

Charlene stood up and pulled out a chair from a small, square dining table. She dragged it across the floor and placed it facing the couch, in reaching distance from the rest of them. As soon as this happened, they synchronized a shift to the left on the sofa, now with a few inches of space between them.

Acres brought up her knees to her chest.

"Why did you leave?" Larry asked, trying to scoot up to the edge of the cushion, as he had started to sink down into the crack at the back.

Acres ran her fingers over her braids. "It just wasn't for me."

"Why not?" Charlene countered.

Acres breathed in deeply. "It just wasn't what I thought it was." She looked down at her bare knees.

"Bridgette." Charlene leaned forward in her seat, resting her elbows on her knees. "You know that Samantha Baylor was murdered."

Acres nodded.

"Samantha Baylor pledged at the sorority."

The statement snapped Acres head up. She now looked at Charlene, her eyes showing signs of sadness.

"Tell me about the sorority, Bridgette."

Acres hugged her knees. "Before I actually joined, the girls acted really nice and seemed interested in me. They went out of their way to invite me to things, and it seemed genuine and exciting." Her eyes unfocused, as if off in a distance. "But as soon as I joined, though, things changed."

"How so?"

"I don't know. It just wasn't the same. Not just for me, but all the freshman who joined."

"What happened?" Watters asked.

"We got pushed to the side, nobody wanted to get to know us, especially me."

"Why you?"

"I didn't party and I had a steady boyfriend. It can be really confusing because you think you're making the right decision by joining, but then it all seems so fake. I refused to do things they asked me to do."

"Like what?"

Acres looked down again, as if embarrassed. "My least favorite part about pledging was how much the girls stabbed each other in the back, and how ruthless they were. We didn't know anyone, and once the rush ended, the older girls who had been really nice to us turned sour, and acted like we weren't worthy of being members until initiation."

"What happened at initiation?"

"We had to do things blindfolded with the pledgers from some of the fraternities."

She didn't go further, and Charlene didn't push her.

"Rory Cummings told me that she had requested to be Samantha Baylor's big sister. What's that all about?"

Acres nodded weakly. "Every pledge gets set up with a Junior, a big sister to show them the ropes, I guess."

"Who was your big sister?"

"Emma Moore."

This time Charlene looked up from her notepad at the mention of Moore. Calvin made a sound on the couch. He massaged his temples, looking unhealthy.

"You okay," Charlene asked Calvin.

Watters blinked a couple of times. "Fine, but that name is familiar."

"You know Moore?"

"I think so, and I don't think she made a good first impression."

"With me either."

Charlene turned back to Acres. "How was Moore as a big sister?"

"Demanding. She knew that she would be the head of the sorority when she became a senior, so she wanted to go above and beyond to impress the sisters. So she pushed and pushed me until I couldn't take any more."

Acres had started to cry quietly. She didn't make any loud sobbing sounds, but tears sneaked down both cheeks.

Charlene reached over and placed a hand on Acres' leg, to settle her trembling knees. "It's okay, Bridgette."

Then Acres lost it, her sobs growing louder and, sniffing back the urge to lose control totally, Larry handed the sophomore a crumpled up tissue from his jacket pocket. Charlene wondered how old the Kleenex was.

"I'm sorry," she whispered, taking the tissue.

"You have nothing to be sorry about," Charlene said.

"Did you ever report any of this?" Calvin asked. "USC has people to handle this sort of hazing."

"No," she choked out between sobs. "Delta Gamma has a long history, and I didn't think anyone would believe me. I thought the easiest thing to do was to just quit."

"Last question, Bridgette, and then we will leave. Do you know who Samantha Baylor's big sister was?"

Acres dropped the tissue down into her lap, and looked up with red, wet eyes. "I heard it was Mia Davidson."

Chapter 26

The field turf felt soggy, thanks to the condensation from the evening fog. They crossed over to the LAPD CSI team, who was already set up and working by the time they made it back to the Coliseum. The detectives had already prepped them so they knew what to look for.

Calvin struggled, feeling the ever-growing side-effects of his concussion. A migraine had made a home in the back of his skull, a throbbing pain that felt like a thousand hornets buzzing fire inside his temples.

"Mia Davidson, seems fitting," Taylor said.

"Why's that?" Calvin's mind swam, and his attention and energy drained.

"She's tight with Moore, and it looks like Davidson is next in line to take over as head of the sorority next year when Moore graduates."

"Which means she probably pushed Baylor as hard, if not harder, than Moore had pushed Acres the year before," Larry said.

"She'd want to impress Moore for sure." Taylor looked at Calvin. "What was your take on Moore?"

Calvin blinked long and hard, but his vision blurred. The detectives looked like fuzzy, colored shadows through his eyes. He squeezed his lids closed, barely able to fill his lungs with air.

"Not sure," he replied.

"You sure you're okay?"

Calvin opened his eyes back up. "Fine."

Taylor nodded towards CSI. "Let's find out what's going on."

Calvin paused in mid-stride, then involuntarily dropped down to one knee, a dizzy spell forcing him down. He reached out to the wall to avoid falling completely over.

"Calvin." Taylor's voice was high-strung, and sounded as if in the distance, but she stood only a few feet away.

He felt a small hand under his armpit, pulling forcefully on him. But the hand belonged to someone without the strength to lift Calvin. Then the PI felt a second hand under his other armpit, this one bigger, meatier.

This time Calvin was lifted up to a standing position, but his legs wobbled, threatening to give out.

"Grab that chair," Baker's voice authoritarian.

A scraping noise tore at Calvin eardrums as a metal chair scuffed across the pavement. His body lowered onto the cold steel, his bare leg, under his shorts, against the cool metal.

He breathed in and out several times, as the noise around him drowned out by the pounding of his own heartbeat. Once his breathing steadied, he wiped the sweat from above his upper lip and opened his eyes.

His vision became clearer, and the PI saw the detectives staring at him. A look of concern arched Detective Taylor's pretty face.

"Maybe we should get him back to the hospital," Baker suggested.

"I'll be fine," Calvin said. When he looked up, Taylor squatted beside his chair. "Just let me sit here for a few minutes."

"You've been sitting down for fifteen," Taylor said.

Calvin searched his pocket for his phone and took it out, checking the time. She hadn't lied, that much time had passed.

He pushed himself up off the chair. "Let's do this."

Working with Dale and the LVMPD these last couple of years, Calvin had seen his fair share of police scenes. He followed the detectives, sluggishly, carefully monitoring every step, over to where a tech swabbed the dried blood stain from the concrete wall.

The specks were so slight that it was easy to see how it would have been missed by cleaners. Evidence markers had already been placed around the blood drips on the concrete floor.

CSI scraped off the dried blood without smearing any prints, and lifted several hairs without disturbing any trace evidence. The wall had been blackened by magnetic powder print dust, used to enhance fingerprints on non-polished surfaces. From what Calvin could make out, there were no signs of fingerprints.

"Definitely human blood," the tech said. "We'll bring it back to see if it belongs to Samantha Baylor."

"I think it belongs to Baylor," Taylor said, now talking between the three of them. "Remember that cut on her forehead, above her right eye?"

"The only open wound on her body."

"So how did it get here?" Calvin asked. He felt slightly better, or at least he told himself that. But the former running back knew he couldn't mentally will this injury out of his body, as he'd done when he'd played football.

"No idea, yet."

Calvin had never seen a woman with such confidence, such conviction. From what he'd seen of her, Taylor let nothing stand in her way. She worked with mainly men, and had already made a name for herself. He was sure she'd stomp on anyone who stood in front of her.

"Doesn't look like there's any other trace evidence here," the tech said. "No prints, hair follicles, scales of skin or pieces of fingernails."

"Okay, thanks." The detective turned to face Calvin. "You feel up to going back to Tiana Washington's house? I'll make sure her kids are there to meet us."

"Absolutely. They'll know if something is out of place."

Calvin had tried napping on the way to Tiana's house, but the throbbing headache penetrating his skull interfered. His blood pressure started to build. The sunlight stung his retinas, but every time he closed his eyes, the blood rushing to his brain created a pounding sensation that touched the back of his scalp.

So he kept his head down, laying back on the head-rest, and slid on his sunglasses. His eyelids felt heavy.

Taylor appeared relaxed, driving with one hand on the wheel. She stole glances at him in the rear view mirror, a forlorn look in her eyes.

Her cellphone chimed, and she pressed the hands-free speaker so everyone in the car could hear the conversation.

"Taylor."

A male voice said, "Detective, this is Officer Daniels. You asked me to put a trace on Tiana Washington's cellphone."

Taylor yelled even though she didn't need to. "What did you find out, Officer?"

"Nothing. The cellphone can't be traced."

"What do you mean? Why not?"

"Whoever has it has removed the battery. A trace is impossible because the GPS tracker isn't functional."

She pounded the steering wheel. "Smart."

"We also confirmed Francisco Sierra's alibi. A few neighbors remember seeing his truck parked at his home and it never moved all night. They never noticed Sierra leave or anyone come around."

"Okay, thanks."

"What else can I do?"

"Sit tight for now. I'll call you if I need anything." She hung up.

Tiana Washington's sons and mother-in-law stood in the front yard when the detective wheeled the car into the driveway. The house loomed, still marked with police tape and evidence markers, closing the residence from any intruders. A crime scene still in progress.

The tiny neighborhood had seen its share of crime and violence. Still, the house seemed out of place—scarred by a local murder, and stained from an ongoing criminal investigation.

Calvin didn't like what he saw when he looked into the faces of Washington's children. He only hoped that the younger one, Jeremiah, was still too young to totally comprehend the situation and understand what happened. But at eight years old, Calvin doubted it.

The older one, Elijah, knew exactly what was going on. From what Calvin knew about the young boy, even though only ten years old, he was still inquisitive and bright. At this time in his life, that would be a curse. He understood the impact this would have on him and his brother.

They got out of the car, Calvin lagging behind, involuntarily, his body weary.

"Ma'am, I'm Detective Taylor, this is Detective Baker." Taylor showed her badge.

The old African American lady stood tight-lipped, arms crossed, as if to dare the detectives to budge her even slightly. Calvin knew the type, and was sure the detectives had seen the kind many times.

Flora King, a victim of the streets, grew up in a time when cops were seen as the enemy.

"Well, you got us here," King said, far from impressed. Her southern drawl added to a sarcastic undertone.

"Thank you for coming, Ms. King," Detective Taylor said.

"What do you want with us, Detectives? These boys have been through—"

She stopped when she noticed Calvin hanging back, following in behind the detectives. He had been shielded by Baker's large span, and when he came into view of the old lady, he knew he attracted her attention.

"Calvin? Calvin Watters? Is that you?"

"Yes, ma'am," Calvin replied shyly. Momma King had always intimidated Calvin slightly, with her no-nonsense talk.

The old lady moved towards Calvin, slower than the former running back remembered her years ago. Her face had aged, more lines and wrinkles than he recalled. Her hair slightly lighter in color and thickness. Her large square-framed glasses still covered brown eyes filled with wisdom, but now partially covered by small cataracts.

She wrapped her arms around Calvin, but her hands were too short and fragile to reach each other. Holding him close, she cuddled him gently. He squeezed back timidly.

"Oh, my God, it's been too long." She pulled away, eyeing him from top to bottom. Her eyes misted. "What are you doing back in these parts?"

"I'm a private investigator now. I'm working on a case."

"Calvin," Taylor said. The look she gave him, with squinty eyes, as if to shut him up, kept him from talking about the ongoing investigation.

He put up his hand to the detective. But Momma King deserved to know that her daughter-in-law's death might be connected with another murder. The one thing that Calvin knew, was how to talk "street talk".

He knew he had a way with people, how to speak with them, play to their sympathies and blend into any situation, and the PI wasn't so blind as to see that the detective probably let him hang around for that one very reason.

"And this case involves Tiana?"

"I…we, think so."

Momma King sneered towards the detectives. "Well, if Calvin says it's so, then it must be. I trust him. I don't trust no cops."

"We hoped you could help us," Baker said.

"Who said I was talkin' to you?" Momma said bluntly.

Baker's face reddened, and he tugged at the tight collar collapsing his bulky neck.

Detective Taylor stepped back and placed her hand on Calvin's back, guiding him forward in front of the detectives.

"See what you can do," she whispered.

Calvin had to hand it to the detective. Of all the stories he'd heard about her, from his brother and Dale, about her 'cowboy' style, always in control, wouldn't take a second seat to anyone, she seemed smart enough to know that she couldn't beat Momma King. Calvin was their best bet, the only one who would get any kind of cooperation from the old lady.

He stepped forward, his legs threatening to give out. His migraine had weakened, but was still present. The sun felt warm on the back of his neck, his shirt partially damp.

"Momma, I hope you and the boys can help us."

"What can we do?" When she spoke to Calvin, her voice softened.

He waved at her. "Come inside."

Calvin hated putting them in this position, especially the boys. Normally, he would never do this, but he agreed with Taylor that they would have an easier time identifying anything that had been taken, anything that looked out of place or missing.

Calvin was in no condition himself to remember things from his last visit only days ago. The rap on the back of his skull had at least temporarily, if not permanently, deleted any memory he had from the inside of Tiana's house.

This became the LAPD's call, and he wanted to help solve this case in any way that he could.

Momma turned her back to Calvin and looked at her boys. They stood back, timid, the younger one slightly scared. Elijah stood tall, as if knowing that as the older, he had to be strong for his little brother.

Calvin recognized that strength.

"You stay outside with Jeremiah. He needs you right now," Calvin said to Momma.

His stomach had joined his head; it ached putting the boys through this.

"What about Elijah?" the old woman asked.

"I'll take him in with me."

Momma King looked back and forth between Elijah and Calvin. The one-time Calvin Watters jersey strapped to Elijah's upper body now looked looser, as if the boy seemed smaller now after his mother's death.

"I trust you'll take care of him, Calvin."

Calvin placed a hand on the woman's shoulder and moved passed her. He heard the detectives following him.

He put his arm around Elijah, the boy shrinking into Calvin's thick limb.

"You okay with this, buddy?" Calvin asked.

The boy nodded, staring at the front door to the house.

"I want to help." His voice shallow, weak.

Calvin carefully guided the twelve year-old towards the house. The boy moved willingly, allowing Calvin to direct him.

Calvin pushed open the front door and all four of them stepped inside.

"Let's go room to room," Detective Taylor said.

"Okay."

They did, covering each room, and each time Elijah admitted that he saw nothing gone, other than all of their electronics.

In the living room, Taylor asked, "When did you get this brand new TV, Elijah?"

The boy touched the TV. He swayed back and forth from foot to foot. "Couple days ago," he answered quietly, barely above a whisper.

"That's an expensive TV," Baker said.

They had already noted the television in their first visit after Washington's murder. Something was off about it—no way that a single mother, working a minimum wage job could afford the purchase.

"Where did you get it?"

The boy shrugged his shoulders. "Mama bought it."

Calvin had known Tiana for a long time. She didn't just buy things that weren't 'needs'. She lived conservatively.

"We are looking into any part-time jobs Washington may have had," Taylor said to Calvin, as if reading his mind.

Was he that transparent?

They visited Tiana's bedroom last, a complete mess of clothes and broken furniture, having been tossed like the other rooms. Elijah stopped just inside the doorway, the only one inside the room, the rest of them blocked from entering by his tiny frame.

His eyes wandered the room, taking everything in.

"Something off, Elijah?" Calvin asked.

The boy said nothing. He stepped inside further and they followed him. He made a beeline for the closet and stepped one foot inside, then stared up towards the ceiling.

"What is it?"

Taylor charged over to him. She moved him aside and cocked her head to look up into the corner of the small closet, her head just barely fitting under the bar that hung Tiana's clothes.

The detective pulled out a tiny flashlight and shone it up towards the corner.

"I can't see anything. The shelf is blocking my view and I'm too short to reach up."

She looked towards Calvin, so he walked over, trying to squeeze his square build into the cramped quarters. He reached up, his six-foot-four height aiding. His hand brushed against a knob of some sort.

"I feel something," he said.

"What is it?"

"Not sure. Feels like something sticking out of the wall."

"Pull."

He tugged gradually but nothing moved. Whatever he pulled on seemed stuck, unwilling to budge.

"It doesn't want to come."

"Don't be afraid to break it," Baker said.

Calvin yanked hard, heard a snap, and a square wooden piece fell, grazing his shoulder before banging on the floor. A half-second later, hundred dollar bills spilled to the ground, followed by a crumpled up white envelope. It was wrinkled, as if having been opened and closed multiple times. It had a stamp and Washington's address, but no return address.

Calvin looked down at the floor, where several green bills scattered, and a few more still lodged tightly inside the blank envelope. He bent down.

"Don't touch that money," Baker ordered. "That's evidence."

"Washington had something on the side," Taylor said.

"Taylor," Baker scolded her gently, looking at Tiana's son who had stood back and watched the episode carry out.

"Do you know where this money came from, Elijah?" Detective Taylor asked.

The boy shook his head.

"Do you know when she got it?" Calvin asked.

"Yesterday. I snuck in here and watched her put that envelope up there."

Calvin went to the boy and knelt down beside him. "Did you ask her about it?"

His eyes were large. "Yes, sir. I asked her what it was."

"What did she say?"

"She said it was nothing I needed to worry about."

Baker said, "How did she seem?"

"What do you mean?"

Taylor pursed her lips. "He won't know that, Larry. He's a kid."

Calvin turned the boy to face him. "When did she put it up there?"

"When we got home."

"Home from where?"

"The post office."

"I know that post office, it's not far."

They returned to the car, Charlene driving. She liked driving, hated being in the passenger seat and not in control of the vehicle. Just another of her traits that turned many men off, but Larry seemed to enjoy the laid back position of passenger.

She backed out of the driveway with a rev of the engine, the tires spitting up loose sand and stones.

They had taken longer than she had planned, wanted to get the hell out of there and chase this lead, but she gave Calvin time to offer his condolences and console the three family members of Tiana Washington. She could at least do that for them.

Now she wanted to move, and quickly. She caught a scent, and although she'd learned as a cop never to get too high, a smidgeon of hope mixed in with her determination.

The post office Tiana Washington's son had described popped up at the corner of Hill Street and West Thirty-Seventh Street, not far from USC.

Charlene looked at Calvin in the rearview. "Check that bag on the seat beside you. There's some extra strength Tylenol in there. Should help with the headache."

Watters rummaged through the bag and removed two pills from the bottle, dry swallowing them. Relief flashed across his face. Then he said, "Thanks. What do you hope to find at the post office?"

"The exact date and time Washington opened that box," Larry replied.

Charlene said, "The US Postal Service deploys IPv6-capable video surveillance systems using EnableIT PoE Extenders."

"What does that mean?"

"Long distance, high-quality video surveillance. Maybe we'll get lucky."

"Why does a post office need such high-tech surveillance?"

"Video surveillance is critical to prevent and investigate burglaries and other security incidents that occur inside and around USPS facilities."

Calvin shook his head. "But a post office, really?"

Charlene had asked that same question to a senior detective before, when she'd worked a scene as an officer. "A post office is a potential target for criminals just as surely as any other government building is. The US Post office also has internal theft and incidents of workplace violence that need to be under surveillance to reduce occurrences.

"What about the money?" Calvin asked.

"It will be processed by the crime lab."

"Fingerprints?"

"Hardly," Larry scoffed. "There will be hundreds of prints on those bills."

"We'll attempt to trace it back to where it came from, but we will have to involve financial crimes detectives, who have experience tracking money movements. Maybe we'll get an ATM withdrawal, but that's a longshot and takes time."

They had already called ahead so they were ushered inside the post office and guided to the back of the building, where the surveillance monitors ran twenty-four-seven.

An overweight lady with glasses and an old-fashioned hairstyle opened the conversation. "Do you know the box number?"

"No," Charlene said.

"That would be helpful."

Charlene breathed out loudly, hoping the lady would get the urgency of their visit.

"The name is Tiana Washington."

"We have no box registered to that name here."

"She wouldn't have used her real name," Watters said.

"Good point." Charlene turned to the lady. "Do you have the tapes ready?"

"Yes."

They watched the video feed from yesterday, when Elijah reported his mother had stopped in. They saw Tiana stroll into the building early in the morning, probably having just left work for home.

The moment Washington popped up on the video, Charlene's senses tingled.

"There's the box," Charlene pointed. "What number is that?"

The lady zoomed in on Washington, and closed in on the box number. "305," the lady said.

"Check it."

She hurriedly tapped keys on the keyboard and the information came up on the screen.

"That box is registered to Mrs. Flora Washington."

"She used her mother-in-law's first name."

"Not very crafty," Larry remarked.

"She's not a lifetime criminal," Watters said, a defensive tone in his voice.

Charlene knew of Calvin's relationship with the security guard. She knew her murder pained him, but he was handling it well.

"When was it opened?" Charlene asked.

The employee smacked on gum. "Tuesday morning."

"She planned something," Charlene noted. "What do you think, Calvin?"

Checking to see if Watters was as clever as everyone said, and if on the same page as she and Larry.

He whispered, "Hush money?"

"That's what I think too. She blackmailed someone. But what did she have on that person?"

Charlene acknowledged the lady. "Can you trace where the mail came from?"

"Return address on the envelope?"

"No?"

She blew a bubble. "We can trace what city it had been mailed from."

"Forget it. We know where it came from."

"LA," Calvin and Charlene said together.

Larry's phone rang, and he flipped it open. It amazed Charlene that Larry still owned a flip-phone.

He checked the number. "It's Clark." He answered. "This is Baker."

The name surprised Charlene. What would the DA be calling Larry about? She watched Larry's tense facial expression as he listened to Clark.

"Yes, sir. We'll be there." He flipped the phone shut. "Ryan Turner and his father want to meet with us."

"The quarterback?" Watters asked.

"The one and only," Charlene replied.

Chapter 27

When they stopped for a late lunch at a downtown deli, Charlene filled Calvin in on Turner's connection to the case, or apparent connections. Watters listened carefully, seeming to take it all in, but said nothing.

Watters had a strong relationship to USC, and any college alumni felt a strong bond to their school, and anyone who attended, especially the football family. The bond was tightly wound, unbreakable, and Charlene wondered how the former running back would handle investigating one of his 'brothers'.

So far, he passed with flying colors, but they hadn't yet gotten dirty. It was about to get nasty.

She hadn't really been prepped, and the thought of walking into a meeting unprepared put Charlene on edge. This was the second time in this case that Charlene and Larry had been called into a meeting with a suspect and his parents.

For all she knew, Turner's father, a rich Hollywood big shot in the real estate game, wanted to meet with her and Larry, after Turner had been ordered to give a blood sample.

"Calvin, unfortunately you won't be allowed inside the room during the interview," Larry said. "This is police business, and you're not a sworn-in officer, so we can't do anything to get around it."

"That's fine. You must have a place for me to watch, though?"

Charlene smiled. "Sounds like you've been in a precinct before."

Watters returned her smile. "Once or twice."

"I won't ask."

Once they entered the building, Charlene took Calvin to a windowless room at the end of a long, narrow hall.

"Wait in here," she told him. "You'll be able to watch the interview and give me your take on what you see and hear."

The small square room sat adjacent to the interview room, a two-way mirror dividing the two rooms. Usually this room was designated for the "higher-ups", who wanted to sit in on interviews, so Charlene knew that Watters would be comfortable.

"Do you think Turner would do anything to jeopardize his future? He has billions of dollars waiting for him in the pros," Watters asked.

"Good question, maybe he didn't do anything," Larry replied.

Charlene gave her partner a jagged look. "Then why call this meeting?"

"Damage control? Trying to get ahead of this thing. I think something happened that they need to explain before the press gets involved.," Larry suggested.

Calvin asked, "The baby angle?"

"More than likely. You want a coffee or anything?"

Watters shook his head.

"You don't look great, Calvin," Charlene said, and it was no lie.

The man's bloodshot eyes held a cloudy gaze, and he constantly used the things around him to steady himself, even if he tried to conceal the fact that he needed those crutches.

Charlene had been diagnosed with a minor concussion before, when she'd been knocked unconscious by Sean Cooney, a former LAPD member turned serial killer.

Even though it had been only a partial concussion, Charlene had felt the wrath of the side-effects, so she couldn't even begin to imagine what Watters' body and mind, after a full force blow with a steel pipe, was fighting through right now.

Watters plopped down on a steel chair with no cushion or cover. Charlene and Larry left the room to confront Turner.

"How should we handle this?" Charlene asked.

Larry snorted. "Like it matters what I say. We both know how you want to handle it."

"I just think a direct line of questioning is the way to go."

"You always think that."

Larry shouldered open the door.

Three men sat at the table, and all three stood when the detectives entered the room.

Very courteous.

Charlene recognized Turner from the pictures splashed all over the media—social, TV and newspaper—and from the posters hanging around the Coliseum: young, handsome, well built and an arrogant grin that really bothered the detective. He wasn't smiling today.

Turner's father had the same features as his son, only more handsome, aging well. He had brown feathered hair and a strong jaw. His face was lined, but looked well preserved. Carson Turner, a typical headline grabber, had taken over as his son's sports agent/manager, so his face was as recognizable as the USC quarterback's. The father already had a reputation as a hard-baller, someone who may hurt his son more by interfering in and disrupting his son's certain future in football. It had happened before with athletes.

The third man Charlene didn't know, but the detective figured him to be the Turners' attorney. He wore an expensive suit, glasses, and his hair was parted perfectly to the side. His thin face and pointy nose made him look younger than he was.

"Did you bring the blood sample?" Charlene asked.

"That's direct," Larry whispered.

"Good evening, Detectives," the well-dressed man said. "I'm Harvey Baringer. I'm representing Ryan and Carson Turner."

"Representation, how nice," Larry said.

Charlene repeated, "Since you're here, I guess you received the request, and you know why we are requesting it. So where's the blood sample?"

Charlene approached the table, and the detectives plunked down. The three men did the same. The detective removed a recording device and placed it on the table.

"What are you doing, Detective?" the lawyer asked.

"Recording this."

"I don't think so. This isn't an interrogation."

Charlene looked at Larry. Her partner shrugged so she put the device back in her pocket.

"Blood sample?"

"There is no need for a blood sample," the attorney said.

"Why's that?" Charlene figured they would try to twist their way out of this one.

"It was my baby," Ryan Turner said. He refused to make direct eye contact with the detectives.

"How do you know?" Charlene asked.

"Samantha told me."

"And you believed her?" Larry said.

Ryan shrugged his shoulders, which looked toned through his white t-shirt, but now slouched as if in defeat.

Charlene crossed one leg over the other. "You have a bright future. Ever worry about a girl trying to take advantage of that?"

Turner shook his head.

"She also slept with Mark Simon," Charlene stated.

"We would have requested a paternity test to confirm," Carson Turner said. "But obviously that's not necessary, now."

Charlene wasn't sure if the senior Turner realized the implications of what he had said, or just saw the stares and slack-jaws from everyone at the table, but he hung his head slightly, as much as a rich, arrogant Californian could, anyway.

"When did Samantha Baylor tell you about the pregnancy?"

"About a week ago."

"Was she happy?"

Another shoulder shrug. "Maybe, but she seemed kind of scared. Like she wasn't sure what she should do."

"What did you say to her?"

"Nothing. I was stunned. I'd only slept with her that one time."

"It only takes one time," Charlene muttered sarcastically. "Did you sleep with her after the party, the night of the fight and breakup between her and Simon?"

The quarterback nodded.

"Was that the only time?"

"Does it matter?" the attorney cut in.

Charlene looked at him. "I'm just confirming if Ryan here had a relationship with Ms. Baylor or if it was just a one night stand."

"That was the only time," the USC senior said.

"Did you see her again after that?"

"Just when she told me about the baby."

"And the night she died," Charlene snapped.

Ryan looked at his father, who in turn looked at the attorney.

"What do you mean?" the lawyer said, giving them a stern look. But Charlene could read his face.

"We have an eye witness who can place you and Samantha Baylor together at the Coliseum on the night of her murder, not long before she died."

Now the three men, who had seemed so smug and confident at the start of the meeting, huddled together. Charlene couldn't make out the words, but the attorney did the bulk of the talking.

When the huddle broke, Ryan said, "Yes. We left the party to talk about the baby."

"Why did you go to the Coliseum?"

"I don't know. That's where we ended up."

"Because you'd be alone?"

"Yes. What? No," he said, backpedalling.

The attorney placed a soft hand on Ryan's arm. The QB seemed to get riled up, even though he was known as a player who never buckled under pressure, who had ice water running through his veins.

He let out a breath. "We both liked the Coliseum, we felt at ease there."

"So what did you talk about?"

"The baby."

"What about it?"

"Sam said she wanted to keep it."

"And how did that make you feel?"

"I don't know. I didn't want her to have an abortion. She told me that she could tell Mark that it was his if I wanted her to. But she wanted me to know that it was mine."

"What did you say to that? Did you agree to it?"

"Nothing. I didn't know what to say."

Spoiled brat. "Did anyone else know about the baby?"

"What do you mean?"

"Did you tell anyone about Ms. Baylor's pregnancy?"

Ryan looked at his father, than back at the detective. "No."

"So what happened when you finished talking?"

"Nothing."

Charlene rubbed her hands together and then said, "Did you sleep with her?"

"No," he said quickly. "I just left."

"Did she go with you?"

"No, she stayed there."

"Where did you go?"

"Back to the party."

Lewis Mahoney had said the same thing. "And you didn't bring her with you?"

"She said she wanted to be alone."

"Did you kill her?"

He paled. "What? Of course not."

"Detective," Baringer said, as if a warning.

The threat didn't even scratch Charlene's skin. She noticed Larry smiling.

"Was she hurt when you left her? Bleeding?"

"No. We just talked and then I left."

"What time did you leave at?"

"I'm not sure."

"How convenient."

"Wait." Ryan Turner fiddled in his pants pocket and removed his iPhone. "I sent a text to Jumbo as I left the Coliseum to tell him I was on my way back to the party." He looked at the phone. "10:12pm."

Charlene took the phone and looked at the text messages. Turner wasn't lying, he had sent that text at the time and was replied to. Whether or not he was actually leaving or this was a set up was another reason it had to be verified again.

"Who's Jumbo?" Larry asked.

"Sorry. My center, Jacob Cartwright."

Charlene wrote down the name and handed back the phone. They would follow up with Cartwright and find out at what time Turner showed up back at the party. The detective knew how long it should take to walk back to the frat house, so she would know if Turner had actually left when he said he had, after sending this text. Or did he wait around a little longer to finish the job.

"Okay, Mr. Turner. Let me tell you what we have." Charlene flipped through her notepad, not because she had a book full of notes on Turner, but more for dramatic effect, to get them squirming. "The time of death for Ms. Baylor from the medical examiner stated around eleven o'clock Saturday night. You were the last person to be with the victim, at the scene, before her death. We have no evidence that anyone else was connected with the victim between the time you left her, and the time she was murdered." She looked up from the paper. "What would you think, Mr. Turner?"

The QB shifted in his seat.

"I'd say you have some investigating to do then, Detective," the attorney said, a slight smile tugging at the corners of his mouth.

Charlene felt like reaching across the table and slapping it off his smug face. The room quieted, the tension thick.

"I saw her," Carson Turner said.

Every head turned towards the senior Turner. The silence had been broken, shattered, by that sudden statement.

"What?" Charlene said, shocked. She looked at Larry, who seemed equally surprised.

"What?" Baringer said.

The senior Turner tightened his tie and shot his cuffs "I saw her after Ryan left."

Ryan Turner's stunned expression hit home. "What? Dad?"

When his father put up his hand, Ryan's mouth immediately closed. He slumped back in his chair, still looking as astonished as the rest of them felt.

"I followed Ryan to the Coliseum that night."

Charlene leaned back in her seat. "Why?"

"He's my son. I was worried about him. He told me about the baby."

Charlene looked at the quarterback, who stared at the ground as if in embarrassment. He had lied to them about not telling anyone. What else had he lied about and who else had he told?

"Go on," was all Charlene could think to say. She wasn't ready for this, hadn't prepared any kind of interrogation questions in advance. This was news to all of them.

"I saw them enter the back way to the Coliseum, so I waited. When Ryan came out alone, I decided to go in?"

Larry asked, "Why?"

"I wanted to talk to the girl who accused my son of impregnating her."

"You weren't happy," Charlene said, more of a statement than a question.

"I didn't believe her."

"Your son is going to someday be a wealthy young man. He has a long, bright future ahead of him. You didn't want anything to get in the way of that," Charlene said, starting to put the pieces together.

"Something like that. Ryan wasn't himself; it showed in his play in practice, and off the field."

"So you confronted her."

"I just wanted to talk, feel her out."

"So what happened?"

"I found her sitting at midfield, on the 'SC' emblem, with her back to me. She must have heard my footsteps because she turned around and got up when I approached her."

"What did she say?"

He shook his head. "Nothing. I told her who I was. We talked about the baby. She told me she was keeping it."

"That would put a cramp in your plans for your son."

He nodded. The blood had drained from his face. "I offered her money."

Charlene's heartbeat quickened. "For what?"

"I don't know. To leave my son alone. She could have an abortion or just keep it, but not mention my son, leave him out of it completely."

The QB looked bewildered. "Dad."

When Carson Turner looked over at his son, his stern face quieted Ryan. "I'm sorry, I thought it was the right thing to do. I even had a check with me."

"How did Ms. Baylor react to your offer?"

"When I tried to hand her the check, she swatted my hand away and took off running."

"Did you chase her?"

"Sort of. I went after her, but the grass was slick from the sprinkler system. When she hit the pavement to the locker rooms, she slipped and went head first into the wall."

"Was she hurt?" Even though Charlene already knew the answer.

"Unconscious, but I checked on her." He looked at Charlene. "Still breathing, just knocked out. She had a bump on her head. She was concussed probably, but it wasn't life-threatening."

"What did you do?"

"Left her."

"You left her laying on the cold pavement, unconscious?"

He nodded, but looked down. "I didn't know what to do."

"Did you tell anyone about this?"

Headshake.

"Did you tell anyone about the baby?"

Headshake.

"So she was alive when you left?"

"Yes."

"What time?"

"Maybe twenty minutes after Ryan had left."

If true, they still had a timeline that didn't fit. Who else would have involved themselves, gone to the Coliseum and killed Baylor between the time Carson Turner left and Samantha Baylor's time of death?

Charlene looked at Larry. "What do you think?"

He pressed his lips together. "Nothing else."

"We'll be in touch," she said to the attorney. Then she looked at the Turner men. "Don't leave town."

They took ten steps and found themselves back in the claustrophobically small witness room with Calvin.

"Did you see that?" Charlene asked.

Calvin nodded. "All of it."

"What do you think?"

"Quite the story."

"Do you buy it?"

"They seemed genuine enough."

Detective Dale Dayton of the Vegas police department had told Charlene that Watters acted like a human lie detector, and could read facial expression and body-language better than anyone Dayton had ever met, even those trained in the field and worked for the force.

"So we have a missing piece to the puzzle," Larry said.

"A major piece."

"What's our next move?" Watters asked.

Before Charlene could reply, a ringing grabbed her attention.

Calvin covered his ears with his hands, as if to make it stop. His face showed signs of anxiety, as his palms probably only drowned out the sound slightly, not cutting it out completely.

Charlene tugged on his t-shirt.

When Watters opened his eyes, Charlene pointed to his shorts. Calvin uncovered his ears.

"Your phone is ringing," she informed him.

He looked down at his pocket and pulled out his cell, scanning the screen.

"It's my brother," he said. Calvin held the phone to his ear. "Josh, what's up?"

Charlene could only hear Calvin's end of the call, which always frustrated the detective.

"Fine." His hand shook, the phone maybe heavy in his grip. "At the precinct."

They both watched him, with no time for privacy or consideration.

"Yes. They're both right here."

Charlene perked up at the mention of her.

"I said I was." A few seconds of silence. "Flora King?"

"That's Tiana Washington's mother-in-law," Charlene said, stepping in closer to Calvin.

"What does she want?" Calvin asked into the phone.

Calvin started walking, the phone still pressed against his ear. Charlene followed, Larry at her side.

Calvin didn't speak again, only listened. He put the phone away when they reached the parking lot, which unnerved Charlene. He rounded the vehicle and waited at the backseat door, which told Charlene to unlock it and get ready to move.

"You gonna tell me where we're going?" she asked.

"Once we're on the road."

Charlene wasn't patient by nature, and Watters drove her to the edge. She started the car and merged onto the freeway.

"What does Flora King want?" she asked.

The detective drove hard, hearing the excitement in her own voice, wheeling the vehicle off the One-Ten to join the Santa Monica Freeway, on their way to Flora King's home. She could feel the adrenaline coursing through her veins. She lived for this.

"Elijah, Tiana's oldest son, wants to talk to me."

"About what?" Charlene checked out Watters in the rear view mirror, and she didn't like what she saw. He looked meek, pale, and fragile. His eyelids heavy.

"Flora wouldn't tell my brother. She doesn't exactly trust cops, even if Josh is my brother."

"Well, it has to have something to do with his mother. Why else call Josh to see you?"

"I don't know, Detective. It could have nothing to do with his mom at all." Watters' voice faded.

Charlene shook her head. "No way. I know this has something to do with it."

She steered the vehicle off the freeway early to avoid the late-evening rush hour traffic.

Chapter 28

A sharp rap on glass stirred Calvin. He opened his eyes. Groggy. Blurred vision.

It took him a full three seconds for his surroundings to click—the back seat of an unmarked LAPD detective car. Another knock turned his head.

Detective Taylor stood outside his backseat car door, her bony knuckles knocking on the rolled up window. She opened the door.

"You up?"

A partial grin. "I am now."

"Sorry."

"How long was I out?"

"The car ride, about twenty minutes. How you feeling?"

"Better," he lied. But the nap had helped, a bit. He felt slightly better. The Tylenol had kicked in.

"I wanted to let you sleep, but they refuse to talk to us."

Now Calvin smiled completely. They didn't trust cops. He struggled to his feet, one leg at a time, pushing himself into a standing position.

"You up for this?" Taylor asked.

"Yes."

He would do anything to help these people. Even if he wasn't one-hundred percent, physically or mentally, it would take nothing less than a massive heart-attack to keep him from supporting this family.

Flora King and her grandsons stood on the paint-peeling front porch of a run down, century-old Spanish-style home. It wasn't the kind of neighborhood where Calvin would ever want his children growing up, but he understood that Tiana Washington had no other options, no choice but to allow her children to stay there with their grandmother while she worked.

The city of Los Angeles topped the list of US cities with the poorest people laboring under heavy rent burdens, living in substandard housing, or both. More than half of Los Angeles' one million lived in very poor households, spent more than half of their income on rent or resorted to undesirable housing.

The steps creaked and threatened to give way as Calvin ascended to meet the family. He hugged Momma Flora and put his arms around the boys.

"You doing okay?" he asked.

Flora nodded.

"The boys holding up?"

Another nod. "Elijah has something to show you."

Calvin looked down at the boy. He wore Calvin's jersey, but the cardinal red color had started to fade from years of use, and the sleeves were so short that most of his forearms were revealed. The PI wondered how long he'd been wearing it and when was the last time it had been washed.

The former running back knelt into a squat, the bones in his knees cracking and his muscles balking.

"What's up, big man?"

Elijah forced a smile, but there was nothing behind it. He didn't say anything to Calvin, instead, he held out his phone. Calvin remembered Tiana telling him that Elijah took over her old phone, using it as an iPod for music and movies.

Calvin held up the phone for the detectives to see, and they started walking towards the house, joining them on the front steps.

"What is it?" Taylor asked.

Elijah took it back and punched in the password to light it up. Once in, he swiped over and pressed the camera icon. Then he handed it back to Calvin.

The screen showed the start of a video that had been taken at night, looked like from the coliseum.

"It's a video," Calvin said. He stood up so Taylor and Baker could crowd around him. "Tiana told me that this was her old phone but they shared the account, so they are synced together, meaning anything saved on Tiana's phone would also be saved on this one."

Taylor said, "Play it."

Calvin licked his dry lips. The play symbol, a large triangle pointing to the right, loomed in the middle of the screen, like a nuclear bomb button. He pressed it.

The scene commenced from a side view: a large man, both tall and wide, carrying a body, fireman style, across the football field and setting her down gently, as if caring for a baby.

"You recognize him?" Detective Taylor asked.

Calvin didn't, so he shook his head, continuing to watch as the man got down on one knee next to the girl, like a football player huddled around as the coach gave a speech.

"An athlete?" Calvin said. The way the man moved, carried himself in a manner of an athlete, told the PI that he had a past in sports.

Then the camera zoomed in on the girl, lying on the grass. She moved slightly, her left arm wiggling, as if she'd just woken. Her lips moved, obviously saying something to the man, but there was no way for them to hear the words. Whoever recorded the video, undoubtedly Tiana, stood too far away from the scene and hadn't been detected, using only a phone for recording purposes.

Then the camera zoomed in on the man's face.

"Oh, Jesus," Baker said.

"That's not Jesus," Taylor answered.

"Definitely not," Calvin repeated, lost for any other words.

The man's lips moved, as if talking back to Samantha Baylor. They held a twenty-four second conversation, then the man straddled her with his knees, shifting his body weight and leaning into her. She struggled, but the man outweighed her greatly and Baylor's petite frame stood no match, and she could not defend herself.

Baker spat. "Christ, he's gonna kill her."

The man placed his hands on Baylor's neck and squeezed. Using both hands from the front, his fingers targeted and compressed the carotid arteries.

Baylor panicked, slamming her head back and forth trying to resist, the rest of her body paralyzed. The man crushed her chest with his weight, forced Baylor's body underneath him where she couldn't fight back, defenseless.

The young freshman struggled and fought it as much as she could, but after several seconds of restricted airwaves, her body went limp. The fact that Baylor struggled for her life increased oxygen use and hastened unconsciousness and brain death.

"She's unconscious," Taylor said.

The killer, showing no remorse or compassion, continued putting pressure on the victim's throat, even though she was obviously dead.

"That's probably where he crushed her windpipe," Calvin said in a whisper, so the children couldn't hear. Nausea set in.

Seconds to induce unconsciousness, minutes to ensure death.

The man stood up and stared down at Baylor's lifeless body. Then he walked away without looking back.

It was late at night when they parked outside the Los Angeles Memorial Coliseum. The Trojans final walk-through practice, the day before their game, had ended and the team was showered and gone. The stadium lay empty, except for one man. A man who worked tirelessly, stayed late every night, and dedicated his life to USC football.

"We have the evidence," Larry said. "There's no need to confront him. We have a solid foundation here for building a court case."

"I disagree," Watters commented. "I think we *need* to confront him."

"I'm with Calvin," Charlene admitted. "I want to arrest that son of a bitch, immediately."

Baker exhaled through his nostrils. "That's the problem."

Charlene looked over at her partner. "What's the problem?"

"You two working together. You both have the same style—straight ahead, through a concrete wall if need be. Sometimes the safest, most appropriate action is to go around said wall."

"Not if you keep your head down and charge," Watters said.

Charlene put her hand on the car door. "Thanks for the lesson, Larry. But I like the element of surprise, before a criminal lawyers-up."

They took the stairs, the office situated at the top level. They slowed, as Watters labored, his breathing heavy, and he used the hand railing to heave himself up each and every step. Charlene doubted he would make it the whole way.

Ninety-three rows of stairs in the Coliseum ran from bottom to top, and Larry's smoker-lungs started wheezing about half way up.

As they reached close to the top, Watters, moving with difficulty, stopped.

"You okay?" Charlene asked.

"I need a break."

Sweat beaded on his shaved scalp. He breathed heavy, his grimacing face showing signs of discomfort. Larry also bent over catching his breath.

"We'll go ahead up," Taylor said.

"We will?" Larry seemed upset. He coughed without covering his mouth.

"Yes, we will. Calvin, you come up when you're ready."

Watters nodded and dropped down into a sitting position right there in the stairwell, extending his long legs down three steps, and drawing in long breaths. Charlene and Larry started back up and reached the top a couple of minutes later.

The Coliseum grew dark, quiet, foreboding. The detectives hadn't seen the security guards who maintained the lower level, outside the stadium. The empty hallways echoed their footsteps as they moved.

The Athletic Director's office was the only one on the top level.

"The light's on in the office," Charlene told Larry.

The door remained open, and the light from a single desk lamp cast into the dark hallway, shedding a bit of visibility a few feet outside in the hall.

They reached the office, and Charlene poked her head inside to have a look. Jordan Price wasn't at his desk, the modern office sat empty. A large oil and pastel painting hung centered on the wall behind the desk— eclectic taste to say the least.

"Detectives."

Price's voice from behind spun them around. The AD, thick chested and wide-shouldered, blocked most of the hallway. He stood casually dressed, looking unsurprised by an LAPD detective visit so late in the evening.

"Mr. Price, sorry to bother you this late," Larry said.

"We came across a video tonight from Tiana Washington," Charlene cut in.

Price moved closer to the office. "Really?"

"Would you like to see it?" She started walking towards him, Elijah Washington's phone outstretched in her hand. They had already forwarded multiple copies to safe email addresses.

"Stop right there, Detective." Price pulled out a gun, pointing it at Charlene. "I've already seen it."

Charlene stopped, looking down the barrel of probably the same gun that had been used to shoot Tiana Washington. Would Price be dumb enough to keep the murder weapon? Probably not, he would have discarded that one and gotten himself another.

"You and your partner throw your guns over here," Price ordered, a look of mirth in his eyes.

Charlene and Larry slid their weapons across the cement floor.

"Are you really going to shoot two LAPD detectives, Price? How will you talk your way out of that one?"

"We've already had one murder around here, two people snooping around in the dark, shouldn't be much of a stretch that I got nervous and shot them."

Charlene glanced around furtively, checking for any kind of weapon she could use against Price. But the detectives stood in the middle of the hallway, not within reaching distance of any walls.

"Why did you kill Samantha Baylor?" Larry asked.

"She jeopardized my season."

That answer gave Charlene pause. "What?"

"This is my bowl season."

"What do you mean?"

Price clutched the gun tighter. "Do you know that I'm the only AD in the USC modern-day history to have never taken his football team to a bowl game? This cheerleader was threatening to ruin my legacy. I couldn't let that happen."

"You knew she was pregnant?"

"Ryan hadn't been himself. He is my meal ticket. I could tell he was off, then I saw them standing on the field Saturday night. I got close enough to hear what they were saying. Ryan has his whole future ahead of him to achieve greatness. I thought Carson Turner would kill her for me, but the boy's own father didn't even have the guts."

Having been a college football fan all her life, Charlene knew what a bowl game, let alone a national championship, could do for a school, as well as job security for the athletic director.

Winning a national championship had a significant impact on a team's revenues. Title-winning teams moved more merchandise, had greater demand for game tickets and received much more money in the way of alumni contributions.

"You're insane," Charlene said. "All this over a football season."

Price shrugged. "Collateral damage."

Larry asked, "How did you figure out it was Washington blackmailing you?"

"I followed her home from the post office, saw my letter in her hand. Not exactly all-covert, 007 shit. Selfish bitch."

"So this is your plan, keep Ryan Turner happy, throwing touchdowns, and tie up any loose ends?"

Price shrugged his shoulders. "I come up to my office, see two figures sneaking around in the dark, get nervous, and shoot them. Doubtful anyone would blame me."

Charlene moistened her lips. "Is that the gun that killed Washington?"

"You think I'm a fool, detective?"

"Yes, I do."

Price gripped the gun with both hands. "Enough jokes. I'm done with you."

Charlene braced herself for the shot, but while Price's attention drew to the detectives, a blur flashed in front of Charlene's eyes, and side-swept Price as he fired off a shot.

The bullet narrowly missed both her and Larry, splitting the difference between them. Charlene dove to the ground, instinctively.

Watters took down Price, both men rolling across the concrete floor. Price's grip loosened around the gun as they wrestled, and the pistol fell to the ground. They struggled to their feet, neither man letting go.

Since no light lit up the hall, Charlene could only make out shadows and forms. Watters and Price stood about the same size, thick men throwing hammer-like fists at each other, both connecting. They grunted, breathing hard, trying to be on both the defensive and the offensive at the same time.

Charlene surged to her feet and scrambled to where she had pitched her gun. She felt around on the cold, bare concrete floor and felt the cool nozzle of a gun. She picked it up, found the trigger and pointed it towards where the two men fought.

Calvin thrust a punch at Price's Adam's apple, and a gurgling emanated from the man's throat.

Larry stood beside her now, also with his gun. Charlene took out her phone for the light, shining it at Watters and Price, while aiming the gun with her other hand.

"Freeze, Price." But she didn't have a shot.

"Go ahead and shoot, Detective," Price spat out.

He had Watters in a choke-hold, holding Calvin in front of him like a human shield.

"Shoot," Calvin said, but his voice was low, barely a whisper as the breath choked out of him.

She couldn't. There was no way to risk a shot without hitting Watters, who she could tell grew weaker with each moment that passed. When Watters' legs gave out, both men dropped to the ground, the choke hold still held firmly in place, Watters' eyelids closing.

Price reached out for the gun he had dropped, only about three feet from where he and Calvin grappled. If Price got that gun in his hand, the whole scene wouldn't end well.

"Don't do it, Price," Charlene shouted.

Charlene aimed for the gun on the ground, considered the distance from Calvin, and determined that it would be safe to fire without hitting the PI. She pulled the trigger, but instead of the bullet knocking the gun further away from Price, it hit the athletic director squarely on the palm of the hand.

The AD let out a howl, bringing his bloody, bullet-holed hand to his chest, all the while loosening the one-hand grip he had on Calvin. Price appeared beaten, his face paled, and he looked like he might pass out.

Watters seemed to find just enough strength to pry himself loose, turn around and, while still partially on the ground, hit Price with a roundhouse right that connected with the AD's jaw, sending the big man all the way to the ground.

Watters propped up on his knees, heaving in oxygen, then fell onto his back, his chest rising and falling trying to find air. Price lay unmoving, as Charlene approached them carefully, gun still drawn, not taking any chances.

She hovered over Calvin. "You okay?"

He raised his hand and gave her a thumbs up.

"I guess we're even now," Charlene said.

Epilogue

Split Second

"Well, looks like the prodigal son has returned home."

Calvin didn't exactly feel like the prodigal son, and never, ever thought he'd be returning to USC, not after how things had gone down all those years ago.

He had received a very nice applause from the Trojan faithful in attendance, as over ninety-thousand fans jammed into the Coliseum for the USC-UCLA game, a game always well attended.

A number of titles had been applied to the football game such as: The Los Angeles City Championship, The Crosstown Showdown, The Battle of L.A., or simply the Crosstown Rivalry.

Rachel had her arm interlaced inside Calvin's and gave a prideful squeeze when he'd been introduced to the crowd. The smile on her face showed Calvin all he needed to know about how his girlfriend felt. She remained close to him on the sideline as they watched the game.

Calvin turned to look at Detective Taylor. They'd all been granted a sideline pass for the game, after their work on the murder case, bringing down Athletic Director Jordan Price. Calvin hadn't known what to expect when agreeing to partner with Taylor, but she proved a reliable associate, and a competent investigator.

"Maybe I still have a few fans around," he said.

Taylor smiled. "This case might have even saved your legacy here at USC. Maybe someday your number twenty-one jersey will be retired and receive prominent placement in the Coliseum during Trojan home games."

"Definitely," Rachel added with a smile.

Calvin couldn't admit that he had never thought about it. The USC football program had only ever retired six different numbers: Carson Palmer's number three, Matt Leinart's number eleven, Charles White's number twelve, Mike Garrett's number twenty, O.J. Simpson's number thirty-two and Marcus Allen's number thirty-three.

All those players had won a Heisman Trophy, and Calvin had won two, and yet his jersey still hadn't been retired. Maybe now that Price was out of the equation, that distinction became a possibility once again.

A scream of agony at midfield drew their attention. A group of players from both teams had packed onto the ball, and when they'd finally broken up, Isaiah Watson, the Trojan starting RB, lay on the ground holding his knee, crying out.

The scene of Watson, while groups of concern-faced players huddled around him, sent shivers down Calvin's spine. The scene all too familiar. A hush fell over the boisterous crowd, as trainers ran out onto the field while a gurney and golf cart immediately rolled out to midfield.

The team of doctors looked over Watson. Calvin felt like running out onto the field, but his feet stayed planted in place, his body numb and tingling. The PI worked on maintaining a steady breath, allowing his pulse and heartbeat to find its normal cadence.

The staff doctors heaved Watson up onto the gurney, and as they rolled him off the field, Watson extended his arm and gave the USC crowd a thumbs-up sign to show them that he would be okay.

But Calvin knew otherwise.

As Watson wheeled through the USC sideline, his team members slapped him on the shoulder, high-fived him, and shouted words of encouragement. When Calvin came face to face with Watson, the former running back saw the tear-stained cheeks, the sad eyes, and maybe Watson's recognition.

"I gotta go," Calvin said.

The detective nodded. "Sure."

As he turned, Rachel reached out and grabbed his arm. "Calvin, no."

He looked into Rachel's face. "I'll just be a minute."

Her eyes narrowed, showing worry. "Calvin, I know that look. Let it go. This isn't your problem."

"I'm fine, Rach."

"Calvin, don't. Please," she pleaded.

He raised his hands in a calming motion. "It's all good."

Calvin heard Rachel whisper something to the detective as he followed the gurney and trainers back into the locker room. Her words were drowned out by Watson's sobs, and Calvin knew the RB had no family in the area to be with him.

The team doctor, a man Calvin despised, turned and saw him following. He pointed at Calvin.

"Make sure he doesn't come back here," the doc told the assistant trainers. "USC player personnel only."

They took Watson into the back room and the doors closed on Calvin.

Dr. Christopher Reece had an ego the size of the state of California—an LA playboy who used his USC football ties to scam college girls, and never had his players' best intentions when making medical decisions.

Reece became a product of the system, keep them playing, winning games. The USC program, here and now, mattered most to them.

Calvin was just a touch bitter about how he'd been treated by Reece.

The PI counted four trainers exit the room, everyone who'd gone in, except for Reece and Watson.

"How is he?" Calvin asked the last trainer to come out, a pale skinned, young looking med student.

The boy shook his head, and then followed the rest out onto the Trojan sideline, awaiting the next injury, which would surely come. Of all college sports, football had the highest injury rate with 36 injuries per 1,000 male athletes. In addition to the high number of collisions in football, it also had the highest number of knee and ankle injuries.

Once the last staff member had left the hall, Calvin looked around and then pushed open the locker room door. He knew exactly where the medical room was, and walked directly through the dressing room to the back.

The door dividing the locker room and medical room was closed, but Calvin could see Watson laying on his back, on the black leather-topped bench. With his pant legs rolled up, his good knee bent, the injured one flat on the table. Watson's upper-body gear had been removed, arm slung over, bent, covering the boy's eyes as if fighting off the pain. Perspiration dotted his cheeks.

Reece swiveled on a stool next to where Watson lay. The doctor's attention focused on the needle in his hand, as he squirted out a bit of fluid from the needle point.

Calvin closed his eyes, remembering the number of times that needle had punctured his knee to cover the pain, allow him to carry on, finish a game and worry about tomorrow at another time. It had extended his season, but cut short his career.

Calvin barged in, slamming the door with his shoulder.

"Don't do it," he said.

Reece wheeled around on the stool to face him, and Watson's arm fell to the side, his face turning and looking at Calvin, who now stood in the doorway.

"What are you doing here?" Reece spat. "This area is for USC personnel only."

"Calvin?" Watson's voice grew hoarse, his eyes puffy and wet.

"Don't let him stick that needle in your knee, Isaiah. Trust me."

"Doc?" Watson looked at Reece.

"Don't listen to this guy, Isaiah. You want to help this team win, don't you?"

Watson nodded emphatically. "Of course I do. I just want to play ball."

Calvin balled up his fists. "That's what I thought too, Isaiah. But look at me now. Those cortisone shots will help you now, but they weaken your knees, and hurt you in the long term."

"Is that true, doc?"

Reece shook his head. "Of course not." He looked back at Calvin. "Get the fuck out."

Calvin took a step towards the doctor. "I'm warning you, Reece. Don't put that needle anywhere near that boy's knee."

Reece turned his back to Calvin, towards Watson, and Calvin charged. The doctor must have heard him coming because he turned back around and stood up just as Calvin catapulted himself through the air.

When Calvin connected with Reece, the needle slipped out of the doctor's hand and fell to the ground. The momentum of the impact sent both men sprawling over the bench and onto the ground, where they wrestled.

Although Reece had nowhere near the size and strength of Calvin, the doctor had a fresh body. Calvin was still exhausted, sore and stiff from his recent injuries. Not at full strength, Calvin had to work hard to match Reece's strength and the adrenaline that flowed through the doctor.

The medical room door banged open and a group of trainers ran in to break up the fight, getting between Calvin and the USC doctor until both men pulled away, breathing hard. Reece's expensive button-down shirt had been ripped from his body, his gelled hair disheveled, and Calvin had a scratch across his left cheek. Blood dripped from the cut.

"This guy's fucking nuts," Reece screamed, spit foaming at the corners of his mouth.

"I don't want that needle in my knee," Watson said. He held a bewildered look on his face.

The trainers looked down at the needle on the floor.

The head assistant eyed Reece. "Chris?" he said.

Reece looked away from his medical staff, and tried as much as he could to fix his torn shirt. "I don't answer to anyone in this room."

The assistant turned to the volunteer students, still holding Calvin. "Get him out of here."

"Higher, Charlene." The immature squeals of a little girl, like music to the detective's ears.

Three days had passed since Jordan Price's arrest, and the college had become a state of anarchy. Not only was the AD's actions under scrutiny, but the football team's head medical doctor was also under investigation.

The case had been handed over to the district attorney. Clark had everything he needed to put away Price. As far as Charlene, Larry and the LAPD was concerned, they officially closed the case, the paperwork stamped.

Sometimes, it all came down to luck—something happens suddenly, out of the blue, to crack a case. You can't predict it, and you're rarely ready for it.

The detective didn't overlook the fact that they'd caught a break. Some cases just went nowhere, go cold and are never solved, and others hope for a lucky break—being in the right place at the right time.

But it's that one shred of evidence that makes every other puzzle piece fall into place.

If that video had never surfaced, or if Tiana Washington's son had never come forward, they probably would never have solved the case. Price had covered his tracks almost perfectly, and the truth could have been lost had it not been for the video.

USC now searched for a new athletic director, and a new football team doctor. But Charlene doubted any of this would interfere with the football season that was off to one of their strongest starts in years. So far, undefeated but they'd only go as far as Ryan Turner's golden arm would take them.

So many people had been impacted from that case. Parents had lost a child, a cheerleading team had lost a teammate, a school had lost a valuable student, and a friend was gone. Samantha Baylor's roommate's jealousy had created a domino effect that spiraled downward, out of control.

Charlene had placed an anonymous call to the USC Fraternity & Sorority Leadership Development committee, and although the way the sisters at Delta Gamma had treated Samantha Baylor hadn't specifically contributed to her death, the sorority would be under investigation for unethical practices. They had nothing to do with the death, but their actions had changed Baylor, in a round about way.

With an ordered day off, Charlene had pulled Lauren out of school early and brought the seven year-old to a local park to play on the structures. It still remained one of Charlene's favorite places to come, get Lauren out of her house and spend some quality time together.

The detective tried to spend as much time as she could with Lauren. She'd first met the little girl when Charlene worked as an officer—a domestic disturbance had brought her to Lauren's house. Charlene had seen signs of abuse on Lauren's body, but she couldn't prove it, yet. But she would keep trying.

"How is school going?" Charlene asked, giving Lauren another push in the back and watching the little girl arc higher on the swing.

"Good. Higher." She laughed.

Lauren leaned back in the swing, tilting her head and closing her eyes, letting the wind blow through her blond curly bangs.

Charlene wished she could read the young girl's thoughts. The detective didn't know anyone with Lauren's strength. She lived every day in a house full of evil, listening to angry words, the yelling and shouting, and yet the tiny kid stood strong with a smile on her face.

The little girl reminded Charlene to appreciate what she had, and taught the detective to stay positive. Even though sometimes, as a cop, seeing the dark side of humanity, staying strong wasn't always easy.

Charlene's phone rang. She pulled it out of her pocket with one hand, while giving Lauren another push with the other.

A two-zero-two area code, Washington, DC.

"I need to answer this," she said to Lauren.

"Hurry back, Charlene. I want to go higher," the girl sang.

Charlene walked away from the swing set and watched Lauren using her arms and legs to gain momentum to push herself higher on the swing. She got the hang of it, and before long would be able to do it all by herself.

Charlene answered the phone. "Hello."

"Detective Taylor, this is special agent Nicholas Smith of the Federal Bureau of Investigation."

"I know who you are, Agent Smith."

Charlene had met agent Nick Smith in Denver, at the same time as she'd met Matt, while working a kidnapping case.

Smith was a veteran agent, with a multitude of career accomplishments. The man's reputation preceded him, with over twenty years of service with the FBI. He sat high up the rung on the agency's ladder, with a high success rate on cases worked.

"Have you heard from Agent Stone, Detective?"

"Not since he left my house last week. Why?"

"We've lost contact with him."

Charlene swallowed. It wasn't like Matt to not check in with Smith. "When did you last speak with him?"

"It's been five days."

Charlene tried to control her breathing. Matt rarely called her during a case, so not hearing from him hadn't given her a second thought.

She looked at Lauren, hoping the sight of the girl, playing and laughing on her own, would help ease the detective's troubled mind. But it didn't help.

Her throat tightened. "Let me call you back, Agent Smith."

She disconnected the call and texted Matt, and then called his cell. It immediately went to voice mail without even one ring. Charlene closed her eyes, a chill running up her spine, listening to Matt's recorded voice.

"Matt, call me."

She called Smith back.

"Hello," Smith answered after the first ring.

"Tell me everything you know."

THE END

If you enjoyed this book, please consider writing a short review and posting it on your favorite review sites (Amazon, Goodreads, etc.). Reviews are very helpful to other readers and are greatly appreciated by authors, especially me. When you post a review, drop me an email and let me know.

~ Luke
luke@authorlukemurphy.com

Dear Reader,

Thank you for picking up a copy of Red Zone. I hope you enjoyed reading this novel as much as I did writing it. My goal was to take these characters to another level. I hope I succeeded.

You, the readers, are the reason I wrote this novel. Having my two main protagonists, Calvin Watters and Charlene Taylor, work together, was something I had never imagined…until you suggested it.

It was so much fun writing from both Charlene and Calvin's points-of-view in the same story. Red Zone is the first novel I've written where I didn't completely plot out the whole story. I just let it flow, and watched where the characters took me.

Definitely a rewarding experience.

I have no idea if Charlene and Calvin will appear in another story together, but there's always a chance. If I receive enough positive feedback from readers, maybe I will someday let them work together again.

This is a work of fiction. I did not base the characters or plot on any real people or events. Any familiarities are strictly coincidence.

For more information about my books, please visit my website at www.authorlukemurphy.com. You can also "like" my Facebook page and follow me on Twitter and Instagram.

I'm always happy to hear from readers. Please be assured that I read each email personally and will respond to them in good time. I'm always happy to give advice to aspiring writers, or answer questions from readers. You can direct your questions/comments to the contact form on my website. I look forward to hearing from you.

Regards,

Luke

Books by Luke Murphy

CALVIN WATTERS MYSTERIES
Dead Man's Hand
Wild Card
Red Zone
(featuring Charlene Taylor)

CHARLENE TAYLOR MYSTERIES
Kiss & Tell
Rock-A-Bye Baby
Red Zone
(featuring Calvin Watters)

Find all of Luke's books at his website:
www.authorlukemurphy.com

Luke Murphy is the International bestselling author of two series. The Calvin Watters Mysteries: Dead Man's Hand (2012) and Wild Card (2017). The Charlene Taylor Mysteries: Kiss & Tell (2015) and Rock-A-Bye Baby (2019).

Murphy played six years of professional hockey before retiring in 2006.

His sports column, "Overtime" (Pontiac Equity), was nominated for the 2007 Best Sports Page in Quebec, and won the award in 2009. He has also worked as a radio journalist (CHIPFM 101.7).

Murphy lives in Shawville, QC with his wife and three daughters. He is a teacher who holds a Bachelor of Science degree in Marketing, and a Bachelor of Education (Magna Cum Laude).

Red Zone is Murphy's fifth novel.

For more information on Luke and his books, visit:
www.authorlukemurphy.com

'Like' his Facebook page: www.facebook.com/AuthorLukeMurphy

Follow him on Twitter: www.twitter.com/AuthorLMurphy

Be the first to know when Luke Murphy's next book is available! Follow him at: bookbub.com/authors/luke-murphy to receive new release and discount alerts.

Made in the USA
Coppell, TX
11 September 2020

37373106R00154